Praise for MAKING MANNA

"A beautiful story of flourishing in hard times against the madness of an irrational justice system—with family, love, and foodie delights! An inspiring triumph of the human spirit."

— William Upski Wimsatt, author of *Please Don't Bomb the Suburbs* and president of Gamechanger Labs

"Eric Lotke is a beautiful writer and he has written a beautiful book. *Making Manna* is a wonderful story of family, redemption, and love that takes the reader from the prison to the school yard in a touching human way that we rarely experience."

— Heather Ann Thompson, author of *Whose Detroit?*

"An inspiring story that shows how difficult society makes it to reach 'heaven'—yet how some reach it nevertheless. I enjoyed it immensely."

— Patrice Gaines, author of *Laughing in the Dark—From Colored Girl to Woman of Color, A Journey from Prison to Power*

"In this astutely drawn and honest story, Eric Lotke guides us through a world that is all too common and yet largely invisible. *Making Manna* brilliantly details the searing fragility of life below the poverty line, where the smallest mishap can send lives cascading toward disaster, and where redemption is hard to achieve but transcendent when it arrives. Both heartbreaking and heartwarming."

— David Feige, author of *Indefensible* and creator of the TNT series *Raising the Bar*

Making Manna

Making Manna

Eric Lotke

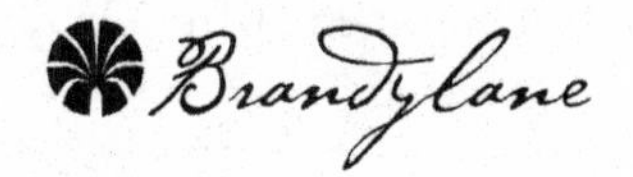

Cover art by Lara Beaudry Byer

ISBN 978-1-9399302-2-4
Library of Congress Control Number: 2014942392

Published by
Brandylane

WWW.BRANDYLANEPUBLISHERS.COM

Acknowledgments

This book was a collective effort. It might not exist if family and friends (Susan W., Joan K., Sylvie M., Darcy G., Laura S., Richard P., Maureen M.) hadn't read early material and been curious about what might happen next.

I received help, direct and indirect, from a community of justice advocates and practitioners. Phyllis Lawrence and sujatha baliga provided crucial insights about restorative justice. Pauline and Charlie Sullivan are saving the world, one family at a time. Jerry Miller, Julie Stewart, Ed Ungvarsky, Tyrone Parker, Rico Rush, and many others are thinking differently about crime and punishment. I owe thanks to all these leaders.

I got help in the background, too. The county library provided a whole shelf of Horatio Alger stories. Anne Greene offered a writer's conference with a weekend of insights. My job gives me weekends off. Striking fast food workers inspired Sheila to gather her coworkers and collectively demand that raise near the end of Part One.

Last came the publishing. Robert Pruett at Brandylane took a risk on an unknown author and dangerous subject. Tamurlaine Melby provided expert editing.

Above all else, I owe thanks for my personal good fortune. I was raised by terrific parents and now have terrific children of my own. Best of all, I got to marry Amy Mortimer. If anything in this story is charming, uplifting, or makes you happy in any way, that part comes from Amy. Sometimes she lets me borrow it.

Part One

Beginning, Beginning, End

Chapter One

Her screams are so loud even the dogs run cowering into the barn. Libby Thompson, fourteen years old, lies on her bed, naked and in labor. She's drenched in sweat, muscles taut with strain. Her knees are up, her outsized belly an island in the middle.

"Who's the father?" asks her mother, Eva Louise Thompson.

Libby says nothing.

"Tell me, please."

The next contraction rips a scream so powerful a cracking sound comes from the windowpane and powder drifts down from the ceiling. Libby's whole body clenches in the spasm.

When it's done, Libby's mother passes her an ice cube from a bowl by the bed.

Libby pops it briefly in her mouth, then spits it out and rubs it gently over her face and belly. For a moment her muscles unwind and she's a tired little girl. "Thanks, Mom."

She's in her own bedroom. Her school medals line one wall—spelling, math, and track—and her favorite books line the shelf. In a photo by the bed she's riding her horse, Shadow Dancer, a dappled gray. Behind it hangs a picture of Shadow Dancer she drew in crayon when she was ten.

The next contractions are less violent and barely elicit moans as Libby bears down hard. She swabs herself with her towel and asks her mother to adjust the fan. It's only ten in the morning, but in the hills of Southwest Virginia in August it's hot already.

"Only a few more," her mother says. "You're almost there. Tell me, now. Who's the father?"

The bedroom door slams open and old Joseph Thompson bursts into the silence. Old Joe, Libby's father, Eva's husband. His black hair is plastered against his head with sweat, and his hands are dirty from some kind of a chore.

"Is she done yet? Is it born?"

Eva Louise leaps to her feet and stands between old Joe and her daughter's wide open legs. "Get out!" she hollers. "Anywhere but here." Old Joe delivers livestock in the spring, but he's never cared about the birth of a baby.

Old Joe steps around his wife and keeps his attention between his daughter's legs. "How much longer?"

Libby aims what's left of her ice cube at his head but misses by a yard. "Go away! I never want to see you again."

"Now, dear, be nice to your father," Eva implores as she takes old Joe by the elbow and guides him out the door, closing it firmly behind him. "This is hard for all of us."

She hurries back as the baby's head comes into view and Libby starts groaning in newfound pain. Libby pulls the towel over her head and separates herself from the world.

Then it's done. One little push. One last groan and one dangerous, delicate moment later, Eva Louise is holding a baby in her hands, pink and slippery and crying.

The whole world falls into place the instant she sees the child. Even as Eva Louise cuts the cord, swabs him clean, and announces he's a boy, she understands why old Joe cares so much about this baby. Now she can see why old Joe refused to whip the truth out of his daughter when she confessed her condition, and why he hovered around when the screaming started. Now she knows why Libby refused to name the father.

The boy in her hands is the spitting image of the man who just left. Thick black hair and flattened chin, she's holding an infant version of old Joseph Thompson, her own husband. Libby's father.

She's always known the mother. Now she sees the father, too.

Libby lies cradling her baby on the bed of fresh sheets and dry towels her mother made. She's wearing baggy shorts and an old flannel shirt, unbuttoned at the moment, so the baby rests smooth against her skin.

Libby didn't know how she'd feel when this day finally came. The past nine months had been endless torture, one punishment following another. She kept it secret at first, quietly enduring the sickness and fatigue, praying for a miracle. Later, when she couldn't hide it anymore, she didn't know how to answer the question that everyone asked.

Who did this to you? How did this happen?

Everyone wanted to know. People treated her like she was keeping a secret.

Libby wasn't keeping a secret. She just didn't know what to say. Her mother had been useless before, and she was even more useless afterwards. Libby didn't know what to do and had nobody to ask.

But now she gazes down at her baby's fragile skin and miniature nose, watches his little eyes squint closed, then open wide, luminous and black. She feels his tiny hand close around her finger, and feels his newborn skin against her breast, softer than anything she's ever imagined. Now she knows how she feels, and why she endured it all.

She did it for him.

He, at least, is innocent.

Now she understands why herds circle to protect their young.

Libby rests with the baby flat against her chest, feeling him rise and fall with her breath, listening to his own breath alongside hers. Downstairs she hears people talking. The words aren't distinct but soon the tone becomes clear.

It's not talking, it's yelling.

She hears her father order her brothers to leave and hears the door slam on their way out. "I don't care!" he hollers. "Don't come back until dinner time."

In the newfound silence Libby closes her eyes. Downstairs in the kitchen, her mother starts at the sink, and the sound of running water covers conversation. Libby doesn't want to listen anyway. All she wants is to fall asleep and for the pain to go away. Finally she dozes off to the sounds of birds singing, her mother cooking, and the occasional wind in the trees.

Sometime later she hears a pathetic whine coming from behind the house, out by old Joe's woodshed. Sometimes shrill and sometimes soft, sometimes loud and sometimes barely a mutter, it doesn't quite penetrate her consciousness, doesn't quite pull her awake. Then suddenly she rises with a start. Her child is missing. Gone from her arms. She blasts down the stairs like a rocket.

Old Joe lies asleep on the couch, shirt off, can of beer on the floor where his arm hangs down. Eva Louise is at the sink, washing the knives and the chopping block she used to make a stew. When their eyes meet, Libby knows exactly what happened. She knows whose stealthy hands, sure in the way of children, had unlocked the baby from her arms and, if Libby had stirred at all, coaxed her back to sleep.

She also knows what the arguing was about.

Libby walks straight past her mother to the woodshed out back. That was no pig she'd heard in her sleep. No dog, no coyote. No animals are scheduled for slaughter today.

The sound leads her past the woodshed to the trash cans behind, lids fastened with the secure knots her father prefers, not the easy clasps Libby and her mother use. Her baby is in the first can, mixed with beer cans and old rags, covered in dust, only a few whines left in his voice.

Libby hauls him out and doesn't bother to seal the can properly behind her. She hears his breath change as she hoists him upright, feels his violent shivering through her shirt.

Back in the house, Libby doesn't even look at her mother. She sets her child, dusty and naked, on the counter top where they trim the beef, pulls on the big heat mittens they use for the heavy boiling pots, and grabs her mother's stew off the stove. Two steps later she reaches Old Joe and empties the pot straight onto his hairy chest. The steam lashes up so she can't see what she hits, but she keeps pouring until the pot is all the way upside down, good and empty. She swings the empty pot once into the cloud of steam. Probably that's his head she hits as he sits up screaming.

She grabs her baby off the chopping block and wraps him in a dish towel, then shoots out of the room as fast as her legs can carry her. "No more!" she yells as she slams the door. "Never again!" She sets out on foot toward the town where Old Joe goes to get drunk and buy supplies.

The sun is setting by the time Libby reaches the main road. She carries the baby comfortably against her chest, but everything else is wrong. Her old flannel shirt keeps slipping off her shoulders and her loose shorts barely stay up while she walks. Her old sneakers pick up a pebble through a hole.

The Safeway truck picks her up on Route 29 like it's been sent from heaven. She sits down in the front seat and the trucker doesn't say a word, doesn't ask her any questions. He leaves her alone to hug her child and nurse her pain. An hour later, he stops at a Walmart and buys her two sets of clothes. "One to wash, one to wear," he says quietly. He pays with cash and gives her the change, plus sixty dollars more from his wallet. He drops her at a police station near the Safeway depot in Fairfax, Virginia, the suburbs of Washington, D.C., as far that night as he plans to go.

Libby names her baby after that trucker. She never learns his name, but she calls him Angel.

Chapter Two

It's closing on midnight as the truck pulls away. Libby climbs a short staircase toward brass doors labeled *Fairfax County Sheriff's Department.* She hauls the doors open and steps over rubber mats stamped with stars.

Straight ahead is a desk. A young black woman sits in the center, dressed in a blue police uniform. On each side of the desk stands a flag, the American stars and stripes and the state flag of Virginia, the bare-breasted woman astride the tyrant.

"I need a place to stay," Libby declares. Angel is fast asleep in her arms.

The woman reaches for a phone without looking at her. "Dispatch 2100," she says. To Libby she says, "Sit down." She points to a bench near the door.

Libby sits down while the sheriff's department shifts around her. She can tell it's late. Just a few people move about, and all of them slowly, but nobody so much as looks in her direction. A big digital clock shows time passing, down to the second. Libby watches the digits speed past in a blur, and wonders what's happening at home.

What are her parents doing now? Her mother? Her father? What is she saying to him?

Do her brothers know what happened? What will her parents tell them? Probably not everything.

Libby's brothers are five and six years older than she is, an age gap that's small between them but so wide before Libby it's like they grew up in different families. The boys had each other and their friends; Libby was the only girl around, and she had only her mother. From playing together with baby dolls to baking bread in the kitchen, her mom was her best friend in the family.

When she looks up again, half an hour has passed. She isn't being impatient. Nobody's coming. She steps back up to the desk. "I need a place to stay," she says again. "I've been sitting like you said."

The woman at the desk turns on her sharply. "Do we look like a child welfare agency to you?"

"No. You look like a police station."

"That's right. Sheriff's Department."

"And I need to go to a child welfare agency?"

"Right again. Or a homeless shelter."

Angel lets out a long breath, like a tire stuck by a nail, but he sleeps without moving. "Any idea how I can get to one?"

"Well, why didn't you just ask that in the first place?"

Libby's no expert at dealing with police, but she's learned how to handle bureaucrats, from the assistant principal at her school to the desk clerk at the feed lot. "I'm sorry if I didn't make myself clear," she offers with the best politeness she can manage. "My baby and I are a little stuck. It's late, you know, and we need a place to sleep. If you can help, we sure would appreciate it."

A uniformed officer walks by as Libby finishes. The desk clerk waves him over. "Finnegan," she says. "Any chance you can take this lost soul to Haven Ministries?"

Finnegan looks like a police officer from TV—older, white, and kindly. He checks his watch and inspects Libby from top to bottom. "New baby?" he asks.

"Very new."

"Come on."

Haven Ministries is a dilapidated building on an empty stretch of street. The door is locked, but it opens when Finnegan pounds, and two elderly white women greet him like midnight thumping happens all the time. "Diapers," one says to the other, who scurries down the hall, trailing yarn from the back of her slipper. Finnegan returns to his car without a word, and the first woman leads Libby to a small, windowless room with two bunk beds, a trash can, and a night stand made from a milk crate. The second woman returns with a stack of diapers, then both disappear and shut the door behind them.

Bunk beds! Libby has always wanted a bunk bed, thrilled by their high-altitude charm on television, but nobody in her world has a bunk bed. She's never even seen one before, except on TV. She tucks her sleeping Angel fast against her shoulder and starts for the top. It's no problem to climb, but the pain splits her in half when she tries to swing her leg over the top. Childbirth all over again. She feels something crack open and new moisture between her legs. She climbs back down, finds a bathroom, and settles on the lower bunk.

What comes next she wouldn't really call sleep, more of an intense blacked-out depth punctuated by pain in her belly that hauls her back to the surface. Her baby sleeps peacefully beside her except for when he wakes up screaming. Libby manages to change his diaper and presses him to her chest, and sometimes drops back into her own blacked-out depths of rest.

Morning breaks like thunder at Haven Ministries. Someone walks the hall chiming a bell. "Breakfast and up," she says. "Breakfast and up." She pushes Libby's door open like she knows it's a newcomer. "Breakfast now, then nothing until dinner."

Libby is sleeping hard when the ruckus begins, but she does what she must and hobbles down the hall with her baby. Every muscle aches and her groin is pierced with nails.

Breakfast is in a room with a long table filled with black women and loud voices. "I've got a job," says a woman as Libby enters. Stitches on her forehead look ready to come out, and a bruise over her eye has all but faded away. "Trouble now is first and last month's rent. The landlord needs both for the lease."

A different woman replies, "When I lost my job, I missed rent for six months before they evicted me."

A few women have small children, sitting beside them or tucked in their laps. Their clothing is old and haphazard, but bright with color. Breakfast is plain oatmeal without milk or sweetener. Libby is happy for the oats, but what she really craves is water. She drains her cup and refills it twice more before anyone notices her. From the end of the table comes an exclamation: "A white woman!" Eyes turn in her direction. "And that there is one new baby."

The room goes quiet as all eyes turn to Libby. She wishes she could disappear in the sudden attention, but she rises from the table and stands still until she's sure of her balance, then bends one knee in an elegant curtsey. "I'm Libby Thompson," she declares. "This here is my Angel."

The table responds with a round of applause. Libby bows acknowledgment and returns to her seat. The woman beside her asks where she's from, and Libby answers as best she can. Fortunately, however, the woman soon loses interest in Libby's half-hearted replies and turns back to the chatter filling the room. Libby sips her water and pays attention only to her child.

After breakfast, Angel needs nursing and diapering, and, by the time she's done, Haven Ministries is emptying. Sarah and Sadie—the keepers of Haven Ministries she met last night—stop by to explain that the Ministries serves breakfast and dinner but everyone must leave during the day. "They can't hang out here when jobs and homes are waiting to be found."

Libby nods her understanding.

"But for you, an exception. How old is that baby?"

"Maybe a day." Libby works it out in her head. "Not quite a day."

"The two of you can stay during the day and sleep. Today, anyway, and maybe tomorrow. Then off with you. Jobs and homes are waiting to be found."

The woman has it exactly right. Libby can't ever remember sleeping so much or so hard, and Angel has mere moments of consciousness between sleep. But nursing goes well, and diapering too. Libby learns the word "meconium" for the thick black poop of a newborn baby. She's seen it in other babies and knows how sticky it is, but Sarah explains that it comes from the fluid in Libby's own womb. Soon, Libby knows, it will be replaced by the yellow, sweet-smelling poop from her milk.

Sarah also explains how to seek paternity tests and child support, but Libby politely declines assistance of that kind. She'd just as soon forget about paternity. The only support she'll get is an offer to return someplace she won't go.

By the morning of the third day, she knows she needs to take the next step. She's feeling stronger, and she can't spend every day dozing in someone else's bed. She doesn't yet know where she'll go, but she's ready to walk out after breakfast and look for work. "How ya gonna work with a newborn?" one woman asks. Libby just shrugs. She doesn't know how any of this is "gonna work." She just knows she can't go home and can't stay in Haven Ministries. The pain has faded to a dull ache and occasional wince, and her legs are strong enough to walk, lift, and help with the chores.

At breakfast on that third morning, all heads turn when a new woman walks into the room. Her clothes match and her head is high. She's tall and broad and very dark-skinned, but she brightens the room like an electric light after a blackout. "Sheila Jackson," she announces, like the sergeant at arms announcing the president.

Two women yell "Sheila!" from the back, and even those who don't know her recognize that she's among friends. Sheila walks the room with handshakes and hugs, greeting and mingling with everyone equally. When she reaches Libby, Sheila kisses her own fingertips and touches them to Angel's head. At the front of the room she announces, "I need a roommate. Who here has a job?"

A woman near Sheila says, "You need a roommate? What happened to Zeb?"

"I kicked him out."

"Zeb? Out? Why?"

"He wouldn't quit the drugs."

"He's not using, is he?"

"No."

"Did he hit you?" asks the bruised woman with the stitches.

Sheila turns like someone pulled a gun on her. "He didn't hit me. He wouldn't hit me. And he's not stoned on drugs." She's defending hard the man she just kicked out, and Libby, like everyone else, doesn't see why.

Sheila stands square and explains. "He's dealing drugs and won't give it up. He says we need the money. I say we both have real jobs and we can make it without drug money. He says we can't. I say we can. Enough said."

"Irreconcilable differences," says a voice in the back, and everyone laughs at the language of divorce court.

"Drug dealer," says a different voice, in a tone fit for the darkest devil.

Sheila draws herself tall in the front of the room and returns to where she started. "I need a roommate. Who here has a job?"

Everyone is quiet. The building's furnace starts with a low throb.

Sheila waits.

Libby doesn't know her name but she's sitting beside the woman with the bruise who said she had a job but not enough for the security deposit. Libby gives her a jog.

Sarah of Haven Ministries sees it and intervenes. "Her boyfriend's dangerous. I want to keep her here until the restraining order goes through."

Still the room is quiet. Sheila keeps waiting but looks more and more disappointed. "You all know what I want, and someone here knows how to find me." She turns for the door.

Most people turn back to talk and breakfast, but Libby follows Sheila out. She catches her in the corridor by the front door. "I don't have a job yet," she says, "but I'll have a job and paycheck before the end of the month."

Sheila looks at her skeptically, with special attention at the baby sleeping against her chest. "How old are you?"

"Fourteen."

Sheila looks at Libby like she's something awful stuck to the bottom of her shoe.

"I'll be fifteen soon. In October."

Sheila keeps sizing her up. Libby's breasts were large even before pregnancy filled them out. She has a nice butt, dark blonde hair, and a pretty face. Sheila asks, "Can you prove you're fourteen?"

"What do you mean?"

"Birth certificate, driver's license? Student ID? Do you have anything that proves you're fourteen?"

"No, ma'am, I don't have anything. You don't understand . . . "

Sheila cuts her off. "I understand enough." She squares up again. "You're not fourteen. You're seventeen. Anybody ever asks you how old you are, you're seventeen. When's your birthday?"

"October 21."

"Congratulations. On October 21, you turn eighteen. Then you're a really big girl." Sheila opens the door and stands aside. "Come with me."

Chapter Three

They leave Angel in Sheila's car in the parking lot.

Sheila puts him on the floor on the passenger's side, covers him with loose clothing and an old newspaper, then seals the windows tight. She walks once around the car, looking inside, then opens it again and throws a handful of rags onto the pile.

"He'll smother," Libby warns.

"I'm not worried about smothering," Sheila replies. "I'm worried about the police. You don't need some friendly passerby to hear him crying. Come on."

She leads them to a small office between a liquor store and a mattress discounter: Happy Jack's Custom Cleaning. Inside is cluttered with mops and detergent bottles, with schedules posted on the walls. Jack sits behind the counter, name tag on his pocket; he looks nothing like happy.

"Who's she?" he scowls at Sheila before she's fully in the room.

"I brought us a new girl."

"Why?"

"Crystal quit last week, remember? We need someone new."

"Bitch."

"Cleaning teams have three. I saved you the trouble of looking."

Jack looks at her like she hasn't saved him any trouble at all. She knows Jack is happy to send teams of only two girls. Customers pay the same rate, two girls do the work of three, and Jack comes out ahead.

Jack turns next to Libby, staring straight at her breasts. "You'll get paid five dollars an hour."

Sheila wants none of it. "Five is the illegal's rate. It's less than minimum. You pay her $7.25 like most new girls."

"Where are her papers?"

"She's an American."

Jack aims his next question straight at Libby. "How old are you?"

"Seventeen." She doesn't skip a beat.

"Where are you from?"

"Virginia."

"What's your social?"

That stumps her. She looks to Sheila for advice.

Sheila answers for her. "She's an American. When did you get all careful about following the law?" Her tone suggests she might reveal some things.

Jack finishes it off. "Six dollars. Start today. Payday is in two Fridays. If you don't make it to payday, you don't get paid."

By the time they reach the car, Angel is starting to fuss. Libby diapers him on the hood and nurses him while they drive to their first job. Rosario, the third team member, is already outside the house, dropped off by her husband on his way to work. Sheila is team leader. She drives the team from house to house every day, then leaves Rosario at a logical bus stop after their final location.

Rosario speaks only a few words of English, but she coos happily at Angel, who is awake after his meal. Sheila pulls a key from under the mat and lets them inside. She knows the house and gets right to work.

But Rosario tugs Libby's arm and guides her to a downstairs bathroom. She fishes through the closet, then emerges with a giant beach blanket. Rosario takes Angel from Libby's arms, turns Libby around, and ties Angel to her chest in a giant papoose. She checks that everything is tight, then gives a big smile and two thumbs up. All of them are now ready for work.

They storm the house from top to bottom. Sheila drives the vacuum cleaner. Rosario makes the beds, dusts the furniture and sweeps what needs sweeping. Libby scrubs the kitchen and bathrooms, familiar motions from her lifetime at home, where mops and rags keep the farm on the outside of the house; though it's trickier with a baby fastened in front. She learns how to bend over without crushing him and manage brooms without whacking him with the handle. Two hours later with the house spotless and Angel starting to stir, Libby returns the papoose towel to the closet and starts to nurse even as they walk to the car.

By the end of the day, they have a perfect rhythm. Sheila always runs the vacuum cleaner, while Libby and Rosario trade off tasks. Libby scrubbed the first house so she sweeps the second. Sometimes Libby wears the baby and sometimes she sets him on the floor while she works, carrying him from room to room and always keeping him in view. The women eat and Angel nurses on the way to the next stop. Libby brought no food but pretends not to be hungry.

Three houses later, Libby is exhausted, but it's the last of the day. "Five tomorrow," Sheila says. "We'll need to move fast."

Rosario's bus is coming as they drop her off, but still she makes time for Libby. She reaches across to give her a proper hug and a kiss on each cheek. "Welcome," she says in English with a perfect accent, and sprints for the bus.

"Monet is seven years old," says Sheila as they pull away. "Spelled like the artist."

"Who's Monet?" says Libby. The artist is also a mystery.

"Monet is my daughter."

They're driving home with Angel asleep in Libby's lap. She cradles the baby and looks out the window. Angel won't be the only child in the house. It ought to matter, but she doesn't know which way. Should it make her happy or sad? A benefit or a drawback? She doesn't know. It's all too new. It's like being asked if the grass will grow, without knowing the field or the season.

They stop at a red light. In her whole life, Libby has never seen as many traffic lights as she has today. She's never seen so many cars, buses, or McDonald's, and she's never been inside houses as large as the ones she's scrubbed every square foot of. Libby has cleaned a lot of stables and logged plenty of cross-country miles, but her legs have never been quite as rubbery-tired as they are this minute.

The space closes in as they drive. The homes here aren't as big as in the neighborhood where they cleaned, and they're packed closer together. At last Sheila pulls into a parking space beside a brick apartment building, three floors tall, with large windows and green wooden shutters. Three identical buildings make a square around a grassy lawn facing the street. Children climb a mulberry tree, Libby's favorite berry every spring.

"Three more flights of stairs," Sheila says as they walk across the lawn. "The top floor gives us more sunshine." They've probably climbed a hundred flights already today, with all the ups and downs in the homes they cleaned; three puts the final goal in mind.

Sheila's apartment explodes with childhood. Crayon drawings of sunshine and flowers, Lego towers in primary colors, a watercolor ship on poster board so big it covers an entire wall, and is covered itself with flowers drawn on post-it notes. Shoes, jacket, and a school bag sit smack in the center of the floor.

"I brought us a roommate," Sheila announces as they enter. She frowns at the pile on the floor but says nothing about it.

In walks Monet, bright and smiling in blue overalls and red T-shirt, her black hair pulled up into a cute little bun. She's seven years old and looks it, small enough for childhood innocence but big enough to understand what's happening. "Where's she sleeping?" she asks.

The question seems to catch Sheila by surprise. She moves Monet's school bag into a corner as she composes her reply. "You'll sleep in my room like Zeb used to. Libby will sleep in your room."

Monet looks none too happy, but Libby steps in. "I'm sorry, honey," she says. "It's just me and my baby, and we need someplace to sleep." She turns Angel so he's looking outward from her chest. His little eyes are open wide.

Monet's eyes open wide in return. Her face lights up. "Can I touch her?"

"He's a boy."

"With a penis?"

Libby laughs. "Heaven knows where he got one, seeing what I think about the things. But he got one, all right." She kneels to bring the baby to Monet's height, and waits as she reaches gently out, touches him on the leg.

"Want to see something else?" Libby says. She unwraps Angel's blanket so his feet poke out, takes Monet's hand and guides it gently toward his feet. One finger she touches softly against the sole.

Angel's foot curls up around her finger, toes clasping it like a little fist.

"He's grabbing me!" Monet exclaims. "He's holding me with his foot!"

"He's just a baby," Libby says. "He's still halfway to a monkey. Later he'll beat his feet into submission. Turn them into shoes."

Monet lingers a while longer, tickling Angel's toes and watching them spread and curl with the dexterity of fingers. "Wait," she says. "I want to fix my room before you move in. Can you stay out here? It might take a while."

"How long?" Sheila asks, looking wary.

"Not too long," Monet replies. "Be patient."

Sheila smiles as her own phrase is used against her.

Sheila shows Libby around the apartment, which isn't very hard. Two bedrooms and a bathroom. A closet filled with coats. The living room is separated by a narrow counter from the kitchen, which is hardly more than a stove and a refrigerator. "You can use my soap and stuff for a while," Sheila says. "Payday Friday we'll go shopping."

In one cabinet are SpaghettiOs and cereal boxes; in the fridge are milk, bread, and peanut butter. Libby asks, "Will you be okay without this Zeb?"

"That's up to you."

"Me?"

"Zeb says we need his drug money to survive. I say we don't."

"He used to deal drugs?"

"He used to load boxes at the Best Buy. Paid nine dollars an hour. He sold heroin on the weekends. He wouldn't stop, and he refused to give up his treats."

"Treats?"

"He'd buy coffee on the way to work and we'd have a restaurant meal on Fridays. Gifts for Monet and that new school bag on the floor right there." She nudges it with her toe. "We had money in the bank when something went wrong."

"That's a big hit, six dollars for nine."

Monet walks in humming the "Happy Birthday" tune. She heads straight for her jacket and school bag on the living room floor, and hangs them neatly in the closet. Her shoes she sets beside the front door. "I'm done," she declares. "You can come in."

Her room has been cleaned to perfection. The bed is made, the decorations are straight, and the surface of her little desk is clear except for a single blue notebook in the center. She's made a nest for Angel out of towels and a box, and set it by the bed, exactly where Libby would have if she'd thought of it.

Libby's eyes tear and a huge smile spreads across her face. She drops to her knees and spreads her arms open wide. Monet leaps into them for a giant hug and they stay together for a long time. Sheila reaches down to touch their shoulders while they cling.

Finally Libby returns to her feet, her eyes moist. Looking only at Monet, she points to the baby in her arms. "His name is Angel," she says. "Now I have two of them."

To Sheila she says, "We're gonna make it."

Chapter Four

Two weeks later and $480 cash is burning a hole in Libby's hand. Happy Jack just paid her in full—six dollars an hour times eighty hours of work—and Libby's heart is pounding with excitement. She scrubbed, mopped, vacuumed, and polished for two weeks, and she's never held this much cash in her life. Nothing even close. Now she really feels like a grown-up.

Sheila doesn't look so happy, though. "Next week she's up to $7.25," she tells Jack, "the legal rate. And none of this cash business. You pay her proper."

Happy Jack pokes a mop handle toward Sheila like a sword. "She gets me a social security number, I pay her 'proper.' Until then, she is who she is."

Libby's listening but she doesn't understand. She's holding a wad of twenty-dollar bills as thick as her old leather work-gloves. She all but pulls Sheila out the door toward the car.

Outside she flips the bills before Angel's wide-open eyes. "We're rich!" she cries, and breaks out in tune. "Hi-ho the dairy-o, a hunting we will go!"

The song doesn't last very long, though. Five minutes later they're pulling into a gas station. Sheila fills the tank, but half the cost comes from Libby's pay. The next stop is the landlord's office to pay the month's rent, and most of what Libby has left goes into his pocket. Now the cash left in her hand feels more like a tissue than a leather pad. She steps wrong coming out of the landlord's office, and her knee makes a popping sound. It pops again on every step climbing up to the apartment; on the last flight it starts to hurt.

But upstairs in the apartment Monet leaps up from the carpet where she's been playing cards by herself. "Payday!" the little girl cries. "Shopping!" she gives her mom a hug.

Sheila asks her to clean up and wait a minute, then disappears into her room. Libby sits on the couch, rubbing her knee and counting her remaining cash. The trucker money has long since disappeared on diapers and wipes. Sheila has been feeding her breakfasts of toast and dinners off the McDonald's dollar menu, and waving her away when she promises to pay her back. "A gift until payday," she said every time. Now Libby's on her own.

Sheila returns to the room and sits on the other end of the couch.

"How did you do it?" Libby asks. "How did you and Zeb stay afloat?"

"Nine not six," Sheila says. "Three extra dollars every hour for a month."

Libby does math in her head. Life on the farm was tight, too. Money was scarce and there was never enough—but they didn't use cash the same way. Eggs came from the chickens and beef from the slaughter, and they swapped peaches for figs with the McAllisters. But still the farm was a business. Seed got bought and crops got sold. Libby helped calculate next year's needs based on last year's prices. The arithmetic could be complicated, and shrewd guesses helped—but it was a longer time horizon, not weekly cash flow like this. Now she's thinking hard about her own situation, and she doesn't like the math. Start with the income; subtract the rent, subtract the gas . . . and they haven't even bought food yet. "It just doesn't seem like enough," she concludes out loud.

Sheila looks up sharply. "You sound like Zeb," she says.

Libby says nothing for a long time. She's looking in the direction of Monet but doesn't really see her, just the bare spot in the carpet where she's playing and the gray sky turning darker with evening. The paint around the window is cracking and an orange stain is seeping through, probably rust from the steel frame. Last week during a thunderstorm the curtains danced in the draft, but now they hang lifeless under a wearying sky. "I can't go home," Libby declares, a thunder crack from nowhere. "I can't go back."

Nobody answers. Monet freezes in place, her playing cards stacked incompletely on the floor. Somewhere down the street, a car skids audibly to a stop. Sheila moves to Libby's end of the couch and the old springs creak under the shift. Libby feels the seat sink under the load as her own body tilts toward her new friend. "Why not?" Sheila asks. "Why can't you go back home?"

Libby says nothing at first. She's looking out the window, but her mind is back at home. The dogs. Her horse. Crawling behind the barberry bushes to the spot where the chickens liked to lay their eggs. She remembers the baths her daddy gave her as a little girl, and how she used to love them, her special private time with the master of the house. And she remembers how it changed. How he started doing things that didn't seem right, and eventually things that hurt. How he made her promise not to tell.

Angel mutters a few little cries from where he sleeps on a towel on the floor. "I can't go back," Libby says again.

Libby remembers gathering the courage to tell her mother. At first she obeyed her father and kept it a secret. But slowly over time, as he went further and it felt more and more wrong, she decided she had to tell.

But her mother didn't believe her. "You must have misunderstood," she'd say. Old Joe had been checking for ticks. Or admiring how you've grown. "Old Joe would never do anything like that."

Specific complaints received the same blanket denial. "He's not watching you in the shower. He just needed something in the medicine cabinet." The more Libby complained, the less her mother listened. She just kneaded the dough, darned the socks, or did whatever she'd been doing while Libby spoke... and quickly changed the subject.

Sheila seems to sense something is wrong. She takes Libby's hand, holds it warmly in her own. "What's wrong?"

Libby doesn't answer, her eyes staring vacantly out the window. Monet finishes cleaning up her card game and takes her coat out of the closet.

Sheila presses on. "Did they kick you out or did you leave?"

Libby lifts herself straight and leans backwards into the couch, her eyes on her child, asleep in his cardboard box of towels, the little nest Monet made for him on his very first day. Her mother and best friend had betrayed her when she needed her most. "They made it so I couldn't stay."

Monet walks over with her own coat zippered and a coat for each grown-up held out in her hands. "Choppity chop," she tells her mom. "Time to go."

Sheila stands up and reaches back down for Libby's hand. "Choppity chop," she echoes. "Time to go."

"Look, Angel!" Libby says as the Safeway comes into view. "It's our store!" She lifts him to give him a view and he coos in expectation.

The Safeway is maybe eight blocks away, a bit long to walk but barely worth the drive. Tonight Monet asks for a ride and Sheila says okay. It's payday Friday and everybody's tired. The gray clouds threaten rain.

On the way Sheila explains how the Safeway club membership works and how to enter her telephone number at the checkout for the special discounts.

"We only buy the discounts," Monet chimes in. "Mommy lets me pick my own box of cereal on payday. Any kind I want!" Sheila joins her and their voices chime in unison, "*As long as it's on sale.*"

Once they're inside they take separate carts and go in separate directions. Angel is too small to sit in the child seat, so Libby makes a bed out of his towel and lays him down in the center of the cart. She walks slowly down the aisles and counts her totals as she goes. Two boxes of spaghetti and one pound of butter; five dollars gone. Toothbrush, toothpaste and soap; another five dollars are gone. She'd like shampoo but none is on sale and she can't buy everything at once anyway. She'll wash her hair with soap until next payday, but she finds a good price on a two-pound package of rice.

The biggest disappointment is the produce. Even on sale she can't bring herself to pay ninety-nine cents a pound for zucchini that looks so sad. Back at home at this time of year she'd have more zucchini than she knows what to do with, fresh and full, gleaming with energy. Her tomatoes would be plump and round, not those pinkish tennis ball things. But one cabbage on the discount rack looks better than the rest, so she puts it in her cart. The three-pound bag of onions isn't on sale but the five-pound bag is, so she buys more onions than she needs. They look pretty decent, too.

She arrives at the checkout just behind Monet, who is pushing the cart for their team. Libby sees three loaves of bread, with peanut butter and jelly. A gallon of milk and a package of oatmeal. Monet holds up a box of Froot Loops. "One Safeway sale," she brags. "My favorite."

While Sheila unloads the cart, Monet turns her attention to the candy rack. "One candy on payday," she explains, "even though candy never goes on sale." In not more than a second she's put a pack of Starbursts on the conveyer belt. She gives her Froot Loops box a hug and arranges it together with the Starbursts on the conveyer.

"Not today," Libby replies, taking the Starbursts off the belt. "Not this payday."

Monet's face turns sour until Libby moves the Starbursts onto her own part of the belt. "This week it's on me."

They unload the groceries, then Sheila and Monet head out for a McDonald's Happy Meal. "Are you sure you don't want to join us?" Sheila asks.

"I'm sure, thanks," Libby replies. "It costs too much."

Sheila shakes her head in bafflement. Nothing is cheaper than the dollar menu, she knows for sure. But she leaves her roommate to her own conclusions.

It's all different when they return home an hour later. Monet's first word when she enters the apartment is, "Wow!"

Sheila enters one step behind her. "That smells great," she says.

Libby has cooked what seemed to her a simple meal. She boiled a handful of spaghetti and fried one sliced onion with an egg in butter. The hardest part was finding the pots under the sink. They were exactly where Sheila said, but buried under layers of clutter and grime. It took as long to wash them until they were fit to use as it did to cook the meal, and straining spaghetti without a colander was a trick. But persevere she did, and as her hosts return, she is finishing a solid, home-cooked meal.

She is starting to accept congratulations when the telephone rings.

"Daddy!" Monet exclaims, running over toward the phone, her face bright.

Sheila cuts her off. Monet rebounds off her hip as Sheila grabs the phone herself. "Who is it?" she growls into the receiver.

A pause.

"He's not here." Her face grows dark.

Libby can hear the voice on the other end of the line but she can't make out the words. Sheila cuts the voice off. "He's not here. I don't know where he is. I won't take a message." She pauses and then repeats herself. "He's not here. I don't know where he is. I won't take a message." Her voice drips with venom. "Thank you. Good-bye." She slams the phone back into the receiver.

Libby sees the cold fury in Sheila's face before she recomposes herself and reaches down to offer Monet a hug. "You know the rules," she says.

Monet looks a little sheepish, like she's made a childish mistake. Sheila gives a pat that all is forgiven and ushers her toward the bathroom and bedtime.

To Libby she says, "I'd better explain."

That much is so clear Libby doesn't bother to say yes.

"It's not my rules that matter," Sheila says. "It's the rules of the court. You answer a question or take a message, you're 'accessory liable for the whole.'" She says it in a way that Libby can hear the quotation marks around the words.

"'Accessory liable?'" Libby asks, using the same quotation marks.

"'For the whole,'" Sheila concludes. "According to the rules, if you help in any way to commit a crime, you are liable as an accessory for the whole thing. So if you take a message from a drug dealer who's closing a twenty-gram deal, you just made yourself part of a twenty-gram crime."

"A twenty-gram crime?"

"That's how they punish drug crimes. You trade ten grams, you go to prison for so many years. You trade fifty and you go away for so many more. Fifty grams will put you away for a long, long time."

"And all I have to do is take a message?"

"It's worse. Sometimes they tempt you into it. 'Please take the message,' they say. 'It will help a lot.' You might not have bothered but now you feel bad. You say yes and *bam*! All of a sudden you're an accessory."

"That's awful."

"Sometimes the police create the whole thing. They pretend to be the drug dealer or pretend to be the buyer, and there's not even a real deal involved. They just hope you'll say yes so they can take you out. They're like scavengers, nibbling for what they can."

Libby sits heavily on the couch and the springs squeak in protest.

"Those are the rules," Sheila concludes. "You don't know anything. You don't say anything. You don't take a message."

Libby is looking at her feet, and Sheila seems to sense something is wrong.

Sheila puts the phone back on the shelf. "Did someone call while I was away?"

Libby doesn't know what to say. She feels like a child. She'd been proud of what she'd done and was planning to show off about it. "I took a message," she confesses.

The dark mask comes over Sheila's face. "Who was it?"

"Hulon," replies Libby. "I told him I'd make sure Zeb got the message that he'd called."

Chapter Five

Nobody knows who Hulon is. Sheila doesn't know and the friends she trusts to ask the next day don't know either. Hulon's not from the neighborhood and he's not someone Zeb did business with in the past.

What they do know is that the bar around the corner has a new sign in front: *Waitress wanted. Inquire within.*

"You go downstairs and check that out," Sheila says as they arrive home from work.

Libby saw it too and she is planning exactly that, as soon as she changes Angel's diaper and tucks him into his nest.

"Flirt yourself into some nice tips," Sheila says, straightening Libby's shirt and giving her hair a tug. "But not too much. We don't need more of those things." She is pointing at Angel.

Libby's eyes make it clear that nothing could be farther from her mind. Then she brushes her hair and heads downstairs, waving good-bye to Monet through the crack as the door closes. The phone rings when she's halfway down the first flight of stairs. She stops and steps back up to listen, taking care not to creak.

"Nobody else is here," she hears Sheila say. "I don't know and I'm not taking a message."

The door opens and Sheila pops her head outside. "Not Hulon," she says.

Libby trots lightly to the bottom of the stairs.

That night for dinner Libby cooks for all three. They celebrate her new job with a home-cooked meal of sautéed cabbage and onions over the rest of that pound of spaghetti, with peanuts on the side. Monet helps chop the vegetables and she's thrilled by what the onions do to her eyes. "They're sneezing!" she exclaims.

Over the next few weeks they settle into a whole new rhythm. Gone is the McDonald's dollar menu. In its place is home cooking. With the extra cash from Libby's job and the savings from McDonald's, they buy some extra pots and improve their ability to cook. Only now does Sheila realize that her ultra-cheap eating habits weren't cheap at all. One night at McDonald's could buy home-cooked food for a week.

Every night they come home and Libby settles Angel in for the evening. She nurses him right away, then sets him in his nest to sleep or on the couch where his big bright eyes watch everything. When he gets bored Sheila or Monet will pick him up and talk to him. Monet loves feeding him a dilute mix of milk and water from his baby bottle, warmed up by soaking in a pot of hot water. Everybody learns the gentle bounce that settles him when he fusses, and that a few softly spoken words can sometimes work wonders. Sheila calls him an easy baby.

Most nights Libby comes home around midnight, and she's so well synchronized with Angel that he's often ready for a meal just as she comes home ready to feed him. Then they both sleep until morning.

Libby shops for meat at the local butcher every Monday. Sheila didn't even know that she had a butcher so close the first time Libby asked. But it turns out to be a short walk away, past a playground that Libby knows Angel is going to love someday. Boys and girls of every age and color soar on the swing set or kick their soccer balls.

Her first trip to the butcher she brings two dollars, planning to bring home as much fresh meat as it will buy. The butcher shop is clean and friendly, with red plaid curtains and spider plants hanging in the window. Behind the counter, the butcher is working some beef on a broad white cutting board, an older white man with his remaining gray hair trimmed short. She stops him as he slides a handful of slop toward a garbage pail. "What are you doing with that?"

He points toward the garbage pail. "On its way out," he says.

"There's beef in there."

"Not worth trimming that carefully," he replies with a hint of remorse. "Nobody will buy it."

"I will." She pulls out her cash. "For the whole thing."

The butcher waves her bill away. He reaches into the garbage pail, selects out a few pieces with care, and bags them along with the slop from the cutting board. He walks around the counter and puts it all in her hand with a smile. "Put it to work," he says. "That's what it's for."

Libby goes home and cooks the best French fries Monet's ever had, fresh cut potatoes deep fried in melted beef fat. Libby opens all the windows while they fry and spends an hour scrubbing the stove top, but it's all worth it for Monet.

On Wednesday she returns to the butcher with a thermos of soup made from potatoes and onions and flavored with fat. "That money you didn't take? I spent it on a thermos. Here's your soup."

He walks to her side of the counter to take the thermos and unscrew the lid, and she can see he likes what's inside. Butcher or not, there's nothing like fresh soup to round out a meal. "Next time you're going to throw something away, think of me," she says. "You fill this thermos with fat, and I'll bring it back with soup."

It becomes a relationship and a deal. Every Monday she comes in and he passes her meat scrap in the thermos. Every Wednesday she brings back the thermos filled with soup. She notices after a while that the slop isn't so sloppy. Often there's more beef than fat. Every now and again she buys some chicken.

With the second job and money changing hands, Libby develops a system for accounting. She puts Sheila's pay stubs in one envelope and her own in another, both clearly labeled with big black letters. Back at Happy Jack's Custom Cleaning, Sheila insists that if Jack is going to pay her in cash, Libby needs some kind of pay stub to go with it.

"I don't want her walking around with five hundred cash and no proof of where she got it," Sheila insisted.

Jack grumbled the first time, but now he scribbles a note or taps some keys and presses a button on his computer.

From the recycling bin downstairs, Monet brings a big red jar that Libby puts her larger bills into—the tens, twenties, and fifties that make her biweekly paycheck. The next day Monet adds a big blue jar that Libby uses for cash from the bar. No stubs for this one—it's mostly tips, plus ten dollars just for showing up during the busy eight-to-midnight part of the evening. This jar has mostly single dollar bills and lots of change—so Libby spends it first for household expenses, not wanting to clutter the drawer with all the small stuff.

After a few months of home-cooked meals, Sheila has lost a chunk of weight. She looks better and says she feels better at the end of the day. "More muscle and more energy," she concludes.

"For less money," Libby chimes in.

"Bye-bye Happy Meal," adds Monet.

People still call sometimes asking for Zeb, but Libby answers just like

Sheila taught her to. Not here, no message—just like that. One time it's Hulon on the line. Libby's heart freezes when she recognizes his voice. "Hey honey, it's Hulon," he begins. "Is Zeb in?"

"He's not here," says Libby, a voice of ice. "He doesn't live here."

"Will he come by later? Can I leave him a message?"

"No, he won't. No, you can't." Weeks of remorse slam the phone back into the receiver, then Libby raises her arms in the air like it's a touchdown in football. "Score!" she exclaims.

"Let's hope that one was recorded," Sheila replies.

By now Angel is less like a newborn baby. He recognizes his friends and family and follows them around the room with his eyes. Monet and his mom are his favorites. His whole face bursts out in smiles when they approach, and he loves a little tickle on the tummy.

His favorite of all is taking a bath in the kitchen sink. Monet fills it up for him and sets him in it like a swimming pool. At first the sink was just for scrubbing, but now that he can sit by himself, he'd stay there all night if they let him, cooing like a pigeon or bellowing with laughter when they tickle his feet. Monet gives him ice cubes to watch as they float around the basin. Sometimes he manages to catch one and bring it all the way up to his mouth where he sucks it until it slips away. His worst screams of the evening are when the bath ends and Monet takes him out, but they've learned to turn even that to their advantage. They pull him out of the sink for his screaming fit after they've cooked and eaten, just before Libby heads out to the bar for the night. She nurses him calm while Sheila and Monet use the sink for dishes, a meal that will last until Monet feeds him from a bottle before her own bedtime.

Life is great and they know it. On Libby's birthday they go out to celebrate. Pizza and ice cream and a movie that Monet's been wanting to see. On Thanksgiving they roast a turkey, and take turns around the table counting their blessings.

"You," says Sheila, pointing at Libby. "You're what Zeb said wasn't possible. All the basics and sometimes even a treat—with no drugs anywhere in sight. You are my blessing."

Monet walks over and grabs her mom's love handles. "But there's not as much of you to bless."

Chapter Six

It's two o'clock in the morning, the week after Thanksgiving. Everyone is at home and asleep, Sheila and Monet in their room, Libby and Angel in theirs. The season is turning cold, but tonight is warm. Early Christmas decorations dot the landscape, and Angel loves the flashing lights in the wreath by the front door of their own apartment building. Right now he's asleep under a bright red blanket Monet picked for him at Goodwill.

The banging on the door shocks Libby awake. Just a few feet away in the corridor, someone is hammering to get in. "Police!" shouts a voice in the darkness. "Open up!"

Libby sits upright. Surely this isn't her door they're knocking on. Someone down the hall must be in trouble. She rests a hand on Angel in his nest; he's still asleep.

The next knock is unmistakably on their own door. "Police! Open up!"

The sudden noise wakes Angel, who starts to cry. Libby lifts him into bed with her and presses him against her chest.

"Police! Open up!"

She gets out of bed and starts her baby bounce, hoping to settle him down while looking for clothes. She hears motion in Sheila's room but can't tell what it is.

"Police! Open up!"

The next knocks are so hard they shake the room. Someone is banging on the door, and someone else is banging on the wall that separates Libby from the hallway. She feels the pounding through her feet. "Let me in," calls the voice by the door. "I demand consent to enter."

She sees Sheila, fully dressed, walking across the living room toward the front door. Sheila doesn't shout as loudly as the police officer, but she's talking straight to the door and her tone is clear. "Go away. We don't want you here."

Angel is screaming by now. Libby is struggling to get dressed and comfort him at the same time. He spits up on her shoulder and she has no rag handy. She moves him to the other shoulder and continues to bounce. She can't see Monet but she imagines her doing what Libby most wants to do, hiding in her bed under the covers.

The next knocks are so hard she hears wood starting to split. "Give me consent or I'll break the door down."

Another voice starts from down the hall. "Shut the fuck up out there. What the hell are you doing?"

Then the officer again, pounding the door at every syllable. "I de-mand con-sent to ent-er."

Sheila is just as loud on her own side of the door. "Consent denied!" Her back is pressed against the door as if she can hold it shut against a flood. "Keep your people out of my house!"

The knocking continues in a steady rhythm. "Final warning. Volunteer to open or I'm coming in anyway." The next knock hits so hard the door frame shakes and Sheila's body shudders at the blow.

Sheila doesn't talk and doesn't move, just presses backwards against the door, head down, hands balled into fists.

The corridor goes quiet. No more banging and no more yelling. Just silence on the other side, like the hall is empty, but without the sound of feet walking away. Angel pauses in his screams and Libby can hear Monet sobbing in the other room.

Then the crash. The officers push so hard against the door the whole thing comes smashing out of its frame and Sheila is shoved bodily into the room. She turns to lash back at them but trips and ends up sprawling sideways into the kitchen. Three officers burst into the room, dressed in black, belts clanging with equipment.

Libby screams. She's never seen so much power up so close. They push past Sheila and stride fully into the apartment. One officer shoves into Libby's room, going out of his way to bump her with his shoulder even as she does her best to stay out of his way. Then he's pulling everything apart, ripping Angel's bright red blanket out of his nest and shaking the whole box empty onto the ground. He strips Libby's bed and flips the mattress upside down onto the floor. The corner hits her lamp, which falls to the floor and shatters.

"Shut the fuck up out there!" cries the voice from down the hall.

Every drawer gets opened and every shelf swept clean. Through the racket she hears the same happening in other rooms. Glass shattering and large objects falling. She hears the toilet tank being opened and the lid cast into the shower with a clang so loud a dog starts barking in the building next door. An officer orders Monet out of her bed and out of the room; Libby sees her shuffling into the living room, hunched forward, wrapped up in her blankets, face gleaming with tears. The officer chases her down and rips off her blankets. "Those stay in here," he says, hurling them back into the bedroom.

Libby steps out to the living room and sees Sheila face down on the floor, the commanding officer leaning over her, giving her one last pat and frisk before standing up and letting her do the same. She rises as fast as a viper and gets straight in his face. "I told you he doesn't live here," she says. "Zeb's gone. That's my new roommate." She points to Libby. "Fresh as a daisy and whiter than you are."

The officer shoves her into the couch and orders Libby and Monet to join her. Libby sits at the far end, and does her best to settle Angel. Monet sits down beside her mother, leans over and snuggles in, tries to sink her head into her shoulder, her face wet with tears. The officer grabs her and shoves her back into her own part of the seat. "Sit! Stay."

Angel screams anew and Libby whispers a few words to calm him down. "Easy, baby. Shhh."

"Shut up!" The officer's hand moves toward his gun.

The officer that had been in Libby's room starts hunting through the kitchen cabinets, sweeping through with his hands, not caring what falls or what breaks. He opens the drawers and soon finds their big red cash jar. "Bull's-eye," he declares. He brings the jar to the commanding officer and resumes his search.

"And what's this?" the officer guarding them sneers at Sheila, as if she's been caught with the crowned jewels of England.

"That's our money," Sheila replies. "Every last nickel of it. Every nickel ours, and every nickel legal."

"You get paid in cash?"

Libby finds her voice. "I get paid in cash," she says.

The officer turns toward her, surprised, like a puppet has come to life. His hand reaches for his gun but it stays in the holster.

Libby continues. "I get $480, every two weeks. The receipts are in an envelope near the jar. The blue jar has my tips from the bar. That's mostly singles and change, but without receipts." Her voice is small and orderly in the tumult. The words alone start to calm Angel down.

Sheila adds, "I get paid by check. My receipts are in a separate envelope." Now she, too, sounds like an accountant.

Nobody speaks while the officer returns to the kitchen and starts opening drawers. Soon enough he has found the receipts and examined them closely enough to report back. "Seems right," he says. "Happy Jack's Custom Cleaning."

The other office returns from the bathroom and bedroom. "Negative, sir," he reports. "No contraband on premises."

Sheila stands up from the couch and steps his way. "Put my cash down on the counter top. Do it slowly. I want to watch your hands the whole time." Her voice is quietly dangerous.

The officer stares back at her but doesn't move. Their eyes stay locked, testing wills, until the officer moves slowly back toward the counter top. He rests both jars on the surface, then steps away, moving slowly, his hands in the clear. "You're clean," he declares. "Today."

Sheila says to Libby, "Count our cash."

To the commanding officer she says, "I trust you'll talk to our landlord about his door."

But he's losing interest by now. The search is finished and the results were negative. The other officers are already walking toward the door. "Any property damage is between you and your landlord," he says. "The police report will say we were given consent to enter."

Chapter Seven

Monet sits motionless on the couch as if she's in some kind of shock. No longer sobbing, she barely even seems to be breathing, just sitting utterly still, a tiny animal whimper on every breath. Her face is glazed with tears and her nose needs wiping, but her hands rest insensible in her lap.

Sheila steps toward her daughter but the door lies flat across her path. As she detours around, the officers beyond the missing door catch her attention. She turns as if to chase them, then stops and turns back. Her eyes come to rest on the cash jars on the counter top, jumbled together with the receipt envelopes, breakfast bowls and a box of cornflakes that's been emptied onto the floor. Cornflakes crunch underfoot as she steps toward the cash jars and, eyes still on Monet, bends down and starts sweeping up cornflakes with her hand.

Libby can feel the urgency of her confusion. Sheila wants to clean up the mess and kick at the rubble; she wants to chase the police and take her daughter in her arms. Libby steps in front of her. "Go to her," she says. "Take care of Monet." Her voice trips on tears of her own. "The mess can wait."

At first Sheila doesn't seem to understand. She seems confused by the interruption—then she looks over to Monet and suddenly has eyes only for her daughter. She races to the couch and takes her in her arms, surrounding her with love. Monet seems to awaken at the contact. She closes her own arms around her mother and burrows into her chest, the animal whimper expanding into full-blown sobs. They stay together, clutching each other, and it looks to Libby like more than one of them might be crying.

Libby starts to walk laps around the apartment, bouncing Angel and cooing in his ear while surveying the damage. Soon enough, the infant falls asleep on her shoulder. Libby recovers his box and shakes his red blanket clear of debris; a few minutes later he's asleep in bed as if nothing has happened.

Libby goes straight to work on the apartment, starting first with the door. She stands it up and leans it closed across the door frame, creating a semblance of privacy. Next she walks around with the trash can, picking up rubble and sweeping up cornflakes and dust so people can walk without grinding and tripping.

Sheila and Monet stay together, clutching each other on the couch. But by the time Libby starts putting the kitchen back together, Sheila has joined her. They retrieve Monet's blankets from her bedroom and settle her down to sleep on the couch so everyone can stay together in the same room. After she's sleeping, Sheila and Libby change rooms and go to work on her bed.

"Some friends owe me a favor," says Sheila as they lift the mattress together onto the frame. "We can probably get a deal fixing the door."

Near dawn the apartment looks close to normal. Not everything has been put in place and much has been broken, but it's no longer a disaster area. They agree to quit for now and rest for an hour before the alarm goes off, though Sheila opts to squeeze onto the couch with her daughter rather than go to bed by herself.

Libby lies down on her bare mattress beside Angel in his box. No sooner has she closed her eyes than a new thumping starts by the door. Soon she hears the door being dragged so someone can step inside. "Landlord," a man's voice declares. "Coming in."

Libby doesn't get up at first. It's Sheila's landlord, and Sheila is in the front room. But as the discussion rises in heat, she decides to join them.

"No," the landlord is saying. "It needs to be my people. I can't have any Tom, Dick, or Harry driving nails into my building."

"They're licensed and insured," says Sheila in a tone that sounds like she's saying it for the hundredth time. "They're professionals." Monet is still sleeping on the couch.

"My people. My people will do the work. I'll bill you for it." He steps outside but keeps talking as he slides the door back into place behind him. "I'll make you a payment plan."

"Thanks for nothing." Sheila tosses a loose corn flake toward the sink and misses.

"Lucky I let you stay here at all, with all the trouble you cause."

When they return from work at the end of the day, the door is back in place, but it looks nothing like new. The face is scratched, trim is missing, and the knob grinds as it turns. The apartment inside is even worse. Fresh sawdust covers the floor and new scraps of wood lie where they fell. Wrappers from McDonald's cover the couch, and dirty dishes sit on the table.

The landlord's workers helped themselves to the refrigerator as well. Monet's precious bottle of Coca Cola, her treat from last week, sits empty in the bathroom. The toilet is clogged with toilet paper and some strange man's waste.

The landlord demands the first payment on their installment plan immediately and in cash, and it decimates their savings. Making payments the next four weeks puts them deep in the red. Libby doesn't even try to replace the lamp in her room; she just lives with the dark.

Cooking is no longer an exercise in independence and a joy, but just one more chore among so many others. Without a break, they spend more time cooking, cleaning, and shopping than ever before, and the savings don't begin to cover the door. Libby's nightly departure to her second job seems less like a step upward than an abandonment.

One night the police call and ask for Zeb.

The next night they call and ask for Hulon.

One night while Libby is at the bar, the police call and ask for her. Sheila says that she picked up the phone that time, and she "gave them an earful." She says it with gusto, but Libby isn't amused. She still remembers that shoulder as the uniformed man forced his way into her bedroom.

Angel is developing a sense of humor. He's fussy at dinner one night, whining, not eating, so Sheila offers him a little rubber duck she picked up lately. It's a cute yellow duckling that sometimes he sucks on or floats around in the sink, but tonight he wants none of it.

Sheila puts it in his hand. He throws it away.

She brings it back. He throws it away.

"You love it!" she insists. "Play with it. Suck on it. Do something! Just get happy."

He throws it away, and now his fitful grumbling teeters on the brink of a full-fledged cry.

So Libby gives it a try. She grabs the duck off the floor and waves it around to catch Angel's attention; then with great flourish, she opens her mouth wide and, with a long arc of her arm, sticks the duck in her mouth.

Angel stops cold.

She takes the duck out, sweeps it away in her hand . . . then brings it all the way back into her mouth again.

Angel busts out laughing.

Libby does it a few more times to riotous giggling—snatching a few bites of her own dinner in between—until Angel reaches for the duck himself.

Libby thinks maybe he'll play with it himself but Angel has other ideas. With a combination of pulls, gestures, and sounds he gets Libby to lower herself next to his chair . . . and he puts the duck in her mouth.

Everyone cracks up. The only one louder than Angel is Libby, and the two of them go back and forth a while, taking turns with the duck, chewing on it and putting it in the other person's mouth, until finally dinner is over. Everyone is fed, Angel's had his bath, and Libby heads out for work.

Angel still loves his bath in the sink, but nowadays he's getting too big to fit. His knees bang up against the faucet and he can almost tip himself out looking over the edge. Soon they'll need to manage him in the cubicle shower.

He's getting too big for his papoose, too. No longer can Libby tie him onto her back and do a full day's work cleaning other people's houses. Now he wants to scooch around and play. She gives him as much freedom as she can, but she can't leave him to crawl around taking things off people's bottom shelves. If the owners are at home, she leaves him in the car alone. She makes quick visits to check on him as if she's going for cleaning supplies, but often that amounts to nothing more than seeing that he's alive and crying. She just leaves him there, screaming for her, and goes back inside to work. She can hear him from inside, and her breasts throb in sympathy.

So Sheila starts hunting for day care. The woman who took care of Monet has long since moved away, but soon she finds a woman called Josephine Baker who tends six children in her apartment.

"Josephine Baker?" asks Libby. "For real?" She doesn't remember exactly who Josephine Baker is, but she knows it was someone famous.

"Yes, for real," Sheila replies. "Her family name was Baker and they started her with something special."

The very next Monday morning at eight they detour to Josephine Baker's on the way to Happy Jack's. She greets them on the first knock. An African-American woman, maybe fifty years old with close-cropped hair and big, black, rectangular eyeglasses, she's talking on the telephone as she opens the door. "Come in," she says. "With you in a minute."

A big-screen television dominates the apartment's largest wall, and two children about two years old watch a Barney movie, sitting on the floor amidst scattered toys and Tupperware lids. Milk crates stacked along the back wall serve as shelves for diapers, baby bottles, and old plastic toys. On the couch opposite the television a woman in a tight red dress sprawls crookedly, holding an infant in her arms. Both appear to be asleep, a pearl of drool gleaming in the corner of the woman's lips.

Leaving her child with a stranger is hard enough for Libby. Leaving him with sprawling drunks seems all but impossible. This place is a mess, with toys everywhere and cups stacked in the sink. Libby says to Angel in her arms, "Let's get out of here."

Angel responds with a fat, wet raspberry.

Josephine Baker is talking on the telephone with her head in the refrigerator as they start for the door. Libby hears her say, "Got plenty. We'll be fine. Bye." Emerging from the refrigerator, Josephine stirs a pot on the stove as she turns to her guests. "Welcome. Good morning."

Libby has no choice. "Good morning."

"Make yourselves at home," Josephine says, but offers them nothing to eat or drink, nor even a place to sit. She notices Libby looking at the woman sprawled across the couch. The woman isn't just small, she's scrawny; all skin and bones, the low neck of her dress showing the ribs around her sternum. The arm holding the infant is tracked with marks from needles.

"That's Meredith," says Josephine as if that explains it all. "I mind her daughter, Malika."

With the smallest edge that Libby might not have caught if she didn't know her, Sheila asks, "Does she live here?"

"I mind her daughter," says Josephine with seemingly full understanding. "And Meredith had a tough night last night. If I mind your child, you're in my family."

The door opens. Arms reach inside and deposit a toddler boy. "Thanks!" says a disembodied voice that's already racing down the hall.

Josephine kneels to the floor and the little boy runs into her arms for a hug. "That was Latisha," she says, looking at her watch. "She's always late to work." Holding the hand of the new toddler, Josephine walks across to the milk crates and digs until she finds a small purple sack. "Here you go!" she says to the youngster, kneeling back down to his level. "Your favorite."

The boy grabs the sack and Josephine stays with him while he works the clasp open and dumps a cluster of purple frogs onto the rug. "Bravo!" she cries. The boy turns his full attention to the frogs as Josephine, satisfied that he's happy, turns back to her newcomers.

"Ninety dollars a week," she explains. "I open at 7:00 A.M. and I like to have them picked up before seven at night—though you can see it doesn't always turn out that way." She picks up a stuffed cat and tosses it into a milk crate as she walks back toward the kitchen. "The price stays the same whether you pick up late or pick up early. Has he been in day care before?"

Before Libby can answer, a gasp erupts from the direction of the couch, followed by a long, low whistle like a balloon losing air.

"Excuse me," Josephine says.

They all walk together to the couch, where Meredith is struggling to sit up, holding her baby tight against her chest, looking exhausted and haggard. The drool is gone from her lip but now Libby sees old bruises on her cheek and a cut by her eye that's not fully healed.

"Good morning," Josephine says.

Sheila is more direct. She kneels beside Meredith like an old friend or a nurse. "Can I get you anything?"

"Water." Meredith's voice is soft and hoarse.

Sheila finds a large plastic cup by the sink and fills it with water from the tap.

Meredith chugs it down in one long draw, without pausing for breath or moving her daughter Malika, who starts to stir as water dribbles on her forehead. Meredith passes the empty cup back to Sheila without looking up. "More."

Sheila refills the cup and returns it to Meredith, who downs it in another long draw. A grimace slashes across her face and she stands up urgently, dropping the not-quite-empty cup onto the couch. She shoves her daughter into Sheila's arms, races to the bathroom and vomits violently into the toilet. On her knees with her back to the door, she wretches long and loud and hard.

Everyone stands mesmerized, listening to her gag and heave, watching her head rise and fall over the bowl. Josephine recovers the cup and blots the wet spots on the couch with a towel while Sheila rocks the little girl, who wakes up and seems confused.

Slowly the noise starts to abate.

"Heroin," says Sheila to Josephine.

"You've been there before."

"My boyfriend sold heroin before I kicked him out."

"May he rot in hell." Josephine hangs the towel on a hook by the sink. "Meredith's dealer pimps her for her fix."

In the bathroom the toilet flushes and the vomiting starts again. Meredith reaches back between heaves to close the door. They can't see her any more, but the thin door can't hide the sound. Everyone recognizes the painful heaves against Meredith's now empty stomach.

"She's trying to quit," Josephine explains. "It isn't easy, and most people would rather she not make it." She walks around the apartment, picking up toys and checking personally on each child to make sure they're okay. The two boys watching Barney are as happy as can be. Latisha's boy with the purple frogs asks for some crackers, and Josephine brings him a handful on a plate.

By now Sheila is making good friends with Meredith's daughter Malika in her arms. They're taking turns touching each other's noses and smiling.

"Nose!" says Sheila every time she touches Malika's with her finger, and Malika erupts with a gust of laughter.

Libby's been holding Angel this whole time and before long she starts playing the nose game with him too, saying "nose" and touching him with her fingertip.

Soon enough Meredith returns from the bathroom, her face washed and looking like a whole new person. She reaches across for Malika, who is excited to go back to her mother and burrows in for a big hug before turning back out to the rest of the room.

"Thanks for the water," says Meredith with a sarcastic smile.

"Anytime," says Sheila, grinning in return. "You didn't keep it very long."

Josephine joins them for a formal introduction, then returns to the kitchen to stir her pot.

Libby follows her. "What's in the pot?" she asks.

"Oatmeal and applesauce," Josephine replies. "Never won an award, but it's good and good for you. Long as you're here, you get what you need, whatever you need. Now let's have a look at him."

Angel senses her coming even as Josephine steps in his direction. He wriggles free of his mother and all but leaps into her arms. He reaches up to touch her big black eyeglasses, then grabs ahold of her ear. When she smiles down on him, he laughs hilariously and keeps on laughing.

The two of them get acquainted while Libby unpacks some clothing and diapers to see them through the day. Josephine's still laughing with Angel when Libby waves good-bye and closes the door behind. Ninety dollars and all he can eat.

Josephine works out fine, but still the math is against them. Day care plus six more weeks of door payments—three pay periods—and they just don't have enough. Libby extends her hours at the bar for a few extra tips, but it barely seems worth the effort.

Spending his days at Josephine's, Angel is being weaned from Libby's breast milk that she used to provide him for free. Now they need to add milk to the budget, and Libby's breasts ache for relief during the day. Bending down to scrub and stretching up to dust an upper shelf pulls on her flesh and reminds her of her missing boy. The ache eventually passes, but still she misses her baby. Nursing in the back seat between houses was at least time together. Now she's lucky to hold him during a bottle between cleaning during the day and waiting tables at night.

Then he gets sick. Angel's never been really sick before, just ordinary baby sniffles and sneezes. But now in his eighth month he develops a terrible croupy cough, barking like a seal, and a horrifying wheeze that keeps the whole house awake at night. Josephine takes a look at him one morning, hears him cough, and won't let him stay.

"I won't charge you for the time, of course." She holds them in the hallway while she delivers the news. "You're welcome back when he's better, but I can't risk everyone getting sick like that." She closes the door quickly as if germs might hurry inside during a proper farewell.

Three days later he still hasn't gotten better. Libby still works her night shifts when Sheila and Monet can take over on Angel, but she skips her day shifts cleaning for Happy Jack. It doesn't affect her daily cash, but it will come out of her paycheck at the end of two weeks. Libby's not sure how she'll pay her share of the rent, and it's not as if Sheila can advance her much. She drops her food ration down to oatmeal and water, and she starts daydreaming about meat. Ham at first, then a steak; it seems like she spends every waking hour thinking about meals she's eaten or meals she could cook.

The third night as she's heading downstairs to wait tables, the rubber sole of her shoe falls off. Her first thought is to wish it were leather, as if she could boil it soft and chew it down, but she returns to the apartment to find a plastic grocery bag. She sits on the couch, twists the bag into a rope and ties the sole back in place.

Sheila watches her while she's waiting for water to boil. "Don't you have family who can help?" she asks at last. She tries to make it sound casual, but Libby can tell she's been nursing that question for days.

Twisting the bag and tying the sole is both difficult and noisy. Libby acts as if she doesn't hear the question.

Sheila walks in front of her so she can't be missed. "Just a hundred dollars. Maybe someone can help get you through the month. Don't you have family?"

Libby does have family. They're not rich, but they could surely find a hundred dollars if she asked. They could find ten times a hundred if they had to. Most of the meat she's been daydreaming about is raised on their farm.

But no. She can't do that. She can't set foot in that house or even call them on the phone. She can't go back to her father who treated her like another farm instrument. Hoe for the garden, oil for the hinge, teenage daughter for the sexual satisfaction. Lie here, rub there, suck that. No, she's not calling him for help. She can't bear the thought of her mother's voice on the phone, her mother who never listened when it mattered.

If she ever goes home it has to be as a happy hero—when she can show off how well she's done without them, not as a lost little girl begging for help.

She doesn't say any of that to Sheila, but can't leave the question hanging. Libby just says, "No."

Sheila leaves it at that.

On the fourth day, Angel's cough seems to be subsiding and Libby is ready to bring him back to Josephine, but in the middle of the night he starts to blaze with fever and cry like he's never cried before. Libby holds him to her breast to comfort him but her supply's run dry, which only frustrates him and makes her breasts ache anew. Now at last they decide that it's time for a doctor. He's tugging at his right ear like he'll rip it off. Sheila drops them at the emergency room on her way to Happy Jack's.

A woman cuts them off on their way inside the hospital. "Need a Visa card?" she asks. "Free credit."

But Libby doesn't need a Visa card. She's heard enough about late fees and outrageous interest rates, and she remembers how the Anderson family lost their farm. What she needs now is a doctor. Feeling almost like that cop in her bedroom, she shoulders past the woman pitching the Visa cards.

And then she waits. She sits all morning in that emergency room. People come and people go; doctors and nurses bustle around, pushing carts of equipment and sometimes beds with people, occasionally bloody and often moaning in pain. The longer Libby sits, the more tired she feels, then she feels dizzy when she stands. She didn't eat breakfast today or dinner last night, and she hasn't slept properly in days. When she closes her eyes to doze, it makes her feel nauseous, and Angel demands her attention anyway. He's crying so much that even in the crowded room, the seat next to her is empty.

As the hours, pass Libby's thoughts turn back to her mother. Somewhere deep down she wants her back. She wants someone to take over, to lay her down to rest and bring her soup. She wants her mother to rub her head like she did when she was a little girl, and tell her how wonderfully she's doing.

Isn't Libby being wonderful, after all? Isn't she doing great? Cooking, cleaning, and paying her way? She's come so far, by herself, with her newborn baby.

But maybe she's not being wonderful. Maybe she's being foolish. Maybe it's time to go home, to forgive her mother and learn how to keep her distance from her father. Maybe it's time to go to where she's sure they'd take her in.

A boy hobbling past on crutches reminds her of the other time she went to an emergency room. When she was twelve years old she'd been thrown by a horse and broken her leg. She got a cast for people to sign, starting with her mother in the emergency room, and her brothers had been nicer than they'd been in years. But she remembers her father, too. How he came to her bed to tuck her in, and what else he did while he was supposed to be taking care of her. She remembers how he made her move even when it hurt her leg.

Around the corner comes an elderly couple looking for someplace to sit, struggling in the crowded room, she with a walker and he with a cane. Libby stands to catch their attention, banishing her memories. "Here," she says, pointing to her own seat and the empty one beside her. "Two seats together."

"Thank you so much," says the man, hobbling gingerly toward the chair, clutching his wife's walker once to steady himself. "It's hard for us."

"No problem," she says, and finds strength to walk amid the rows of chairs with Angel on her shoulder. She picks up a candy wrapper hoping for crumbs, then tosses it in the trash can as if that were her plan all along.

At last a nurse peers from behind the closed doors and announces, "Libby Thompson with child." She shows Libby back to a room and tells her to sit again, though this time alone and with a cup of water that Libby empties and refills immediately. A nurse comes to take Angel's temperature and listen to his chest with a stethoscope. Finally, a doctor arrives to look in his eyes and ears with a flashlight. "Ear infection," he declares almost immediately. He scribbles words on a prescription pad and passes her a piece of paper. "Pharmacy," he says, pointing in the direction of a wall.

Out of the room and through the waiting room, Libby navigates her way in the direction he pointed and to the pharmacy. Again she stands in line until another young man reaches for her slip of prescription paper. At this moment Angel isn't crying, but his exhausted whimper breaks Libby's heart. The young man says, "Amoxicillin," and walks away, then returns a moment later with a little bottle. "Twenty-nine thirty," he says.

The numbers make no sense to her. Is that an estimate? As in twenty-nine or thirty tablets? Twenty-nine or maybe thirty days until Angel gets better?

The pharmacist sees her confusion. "That's the price," he says. "Twenty-nine dollars and thirty cents."

The price hits her like a punch in the stomach. *Twenty-nine dollars?* She doesn't have twenty-nine dollars and might not for two weeks. She doesn't even have thirty cents. Where is she going to find twenty-nine dollars? What can she do to earn that kind of money? Not someday, but this very instant. She needs twenty-nine dollars before Angel wakes up and starts howling again.

But even as she gives up her place in line and leaves the precious bottle behind, she knows what she has to do. She walks back to the woman offering the Visa cards. She fills out forms and does something that every farmer knows is the path to ruin, that goes against everything she ever learned at home with her family. She fills out the form and waits while the woman works an Internet connection and produces a temporary form with a number in the corner. Then she walks back to the pharmacy and buys something with money that isn't hers. She just borrowed money from a stranger to take care of her baby. She's lost.

Chapter Eight

Angel responds quickly to the Amoxicillin, and by the second day he's back at Josephine's. Meanwhile, the Visa card proves to be a godsend. Libby buys groceries for herself and a quart of milk for her Angel, still obeying the Safeway sales but at least putting food in the cart. She understands the lure of credit as she eyeballs fresh spinach and a new pair of shoes she could also get for free—but she still minds her math. Yes to the milk; but Josephine and the door come before spinach and shoes.

On Friday evening, dinner's been cooked and the dishes are clean. Libby's in her room tending to Angel before her night shift, planning to start early and return home late. He seems tired tonight, and he's falling asleep with a bottle. Libby is setting him to bed in his box when she hears unusual footsteps in the hall. A moment later on the front door comes the age-old knock: *Tap tappity tap tap. Tap tap.*

Monet leaps up from the table where she's been doing her homework. "Daddy!"

Libby hears her run across the room and open the door. A deep, new voice says, "Baby girl!" and the door clicks shut.

Sheila emerges from her room and announces, "Well, aren't you a day in springtime!"

Libby expected to meet the drug dealer someday, but not here, not now, and the noise seems to be bothering Angel. He lifts his arms out of his blankets and opens his eyes, uttering the first little hiccups of a cry, just like little Malika when Meredith started dribbling water down her chin. Libby puts her hand on Angel's chest and whispers a few words, coaxes him back down while Sheila and Monet start what sounds like a party in the living room. After a few delicate minutes Angel falls back asleep. Libby pulls on a sweater and steps outside.

Zeb at that moment is swinging Monet around the room, holding her near the shoulders and spinning in tight circles so her legs fly out, filling the room, dodging the furniture like an expert. Zeb is better than six feet tall, a lean, muscular, handsome African American man. It's clear that he'd have no problem finding another girlfriend now that Sheila's kicked him out, but it's also clear from the way he looks at Sheila that he wouldn't be interested.

With one final twirl, Zeb flops backwards onto the couch, Monet in his arms. Libby cringes in expectation of an earsplitting squeak or even total collapse, but the springs pipe cheerfully, as if even they are happy to see him. With Monet glowing in his lap, he looks like Santa Claus in the shopping mall holding a child before Christmas. He looks up and sees Libby for the first time. "Is this the Angel I hear tell of?"

Libby steps forward, arm out for a formal handshake. "I'm Libby Thompson. Angel is asleep in the other room."

Zeb shakes her hand while Monet takes over. "It's not mine anymore, Daddy." Her eyes are bright like she's showing off. "Angel sleeps in it now. He cries sometimes, too."

"Does it bother you?" Zeb wants to know.

"No, it reminds me I love him. And I snuggle in with Mommy."

Her father pulls her in for a giant hug, then, catching Sheila's eye, pulls her in too. The three of them stand together, hugging and rocking. Tallest in the center, Zeb starts to hum the tune "You Are My Sunshine."

At the end of the verse, Sheila pulls herself free. "Sunshine my left foot," she says with a grin. "How are you, stranger? How's life on the street?"

"Life is good," Zeb replies. "There's just one thing missing from it."

"Squeaky couch?" she sits back down and the springs prove her point.

"You, honey. I love you, baby." He sits beside her gently, and the springs don't seem to notice.

"No kissy stuff!" yells Monet with a giant smile.

Sheila's looking only at Zeb. "I miss you too, honey. I've got a great new roommate and warmth in my bed—" she smiles at Monet "—but I miss you wholesome." He's taller than her and it's a tough stretch, but she reaches her arm all the way around his shoulder. "You can come back anytime you want, you know."

"I know the terms, baby. I'll get there. I want to come back. But I won't ask until I'm ready." He stands up from the couch with Monet still on his lap, then lowers her back down beside her mother with muscular ease. "Does it help if I brought gifts?"

Monet lights up.

Sheila frowns. "Did you buy them legal?"

"Honey, I'm a drug dealer. One thing I know is how to track the cash.

Every nickel here came from payroll. Taxes deducted and everything." He's walking across the room to some bags he left by the door as he came in. He bends down and starts sorting through one of them, emerging a moment later with a tiny pink box. He steps back to Monet like a suitor approaching his betrothed. "For my princess," he declares.

Monet can barely contain her excitement. If she were a dog, she'd be running around in circles, tail wagging up a storm, but she holds herself sober for a reply. "Thank you, my prince. I accept your gift."

Inside the box is a chrome charm necklace, colored beads on a silver chain, a cobalt blue whale dangling in the center. Monet doesn't even try to control her response. She launches at her father for another hug, then she's all smiles as she parades the room, showing everyone her prize, modeling it every which way. "I like the blue beads best," she says to her dad, before interrupting herself. "No, I like the yellow beads best. Or maybe no, I like the red beads best . . . but obviously the whale is best. Daddy, I like the whole thing the best!" She gives him another huge hug.

"You know how things are at Claire's," he says, reaching into his pocket. "You can never buy just one thing." Out comes another jewelry box. "The second is half price."

The hugs begin before she even opens it. Soon Monet is parading around with her whale chain and a silver seahorse ring, loving them both and declaring that every single part is the best. The seahorse, the whale, and every single color of bead all have a turn at being best. Libby suddenly realizes how long it's been since this little girl has been a little girl, busy as she is in school all day, then helping with the chores and tending to Angel in the evening. All of a sudden, she's a princess.

Zeb goes sober and strides purposefully into the center of the room where he poses like a TV commercial. "But wait! There's more."

Back to the bags he goes and this time returns to Sheila with a single small brown grocery bag. "For my other princess," he says with a bow. "With your permission." He hands her the bag.

Sheila looks inside and lights up in a smile before she takes anything out. "Perfect," she whispers. "Absolutely perfect." She pulls out of the bag and holds up for all to see one red apple, perfectly shaped and resting naturally in her hand. Zeb gets his hug too, though this one ends with a bit of the kissy stuff.

She retreats back to her place by the couch, studying her reflection in the bright red apple in her hand. "I'll save it for later," she explains for no reason.

Zeb returns to the door, where the largest bags rest unopened. To Sheila he says, "With your permission, I have something for your new roommate. With your permission." His tone suggests that it's actually a question.

"Permission granted," replies Sheila, apple in hand.

Zeb carries to Libby the two large shopping bags. Inside are baby diapers and wipes, two large family packs of exactly what she needs and exactly what's been busting her budget. The diapers are even the right size, too. She doesn't mean to echo Sheila, but she says it anyway. "Perfect. They're perfect. Absolutely perfect."

She doesn't ask permission, just races across and gives Zeb a giant hug, and her eyes prick with tears as she steps away. "Thank you so much," she says. "It's exactly what I need."

"Keep digging," he says. "It's not all you need."

She looks back in astonishment. She can't imagine anything more. But she returns to the bag and digs down to the bottom, removing the diapers, looking past the wipes, to a little bag that hides separately at the bottom.

"What is it?" says Monet, racing across the room, her necklace jingling as she moves.

Inside the bag is a disposable camera, a little instamatic like Libby's seen at the pharmacy, and a prepaid coupon for developing the film.

"Perfect," she says. "You're right. It's perfect." Her eyes are filling with tears.

"Keep digging."

At the bottom of the bag is a frame.

The tears are running down her cheeks by now, as every step makes the gift even more perfect. Sheila too is wiping her eyes.

Zeb wraps one strong arm around Monet. "You might not believe it now, but he won't always be a baby." He gives her a squeeze. "You might want some evidence."

Libby walks across and gives him one more hug, this one with Monet naturally included in the circle. A moment later, Sheila joins them. "Keep him," says Libby. "Please keep him."

Sheila steps back, eyes on her mate. "I always said you were the best of your breed."

Chapter Nine

Monet is still buzzing the next morning. "Daddy's back, Daddy's back," she sings while they boil water for oats. "Oh Daddy, Daddy's back." She dances around the apartment, cleaning as she goes. At a crucial moment she changes the rhyme. "Daddy's back, Daddy's back. Put the spoon in the rack." She lifts the spoon she's been cleaning high for effect, then lowers it dramatically into the dish drainer.

"You're a goof," says Libby.

"Mom's asleep, Mom's asleep. Sleeping in, Mom's still asleep." Monet climbs the stool they keep near the stove top for her, and measures oats into the water. She stirs the pot then holds her new charm necklace out toward the edge. "Did you see my whale?" she says, as if showing the pot. "Look how cute she is!"

Libby lets Monet show the pot then steps in for her own turn. "Can I see her?" She didn't really have a chance last night, racing out to the bar shortly after Prince Zeb appeared with gifts and returning home long after the house was asleep. Now she looks more closely at the sea horse and whale, worn so lovingly by the prince's daughter. They're adorable and picked with care, and Libby says so plenty of times.

While the oatmeal boils, Monet dances around the apartment, showing her charms to everything in sight. "Did you see my whale?" she says to the sink. "Do you like my sea horse?" she says to her shoe. She shows off the colors and shows off the charms, and soon enough she's created a rhyme:

Blue is best.
Red is best.
No, not really;
Daddy's best.

At a crucial moment, Libby interrupts with a rhyme of her own. "Daddy's best . . . *but you're a pest!*" She pounces on her and tickles her, driving her giggling and laughing into the couch. Monet tickles her back, and soon enough they're laughing hilariously together, rhyming and tickling red-faced on the couch.

"Zebby, Zebby, Zebby dad," says Monet. "Best dad I ever had."

"When he's gone you miss him bad," offers Libby.

"Good one!" says Monet, bouncing up and down, the couch squeaking in rhythm. "When he visits, it makes me glad!"

"Better one!" says Libby, diving low to tickle Monet's feet, but leaving her back unprotected in the swoop and getting the worse of the move. Monet has her from behind, tickling her armpits. Libby cracks up in defeat. She's always wanted a little sister, and now suddenly she has one. The age difference between them isn't much bigger than the difference between Libby and her older brothers.

But she's not a big sister, of course. She's a mom. She sobers up enough to stir the oatmeal and take it off the stove before it burns on the bottom. By the time they've finished breakfast, both Sheila and Angel have awakened to join them. Sheila serves herself while Libby expertly balances Angel on one knee while feeding him oatmeal with a spoon.

But he's not having any of it. Instead of placidly opening his mouth for the spoonful, he grabs the spoon from Libby's hand and feeds himself. His first spoonful misses his mouth and spreads oatmeal across his cheek. On his next try he pokes himself in the eye, but the third goes clean into his mouth.

"Yay!" cries Libby. "Bulls eye!"

Angel is so excited he flails his arms so hard he loses his spoon, which flies across the room. Turning to look where it went, he topples his oatmeal bowl on the floor. Soon enough they're all covered with oatmeal, but Libby couldn't be happier.

"Where's the camera?" Monet asks, recognizing the moment.

She comes back to take a snapshot of Angel covered with oatmeal and a snapshot of Angel being fed by his mom. After breakfast she takes pictures of Angel cleaned up, Angel with his mom, and Angel rolling a ball along the floor. The pictures are part of the game, and soon enough the whole roll's been finished.

"Let's go develop them," says Libby. Imitating Zeb, she bows toward Monet. "I'd be honored if the princess would join me."

"Can I?" Monet asks her mom.

"If you're set with homework and everything else. It's Saturday."

"I'm off until dinner time," Libby offers. "I'd love some company on my chores." She loads a bag with some baby gear and slings an empty backpack over her shoulder for shopping. "Let's go!" Angel understands what's happening and climbs into the umbrella stroller that Josephine's letting them use until they can find one of their own

It's a beautiful day in April, Libby's first outdoor taste of spring all year. Daffodils line the courtyards and the trees are fully green. A flock of starlings scatters at their approach, but a robin lingers to work a worm out of the ground, then looks them full in the eye before flying off with the worm in its beak. "She has chicks," Libby says. "She's bringing it back to her nest."

"Nest is best," replies Monet.

"You're still a goof," says Libby as she expertly navigates the umbrella stroller over some tricky pavement by the playground. A girl who'd been swinging on the swing set jumps off the swing, arcing high in the air, and the girl who'd been pushing her takes her place.

"Do you want to stay and look for friends?" Libby asks.

"I want to stay with you." Monet steps in front of Libby and takes Angel's stroller out of her hands. "My turn."

Monet leads them first to the CVS to drop off the camera for developing. "Make sure the coupon works," she warns. They do, and it does, and out they go while they wait.

Near the end of the block they pass Libby's butcher shop. "Pull over here," she says.

Monet doesn't recognize the place but she wheels Angel in while Libby holds the door.

The butcher is behind the counter chopping meat. In a room behind him but with the door open, a woman roughly his age that Libby doesn't recognize is stacking rolls of white paper and plastic wrap. "Gloria!" calls the butcher. "It's the soup fairy."

The woman stops what she's doing and walks out to the center of the room. "Good morning," she says with a smile. "We've never met, but I enjoy your soup every week!" She looks over her shoulder at the butcher, who Libby now guesses is her husband. "We haven't seen you lately."

"I'm sorry, ma'am. We had some bad luck."

"Sorry nothing," she says. "I hope your bad luck is coming to an end."

"It is." Only one payment remains on the door, and she's steady at the bar seven nights a week. She still needs to pay off the Visa bill, of course, but with Angel healthy she feels the wheels coming back into alignment. "I'm out doing some chores and I just wanted to say hello." She spreads her arms to indicate Angel and Monet. "This here is my baby and my sister."

Libby doesn't realize until after the words are out that Monet is obviously not her sister. But it's too late to clarify, and neither the butcher, his wife, nor Monet seem to notice or think anything of it. Gloria bends over in front of Monet. "That's a lovely chain."

"Thanks. My dad gave it to me."

"He's a lucky man."

"He's the best."

"I like the colors too. I like red and I love the blue."

"Blue too," says Monet with a grin, emphasizing the rhyme. "Blue too. Get it?"

Gloria's smile makes it clear that she does. "Hold there a minute," she says, straightening up and returning to the room where she started.

The butcher gives them an "I don't know" shrug and they all wait together, the butcher busy with his work, Libby playing peek-a-boo behind her hands with Angel.

Soon enough Gloria comes out with a little white butcher's bag. "Pork chops!" she announces. "For you. A little gift for the soup fairy and her wonderful family."

Libby looks down in embarrassment. "You don't have to do that!"

"I know I don't. That's what makes it a gift." She presses the bag in Libby's direction. "Take it."

This time she accepts it with a wide smile. "Thank you," she says. "Thank you so much."

"Soup fairy?" asks Monet as soon as they're out of the shop and walking toward the corner.

Libby tells her all about the weekly delivery and the cuts of meat. No, she didn't know about the name, but she knows how she got it, and next week she'll make them something nice.

They need to cross the street, but a red light stops them beside a homeless man who's begging on this corner. An older white man wearing blue jeans and a camouflage jacket, he sits on the ground, leaning back against a signpost, a cup holding a few coins beside his hand. He doesn't seem to be paying attention to anything.

"We need to give him some money," announces Monet.

"But we don't have any money." Their luck might be changing but they're miles from flush.

"Yes we do," insists Monet. "We have more than he does."

Now Libby looks at him for the first time. She sees in him more than just scenery—the beggar on the street, a view familiar from television to movie—but an actual person, a man with a name, for whom life was unkind and the winter doubtless worse. She's almost ashamed by her resistance at first. "You're right," she says to Monet. "Thank you. We just got a gift of our own. Of course we can share." She digs for a dollar bill and passes it to Monet.

Monet puts the dollar in his cup. "Have a blessed day," she says.

The man doesn't respond. He still doesn't seem to know they're there.

BACK AT THE CVS THE pictures are charming. A few show Monet's finger, which gives them plenty to laugh about, but most of them capture the spirit of the family on a happy Saturday morning. "Look! He has oatmeal in his belly button!" Monet exclaims, as they make themselves at home in the corner and flip one by one through the photos. Libby wants to include Angel, though he's as likely to suck on the picture as look at it, so she gives him a colorful coupon from the envelope instead.

"Look at that one," she says, pointing first at the coupon in Angel's hand and next at her new favorite photo. Angel waves the coupon back at her enthusiastically, then passes it to Monet.

"Thank you," says Monet, trading him the coupon for a shaving cream advertisement with a glossy young man.

As they flip through what Zeb called "the evidence," Libby realizes that she thinks less often of her old family at home. *This is my family now*, she realizes. Monet in many ways really is a sister, and Angel of course is no act of imagination. Neither a crime nor a clumsy misstatement, Angel is her son for real. What if she'd never had him? What if he were to disappear? Life without Angel seems suddenly empty.

Libby recognizes with a shock that this is exactly what she's done to her own mother. She made her mother's daughter disappear. Libby had to leave and she doesn't reconsider, but suddenly she looks at it through a mother's eyes. She can feel the empty hole where a child used to be, and she makes a decision.

With Angel happy and Monet in no hurry, Libby detours past the post office. She sets Monet to play peek-a-boo with Angel behind a paper plate someone left behind, and she buys a single envelope and one first-class postage stamp.

On the envelope she writes the address of her old home in Chatham, in the mountains of Southwest Virginia, which seems like a thousand miles from busy Fairfax. She flips through the pouch of photos until she finds a good one of herself. Angel's in it too, of course, but the highlight is a healthy mom with a smiling face. Without writing a note or a word, she puts the photo in the envelope and drops them together into the mailbox.

The telephone starts ringing as they enter the apartment. They can hear Sheila in the other room, but Monet reaches the telephone first.

"Mom, it's for you," she says almost immediately. "It's Hulon."

Libby grabs the phone out of her hand. "She's not here," she declares. "She has nothing to say." She slams the receiver down and looks back at Monet, who looks ashamed of herself, a little girl who made a mistake.

"It's okay," Libby offers in consolation. "Just one small goof. You're still my sister."

Monet doesn't appear to be mollified. She grabs the phone out of the receiver and slowly, deliberately starts pressing buttons. Obviously she's working hard to remember a number and not make any mistakes while dialing.

Libby doesn't know who she's calling, but she can hear when it connects and starts ringing into Monet's ear. Very soon a man's voice answers. "No! No! No!" is all he says, almost shouting. "No!" She hears the line disconnect from the other end.

Monet looks heartbroken. Her eyes go damp and face crunches up as if she's about to cry, then she's off and running into her room.

"Who was it?" Libby calls to her receding back. "Who did you call?"

"Daddy," comes the voice from the other room. "I wanted to tell him about the soup fairy."

Chapter Ten

Two weeks later, the door is paid off and Libby's cut her nights back to six shifts a week. Today is Saturday, and Libby takes a long walk with Monet and Angel. For the first time, she stops at that playground and pushes Angel in the swings. At first he seemed puzzled, but then his big brown eyes open wide and he doesn't want to stop when they finish. Now it's afternoon and the family is gathering to plan a dinner. The doorbell rings from downstairs.

"Are we expecting anyone?" Libby asks.

They're not expecting anyone and they decide to let it rest. The person can ring again if they mean it.

A minute later comes a knock on the door. Not pounding like the police and not Zeb's familiar *tap tappity*, but an ordinary knock as if the person downstairs has gotten inside and is now in the hall.

Sheila opens the door. It's Zeb.

But he's not the same old Zeb; he looks entirely different. He's wearing a suit and a tie, freshly pressed, and carrying a briefcase. He looks like a professional. He's a doctor, lawyer, or Wall Street financier.

Monet isn't fooled for an instant. She gives him a giant hug and gets swung around the apartment by a man in a suit, but soon it's time for explanation.

"I have a new job," Zeb says. "I'm still at Best Buy, but I'm not loading boxes anymore. Now I'm a shift supervisor. I'm on the management team." He keeps a straight face, but Libby can see he's grown to eight feet tall.

"I'm not hourly," he continues. "I'll get paid $36,000 a year, plus benefits. I've never had it this good before. It's all I want. It's all I need. That drug money is gone, gone, gone."

Monet is sitting patiently. Libby can't tell how much she understands, but she's quiet while the grown-ups discuss something important. Finally she interrupts, "Did you bring any gifts?"

"No, honey," he replies, patting her on the shoulder. "No gifts. A proposal. I'd like to move back in together." He looks at Libby. "All of us. Like a family."

"We are a family," offers Monet.

"This place won't be big enough, but I found a townhouse with all the space we need. I'd like to show it to you. It's in a neighborhood where drugs used to get sold, so prices are low, but the trade is moving on. I know that."

"Moving on," echoes Sheila.

"I think we can buy it."

Nobody says a word. This is so sudden and so far beyond anything they know. Homeowners? A red cardinal flutters to rest on the windowsill. All eyes turn to watch until it sails away.

"And I was signing up for health insurance for my new job," Zeb continues. "They take eighty dollars a month from my paycheck and I can see a doctor anytime I want. Medicine costs extra, but insurance pays some of that too."

"Nice," Sheila says.

Libby fully understands about the medicine. She's still working off that Visa bill.

"The form has other spaces to fill in too. For sixty dollars more I can sign up my wife. Sheila, I know you're mostly okay, but your back hurts a lot and you get those headaches. Sheila, will you marry me?"

Sheila's eyes go wide. Her mouth opens but she says nothing.

"And I love you too. Does that help?"

Sheila stays quiet for a long time. She's looking out the window as if the bird might come back, but there's nothing in view but sky and clouds. "We sure miss you around here," she says absently.

"There are spaces for kids too. For $200 I get family coverage. Spouse and kids. It's funny that it doesn't count how many kids I have, as if two costs them the same as four. Or six! But that's their problem." He smiles at Sheila and waits for her to talk. When she doesn't, he carries on. "Monet's our kid and I would sign her up, obviously. Maybe we can even find some way to get Libby and Angel on the same plan."

He looks for Libby's response to his far-fetched scheme. Like Sheila, she has nothing to offer.

"What do you say?" Zeb concludes, looking back to Sheila. "And can we get married? I mean, will you marry me?"

Sheila is still staring absently out the window. It's long past time for her to talk, but still her tongue is tied. Even the clouds aren't moving.

Zeb moves in front of her and takes a knee. He says nothing, but holds the position of suitors through the centuries.

"Say yes," says Monet.

"Say yes," suggests Libby.

The chorus of voices seems to pull Sheila back from a brink. She shakes her head and focuses straight on Zeb. "I'm sorry," she says with another shake. "Did I not say yes yet?"

Zeb stands tall and spreads his arms open wide.

"Yes!" she yells as she flies into his arms. "Yes to everything."

Chapter Eleven

Two months later, just shy of Angel's first birthday, they move into the beautiful new townhouse. The whole first floor is living area, a big living room, a dining room to eat in, and what the real estate agent calls a "fully equipped" kitchen. The next floor up has bedrooms for Libby and Monet, and a bathroom for them to share. The top floor is for Sheila and Zeb, with a bathroom of their own.

The floors are wooden, though the central hall on the first floor has carpet that was left behind, a literal red carpet to greet the new owners. They own hardly any furniture compared to the size of the house, so most of the rooms are empty. Monet loves running across the living room in socks, then stopping for a long slide into the kitchen. The windows all open and, on the tree outside of her room, Monet spies a little bird's nest.

Sheila and Zeb keep the double bed from their apartment, and Libby insists that Monet take the single. The squeaky couch belonged to the landlord, so the living room stays empty. That's just fine with Monet, who treats it like a skating rink.

The living room is Angel's favorite room, too. Learning to walk, he cruises along walls, leaning on them for support and walking unsupported almost exactly as far as Monet can slide. Once he discovers how to use a packing box for balance, he becomes unstoppable. Pushing his box in front of him, he owns the lower floor, cruising hither and yon—though in the living room he often leaves the box off to one side and runs as far as he can before cascading to the floor in a heap of giggles.

Libby's favorite room is the kitchen. It has a bigger stove top with four proper burners—not the dinky double burner in the apartment that took forever to boil water—and there's an oven. The treats continued when Libby opened the oven for the first time and found pans inside. Either they didn't want them or they forgot, but the previous owners left behind a pair of cookie sheets and two loaf pans for baking bread. In the old apartment Libby had dreamed of fresh baked bread but never dared to think it could ever come true.

"Have you ever baked bread?" she asks Monet.

"It's possible?"

Libby holds out the loaf pan and shows how a traditional loaf fits in the rectangular center. "It's more than possible. It's the best thing in the whole wide world." Then she holds up the cookie sheet and intimates in a whisper, "With the possible exception of chocolate chip cookies."

Memories of baking bring back memories of her mother, and suddenly in the beautiful new space, for the first time ever, it seems possible to forgive.

In the new townhouse, even the stairs are exciting. The house has the same three flights of stairs they used to climb in their old apartment, but now each floor is their own. Every time Libby walks up or down the stairs she has a new daydream. A plant could go here. Or a picture there. This house is theirs, and over time they can really make it so.

Zeb was right about homeownership, too. The monthly payment isn't much more than their monthly rent back in the old space, and it's a whole lot less than Sheila and Zeb were paying between them when they lived apart. With three incomes and one home, Libby's math tells her that it won't be long before they can fill the place with the furniture they choose. But they're in no hurry. They can take their time, accumulate savings, and get it right. Libby and Angel are happy to sleep on mats. Even the bed can wait.

Libby and Sheila quit Happy Jack's on the same day. It was a shock to Jack, but not to Rosario, who was told everything far in advance. Before that final day arrived, Rosario found two friends who needed work, and all five of them walked into Jack's office together.

"Hire Rosario's friends," Sheila commanded. "Or our whole team is leaving together."

Jack stared back like a deer in the headlights.

"You have customers who expect cleaning today," Sheila explained. "You can't afford to lose us all. Fortunately, I brought you replacements."

"Fine," Jack said.

"And they all get paid at least minimum wage. The legal rate."

"Do they have papers?"

"I don't know. It doesn't matter. Pay them the legal rate or we all walk."

Jack took a long time to answer. He glared back at her, acting like he might accept her dare, but eventually backed down.

"You want happy customers, Happy Jack," she said, "you pay people proper."

So Rosario got a raise and her friends got jobs. Libby didn't see it, but she imagined that some houses had never been cleaner at the end of the day.

Sheila and Libby find new work of their own, cleaning jobs in the county hospital, not far from the new townhouse, union jobs with benefits. Sheila and Monet sign onto Zeb's health plan. Libby and Angel go onto her own, and Libby keeps her first pay stub with the legal deductions for taxes and health care. Not in an envelope for accounting, but under her pillow as a souvenir. Every night she counts her blessings.

During the workday, Angel stays with Josephine, who isn't so far away from their new location. Libby quits the night job, since her union job alone pays as much as Happy Jack and the bar paid together. There's even a playground with a swing set only a few blocks away from the new townhouse. Libby pushes Angel in the swings after work in the evenings, when she used to wait tables for drunks.

Angel is talking now, though he's tricky to understand. Both Libby and Monet can tell the difference between "Mommy" and "Monet"—but Sheila can't, which drives her bonkers. He's learning so many words so fast, it's hard to tell which one is new or which one came first. But Libby spends every minute she can playing with him and talking to him.

Sheila and Zeb are cute as puppy dogs, newly married after their time of separation. Libby watches them climb up and down the stairs holding hands or looking out the window in each other's arms. Zeb doesn't really take to cooking, but he's a demon on dishes, and he does more than his fair share around the house.

Between setting up telephone service, changing electrical service, and new neighbors introducing themselves, they don't think much of it when the doorbell rings. Someone just hustles down the stairs to answer it.

This time it's Libby who answers the door. And this time it's the police.

The squad car is double parked right out front and a pair of officers in blue uniforms stand in the door, smiling and friendly, but with guns on their belts.

"Are you Libby Thompson?" the first officer asks.

"Yes."

"Can we come in?"

Sheila arrives as Libby is standing there, fumbling. She's uncertain what to say, but it's past time to say something. Sheila cuts in front of her, filling up the door, standing between Libby and the police. Her tone is friendly, but Libby can feel the anger behind the words. "What's on your mind, officer?"

"We want to ask you some questions."

"Go ahead."

"Can we come in?"

"No."

"It will go quicker if we're sitting down."

"I have time."

"It's about Zeb and where you got the money for your change of address."

"Zeb has a new job. Look it up."

"We did. It still doesn't pay for all this."

"Did you look up my job? And Libby's here? Zeb's clean. I have nothing more to say."

"Can we come in and look around?"

"No." She steps out to confront him but her movement opens a space in the door, and the other officer slips in behind her.

Sheila turns in anger. "What the—" but the appearance of the officer inside the house somehow disarms her.

He's standing in the empty living room looking lost. A big old empty room with wide-open windows and he doesn't know what to do. "There's no place to sit," is all he says.

Now Libby chimes in. "We'll buy furniture someday."

Sheila's voice is dripping with sarcasm. "And we'll invite you for tea. But right now, as you say, there's no place to sit. You might as well leave."

"Where's Hulon?" The outside officer has squeezed past Sheila and takes over inside.

"I don't know any Hulon, and I don't know where he is."

"You'll do better if you cooperate."

"I am cooperating. I don't know Hulon. I don't know anything."

Now Libby takes the lead. "It's time for you to go."

"We have nothing you want," Sheila adds. "I'm clean. Libby's clean. Zeb is clean." She says the last with special emphasis.

The officers step out through the door. "But you'll keep your eyes open."

Later that night, too close to bedtime, the doorbell rings again. Both children are asleep but all three adults answer the door together.

Outside are three young black men, two of them dressed like hoodlums, with cargo pants hanging low off their waists, and one dressed like a stereotypical pimp, silk shirt unbuttoned to his midriff.

"Welcome to the neighborhood," says the biggest and most thuggish of the bunch. He's wearing a black T-shirt with the image of a machine gun and the letters AK-47 on the front. "We see you've been talking to the police."

Zeb steps forward, exits the house and stands in front of them on the stoop. Even the biggest of the three seems small compared to the tall, muscular Zeb, radiating energy. "Good evening to you as well," he says. "I'm Zeb Blackstone and I'm pleased to meet you." He holds out his hand for a shake.

The thuggish one in the middle has no choice but to shake Zeb's hand. Zeb offers his hand to each young man in turn, and each of them shakes his hand properly. The formality somehow changes the mood. The three young men seem less like robbers demanding ransom than like visitors on a social call. "Nice weather," Zeb remarks, and the three young men respond in kind. Soon they agree that they're glad it's not raining but hate this boring time of year, after the basketball season has ended but before football has begun.

But they haven't forgotten their purpose. Eventually the leader in the AK-47 shirt turns to business. "What did the police want?" he inquires. "What did you tell them?"

"I don't know what they wanted," Zeb replies. "I only know what we told them."

"Which is?"

"Which is nothing. We're new to the neighborhood and we don't know anything of interest to the police."

"And we wouldn't say anything if we did," Sheila adds.

"Your boyfriend knows the trade," their leader says in return.

"Her husband," Zeb corrects. "And I *knew* the trade." He emphasizes the past tense of that word. "Not anymore."

The young man seems to sense the conversation coming to an end. He puts his hands in his pockets and takes one step backwards. "We'll be watching."

"Like the police, you're welcome to watch. Like the police, you'll find us boring and uncooperative. Now if you please, I need to wake up early for work tomorrow. I'm minding my own business, and nothing but my own business."

Zeb steps inside and his family follows. His final words as he closes the door are "You all have a pleasant evening."

But inside he walks only as far as the lowest stair and sits down hard.

"What is it?" says Sheila, sensing his trouble.

"They think we know something. And they think we told the police."

Chapter Twelve

Monet breaks her arm on the playground. It's no high drama, just a bad fall off a slide, but now more than ever they appreciate what a difference health insurance makes. Signing the cast is great fun in school, and by wintertime the arm is just a story and the cast is the first piece of artwork to hang in her bedroom.

Libby buys a bed from a thrift store, and her own sets of sheets and blankets, her first-ever really grown-up things of her own. The family together improves the table and chairs where they eat, but they decide not to furnish the living room anytime soon. They prefer the sense of the steadily growing savings account. "We might as well wait until Angel learns some manners," Sheila adds.

"But where will the police sit when they come by?" Monet adds, with excellent sarcasm for someone who just started second grade.

The comment is not entirely out of the blue, though, because the police do call or knock from time to time. And so do the young men who expressed their concern on that very first day. Sheila and Zeb maintain their ignorance and expect that the passage of time surely makes their ignorance easier to believe.

The arrest comes as a complete surprise. At two in the morning, bands of armed and armored men storm in black suits through the townhouse. They don't slow down to search, and they break nothing but the door. They're after people. Not weapons or contraband, just people. They want to catch them by surprise, and they succeed.

Within sixty seconds every light in the house is turned on. Every room is entered and everyone shocked awake.

Sheila and Zeb are hauled out of bed in their nightclothes, handcuffed, and manhandled down three flights of stairs to the armored van. Libby is left behind with the tear-stained Monet. Angel spends the entire time shouting "Bad! Bad! Bad!" at the police.

The next day Libby takes off from work (A sick day! Bless the union dues she pays every month.) and learns with both children where the criminal court is located and how to attend something called an arraignment. In a hot room crowded with people, Monet watches her mother and father hauled in handcuffs before the court and charged along with four codefendants of dealing nine kilograms of cocaine.

Three codefendants are familiar from nights on the stoop. The fourth codefendant is Hulon Nesseler, a runty man with bald spots and a pockmarked face who reminds Libby of the dead moles her cat used to leave on the doorstep back on the farm.

Every other defendant has a lawyer next to him, either a hired lawyer of his own or a public defender assigned to his case. Sheila and Zeb do not.

Every other defendant pleads not guilty when the judge demands that they enter a plea. Sheila and Zeb do the same thing when it's their turn (the difference, Libby thinks, is that they actually aren't!).

Arguments are made about bail. Libby watches the other defendants' lawyers stand up and advocate on their behalf. She hears words like "risk of flight" and "danger to the community." She doesn't understand a lot of what's happening but in the end decisions are made and a gavel comes down. Along with the other four codefendants, Sheila and Zeb are escorted by their handcuffs out a side door to the holding pen. Bail has been denied. They will be confined pending trial. Monet's wail is louder than anything Libby ever thought possible, and soon they, too, are being escorted out the door. Not in handcuffs out the side, but by brown-suited guards back into the hallway where they came in. "Learn how to keep her quiet" are the last words Libby hears in arraignment court.

Those good union jobs were the death of them, Libby learns. Poor people—"indigent defendants," they are called—are assigned public defenders to exercise their constitutional right to counsel. Rich people spend millions of dollars on lawyers of their own. Sheila and Zeb earn too much money to qualify for a public defender. But they don't have millions to spend on a lawyer. They're stuck in a trap. Too poor for a lawyer, too rich for assistance. Libby can't begin to guess where to find a lawyer of their own.

Monet closes the door to her room and won't come out for food or water. "You'll need to eat someday," Libby says to the closed door. "What can I bring you?"

The closed door doesn't answer.

Angel sits attentively in front of Sheila and Zeb's door, hour after hour, staring with his big brown eyes like he's waiting for something. When Libby comes by he points to the door and says "Sheila" with perfect diction.

The next day there comes a knock on the door that seems like the answer to Libby's prayers. Attorney Simpson Mellor saw notice of the arraignment and suspected that since they own a home, Sheila and Zeb might not qualify for public defenders.

"Usually a case like this would cost about $40,000 each. Those guys are facing a lot of time."

Libby's head starts to swim. They have some savings, but the money they didn't spend on a living room couch is nothing close to $40,000 times two.

"But I can do you a favor," attorney Simpson Mellor continues. Libby had made Monet go back to school that morning, but she kept Angel at home with her. Simpson Mellor calls him cute and makes small talk. He's wearing a light gray suit and a light blue shirt, a pink tie and a handkerchief folded neatly in his pocket. He has a gray beard trimmed close and a face that's warm and strong at the same time.

"You'll have to sell the house, of course," he says at some crucial moment. "But you have a giant asset. Here's what we can do."

He shows Libby how to sell the house, and estimates what she might clear after paying off the bank, minus the transaction costs and so forth. "As long as it comes out over $5,000, I'll take it as payment in full."

"But the house is all we have."

"The house will be payment in full for *both* cases. Two for the price of one, a grand bargain."

"But the house is all we have."

"I'm the one taking the risk here. If I'm lucky, I'll make ten. I might go home with only five. But it's God's work and I have to do it. I want to keep your family out of jail."

"What if we sell the house and it only comes out with $4,000?"

"We'll have to take that risk together."

"Where will we live?"

"Think of it this way. You're not in jail. Your good friends Sheila and Zeb are in jail. They have a place to live . . . but they're not very happy about it. What do you think? Do you think they're happy about it?"

"No."

"Me neither. You need to do this for them. You need to do this for your baby. You need to sell the house and hire me to keep your family out of jail."

So it's settled. Attorney Simpson Mellor takes their savings as an advance and gets right to work. Libby sells the house and makes almost $12,000 in the process.

"You did great," says the real estate agent who handled the sale. "With the drug dealers moving out and the neighborhood on the mend, you made good money in no time at all. Congratulations!"

Simpson Mellor takes the entire $12,000. Libby signs the check over to him, right there in his office, the attorney having obtained the necessary delegation of authority from Sheila and Zeb in advance.

"Good work," he says as she signs the papers, crying as hard as she's ever seen Monet cry and harder than she's ever cried as an adult. "Two for the price of one. You're doing what you have to do." Attorney Simpson Mellor keeps Kleenex on his desk.

Libby, Angel, and Monet move into a tiny apartment on a middle floor of a tall gray building where the windows don't open and there's no grass out front. But it's near enough to the same neighborhood that Monet can stay in her school and Angel can stay with Josephine, though he changes from being a child who gets picked up early with a family that does favors, to a child who gets picked up late and needs that occasional favor. Meredith didn't make it off heroin and she's back with her pimp. Libby keeps her union cleaning job at the hospital. With two children at home she couldn't work a night job if she wanted to, but she does accept overtime shifts when they come her way.

What happens next is like a rockslide, jumbled, fast, and confusing. Letters arrive from the court, phone calls come unexpectedly, and questions go unanswered. Sheila and Zeb each telephone once from the jail, and each time Monet happens to pick up the phone. Confused by a "computer sounding" telephone tree, she presses the wrong buttons and somehow loses the calls. Simpson Mellor never writes or calls to tell her what's happening, though he answers courteously whenever she calls. "It's moving along nicely," he always says. "I don't think a trial will be necessary. We're working toward a plea bargain."

Libby thinks plea bargains are how guilty people get off easy, not how innocent people prove their innocence, but she doesn't really know. He's the lawyer and she's paid him everything she has to handle the case. She has to trust the expert. And she has to get to work.

She hears through a friend of Zeb's that some of the other codefendants entered a plea. Hulon had good information to trade and informed on others. He got his sentence down to only five years. Minus good time and time served before he entered the plea, he apparently has under four left to go.

If Hulon is getting good news, Libby thinks, surely Zeb and Sheila will do okay too. Probably better. She calls Simpson Mellor to ask what he thinks and what he knows. He doesn't want to talk about the other codefendants. Regarding Sheila and Zeb, he says only that the "inevitable conclusion" is taking shape.

Libby learns that inevitable conclusion in the courtroom a beautiful day in April, almost exactly a year after she first met Zeb with gifts of photos and diapers. Sheila and Zeb are brought to court alone. No codefendants have a hearing at this time, for reasons that Simpson Mellor doesn't explain.

They look awful. Monet starts to cry as soon as she lays eyes on them. Sheila has gained weight and she waddles into the courtroom like a hippo, wearing handcuffs and an orange prison jump suit. Zeb has kept his muscular physique, but he's lost the sparkle of a prince. He looks pale and gray, his eyes gone dim.

"State your names," intones the judge, a white man in a black robe.

"Zeb Blackstone," says the tall man in the orange prison jumper that Libby knows so well.

"Sheila Blackstone," says the woman next to him, and Libby loses control when she hears the married name. They had mere minutes together. The judge hears Libby groan and gives her a dirty look over the problems she's causing.

Sheila and Zeb seem to know what's coming. They understand the procedures; they've agreed to something in advance. They stand before the court and answer questions posed by the judge. Most questions and answers seem obvious, and they answer them in turn.

"Can you hear me okay?"

"Yes."

"Do you understand me?"

"Yes."

"Are you presently under the influence of alcohol, drugs, narcotics, medicines, pills, or any other substances?"

"No."

Libby had never seen either of them under any such influence, not so much as a beer with dinner.

"Have the charges been explained to you by your lawyer, and do you understand the nature of the charges?"

"Yes."

"Are you satisfied with your lawyer's legal services?"

Both of them hesitate on this one. Neither of them seems to want to talk about it.

The judge repeats the question. “Are you satisfied with your lawyer’s legal services?”

Finally Zeb answers, choosing his words with care. “To the best of our knowledge, it appears that our lawyer gave us such legal services as we were able to pay for.”

The judge considers that, but it doesn’t seem to be good enough. “Were you satisfied?”

Silence.

“Were you satisfied? It’s a yes or no question.”

Looking back at Libby, summoning courage like it’s some ultimate act of betrayal, Zeb goes ahead and answers. “Yes.”

Sheila needs some time of her own. She looks hard at Simpson Mellor in the counsel chair next to her, but she agrees in the end. “Yes.”

There follows a whole bunch of court talk that Libby can’t follow and doesn’t try to understand. Something about naturalization privileges and licensing rights for state-regulated professions. They answer “yes” to some questions that Libby thinks aren’t true or in some cases couldn’t possibly be true, but Sheila and Zeb seem somehow resigned to answer each question in the affirmative. Yes, they have been provided a copy of the indictment; yes, they understand the maximum possible term, and that the court is not bound by agreement of counsel. Libby gets increasingly upset as the questions become more frightening and start narrowing toward a conclusion. She hears Sheila and Zeb give up their right to trial by jury and waive the requirement of proof beyond a reasonable doubt. She hears them give up their right to confront witnesses against them.

“What witnesses?” Libby wants to shout from the gallery. But she holds her tongue. She’d be out of order, and she doesn’t know what she’s talking about. Monet drops out of her seat and curls up on the floor under the bench. Libby hears her weeping at her feet.

Finally, the judge reaches some kind of a conclusion. He raps the gavel lightly for perfect attention. “I find the plea to be knowingly, intelligently, and voluntarily made,” he says. “The clerk may enter a judgment of conviction for the distribution of cocaine as specified in the complaint. Notwithstanding prior agreement of counsel, but because of their leadership role in the conspiracy, the quantity of narcotics found in their codefendants’ premises and these defendants’ refusal to accept responsibility, each defendant will serve a sentence of sixty years.”

He peers indifferently toward the clerk seated beside him. “Sentences to be served at the discretion of the Commissioner of Corrections. Remand the accused forthwith into his care.”

The bailiffs step away from the edges and toward the defendants in the dock.

"*Sixty years!*" Sheila is on her feet, hollering like a train wreck. She turns to the counsel chair next to her. "You never said anything about sixty years!" But the chair is empty. Attorney Simpson Mellor is heading for the door.

Libby thinks surely she must be confused. Sixty years? Did she hear that right? Was that a prison sentence? Libby rushes toward the front of the courtroom, runs into the bar that divides the floor of the court from the benches for the audience. Behind her, she hears Monet lose all control under the seat.

Sheila is handcuffed but nearby. She steps toward Libby at the bar, looking like she's on her way to gallows. "He told me to expect three or four," she says. "Minus probably a year for good behavior and time already served."

"What happened?"

"I got sixty years hard time."

"You'll die in there!"

The old Sheila breaks through in a sarcastic smile. "Thanks for your encouraging words."

"You're innocent. I'll hire another lawyer. I'll file an appeal."

"No more lawyers!" Sheila cries. A sob comes from deep inside; her knees give way and she falls against the bar. "No more legal fees. No appeal. Just make me one promise." She's up against the bar and the escorts are coming for her.

"I'll get you out."

"Every nickel you spend on legal fees is a nickel you don't have for my daughter. I hear her crying back there." Sheila chokes up, and a sob escapes her at the same moment as Monet's sob from under the bench. "Promise me, please," says Sheila. "Promise me you'll take care of my daughter. Take care of my baby girl."

Libby takes a deep breath and stands up straight, as straight as Sheila stood when she chased the police out of her new house, as tall as Zeb stood when he chilled the drug dealers at the door with a confident "good evening." She places both hands on the bar and she says as clearly as she's ever stated anything in her life, "Sheila Blackstone, I promise to take care of your daughter. I'll love her like my own, but I'll never let her forget her real mother."

The guards pull Sheila away by her chains.

She's out of earshot but Libby isn't finished: "And I promise to get you out of there."

Part Two

College Candy

Chapter Thirteen

The kindergarten classroom is bright with color. Sunny windows with rainbow curtains look over a grassy playground. The floor is carpeted in blue, scattered with yellow throw rugs and purple pillows. In the center is a cluster of red tables with little green chairs; on each table sits a stack of paper, and jars with pencils, crayons, and little scissors with rounded points.

Angel stands by himself in the corner. His clothes are all new to him, but every one of them came used from Goodwill and The Salvation Army. The room is filled with kids, but nobody seems to notice Angel standing quietly.

Two girls in matching red Elmo sweaters greet each other with a hug, and chatter excitedly about a playgroup called LittleKinz. Two boys in Redskins jerseys dare each other to jump into the deep end of the pool when they get home. One tells the other that his parents can't use their opera tickets on Saturday. "My mom said to tell your mom that you can have them if you want."

The only African-American child is in the center of a little crowd, dressed in bright pink from top to bottom. She wears a pink shirt covered by a pink vest, pink pants with pink socks and shoes, and a pink hat with a pink feather. "We made the biggest dog fort!" she is telling the other kids. She and her sister found "every blanket and towel in the house" and hung them over the sofas and chairs in the living room until "the whole room was full." They crawled around in the space underneath and made space for all their "stuffy dogs" so each one had a room of her own.

"We played in it all day," she says. "But then the maids cleaned it up. That ruined it."

Eventually the teacher moves to the front of the room. "Come on up, boys and girls. Welcome to kindergarten. I'm Ms. Milton and I'll be your teacher. We're going to spend the whole year together!" Ms. Milton is wearing blue jeans and a green blouse with flowers, and her hair is entirely silver-gray.

"Who here knows how to write his name?"

Almost every hand in the class goes up. Angel's doesn't.

"That's wonderful!" Ms. Milton cries. "I thought you looked smart!" She ushers them toward the tables and sets them to work making name tags for themselves. "There are stickers and crayons," she explains. "You can decorate them anyway you like."

Angel stays where he is, rooted in place at the edge of the hurly-burly, while Ms. Milton bustles around setting the kids up and passing out the supplies.

"Done already?" she says to the African-American girl in pink. She peels the back of the sticker that now says *Veronica West* and places it in the center of her shirt. "Everyone else do like Veronica," she says. "Peel off your sticker and put it on when you're done. You can keep drawing until everyone is finished."

Another girl raises her hand. "I'm done," she says.

"Peel your sticker and put it on," Ms. Milton replies.

She turns and all but stumbles on Angel, standing silently in his space. "What have we here?" she asks.

Angel straightens his back and stands tall. "My name is Angel Thompson," he says. "I don't know how to write my name."

Ms. Milton seems almost embarrassed that she hadn't seen him earlier. "Then we'll teach you," she says with a smile. "That's what we're here for." She waves toward a teachers' aide whom Angel only now notices, also standing quietly to one side of the room. She brings Angel to a special table by himself, not far from the others, but clearly separate.

By the end of the morning, Angel is pretty good at writing his name and knows a lot of other letters besides. The teachers' aide, Miss Stephanie, spends most of her time with Angel, though occasionally another child comes over for a few minutes' attention. For lunch he eats the sandwich his mom made for him, peanut butter and jelly, with two Hershey's kisses on the side. "That's what my mom always made for me," Libby had said.

The activity after lunch is drawing. The children are again shown to the desks with the papers and crayons, and invited to draw pictures of their families.

"Can I draw my dog?" asks Veronica West.

"Your dog, your cat, your house. Anything you want," says Ms. Milton. "But start with your family."

Angel is placed into the tables with the other children, but near an edge, and Miss Stephanie gives him special attention.

This at least is familiar to Angel. Miss Josephine's day care had crayons and papers—though not as many colors—and Monet loves to draw at home. With encouragement from Miss Stephanie, Angel draws three stick figures in a row.

"Who's the tall one?" Miss Stephanie asks. She's pretty tall herself, with long black hair and eyeglasses in a big round circle. She wears blue overalls over a yellow turtleneck.

"That's my mom."

"Which one is you?"

Angel points to the smallest stick figure, drawn in the same pink crayon as his mother. "That's me," he says. "My name is Angel." He points to his name tag and his face lights up in a smile. Then he reaches back for the crayons and for a minute it's as if Miss Stephanie doesn't exist. He leans close over his drawing, all his attention on the little figure at the end of the row. Carefully, deliberately, he retraces the lines and redraws the figure. Then letter by letter, he spells out his name under the drawing. He looks back up at Miss Stephanie and points back and forth between the picture and the word. "Angel," he says. "That's me!"

"That's you, all right," Miss Stephanie cheers. She reaches down for a hug and a pat. "You're the Angel." The she points to the third figure, midway in height between Angel and his mom. "Is that your dad?" she asks.

Angel looks at her like she asked which one is the elephant. The question makes no sense. "I don't have a dad," he says.

"Surely, you have a dad somewhere," protests Miss Stephanie. "Are your parents divorced?"

Angel stays silent.

"Does he live in a different state?"

"Mom says he died in a car accident," Angel explains at last. "With my mom's parents too. It's just the three of us that's left." He pauses as if he's going to have more to say, but then nothing follows, and he looks blankly down to the page.

"So who is this?" Miss Stephanie asks, her finger still on the third figure. "Your older brother?"

"She's my sister."

"Why is she drawn in brown?" Angel and his mom are stick figures drawn in pink crayon, but his sister is brown.

"Because she looks like her." He points toward Veronica West. "She says to tell the truth when I draw."

Lights are starting to go off in Miss Stephanie's eyes, as if she is starting to understand. She looks carefully at Angel, who clearly has no African blood in his veins. "Do you and your sister have the same mom?" she asks.

"No," says Angel. "She has her own separate mommy."

"The same dad?"

"Nope," Angel replies. "She has her own daddy too. His name is Zeb. She tells me that I met him once. But I was a baby. I don't remember it."

Now Miss Stephanie is again looking confused. "If you have a different mom and a different dad, what makes her your sister?"

"She's not *legally* my sister," with an emphasis that suggests he's heard it said this way before. "She's in a different foster family but she lives with us."

"Why's that?"

"She likes us better. We're nicer than the foster family. I met them a couple of times. They have lots of foster kids and my mom—my *real* mom—says they only do it for the money."

All this time Miss Stephanie has been standing and leaning over Angel. Now she gets down on her knees so she's nearer his height. "What's your sister's name?"

"Monet. Like the artist."

Miss Stephanie smiles. "Does she like to draw?"

"She loves it! Especially with colors. We draw all the time." He leans in close, takes advantage of her proximity to whisper confidentially in her ear, "She's in sixth grade." Then he gathers himself to say something difficult, and minding his diction, he concludes, "She's in Sidney Lanier Middle School."

"Good work," says Miss Stephanie, beaming. "That's great. I was an intern at Sidney Lanier."

Angel looks brightly back at her. "Her bus leaves at 7:10, a whole hour before mine."

"Thanks for telling me," says Miss Stephanie. "Do you know where Monet's parents are? Her *real* parents?" She smiles as she echoes his way of saying it.

"Yes."

"Where are they?"

Angel slows down and straightens up to tackle something difficult again. "The Virginia Department of Corrections," he says. He pauses to make sure he got it right.

Miss Stephanie stands up and steps away.

"Mom is in Fluvanna and Dad's in Nottoway," Angel concludes with a triumphant smile, naming the prison where each is held. He got it all right.

And just in time, too. Because at that moment, Ms. Milton calls everyone's attention back to the center of the room.

"Time to pack up," she says. "All done drawing. Now it's quiet time."

Miss Stephanie and Ms. Milton shepherd the kids to a giant double-door closet filled with rolled-up soft mats, one for each kid. The two boys in Redskins jerseys have a little push-scuffle about who goes first, but it is quickly broken up, and soon enough each child has unrolled a mat and is lying quietly on the floor. Angel picks a spot on the edge, between Miss Stephanie's desk and the window. He doesn't sleep, but he lies quietly listening to the sounds. Some kids are reading and turning pages in their books. Other kids are breathing in a way that makes Angel think they're asleep. Outside he hears birds. They sound like the same ones he has at home, sometimes singing at random, and sometimes in response as if they're talking to each other. A teacher quickly hushes any children who talk.

What seems like a few minutes later, a church in the distance chimes one o'clock. Ms. Milton starts to circle the room. "Wakey, wakey," she says. "Time to roll." She and Miss Stephanie supervise the kids standing up to roll their mats and use the bathroom. Angel is the first one with his mat rolled and returned to the closet. He helps some other kids roll their mats and work out the tricky elastic bands that hold them shut.

"Thank you very much," says a blonde-haired girl in a blue tank top.

"You're welcome," Angel replies.

Veronica West has her mat rolled but can't get the elastics to stay in place. "Want a hand?" says Angel, scooting in beside her.

She looks at him like he's holding a gun to her head. "I can do it," she declares. The elastic snaps loose again and the mat starts to unroll. She scowls at him. "Look what you made me do!"

Angel reaches down to arrest the mat. "Hold it like this," he suggests.

"Like as if you know," says Veronica West as she rips the mat away from him and sets it down to start anew a few steps away.

Angel leaves her be and stands quietly to the side until all the mats have been put away. Veronica West is last, until Miss Stephanie takes her mat away, fixes the elastics and replaces it gently into the closet.

"Story time," says Ms. Milton. "*Goldilocks and the Three Bears.*" She holds in the air a giant book, with a picture of a little blonde girl and a family of bears on the cover.

Some children shout out in enthusiasm. "Hooray!" Angel hears, and from behind him, "My favorite!"

Other kids aren't so happy. "Not again," says one of the boys in a Redskins jersey. His friend grumbles but Angel can't make out the words.

Angel himself doesn't know the story of *Goldilocks and the Three Bears*. Indeed, he doesn't know many stories at all . . . though he knows he likes them. The other kids all push around Ms. Milton, and she directs them to sit around her in a loose circle. Angel soon finds himself on the outside edge.

Ms. Milton opens the book so it stretches across her lap. He's never seen a book so large in his life. Miss Josephine had a scattering of books, though none nearly so big, and she rarely read them.

"Once upon a time, there was a little girl named Goldilocks," begins Ms. Milton. She holds up the book so everyone can see the giant picture of the pretty blonde girl.

"She went for a walk in the forest." Again she holds up the book to show the pictures. Trees in the sunshine, a deer in the shade and birds flying above.

"Pretty soon, she came upon a house." Ms. Milton holds up the picture of a wooden cottage. "She knocked and, when no one answered, she walked right in."

The audience murmurs in anticipation. Angel, too, senses the possibilities.

Showing the pictures as she goes, Ms. Milton tells the class how Goldilocks explores the house. One bowl of porridge is too hot and one too cold, but the third is perfect so she eats it all up. One chair is too big and one is too small, and the small one breaks when she tries to squeeze in. Then at last Goldilocks comes to the beds. One is too hard and one is too soft. But the third bed is just right. She lies down to take a nap.

"Don't do it!" cries one of the Redskins boys. Other kids laugh.

"Stay awake," warns another.

But Goldilocks can't hear them. Soon she falls asleep in the bed.

Angel leans forward in anticipation.

Soon the owners of the home come back, and they're bears! Ms. Milton holds up the pictures for all to see. A big scary papa bear, a friendly momma bear, and a cute little baby bear. A family of bears who live in the woods. Before long they find the chairs that didn't fit and the smallest one that broke. They find the porridge that Goldilocks tasted and the perfect one she'd finished off. Each discovery makes them angrier than the last. Eventually, they find her upstairs in their bed.

Goldilocks wakes up in horror at seeing the three hairy beasts . . . "and runs straight out the door and into the forest, crying 'Mommy, Mommy, Mommy' all the way home."

The kids all cheer. Ms. Milton holds the giant book aloft, pages open to Goldilocks tearing through the woods with the bears chasing behind.

One girl echoes, "'Mommy, Mommy, Mommy' all the way home."

Another cries out, "Run faster!"

Ms. Milton lets them celebrate awhile, then encourages them onwards. "How'd you like it?" she asks the class.

The children respond with more cheers.

"Do you think she made it home?"

Again more cheers.

"Does anyone have any questions?"

At first the room is silent. The children don't seem to know quite what to say. Eventually Veronica West raises her hand.

"What's on your mind, Miss Veronica West?" Ms. Milton inquires.

"I want to know if bears can have dogs."

"I didn't see any in the story . . . but yes, I suppose they can. I don't see why not."

The blonde girl in the blue tank top whom Angel helped with her mat raises her hand.

Ms. Milton singles her out. "What's your name?"

"Tammy Atford."

"What's your question, Tammy Atford?"

"Does she get in trouble?"

"What do you think?"

"I bet she does."

"Then I bet you're right. Seems like she didn't even make the bed!"

All the kids laugh. Ms. Milton keeps the conversation moving on along those lines, calling on every child by name and sometimes asking them to repeat their names for all to hear. Some kids are worried about the broken chair and want her to say she's sorry. All of them hope she gets home safely. Angel doesn't say a word. But he's sitting in a place with a good view of the book and he studies the artwork on the cover, especially the red cardinal in the tree.

"Is there anything else?" Ms. Milton asks at last. Does anyone have anything else to say or ask?" The room is silent while she looks around.

Finally, Angel sits up straight and raises his hand. Ms. Milton sees him immediately and leans his way in encouragement. "What's on your mind, little Angel?"

"My name is Angel Thompson," he says.

"Thank you, Angel. What's on your mind?"

He gathers himself to speak deliberately. "It's about the porridge," he says. "That's like oatmeal, right?"

"Yes, porridge is like oatmeal." She makes a gesture as if stirring and eating from a bowl in her hand. "Is there something you'd like to say about the porridge?"

"Why doesn't she mix it?"

Ms. Milton looks at him in confusion. "Mix it?"

"One bowl is too hot. One is too cold. She could mix them. Put too hot and too cold together. Then she'd have more porridge that's all just right."

Ms. Milton's eyes open wide in comprehension. Mix the porridge, of course!

Angel forges ahead boldly. "She could still eat the bowl that's just right. But if she's hungry she can eat even more."

Now all of the kids seemed to understand. A positive murmur fills the room. He catches some words behind him. "Mix the porridge, mix the temperature!" Someone else says "hot and cold together" while a different voice says "more to eat!"

Veronica West's voice rises above the hubbub. "She'd get fat."

"Not from one bowl of oatmeal," protests Angel. "And she seems to be hungry." He finishes with words he's heard many times around the house. "You never know where your next meal is coming from."

The kids fall silent and look at him in surprise. They don't seem to have heard that before.

"But she still needs to pay for it," he concludes. He looks deeply troubled, like he's solved one problem but raised another. "I don't know how she can do that." He turns to Ms. Milton for answers. "Does she have any money? Does her mom work at night?"

Still Angel is the only one talking. The room is silent while Angel waits for an answer, but at that moment the school bell rings. The kids all jump up like they know what it means, though Angel waits for Ms. Milton to make the announcement. "All done for the day. See you tomorrow!"

Chapter Fourteen

The boy in the Redskins jersey is named Parker Carlson, and Angel notices that he wears a Redskins jersey every day. Every day a different jersey with a different number and a different player's name on the back. By the end of the first month in school, Angel knows the names of every kid in class, and most of the Redskins.

The other boy in the Redskins jersey on the first day of school is named Walter Roscoe. Most kids call him Wally. He doesn't wear Redskins every day, but most of his clothes have something to do with sports. Most days at recess, he throws a ball with Parker Carlson or other kids in haphazard games of keep-away or tag.

Angel never gets invited to play with the other boys, and he wears almost the same few clothes every day. Most days at recess he walks around the playground collecting leaves. Some leaves come from the trees around the field; others are blown in from nearby and sometimes he can figure out where, though often it remains a mystery. Quickly he notices that leaves come in consistent, distinctive shapes.

When he asks her about it, Miss Stephanie explains that the leaves like a big star are called maples. She says that the leaves with the smaller, narrower star are called oaks. Angel shows her three other distinctive kinds of leaves, all of them roughly oval, some with smooth edges and others toothy. Miss Stephanie doesn't know what kind of tree these come from, but says she'll get a book to find out. In the meanwhile, she lets him make a pile in the classroom for each different kind of leaf when he finds it. She never brings the book, though, and after a while Angel stops asking her.

He watches everyone as he walks around. Parker is clearly the leader of his little gang of boys. He tells them what to play and assigns positions in every game. "Football and I'm quarterback," he yells. The other boys all run around waiting for a pass, though he doesn't throw to all of them equally.

One day Parker brings in a new soccer ball and the gang spends the rest of the week playing soccer.

Parker bullies the other kids, too, especially the smaller ones. Sometimes it's part of a game, a push or a hit during a football play, but sometimes he just pushes them for no reason. One day playing football, Mitchie Daniels falls down trying to catch a pass that looks to Angel impossible to reach. "You stink!" Parker yells.

"I'm sorry," Mitchie says, climbing back to his feet.

It isn't enough. Parker pushes him back to the ground and kicks him until he cries.

The next day Mitchie goes back to play and almost exactly the same thing happens. Mitchie drops a ball and ends up crying, but still he plays with the big boys every day.

Angel picks up trash while he walks the playground looking for leaves and watching things. He doesn't walk with the purpose of gathering trash, but he certainly wouldn't let a plastic bag fly past without catching it, or leave a soda can sitting in the playground after the weekend. The playground has four trash cans and a fifth by the door to the room. The least he can do is gather what he finds and throw it away where it's easy.

On days when it's raining or he doesn't feel like going outside, Angel likes to play with dice. The classroom has a whole wall full of games, many of them with dice. There's a can on the shelf filled with dice, mostly white, a few in colors, all of them with six sides and tiny black dots. Angel likes to grab two of them—any two, it doesn't matter which—roll them and watch the results.

One day while he's rolling, Miss Stephanie kneels down beside him and asks if he doesn't want to go outside.

"No thank you," he says, rolling the dice, then he looks up as if sharing a treasure. "Seven comes up most of often."

Miss Stephanie seems confused. "There is no seven."

Angel holds out two dice to explain. "Not one dice alone," he says. "But two dice together plus up to seven." He holds out a six and a one to demonstrate and explains again. "Two dice plus up to seven more often than they plus to any other number."

"Really?" says Miss Stephanie. "I didn't know that. We don't call it 'plussing,' though. We call it 'adding.' Six *plus* one *adds* up to seven." She stresses the words she wants in his vocabulary.

"Watch," he says.

He rolls the dice but they don't cooperate. A pair of twos. "Four," he says disappointedly.

Then a two and a three. "Five."

Finally he gets a four and a three. "They plus to seven," he says. "I mean they add," he corrects himself sheepishly.

"That's right. Four and three add up to seven."

"I get more sevens than any other number, except maybe eight. It doesn't matter what color they are."

"That's right. Color doesn't matter. Do you do math like that all the time?"

"Two dice is most fun. Five dice get confusing."

"Five dice sounds confusing!" She smiles supportively. "What happens if you add three plus six?"

"Nine." He answers immediately.

"What about three plus ten?"

"Thirteen."

"Two plus three plus four?"

"Nine again." He's enjoying this game.

"One plus one?"

He smiles in recognition of a question that's so easy it's a joke, and holds up two fingers.

Miss Stephanie doesn't stop. "Ten plus twelve?"

"Twenty-two."

"That's amazing!" Miss Stephanie exclaims. Most kids in kindergarten can barely add two plus two, and many can't count past ten. "How did you do that?"

"Do what?"

"Add ten plus twelve."

"It's twenty-two."

"I know. But how did you figure it out?"

Angel freezes. His smile disappears and he looked suddenly alarmed, like he's done something terribly wrong.

Miss Stephanie persists. "How did you do it? How did you know?"

Angel doesn't answer. He collects the dice, returns them to their can and hurries back to his seat. "Twenty-two," he says over his shoulder as he scurries past, his smile replaced by a terrified uncertainty.

The next day during class, Miss Stephanie pairs Angel with Tammy Atford, the girl he helped with her mat on the first day. "You two will work well together," she declares.

"Why?" Angel asks.

Miss Stephanie doesn't answer but Tammy steps right in. "It's okay," she says. "Let's work together." She's wearing a red sweater over a blue turtleneck.

Halloween is two weeks away and they're decorating the classroom. The first activity is drawing pumpkins. Tammy and Angel work together to cut orange construction paper into big circles and draw faces for a jack-o'-lantern.

Tammy points to Parker Carlson's pumpkin with a mean scary face and horns. "Let's make ours nice," she says. Soon they have a collection of friendly, smiling pumpkins in sizes ranging from circle traces around a Dixie cup to a pumpkin so large they taped two pieces of paper together before they cut. Angel has fun the entire time.

For the next activity Ms. Milton asks the kids to estimate how many jellybeans are in a jar. "When you're finished we'll have recess and lunch," she explains. "Maybe we'll even eat some jellybeans."

Miss Stephanie walks around the room giving jars of different sizes and shapes to the teams of kids, each jar filled with large jellybeans in happy pastel colors. Angel and Tammy get the biggest jar.

"No fair!" says Parker Carlson.

"They get more jellybeans but they'll need to work harder for them," says Miss Stephanie.

"You can have some of our jellybeans," Tammy adds.

"Now estimate!" Miss Stephanie commands. "After you estimate, count." She walks around the classroom explaining what it means to estimate and helping kids count.

Angel and Tammy look together at the jar of jellybeans, a mosaic of color. Angel thinks the jar once had jam in it, though the label's been removed.

Tammy shakes the jar around. It makes a satisfying rattle, but Angel can tell she's confused. She examines the jar from every direction, then shakes it again. "A million," she says. "That must be a million jellybeans."

Angel gently takes the jar from her hand and examines it himself. From the bottom he can see five jellybeans in a circle. He guesses that the jar is maybe six jellybeans tall. He shakes the jar while Tammy watches. When she smiles he shakes it again. "Thirty," he says.

"Thirty jelly beans?"

"Uh huh." He shows her how he worked it out, showing the number on the bottom and the height up the side, their heads nearly touching as they look together at the jar, and she agrees. They tell Miss Stephanie what they've done, and she tells them to dump the jellybeans out and count them. Parker next door has already started on his smaller jar. It looks to Angel like a mustard jar, though he knows from shopping that mustard in jars that small is very expensive per ounce, and it's cheaper to buy a bigger jar.

Angel's jar is still in his hands so he unscrews the lid and pours them out, but he's momentarily overwhelmed by the mess he's made.

Tammy has a plan. "Let's break them up into fives," she says.

"Good idea," Angel replies.

Together they start pulling the pile into smaller groups. Soon enough they've created six little groups of five, plus two jellybeans more. "Thirty-two!" Tammy yells out loud. "Miss Stephanie, we have thirty-two."

"How many did you estimate again?"

"Thirty," says Angel. He's embarrassed because he was wrong and feels like it was his fault.

"That's wonderful!" Miss Stephanie exclaims. "That's an amazingly close estimate on such a big number!" She pats Angel on the head and he remembers what it means to estimate. It's not the same as counting. He goes from embarrassed to proud.

Miss Stephanie looks around the classroom. Most kids are finishing up by now. "Let's clean up, then we'll have recess and lunch."

Angel and Tammy put the jellybeans back in the jar, and Angel uses his hands to sweep some sugar dust up from the floor. Miss Stephanie is complimenting them both on a job well done when Tammy's girlfriends come by on their way outside.

"We're playing hopscotch," says Joanna Baye. Her hair is dark and curly, tied with a red ribbon at top. "Let's go."

"Want to join us?" Tammy asks Angel.

Joanna makes a face like Tammy made her drink glue. "He doesn't know how," she says.

"Sure he does," Tammy replies.

Angel keeps sweeping the floor with his hand, though the dust is long gone, acting as if he doesn't hear.

"Don't you?" Tammy asks him.

"Not really." He's still looking down at the floor. He doesn't even know what hopscotch is.

"See," Joanna says.

"We can show you." Tammy is undefeated.

Miss Stephanie sees all of this. "Great idea," she adds. "He can learn. Hopscotch is great fun."

But Joanna is still scowling like she's drinking glue.

Angel says, "You go ahead. I'm okay." He picks up a pinprick of dust with his fingertip, then stands and passes the jellybeans back to Miss Stephanie.

"Let's go," says Joanna, tugging on Tammy's arm.

Tammy looks at Angel to be sure he really is okay, then follows her girlfriends out the door.

Angel watches her walk outside, and keeps on watching as they start the game. So that's what hopscotch is. He's seen them play before, and now he knows the name. It does look like fun.

But an empty can of Dr. Pepper sits in the grass just outside the door. Angel steps outside to throw it away, and spends the rest of recess collecting leaves by himself.

Chapter Fifteen

On the first day of first grade, Angel brings in a whole pack of Starbursts with lunch, a gift Monet bought him with her babysitting money. Lunch is at a different time this year but it's still in the same cafeteria and the kids all sit in their same places. Parker Carlson and his football friends sit at one table. Veronica West and her gang take over two whole tables near the front. Tammy Atford sits with Joanna Baye at a table near the window.

The cafeteria is the biggest room in the school, used not only for lunch but assemblies and after-school programs, too. The walls on the first day of school are decorated with permanent art—scenes from *The Wizard of Oz* and a portrait of Thomas Jefferson—but it will soon be decorated with artwork by the students, changing with birthdays, seasons and holidays.

"Look, a rabbit!" Joanna shouts, and her whole table jumps up to look out the window.

Angel's table is farther from the window than Joanna's, but he can see the rabbit without getting up from his chair. He catches a quick glimpse of the small gray bunny nibbling grass near the building before the view is blocked by Joanna's friends rushing the window.

Angel doesn't sit by himself because there aren't enough tables that everyone can have their own table if they want. Angel sits at one end of his table, and Mitchie Daniels sits at the other. A blond boy called Huck sits between them, though they rarely say a word to one another.

Angel is hungry today and he wolfs down the sandwich of bologna and mustard he made himself over breakfast. He sweeps the crumbs into his hand and tosses the collection into his mouth, then unwraps his Starbursts. He works to open the foil from the top, peeling it down to release three little squares of candy—red, pink and yellow. The wrapper shows four different colors, so he peels down a little farther, passing two more reds before reaching the last color, an orange.

Angel doesn't get candy all that often at home, but Starbursts are his favorite, with their chewy burst of flavor and long-lasting tang. Now he has six Starbursts open in front of him, one of each color plus two extra reds. He stacks them on top of each other—reds on top—and notices that together they stand the same height as the unopened part of the package. The whole package probably contains twelve little Starburst squares.

He's just deciding to eat one with lunch and save the rest for later when he suddenly feels crowded. Parker Carlson is standing over him, barely a football's length away. "You have candy today," Parker observes, staring straight at Angel's Starbursts.

Parker often has followers, but now it's just him alone. His hand is resting on the table by Angel's treats. "Can I have a piece?"

Angel says nothing.

Parker leans in closer. "I said, *You have candy today.*"

"Yes," says Angel. "I'm lucky today."

"Can I have a piece?"

"No, thank you," says Angel.

At the other end of the table, Mitchie Daniels stands up to leave, and so does Huck. They gather their trash and move swiftly toward the exit, without crossing Parker Carlson or looking back at Angel. Mere crumbs rest on the table where moments ago sat two classmates.

Parker steps even closer, looks Angel hard in the eye, then turns his full attention to the Starbursts on the table. He lifts the top Starburst on the stack—a red one—and holds it before his eyes. "Red like the Redskins," he says. He leans in toward Angel and pushes the Starburst into his face. "Can I have a piece?"

Angel feels suddenly dizzy, like he stood up too fast or all of his air has disappeared. The room starts to spin and he leans against the table to hold everything still. Parker is still standing above him, red Starburst held in Angel's face. "Can I have a piece?" he repeats.

"Not for free," says Angel gently but with a hint of possible compromise. "You can have two for a quarter."

Parker cocks his head in surprise.

"You can buy as many as you want. They cost two for a quarter." Angel says it like it's obvious. "Do you have any money?"

Parker still seems confused, but he reaches his hand into his pocket. "I have a dollar," he says.

"For a dollar you can buy eight of them," Angel does the math for him. "Plus the one in your hand you can keep for free."

Parker raises that hand high in the air like he got a deal. "Score!" he declares. He passes his dollar to Angel, then takes his time sorting through the Starbursts in the line. Like Monet at home and Angel just moments ago, he chooses his colors with care, setting some aside and moving others into groups, then changing his mind and moving different colors up front. Finally he picks eight Starbursts plus the extra red one he kept in his hand the entire time. "Perfect," he says. And he smiles at Angel, looking less like a bully than a young boy with brand-new candy.

"More tomorrow?" Angel asks.

Parker looks a little embarrassed. Then quickly and without answering, he gathers his winnings and charges back toward his friend at the other table. "Score!" Angel hears him say as he rejoins them, two fists full of Starbursts held high in the air.

After lunch Tammy Atford and Joanna Baye are playing with dominoes. They balance them upright and line them up in a long arc across the floor. When the last domino is up, Joanna counts, "One, two, three . . . go!" and knocks down the first domino in the row.

Angel has never seen this game before and he exclaims out loud when the dominoes knock each other down, tick, tick, tick, the whole length of the floor.

He watches eagerly as they set the dominoes up again, this time thrilled in anticipation of the climax. "Do you want to start them falling?" Tammy asks Angel as the last piece takes its place in the line.

He never answers. Whether by design or miscommunication, Joanna has already started the chain reaction. Angel and Tammy simply watch together as they all fall down, and applaud the tight little curlicue at the end. Then it's time for class.

Angel detours past a 7-Eleven with a dollar to spend when he gets off the bus in the afternoon. Starbursts cost seventy-five cents a pack, plus three cents tax. He buys one pack and pockets twenty-two cents of change, two each of pennies and dimes. He lets himself into the apartment, reads his favorite books from last year, and turns pages in the magazines and advertising flyers he picked up for free at the 7-Eleven.

An hour later when Monet gets home from her own first day of school, he gives her an especially big hug and thanks her all over again for the Starbursts. He keeps the details private for now, but he still has three Starbursts left from the day. One he eats and one he gives one to Monet; the last one he returns to his backpack for tomorrow. Mom promised them a nice dinner tonight, but they decide not to wait. They put potatoes in the oven to bake, and start to reheat a big pot of soup from the weekend. They can eat as soon as she arrives.

The next morning at school, Parker stops Angel in the hallway before class. "Are we on?" he asks. Parker is walking with Wally Roscoe, who doesn't seem to know what Parker is talking about.

Angel feels no need to explain. "Yes," he says. Behind him as he walks away he hears Wally ask Parker what they're up to, and when Angel turns to look, he sees them joke-wrestling until a teacher walking by breaks them apart.

At lunch Angel sits in his usual place, again with Mitchie and Huck sitting silently. Parker sits with his crowd near the door but no sooner has Angel unwrapped his sandwich than Parker sits himself down alongside.

"Two for a quarter?" asks Parker, holding out a crisp, clean dollar bill.

"Eight for a dollar," says Angel, pulling out his Starbursts package and working off the wrapper. "Plus one extra."

Parker immediately pulls one red Starbursts aside and sets it lovingly in the corner. Then he takes his time counting out eight more. "Orange for the Bengals," he says. "Yellow for Steelers. I hate them!"

When he's all done there are still three Starbursts remaining, plus one from yesterday. "Tell the other guys at your table that they're for sale. Two for a quarter."

Parker returns to his table like a conquering prince, showing off two fistfuls of Starbursts to a crowd of boys on tight candy rations at home. Angel watches him carefully, catching a few words as a red Starburst tackles a yellow Starburst to laughter all around . . . then surely the message is delivered. Parker points back toward Angel's table and all the heads turn. Wally Roscoe leads the crowd that runs in his direction, and soon enough Angel has fifty more cents in his pocket.

Angel races through the rest of the school day, trying to pay attention, getting caught once when he's supposed to be drawing but he doesn't want to take his hands out of his pockets. He never takes it out to count, but including yesterday's change he knows it's $1.72, more money than he's ever held in his life. When he gets off the school bus at the end of the day, he heads straight to the 7-Eleven and buys two new packs of Starbursts for $1.50 plus tax. He walks home with sixteen cents jingling in his pocket, and he receives an especially friendly smile from the man driving the ice cream truck.

The next day he sells it all. Eight Starbursts plus one to Parker for a dollar, and he still has fifteen more. Fourteen of them he sells for seven quarters, and the last one he pockets until tomorrow. He returns to the 7-Eleven with just a few pennies shy of three dollars in his pocket.

Two packs of Starbursts are a given. He'll buy those for sure. He has little doubt that he'll sell them tomorrow, and he succeeds with ease. No announcements are needed nor encouragement required. The kids simply flock to his table at lunchtime and swap quarters for Starbursts. By Friday, the last day of the first week of school, he has enough cash to experiment. He adds to his Starbursts a pack of Wrigley's Spearmint gum, thirty-six individually wrapped sticks for $2.50. He thinks he can sell sticks of gum for a dime apiece, making a profit of roughly a dollar including tax.

He doesn't know if he'll be able to sell them all in one day, or whether he'll get in trouble with the teacher, but he runs home with his little bag clenched tightly in his hand. He'll find out.

Chapter Sixteen

Most evenings Libby gets home around six o'clock. She still works at the hospital, the same place she worked when Sheila and Zeb were taken away, though her job has changed through the years. Now she spends less time cleaning than supervising other people and keeping the supply inventory.

Except when she works overtime—which she does whenever she can—they have dinner together. Usually they start to cook when Libby gets home and they eat by seven o'clock. They do their homework—especially Monet, who is in seventh grade—and sometimes play a game. Angel goes to bed a little before nine and Monet a little after. They all take turns in the tiny bathroom.

On nights when Libby does work overtime, Monet and Angel take care of themselves and leave leftovers for her. Every night of overtime means ice cream the next night, a rule that at first they resisted because they wanted their mom, but now they enjoy. If Angel wakes up when Libby comes in, he runs out of bed to give her a hug, even though she scolds him and tells him to get back in bed.

On the second Friday of the school year they eat early and Angel is so excited he can barely sit through dinner.

"Sit down," his mom says again and again. "I made your favorite."

Angel's favorite is something he and his mom contrived together one night when the refrigerator held no obvious combinations. They boiled up some rice, melted cheese on top and mixed in olives from a jar. All of them loved it and they made it a regular, though Libby adds Tabasco to her own. Tonight, because she grabbed an opportunity on sale, they have cashews on the side.

They eat the dinner, bus the dishes, and then learn why Angel was wiggling through dinner. Libby and Monet return from a trip to the sink to find a ten-dollar bill and three quarters sitting at Monet's seat at the table.

"For you," Angel explains.

"Ten seventy-five!" she cries. "Exactly what I need!" She doesn't ask who gave it to her or where it came from, just launches for Angel with a giant hug. "Ten seventy-five," she says again. "You're perfect."

"It's for your phone call," he says.

"You're perfect," she says again. All of them know that tonight is Friday. Monet's only contact with her parents is Friday phone calls—every other week with her mom, less often with her dad—when she accepts a collect phone call from the prison. Their apartment has no telephone and Monet's foster parents refuse to accept the charges, but a little organization called CURE—Christians United for the Restoration of Errants—fills exactly this gap.

People in prison obviously don't have regular phones, and the only way they can talk by phone is to call collect. The family that gets the call then pays. The trouble is that people in prison can only use the prison telephone company, and the prison phone company can charge any rate it wants. Monet learned that prisoners can't use prepaid calling cards, 1-800 dial-around services, or anything else to reduce the price. Prison phone calls cost ninety cents a minute plus a $1.75 connection fee, limited to a ten-minute maximum. Do the math and a ten-minute phone call comes in at exactly $10.75. Monet and Angel have done the math many times together.

CURE is willing to accept the charges for the phone call if the person receiving the call repays CURE in cash at the time. Libby has built a ten-minute call into the family budget for every other Friday.

"Where did you get the money?" Libby asks.

"She gave it to me." He points to Monet with a sly smile.

Neither of them gets it.

"Remember those Starbursts from the first day of school?" Angel explains how he sold them to Parker Carlson and turned his profits into future sales.

"Parker Carlson's sister is in my class," Monet offers. "She's a jerk. At least Parker's a nice guy."

"I didn't say that," Angel replies. "I just said he buys my candy."

Everyone laughs in understanding. Libby asks, "Does the teacher know you're doing it?"

"I don't think she minds. But I don't think the kids tell their parents."

"That's fine by me," Libby says, then adds with a foreboding tone, "as long as it's only candy."

Angel doesn't understand what she means but it doesn't slow him down. "Here's my goal," he announces, like a politician on a podium. "I want to sell enough candy to buy Monet a phone call on Friday nights. If I do that, then Monet's babysitting money and Mom's extra money can go toward a bus trip. Maybe someday you can take one of those CURE bus rides and visit your mom for real. That's my goal, anyway."

The whole family knows that once a month CURE sponsors a van ride to one of the Virginia prisons. CURE fills the van with family members and charges people only the cost. Twice in the five years since Sheila's been gone, the van has traveled to Fluvanna, the prison where she's held. Neither time was Monet able to go.

Monet steps over to Angel and kisses him on the forehead. "You are so much not a jerk," she says.

"You're welcome," he replies.

"I'll finish the dishes," Libby says. "Monet, it's almost time for you to go."

Everyone checks the clock and agrees. Monet's advance agreement with her mom is to be at the CURE office at seven o'clock. She needs to arrive early and maybe stay late because Sheila can't time the phone call with precision, but hopefully she'll get the full ten minutes at seven.

"Thank you again," Monet says as she scoops the $10.75 into her pocket. "I'll tell Mom all about Angel's Starbursts and the first week of school. I have enough time to walk to CURE. It's a nice night and I'll save the bus fare. Bye."

Libby and Angel do the dishes and the full Friday night of housework. Angel tells her about his first week of school and shows her the homework he started in his new notebooks. He's especially proud of the charts he made by arranging colored dots into regular patterns.

Barely an hour has passed before Monet again returns to the apartment. She tromps up the stairs and shoves open the door and slams it back behind her.

"Fluvanna's on lockdown," she says in a voice of despair. She takes off her coat and jams it into the closet as if it's fighting back. "Someone flushed socks down the toilet and clogged up the system. Everyone's punished. One hundred percent cell time. No work, no rec, no classes . . . no telephone. Just sit in your cage and keep quiet." She takes the $10.75 and gives it back to Angel.

"Keep it for next week," he says, pushing it back at her.

"I'm sorry, honey," Libby offers. "Do you want to write her a letter?"

Monet doesn't answer. She just stomps around the room, opening drawers and closing them, hardly looking inside. Realizing that she's still wearing her hat, she yanks her coat out of the closet, shoves her hat into the pocket and throws it all on the floor. "Lockdown!" she says.

"I can draw a picture for her," Angel says. "For the letter."

Monet kicks her coat into the closet and slams the door.

"Do you want some dessert?" Libby tries.

Monet just stomps into her room. "I don't want dessert!" She slams the door behind her. "I want my mother."

Chapter Seventeen

Everyone is talking about Amanda Hayley. Angel hears about her when he listens for weather on the radio, and when parents pick up their children at the schoolyard. Angel sees her picture in the newspaper boxes on the way to school and on the television display at the Radio Shack near his 7-Eleven.

At first, Amanda is simply missing. The twelve-year-old girl from a wealthy suburb of Atlanta wasn't home when her parents returned from an office party. Amanda's mom had landed a big contract, and the party was held in her honor. Both parents went.

"It was the first time I left her home alone," Mrs. Hayley tells *Fox News at Five*. "I thought she was old enough."

Mrs. Hayley had arranged for Amanda to call her husband's brother, Uncle Dan, if anything went wrong. Uncle Dan said he would be home that evening and happy to be backup. By the age of twelve Amanda knows how to call 911, of course; she knows how to pour her own soda and heat her own popcorn in the microwave. What went wrong?

The first stories are missing person alerts. Police in the neighborhood and citizens everywhere are told to look out for her. Her image appears everywhere: a baby picture provided by a neighbor, a yearbook photo provided by her school.

Additional details soon emerge. Amanda had a long phone call with a friend shortly after her parents left. She checked her email while she was talking, and stayed online for ten minutes after she hung up. Most important of all, her father's brother, Uncle Dan, is also missing. He was the first person the parents called when they returned home, a little later than they wished, and Amanda wasn't in her bed. Dan didn't answer his phone that evening, and he hasn't answered it since. "Uncle Dan will have a lot to answer for," the radio concludes with ominous ellipses.

"He did it," Libby replies.

Angel has never seen his mother focused on the news, but this story has her on edge. She buys newspapers and tunes in for radio updates. On a piece of paper by the refrigerator, she keeps tally of how many days have elapsed since Amanda was last seen, and every morning she adds another hash mark after the news.

On the morning of day nine the radio reveals that Amanda's body has been found, left by the side of a road in northeastern Texas. On day ten the autopsy reveals sexual contact without evidence of violence. Libby listens, transfixed by the forensic analysis, while she burns her toast and eats it anyway. It was Amanda's first time, of course, but there were no scratches, bruises or signs of force.

Death came later, by strangulation, as if an afterthought.

"She said she would tell," Libby explains to nobody in particular, as if the radio were listening. "That's why he did it."

"Who did what, Mom?" Angel asks. She isn't making sense, and Angel can't even tell who she's talking to. The breakfast on her plate is barely touched.

"They'll find him," she says, as if that's an explanation. "He's no criminal mastermind. Just a loser. A confused loser."

Angel buses his breakfast dishes. It's getting late and he hasn't made his lunch yet.

"He's on his way to Mexico." Libby doesn't explain but won't let it go. "Pathetic."

ON DAY TWELVE UNCLE DAN is caught at the border crossing at Nuevo Laredo.

Monet stayed after school with some friends, but Libby and Angel had agreed to buy her graph paper for her math class. They'd bought her graph paper earlier in the year but it proved to be the wrong dimensions, so that purchase was wasted and they have to go out again. Now, mission accomplished, they're walking out of the Staples past the display TV at the Best Buy. Amanda's face is on the screen under the banner, *Breaking News*. Libby hauls them to a stop.

"My poor baby," Amanda's mother is saying.

"No comment," says Amanda's father, asked about his brother, the man who likely raped and murdered his daughter.

The segment ends with another photograph of Amanda, different from the stock photos they've seen all week. Not a baby picture or an official school photo, this is a recent picture provided by a friend. This photo shows how well she's developing—her young breasts impressive already, her hips filling out. The television lingers over the looseness at the top of her blouse, inviting the viewer to look more closely . . .

"We need to go," declares Libby, yanking on Angel's arm as if she weren't the one who made them stop, her face a strange color, burning red and pale as a ghost at the same time. "We'll be late."

"What's the matter, mom?" Angel has never seen her angry in this way, for no reason that he can see. "Aren't you glad they caught him?"

"We need to go. We'll be late." Angel's not sure what to do, but one thing he knows for sure: to walk obediently beside his mother and not say a word. He notices that the trees along the sidewalk have leaves in little stars, like miniature maples.

The next day in school Angel's class starts a new subject called "Good Touch, Bad Touch." The teacher says it's in response to Amanda Hayley, so Angel tells his mom about it right away. Knowing how much she cares about Amanda Hayley, he thinks she'll be happy to hear. Besides, they gave him "Good Touch, Bad Touch" forms that he's required to show his parents and bring back signed to prove that he did.

Diligently he shows her the forms and carefully he explains the different kinds of touches they discussed in school. He doesn't think he's doing anything wrong but he feels his mother starting to burn. He points to the pictures on the form and sings the theme they practiced in school, "Good! Bad! Good, good. Bad!" His mother seems to be only tolerating his explanations and Angel is certain he must be making a mistake. He demonstrates a good touch by patting her on the shoulder, but it doesn't help. He tries a hug but he feels her wincing underneath. He reaches toward her thigh to demonstrate a bad touch and she all but hits him.

He's quiet for a while, and when he tries another hug his mother seems to be on another planet. Finally he can't stand it any longer.

"Mom?" he says.

Libby says nothing.

"Mom?"

Still no answer.

"Did I do something wrong?" The ultimate question.

The ultimate question seems to penetrate and suddenly his mother opens like the sky after a storm. "No," she exhales. "You did nothing wrong." She sweeps him up in a hug so big it can only have one interpretation, rocking him back and forth in her arms. Angel snuggles into the hug, but soon she tightens again. "You spent a whole hour at this?" she asks.

"Hours and hours." He didn't really measure the time, but they kept talking about it all day.

"Did they tell you what to do if you get a bad touch?" Her voice is a pane of glass standing on its edge; a push in any direction will tip it to shatter.

Angel hesitates. They didn't spend much time on that, and he doesn't want to get it wrong.

She asks him again. "Did they tell you what to do if you get a bad touch?"

Angel ventures a guess. "Tell someone?"

"Right," says his mother, but there are no congratulations in her tone, the glass still on edge. "Who should you tell?"

"Tell your parent?" says Angel, still guessing.

Something seems wrong. A stone is heading for the glass. "What if your parent is the one who's touching you wrong?" His mother asks in a spooky whisper.

"That's not possible!" Angel exclaims. "Parents don't ever touch wrong."

"Is that what they tell you?"

"No . . . " Angel is struggling now. "But it's not what they talk about. They say to look out for strangers. Be careful at the bus stop. Stuff like that."

"What if one parent is touching you wrong, and the other parent doesn't believe you?"

It's like she's telling him that up is down. "I don't know," he replies lamely. He doesn't even know what it's like to have two parents.

"They don't tell you?" She's going after somebody now, and Angel is in her line of fire. "They don't tell you what to do?"

"Call the police?" It's a question, not an answer.

"Would you call the police on your parents?"

It's too much. Angel doesn't even try to answer. He pulls the Good Touch forms up over his face and pushes himself back into the couch.

Libby realizes she's gone too far, way too far, and she comes back to him. "I'm sorry," she says, her arms open wide. "Can I have a good hug?"

Angel launches himself into her arms and they stay together on the couch, the forms to be signed all but forgotten, buried in a hug of happiness together. After a while he looks up and, from this proximity, notices a fleck of food near her lip. He reaches up to wipe it clean, but when his hand touches her mouth she slaps it away like she's never slapped him before. Her eyes glow with fire and the glass is shattered.

"I'm sorry," she says again.

Angel accepts her apology hug. He knows something is wrong, but he doesn't know what.

Chapter Eighteen

"Where are we from, Mom?" Angel asks Libby as soon as she returns home one evening, about a week after Amanda Hayley has faded from the news.

It's not late but it's already dark outside as the sun moves toward winter. Today on the playground Angel wished he had a warmer jacket. Right now he is in the middle of the floor surrounded by drawing paper and magazines he took from the recycling bin in the lobby downstairs.

Monet is doing homework at the table. "We're having spaghetti for dinner," she says. "There's water on the stove."

"Where are we from, Mom?" Angel asks again. She seems not to have heard him the first time. Angel can hear that the water is almost boiling, and his mother is giving it her full attention. She looks under the lid, checks the heat, then looks under the lid again.

Even Angel knows that checking under lids is useless. "Where are we from?" he asks.

At last she turns his direction. "We're from Virginia," she says.

"I know that!" he says disapprovingly. "I mean before that. The teacher wants us to find out where our parents were born, and where their parents were born before them."

"Why does he want to know that?" Libby breaks open a box of spaghetti.

"We're studying immiglation," he replies and then interrupts himself, knowing he got it wrong. "I mean immigration." He corrects himself.

"That sounds cool, studying immigration," she replies, slowing down to emphasize the pronunciation.

"Daniel Franco says he's from Peru."

"That's cool."

"He's not really from Peru," Angel says, correcting himself. "His parents are from Peru. Daniel was born in America. Virginia, even. He says his parents point out the hospital every time they drive past. He says that means he's an American."

"That's right," says Libby. "If he was born in America, then he's an American. We're Americans too. Virginians, even. You were born in Virginia."

"My hospital was in Virginia? Can you show it to me?"

Libby turns toward the stove so Angel can't see her face. She breaks the spaghetti in half and drops it in the water, then concentrates on stirring it around.

"What about you, Mom? Where were you born?"

"Virginia."

"What about my dad? Where was he born?"

Libby keeps stirring, holding Angel at her back. "Do you want the tomato sauce I made over the weekend?" she calls over her shoulder. "Or just butter?" She opens the fridge for sauce and takes a bag of frozen peas out of the freezer.

"Do you know where Dad was born?"

Libby rips open the peas and pours some into a cup; she fills the cup with hot water from the tap and returns the bag to the freezer.

"How about your parents? Where were they were born? Do you know?"

Libby pours the thawing peas in the colander, swirls them dry, then returns them to the cup and refills it with hot water. A few more cycles are enough to heat the peas thoroughly, Angel knows. He's done this plenty of times himself.

Libby leaves the peas drained in the cup to serve with the spaghetti.

Angel tries again. "Veronica West says her great-great-great-grandparents were slaves. She says it like it's cool. I didn't think being slaves was cool."

"Slavery wasn't cool," Libby replies. "But being the great-great-great-granddaughter of a slave, whose dad is a rich orthodontist—that's kind of cool, in a very American sort of way."

"Our teacher says that's what makes America great. Can you show me on a map where you were born?"

Libby drains the spaghetti into the same colander. "Dinner's ready," she says to the room. To Angel she says, "Sure . . . but I don't have a map of Virginia very handy. Let's eat."

Monet closes her textbook and helps scoop the spaghetti onto plates. "I'm starving," she says, and everyone's parentage is forgotten—but only for the moment, Libby realizes. These questions are only the beginning. She's kept a lot buried these past few years. They'd flown past while Angel was young and she was busy. By now the problem isn't only what to say, but explaining how long she kept it secret.

What's the answer to that one? How would she say it? How would she tell her son that she'd been lying all these years?

It will only get worse with time—but knowing that still doesn't tell her what to do. How long can this last?

At school the next day the kids are divided into pairs to draw pictures of Thanksgiving. "We have much to be thankful for," Mr. Seigal declares. "Including our ancestors."

Mr. Seigal talks about the waves of immigration that came to America. First the Pilgrims and Puritans. Eventually Irish and Italians. He spends a lot of time talking about Catholics, Protestants, and Jews.

Angel doesn't understand all the names but he knows what Mr. Seigal is driving at.

"We're a melting pot," Mr. Seigal concludes. "Who has ever heard of a melting pot?"

All the kids raise their hands, and Angel has learned that at times like this he should raise his hand too. But the melting pot makes him think about the stew he makes with his mother on weekends, and it's almost lunchtime.

Angel happens to be near Tammy Atford when they're divided into pairs for drawing, and the two naturally turn to each other. Tammy goes after construction paper and crayons; Angel goes for scissors and a glue stick.

A minute later they're back at the desk. "Call me Tamantha from now on," Tammy declares as they sit down together.

"Tamantha? I don't get it."

"My cousin is called Sammy but her real name is Samantha. So if she's Sammy/Samantha, I think I can be Tammy/Tamantha? Get it?"

Angel is already smiling. "Okay, Tamantha. I get it."

"My cousins were at our house all weekend. It was fun. They live in Bethesda on the other side of Washington, D.C. Usually we meet them to go to the Smithsonian together, but this weekend they came to our house. Their parents went away the whole weekend for their anniversary. It was fun."

"What's an anniversary?" Angel feels like he ought to know.

"It's like a birthday. But instead of being the day you're born, it's the day you got married. Do your parents celebrate an anniversary? My parents kiss a lot on their anniversary. It's disgusting." Suddenly she interrupts herself. "Oops, sorry," she concludes. "I guess you don't have anniversaries in your house."

"It's okay, Tamantha," Angel says. "I don't even have cousins."

Together they make family trees. Tamantha's is especially beautiful, with roots from all four grandparents, branches of parents and leaves of all kinds of aunts, uncles, and cousins. They decorate it with colors, and add sun and clouds to the sky above the tree.

Angel's is simpler, just him and his mother.

"We can still decorate it," Tamantha suggests. "We can still make it pretty."

"It will still be little," Angel replies with a frown. "Tell me more about your father."

Chapter Nineteen

November 16 is the day. Monet's been looking forward to it, counting down to it on the calendar. Now it's here. Saturday, November 16, CURE is hosting a van ride to Virginia Woman's Correctional Center at Fluvanna.

Monet reserved her ticket as soon as the date was set. Her whole life has been organized around being free this day, and she's been holding her breath until it arrived. Now it's here. Saturday, November 16. She's going to visit her mother.

They had talked plenty about who would take the trip. Monet, obviously, and maybe Libby, who would have liked to visit her old friend and keep Monet company. Even Angel was curious, and he could travel for half price if he were willing to sit in someone's lap if it got crowded. But in the end they decided that Monet should go alone. Partly it was a matter of cost, but mostly it was a matter of whose mother it is. "This trip is for me," Monet decided. "Me and my mom."

"But you'll send our love," said Libby. "And you'll tell us all about it."

"Of course."

"Me too," Angel chimed in.

Visiting hours start at 10:00 A.M. It's a two-hour drive, plus an hour to clear security; add some time for slack and the van leaves at 6:00 A.M. CURE organizes trips like this all the time, and they know what they're doing.

Last week ended Daylight Savings Time, so the sun rises earlier, but still it's pitch dark when Monet wakes up. She hardly slept, of course, worried that she might miss the alarm, waking up every hour afraid she'd slept through it by mistake, and waking up for the last time just a few minutes before the alarm actually goes off. She puts on the clothes she chose last week and laid out on the chair last night: a pink T-shirt, her new blouse with the pretty flowered collar, and her favorite blue cardigan. Inside is cold and outside will be colder; she has no idea what the temperature inside the prison might be.

Libby must have heard her stirring or set her own alarm, because she's already in the kitchen. Together they make Monet a cheese sandwich for breakfast, and two more sandwiches plus a bag of crackers to get her through the day. Neither says a word as they go through motions familiar from school days. Before Monet leaves, Libby wraps her up in her warmest coat and hat, and gives her a little kiss on the cheek. "Good luck, honey. Send her my love."

Monet wraps her arms around Libby and kisses her on the forehead. "You're my mom, too," she says. "I love you. Thank you for everything."

Monet has been many times to the CURE office but never so early in the morning. In the parking lot a van is waiting with the engine running, a battered, full-sized van that looks like it was once used for deliveries of some kind, the logo of an air conditioner shop partly painted out on one side, looking nothing like the minivans that clog the school parking lot every day after school.

Monet walks into the office and greets Mary Anne, the director, whom she knows from her Fridays and who knows full well how much Monet has been looking forward to this trip. Mary Anne founded CURE thirty years ago with her husband, Jonathan, the minister of a small Presbyterian ministry near Reston Town Center. Monet sees parish volunteers in the office every Friday evening, answering inmate mail and calling for donations. A few other people are buzzing around the office, though none of them looks like a parish volunteer. Everyone in the room is African American except Mary Anne, who is white.

Behind Mary Anne is a poster picture of Jesus, hands clasped, peaceful and calm. "To God, all things are possible," it says. "Matthew 19:26."

Just to the left is another poster, smaller and without artwork, yellow text on a blue background. "Do good to them that hate you. Luke 6:27." Similar posters cover the walls all around. "For the Lord hears the needy and does not despise his own people who are in prison. Psalm 69:33."

Monet knows these posters well, has read them all on Friday evenings waiting for her mother to call. She turns to look at her favorite by the door, a quote not from the Bible but Pope Paul VI: "If you want peace, work for justice."

Mary Anne can see where she's looking, of course. "I have something for you," she says, stepping across to her desk.

Mary Anne puts two Hershey's kisses in Monet's hand, then she kisses her own fingertips and touches them to Monet's forehead. "Go ahead and get on the bus," she says. "We're full today. Get a good seat."

The door on the side of the van is still open, and Monet bounces up the step.

Maybe half a dozen women of all ages are chattering inside, wearing their Sunday best, looking like they're on the way to church. Monet hears and feels the heater blasting at full power, but it can't keep up with the open door. "Good morning," she hears, as soon as she crosses the threshold.

"Good morning," she says to the crowd. "It's dark outside!"

"And cold!" says a voice in the back.

"But it's warm in here," says a large woman wearing a puffy, fiber-filled coat like kids wear on the playground. "And it's morning of another day. God saw fit to give us another morning."

"Amen!" answers a chorus around the bus.

Monet sits down on a row by herself, midway along the length of the van, on the driver's side, opposite the open door. With the cabin light on from the open door, she can see herself in the window. To her surprise, she fits right in with the crowd. A young black woman dressed in her favorites.

Several more people soon arrive, two women she just saw in the office and a third that Monet recognizes from her Friday evening phone calls. People exchange good mornings all around, and many seem to know each other. They all shuffle around, finding seats. A minute later comes an older man, slender and clean-shaven, dressed in a brown suit with a green shirt and burgundy tie. He has no hat and no overcoat, just the suit, the only man in a van full of women. He sits by himself near the back of the bus and nods courteously when greeted, but nothing more.

Only the seat beside Monet remains empty, and she starts to worry that she's doing something wrong. She looks around for somebody who's crowded or needs the space, but everyone is sitting nicely, chattering with her neighbors. She watches a blue jay hop along the edge of the parking lot and dip its beak in a puddle from a recent rain.

A few minutes after six o'clock the driver arrives, and along with him a monumentally large woman wearing a light blue running suit and a bright red cap. The driver muscles the passenger door shut after the woman boards, then moves to his place in the front.

The giant of a woman settles in beside Monet. "Good to meet you," she says. "I'm Alabama."

Monet has never heard of such a name, other than first in the alphabetical list of states she memorized in kindergarten, and it must show on her face.

"Yes," says the woman. "Like the state." She adjusts her coat and works to fit her large body into the small space.

"I'm Monet," says Monet, pulling herself together and moving to make room.

"Monet? Like the artist?"

"Like the artist."

"With a *T*?"

"With a *T*."

Alabama opens into a smile as big as a state. "You are one lucky girl, with a name with a *T*. Not some obvious *T* like Trixie or Tracy, but your own little secret *T* at the end. Good work."

Monet is tickled from top to bottom. That special *T* has always been a favorite of hers, though she's never heard it said in that way. "T-thank you," she says with a smile, artificially sounding out the *T* at the beginning of the word.

The driver starts the engine and turns to his crowd. "Bound for Fluvanna," he says. "Bail now if you don't mean it." The crowd cheers as he starts to roll.

Alabama takes off her hat and cranes around to get a good look at the space they're leaving and the space they're in. When she's seen it all and turned all the way around back to Monet she says, "You're going to Fluvanna to visit your mother?"

Monet nods in the affirmative. She so rarely says her mother's in prison in words out loud, it doesn't come easily.

Alabama gives her time to say more, but she doesn't. "We're like mirrors," Alabama offers at last. "Two sides of a window looking at each other."

"You're going to Fluvanna to visit your mother?"

"No. My daughter."

The driver hits the brakes for a red light and everyone lurches forward; Monet presses her hands against the seat in front of her to keep from hitting it. Stable again, she turns to Alabama. "Two sides of the same window," Monet repeats, shaking her head in amazement. She looks the older woman full in the face. "I'm sorry about your daughter."

"And I'm sorry about your mother."

A woman walking a dog crosses in front of them at the red light. Monet takes out the two Hershey's kisses from Mary Anne, and offers one to Alabama.

"Heavens, no!" she exclaims with a laugh. "Thank you kindly, but the Lord God knows I don't need it." Everyone is thrust back against their seats as the light turns and the driver accelerates hard.

Monet eats her first kiss, the chocolate mixing nicely with the mint taste left over from brushing her teeth. Outside the scenery is familiar at first, streets and stores she knows, soon followed by streets and stores that she doesn't know but aren't so different. When the van gets on the highway going west she knows it's new. D.C. is to the east and every time she's been on this highway she's gone that way. As they accelerate down the ramp she looks out to a truly different horizon.

Alabama is looking out the same windshield. She asks, "Have you been here before?"

"Fluvanna? No."

They've merged and they're up to speed before Alabama finishes. "Have you visited your mother since she's been in prison?"

Monet is almost too embarrassed to answer. Her mother went away when she was in second grade and now she's in seventh. But she realizes that she doesn't need to explain all that to Alabama. "No," she says.

"Are you nervous?"

Monet looks outside before looking back at Alabama. "A little."

"Don't be scared," Alabama says. "That's all I can say. Don't be scared."

Monet doesn't answer for miles. They pass some kind of shopping mall by the side of the road, with giant McDonald's golden arches dominating the skyline. A car ahead of them makes a late decision and cuts abruptly for the exit ramp. They pass under an overpass, then a pickup truck merges ahead of them on its way out from the mall. Finally Monet asks, "What's so scary?"

Alabama turns from the window and gives Monet full attention. "Everything about it is scary," she says. "The razor wire. The bars. The guard towers with guns."

"They have guns?" Monet realizes she's been thinking about her mother, not the place she's held, the place they're going to now. Her daydreams were hugs and kisses, not razor wire and guns.

"And they follow you while you move," Alabama continues. "Everybody's giving orders. Nobody's having fun." She leans away from Monet and examines her critically. "You're so cute you'll probably get extra attention in the pat-down frisk, if you know what I mean."

A group of birds on the shoulder of the highway takes flight as they approach. A dead animal, maybe a raccoon, comes into view as they pass.

"Finally you get inside and you see your mother. That's even scarier."

"Or your daughter."

"The first time I saw my baby girl she was in belly chains. That's what they call the shackles that tie your hands together at the wrist, and tie your wrists together to your waist. She had ankle shackles too. So she comes hobbling out, can barely walk with all the chains, clattering like a garbage truck, trussed up so she can barely look at me. And she's on the other side of bars! In a low-security facility! I mean, what were they doing with all that security? Bars were bad enough, bars between me and my baby girl. But the chains?

"I wasn't brave," she says, sounding like she's never forgiven herself. "I started to cry as soon as I saw her. That was my baby in those chains! That was my baby girl behind those bars." Alabama catches herself and stops, takes a breath and changes her tone as if she's teasing herself. "*She's* the baby but *I'm* the one who's crying? *She's* in prison but *I'm* bawling my eyes out? Imagine that! I made *her* work to comfort *me*! 'It's okay, Mom. I'm fine. I'm used to it. Etcetera, etcetera.' I never should have done that to her."

"I'm sorry," says Monet

"Be brave, baby girl. We're all going to visit people we love. Every one of them is being treated like a criminal. Be brave in there."

"Thank you," Monet says quietly. "I'll try."

They both sit quietly for many miles, the low hum of the highway like a murmuring child. There's hardly any traffic, early on a Saturday morning and far beyond the D.C. suburbs. Outside are fields and trees, and only the occasional street sign or billboard; even the exits show hardly more than a gas station and a fast food restaurant or two. The sky is blue with a few big billowy clouds and a large bird circling on a breeze. The moon is still in view, mostly full and near the horizon. The chattering has stopped and everyone is silent; people sit quietly in their own thoughts.

After a while Monet grows uncomfortable. Her knees are squeezed, her back is cramped and Alabama is, after all, very large. It's hard enough to sit still in class. This is more boring and less comfortable. She checks her watch; they're less than halfway there.

Suddenly, a woman near the back starts to sing; out of the silence comes a tune Monet has known her whole life.

This land is your land
This land is my land
From California
To the New York Islands

At first she's alone but others soon join.

From the redwood forest
To the Gulf Stream waters
This land was made for you and me.

Alabama joins at the next verse and a heartbeat later, Monet does too. She couldn't have told you the lyrics in advance, but with everyone singing she remembers as she goes. Soon the whole van is singing together.

As I was walking a ribbon of highway
I saw above me an endless skyway
I saw below me a golden valley
This land was made for you and me.

The chorus is even more amazing. While some people continue to sing, others hum a background harmony, entering on the beats and adding resonance to the tune, as if they've been practicing together for months, performing complex melodies in concert. *This land was made for you and me.*

On and on it goes. The miles pass on the highway while they sing one song after another: "Go Tell It on the Mountain," "Down by the Riverside," "My Country 'Tis of Thee." As each song ends, somebody starts another, adding harmonies, sharing the experience, a bus full of people traveling to visit their loved ones in prison, singing "sweet land of liberty" as they go. They bounce to "He's Got the Whole World in His Hands" and "When the Saints Go Marching In," laugh but join in when somebody starts the theme song to "Barney," and slow down for the most miraculous "Amazing Grace" Monet has ever heard.

At some point they exit the interstate and turn onto a country highway, far more rural and with the occasional stoplight. They pass cows and red barns with domed silos that Monet has only seen in picture books. Everyone stops to hold their breath as the driver passes a truck full of sheep on a road that's not quite wide enough, and when they start again, it's Christmas carols: "Rudolph the Red-Nosed Reindeer," "Frosty the Snowman," and more. "The Twelve Days of Christmas" ends with drummers drumming and an intersection with a road sign: Fluvanna, six miles. There's a scattering of applause, then silence, a collective rest as everybody gathers strength in their own private way. Monet grabs Alabama's hand beside her and holds it tight.

Be brave, Monet thinks to herself. *Belly chains.*

At first the van is silent, but a few miles later comes another voice. Alone in the back of the van, a man's voice, deep and dark and haunting. The man in the brown suit with the burgundy tie sings by himself.

Nkosi sikeleli Afrika
Maluphakamis'upondo lwayo

Alabama leans against Monet and whispers into her ear, "The African National Anthem." The man keeps singing.

Yizwa imithandazo yethu
Nkosi sikelela, thina lusapholwayo.

The van is silent but for his voice, strong and soft, with everyone leaning in to hear him better. They've slowed down and the pavement is smooth, as if even the highway wants to listen. His song is bold but gentle, joyful but mourning, like the sun rising and setting at the same time. In the end, everybody joins for the chorus, sharing words that only Monet has never heard.

Se tjaba sa heso
Se tjaba sa Africa

The prison is now in sight, alone in a clearing, trees cut all around for an unobstructed view. Monet sees the guard towers. The razor wire. Everything Alabama warned her about. They pull into a small parking lot with a few regular cars, a police car, and some kind of armored truck.

But Monet doesn't see any guns, just the blue sky of morning. Birds fly overhead and Alabama is still holding her hand. The song ends as they enter the gate, and everybody breaks out in applause. Alabama gives Monet a giant hug as the van coasts to a stop in a parking space near the door.

"Be strong, baby girl. I love you."

"I'll be brave. Send my love to your daughter."

Chapter Twenty

It happens so fast. Years of waiting. Hours of driving. All of a sudden there she is. Right in front of her. Her mother.

Security isn't as bad as Monet had feared. She passes easily through the metal detectors and a nonchalant pat-down frisk from an officer who couldn't seem to care less; she has no personal belongings to examine since CURE advised them to leave their handbags and even their heavy coats in the van. Moving into the compound, she sees women walking around in orange prison jumpsuits, the VDOC logo on the front and "Virginia Department of Corrections" stamped across the back. They look surprisingly ordinary in their work, small groups of young women washing windows and scrubbing floors, the same jobs Libby does at home, though she wears a blue jumpsuit for the hospital, not orange for VDOC.

The visiting area has no bars. It's a row of stalls in front of Plexiglas windows, like tellers' windows at the bank where Libby goes to get her checks cashed. Each stall has a stool fixed to the floor on the visitor's side and a matching stool on the prisoner's side. Like at the bank, there's a ledge at the bottom of the window and a slot for passing papers to be signed or read, and a small screened hole in the center of glass so visitors and inmates can talk to each other through the hole or, if they prefer, through telephone handsets hung up by the stools on each side of the Plexiglas.

Monet is assigned to stall number six, last in this bank of visiting stalls. Two other CURE visitors, neither of them Alabama, have been assigned to this visiting area. The two women insisted that Monet go first so the stalls are empty as her security escort brings her down the row. Monet sees no visitors other than those from the CURE van, which has clearly been scheduled and coordinated in advance. Each visitor will get fifty minutes.

Sheila is on her stool when Monet arrives, sitting patiently on her side of the window, not knowing exactly when her daughter will appear.

Then all of a sudden both of them are on their feet, hugging and kissing at the glass.

Sheila is wearing an orange jumpsuit, of course. Monet isn't frightened, warned as she was by Alabama and accustomed as she became by the women she saw on her way in. Sheila isn't shackled and her hands are free. Monet looks straight past the jumpsuit and sees only her mother, smiling with her entire body and crying tears of joy, not horror as Alabama had warned.

She looks just the way Monet remembers her and exactly as she does in the photograph she left behind. The couple of years hasn't changed her age or her image much at all.

Sheila doesn't seem to feel the same way. "You're so big!" she exclaims. "Turn and spin so I can get a good look at you. Oh my God. You're so big."

She's on the far side of the glass, but Monet has no trouble hearing her, her voice dampened some but plenty loud. "Oh my God!" Sheila says again. "You're so big."

Next they're both on the stools, reaching their fingers under the glass through the tiny slot meant for lawyers to pass papers and pens. When their hands connect the tears start to flow anew. It's like a zillion volts of electricity passing through their fingers under the glass. Mother and daughter, holding hands.

They just sit there holding hands, not uttering a word for what seems like hours, crying together. Together at last.

Finally, Monet breaks the silence. She wants to talk, but she has nothing to say. "So what's new?" she whispers through the little screen hole in the window.

Her mother cracks up laughing. *What's new?*

Monet would be embarrassed if she weren't laughing just as hard. Surely a dumber question has never been asked.

They do settle down at last and find a way to actually visit. They talk on the phone and send each other letters, so they know plenty but still have plenty to say. Face to face and holding hands makes it different. Even the silly small talk really seems new.

"I'm growing a garden," Sheila says.

"A garden?" That's a surprise.

"For real. A garden. Not a fancy garden like Libby would probably make—with tomatoes and zucchini and watermelons as big as a house—but a little thing in a corner where there is no concrete. It's pretty little weed flowers and you'd love them. Dandelions and buttercups. Something purple, like a violet.

"I found a moss growing in a crack in a section of sidewalk by the far wall that makes a tiny pink flower. It was easy to dig out from the sidewalk but devilish hard to grow. I managed it, though. You'd love the tiny little pink flower it makes."

"I'll look for them in sidewalks at home."

"Great idea! We can garden together. I asked the people who tend the lawn not to cut it down, and I snuck out with water in the summer. So far so good, but now it's winter and everything is dying. I hope everything comes back next year. Especially the moss."

"I'll tell Libby about it. She'll be so proud of you."

Sheila beams like it's a birthday party. "And you'd be proud of your daddy. He's turning into a real lawyer. The best jailhouse lawyer around, some say. Just yesterday he got some man's leg back."

"Got his leg back?"

"Not yesterday. I just got the letter yesterday. Maybe it happened three weeks ago. Institutional mail is slow to leave his facility, and slow getting into this one. Everything takes a long time. You know how it is."

"About that leg . . . "

"Right. This guy has some kind of disability. His leg is messed up so he can't even walk. The prison medical staff gave him a brace so now he can walk around."

"Sounds good."

"But the brace isn't on the approved property list so the security staff took it away."

"Oh no!"

"That's where your daddy came in. He wrote some letters, documented responses, threatened a lawsuit . . . and now the man got his leg back!"

"You mean his brace. That's so cool. Go, Daddy, go!"

"He helped another man with his canteen account. His mom sent ten dollars every month so he could buy soap and toothpaste, stuff like that. Dental floss. She could prove that she sent the money but it never showed up in his canteen."

"Daddy found it?"

"He fixed it so now it gets there. We may never know what happened to the money that came in before. Or who got it."

"Do you have soap? Do you need money?"

"I have a good job. I'm paid fourteen cents an hour to scrub. You know I'm good at it, and it's enough to buy my own soap. The prison soap makes your skin fall off, so I fork over two dollars for Dial, just like I did at home. I also buy stamps to mail back and forth with you and Zeb.

"I'm near the top of the line for another job. If all goes well, next year I'll have an outdoor job that pays twenty-two cents an hour or a kitchen job that pays twenty-six. Maybe I'll be in charge of the grass near my garden."

A door on her mom's side of the pen opens and a new prisoner walks in with an escort on either side. They bring her to a stool a few windows down and Monet can see that they're telling her to sit.

The door on Monet's side opens too, and an escort shows the two other women from the CURE van to their stools. Monet can see and hear the exclamations between the inmate and visitor closest to her. The visitor in the farthest stall sits by herself to wait.

Monet can't let the lawyer get away. "How's Dad's own case going, Mom? How is your appeal?"

"You know the story. Our challenges to the plea were rejected. That took almost three years. You know, the finality of judgment is worth more than actual innocence and all that."

"That's what the judges say."

"But the judges are in charge. Our lawyer told us one thing, the judge at sentencing said something else. We said yes without thinking fast enough and it's done. The judges won. The judges are still winning."

"You sound like you're giving up."

"I'm making peace with it. I'm tending my garden and counting my blessings, such as they are. You're one of them. You have no idea how much those phone calls mean to me."

"Don't change the subject, Mom. I'm not giving up and neither is Dad."

"He's going after our lawyer. Since Zeb started studying, he learned just how much that man did us wrong. Did you know the same lawyer isn't supposed to handle two codefendants in the same case? He's not even supposed to handle both husband and wife without special permission. He was wrong before we even started."

"We thought we were getting a deal."

"Pretty good deal, eh? Anyhow, Zeb launched another appeal based on ineffective assistance of counsel. That one's sitting in the courts right about now."

"How long will it take?"

"I try not to think about it. Tomorrow I hope. Or maybe the day after. Hopefully you won't be one millimeter taller when our appeal comes through. But I'm not holding my breath, either. I'm counting my blessings and growing my garden, baby girl."

Baby girl. Her mom is the second person today to call her baby girl, something she doesn't think she's ever been called before. But with Alabama's term comes Alabama's memory. She's not here to feed her mom's frustration and complain about the courts. She's here to help.

"Okay, Mom. Count your blessings. Count me in. What do you need me to do?"

"That's my baby girl. Now here's the secret underside of the appeal. Here's where you really fit in."

Now at last the final inmate enters the chamber. She's brought in from the door behind Sheila and escorted to her visitor at the farthest stool. Returning to the entry door, the security escort taps each inmate on the shoulder and points to the security cameras in the ceiling. Monet can understand the message from her side of the glass: you are not alone. Last before leaving, the officer taps Sheila on her shoulder and points to the clock on the wall with another message: time's running out.

Sheila continues without interruption. "The lawsuit gives me access to the library. Recreational use is highly restricted but legal use is privileged. A pending case allows me to use the library—even though Zeb does most of the work."

"Do you have Internet?"

"Highly restricted, but yes. That's your part."

"Me?"

"Yes, you. I've been Googling about you. The security restrictions don't stop me from looking at colleges. College is every prisoner's daydream, and I've been dreaming about you.

"You're in seventh grade right now and your grades are fine. The next few years are the ones that matter. Pump yourself up to straight A's and go to college."

"Then law school?"

Sheila smiles as their dreams overlap. "One step at a time. Right now, Zeb's all the lawyer we need. Your job is to get the grades and go to college. No night job for money. No sending me nickels for soap. No weekend road trips when your friends start to drive. Just college. Will you do that for me, baby girl? Will you study hard and get yourself into college?"

The door beside Sheila opens up and the officer takes the short step toward her mother. Monet would stay forever holding hands, but the moment comes quickly to conclusion as the officer pulls her mother toward the door.

"Piece of cake. Just you watch."

Chapter Twenty-one

Angel is so happy about Monet's trip to Fluvanna, he holds a giant sale on candy. The next day at school he brings his entire stock of candy with him, and sells it all at cost.

His earliest customers get the biggest selection and the biggest haul, but word travels fast. "Hey guys!" yells Parker Carlson. "Candyman is having a sale!"

The sale creates so much excitement and buzz around the school that kids Angel doesn't know and has never sold to start pulling him over between class to buy a Kit Kat or a Twix bar or a single stick of Wrigley's Spearmint gum.

As always, Angel only sells candy that comes individually wrapped. Wrigley's Spearmint gum, not Chiclets.

He's such a hit that even U8 moves to second place. "Fill out your U8 form later," Parker orders Mitchie Daniels. "You won't make the team anyway."

Angel has noticed lots of kids passing around and filling out forms that say U8 at the top and have lots of empty lines and spaces underneath. Some kids have color leaflets that say U8 with pictures inside.

When Mitchie comes over to buy candy, Angel asks him what U8 is all about. "Did you finish the form?" Angel wants to make sure. "If you need more time I can hold something for you."

"I'm done enough," Mitchie replies, patting his pocket. "The U8 form is for travel soccer. It's a special team. The best kids from our school play the best kids from other schools. I'm gonna make the team!"

"Why's it called U8?"

"Oh, that just means 'under eight.' Everyone on the team has to be less than eight years old. We're all U8. Next year is U9."

"The form just asks your age?"

"The form asks all kinds of things. I only filled in my name. My mom has to fill out the rest and show them my birth certificate."

"Birth certificate?"

"To prove your age. So a ten-year-old doesn't play U8 and look better than he really is. How much are the Twix bars?"

Angel has just enough time to sell Mitchie a Twix bar before he has to dash into his first class, and two students are waiting for him as he walks out. By lunchtime he's almost out of candy. Twix and Starbursts went fastest, as usual, though at these prices gum tended to go in entire packs rather than individual sticks.

On their way out to recess, Tammy Atford is making some kind of arrangement with Joanna Baye. "Do you have the chalk?" Joanna asks.

Tammy replies by holding up a little red bucket. At exactly that moment two fourth grade boys come whizzing around the corner and knock the bucket out of her hand. "Hey!" Tammy yells.

The boys keep running. If they know what they did, they don't look back.

Tammy bends over to pick up chalk now scattered around the corridor. Tammy looks up toward Joanna as if for help, but Joanna is walking the other direction.

Angel steps toward Tammy. "I can give you a hand," he says. "Tamantha."

"Thanks," she says, inadvertently shooting a dirty look in Joanna's direction. "Why the big sale?"

Angel isn't sure what to say. A real answer would take too long and be too complicated. "I had a good weekend," is all he says.

A boy comes by and stands over the Candyman. "Do you have any more Starbursts?" he asks.

"Later," says Angel. "I'm in the middle of something." He scoops up some chalk and dumps it into Tammy's bucket. "It'll go faster if you help us."

The boy walks on.

Tammy picks up the last few pieces of chalk and peers carefully under ledges for any strays. "Thanks again," she says as she stands up with her bucket.

Angel too rises to his feet. "One more thing," he says, fishing through his diminishing candy supply until he finds a Starburst. "For you."

On the bus ride home, Angel's backpack is empty but his pockets are full. He hasn't technically made any money—selling everything at cost—but it sure feels like a lot in his hand. He decides to take a few days off. He'll restock again at the regular weekend shopping with his mom, and after his newly gorged customers are hungry again. Maybe some of those new customers will come back, too.

Angel sits by himself on the bus. Parker Carlson and Veronica West take a different bus, and Tammy Atford rides every day with Joanna Baye. Angel knows plenty of kids on his bus and many of them buy his candy, sometimes on the bus. But nobody wants to sit with the Candyman.

At home Angel doesn't even mention the sale. Monet has stayed after school to use the library and his mom won't be back until dinner time. By then the money has all been counted and recounted and stacked neatly in a safe place. Angel is making his plans for his next shopping trip and Monet's next phone call to Fluvanna. He has no idea how much college costs, but he wonders if he can sell enough candy to send Monet.

He boils a pot of rice on one burner and a pot of lentils on the other. He doesn't have an exact plan for dinner but he starts the things that take time; his mom will make combinations and add flavorings when she gets home, and turn this hour of boiling into a nice dinner in no time at all.

After dinner it's all about U8. "Can I join the team, Mom?" he asks. "Can I try out?"

He brought the color flyer home, but Monet has it in her hands. "Soccer?" she asks suspiciously. "You've never played soccer in your life. Why now?"

Angel hadn't really thought about that, and Monet can tell. "You won't even make the team," she says.

Libby meanwhile has been reading the application form. "Look at all these expenses," she says. "Fees. Equipment. Shin guards, uniforms, travel costs. We don't even have a car. Are you sure you want to do this?"

"I just want to apply."

"You want to apply or you want to play?" Libby seems confused.

"Do we have to buy all those things—shin guards and all that—if I don't play?"

"The application requires only the application fee. No shin guards. Yet."

Now Monet swoops in from the outside. "Why do you want to apply if you don't want to play?"

"For my birth certificate!"

Monet sees the trouble coming and stands up. "Homework," she says. "I have a lot to do before college." She busses her dishes, gathers her books, and heads to the little bedroom.

"I love you, sweetie," says Libby to Monet as she leaves the room. Then she turns her attention only to Angel. "What's on your mind?"

"I want to see my birth certificate. You need it to apply. To prove how old you are."

"All this for a birth certificate? Why don't you just ask for it?"

Angel cocks his head like he's been outfoxed, but then he accepts the question on its own terms. "Okay. Can is see my birth certificate? Forget travel soccer. I won't apply if I can see my birth certificate."

"That's the trouble. I don't have it. You don't have one."

"I don't have a birth certificate?"

"You were born. Do you doubt it? Do you need proof?" She launches for his tummy and tickles him until she finally gets a giggle. "There. You were born. I proved it. People who weren't born can't be tickled."

Angel tickles her back, and for a minute they laugh and wrestle instead of cleaning dishes, but Angel still isn't satisfied. "I don't just want a birth certificate. I want family too. Danny Franco is going to Peru at Christmas. He's going to visit his whole family. Grandma, grandpa, aunts and uncles and cousins. He talks about them all day long. Can I do that too?"

"Go to Peru to visit Danny Franco's aunts and uncles and cousins?"

"No, Mom. I'm serious. I want to visit my family."

"You are. You're visiting me. And Monet."

"But that's all! Don't I have any cousins?"

"Nope. No cousins." She says it lightly as if to make it a joke, but Angel doesn't take it that way.

"Do I have any aunts or uncles?"

"No. Your aunts and uncles would be my brothers and sisters. I don't have either. I'm an only child."

"Don't I have grandparents? Your parent's parents?"

"No."

"You don't have parents?"

"Not anymore."

"It's not fair! Everybody has everything. Monet has a dad, even if he's in prison. Mitchie Daniels has a dad even though his parents are divorced. I don't even have a dad."

Libby starts to tell him again the story of the car accident, how she too is sorry that everybody died.

This time Angel doesn't accept it so easily. "It doesn't even matter if they're dead. Paulie Soltz's dad is dead. He died in Iraq. Everyone knows it, and Paulie's whole family goes to visit his grave.

"Where is our family buried, Mom? Can we go to visit my dad? Don't you want to visit your mom?"

Libby seems at a loss for words. She's told him about the car accident before. He knows she is an only child and that her parents are dead, but the graves seem to have struck a nerve. He repeats himself relentlessly. "Don't you want to visit your mom? Even if she's dead? Don't you want to visit her?"

She seems so much to want to say yes. If she were a classmate, Angel would think she's about to cry. She seems to be hiding something, and she seems about to change her mind. But then Angel says something disastrously wrong: "Don't you want to visit your dad?"

Libby's sadness changes to anger and suddenly she's on her feet. "No!" she yells. "I do not want to visit my dad." She starts bussing dishes and slamming things around the sink, packaging leftovers and slamming the refrigerator door so Angel hears the bottles clanking around inside. Instead of stacking dishes and making few trips to the sink, Libby moves each dish one at a time so it takes forever.

Ordinarily Angel would help, but tonight he just moves to the wall and stays out of her way.

With everything bussed and with her hands in the sink, finally his mother speaks again. "By now it's just us. It has to be us." She says it like she's convincing herself, taking a side in someone's argument. "We're the family. You and me and the lovely girl in the next room who's going to college. I have no parents. You have no grandparents."

Libby finishes the dishes and turns off the water. "And you have no birth certificate. You aren't going to apply for U8 either."

Part Three

Love and Loss

Chapter Twenty-two

By sixth grade everything is different. Angel is starting middle school and Monet is finishing high school. Classes are bigger and homework is harder. But the biggest change is Molly Swann.

Kids still call Angel the Candyman, though his candy has mostly run its course. First and second grades were the boom years. Angel outgrew the 7-Eleven and started shopping at the Safeway with his mom on the weekends, where he could buy more candy for less money. Angel knew what every kid liked best and he made sure to have it when they wanted it. He had special deal spots arranged with kids in different locations all day long—though if he saw their wrappers floating around he threatened to cut them off.

As the kids grew bigger, so did Angel's sales. Kids got bigger allowances, and bigger cash presents on their birthdays. They moved up from one square of chocolate to whole bars, from one stick of gum to two.

But by fourth grade sales started to wane. Kids had more freedom at home and greater ability to manage their own lunch boxes. They didn't crave candy at every opportunity, and their tastes advanced from Hershey's to Slurpees, which Angel couldn't supply. Parker Carlson and Walter Roscoe even learned how to save up their allowance to buy iTunes.

Angel still keeps a few treats handy in case someone asks, but for most purposes he has simply disappeared. Even during the boom years, nobody talked to him except for business; certainly they never invited him to play their games or come over after school. He was the Candyman, nothing more; if they didn't need his candy, they didn't need him.

Everything changes with Molly Swann. "A new student will start tomorrow," says Angel's homeroom teacher, Dr. Barry Eisman.

Up front, beside Dr. Eisman, stands a wonderful new girl, well dressed like the rich kids but somehow less snobby looking. Her long dark hair falls straight over her green polo shirt, tucked neatly into her blue jeans. Her jeans look new but her sneakers well worn; around her neck is a silver heart-shaped charm. She looks comfortable even in front of a whole class of strangers. "Everybody welcome her."

A few kids clap and someone says "Welcome," but most kids pay no attention. Homeroom is time to take attendance, mumble the pledge of allegiance and make the occasional announcement—and a new student announcement is barely worth listening to. Most kids turn pages in their notebooks, snatch glances in their magazines, and ignore Dr. Eisman.

Except for Angel. Angel can barely take his eyes off her long dark hair and heart-shaped charm. Is he the only person who notices the strand of hair loose against her forehead? Does nobody else notice that she's left-handed when she reaches up to capture the strand?

Angel spends the morning and the rest of the day thinking about the new girl who appeared and disappeared with only that brief introduction, the girl who looked smart and pretty and nice at the same time. He meanders through the day, half-listening to teachers and halfheartedly going through the motions of one class after another.

What happens the next day is utterly foreseeable, or at least it should have been foreseeable. As soon as it happens, Angel knows he should have seen it coming, because seats in homeroom are arranged alphabetically.

Dr. Eisman walks in with Molly at his side, looking radiant in a pink button-down shirt and white slacks. "You'll sit here," he says to Molly Swann, pulling out the chair next to Angel Thompson. "Molly, this is Angel. Angel, Molly. Take good care of her." And he walks away.

It's like birthday, Christmas, and New Years all at the same time. Angel won the lottery and flew to the moon. He's speechless at first but he knows he needs to get this right. The ball's in his court. Dr. Eisman hit it to him, nice and slow. Molly is wearing little blue earrings, tiny crystals that sparkle in the light. Her hair is in a ponytail, held together by a red rubber band, which flops over her shoulder as she takes her seat.

The ball's in Angel's court but Molly goes first. "Good morning," she says.

Angel thinks hard and gathers his wits. He so rarely talks to children at school. Candy sales, sure, and schoolwork as assigned, but Angel never says good morning or chats in the hallways with kids who always have someone else to talk to. He pulls himself together. "Good morning," he says, but he doesn't stop with the minimum. "Welcome to the neighborhood."

"Thanks," she replies, looking maybe actually a little sheepish, then: "I forgot. Is his name Dr. Eisman?"

"Barry Eisman," says Angel, taking good care of her. "He likes people to call him 'doctor,' not 'mister.'"

"Dr. Eisman. Thanks. Is your name really Angel?"

"That's me! Angel. You can call me Angel," he adds with a smile.

"Not doctor?" She smiles back.

"Are you sick?"

And so it goes. They actually chat, making small talk during homeroom, like so many other kids do but Angel never has before. What seem like seconds later, homeroom is ending and they're grabbing their bags.

Molly stands up, then sits back down as if she's forgotten something.

Angel sits with her.

Molly fumbles around her backpack until she finds a schedule. "I need to figure out where I go next. I'm so silly. I forgot."

Angel ignores the comment and examines her schedule over her shoulder.

Their next class is together, advanced math with Ms. Fitzsimmons in room 224. "We're in math together," he says. "I'll show you the way."

They study her schedule as they walk together down the hall. Homeroom and math are the only classes they have together, but he makes sure to show her where her other classes are as they traverse the corridors. "Social studies will be hardest," he explains. Molly will need to move all the way from history in room 116 to social studies in room 388 in the allotted four minutes.

"No water between history and social studies," she says with full understanding.

"And no talking!" he pretends like a teacher offering a scold.

They're still talking as they sit down in math class. Seats here are unassigned, but they sit together by themselves as if it's entirely natural in a room with lots of empty seats. Only twelve kids are in the advanced math class, studying eighth grade algebra in sixth grade. Tammy Atford is talking with Emily Hudson at a table by the far wall, and Mitch Daniels, the only other boy in the class, sits by himself in the back.

Molly and Angel keep chattering until Ms. Fitzsimmons calls the class to order. Indeed, for the first time ever Angel is among the last ones talking when the teacher gets sharp and tells everyone to pay attention and quiet down. Immediately Molly pulls out a piece of paper with the facility of long practice and starts to write. A moment later, when Ms. Fitzsimmons turns to write on the blackboard, she slides the paper smoothly in Angel's direction.

A note! How many times has Angel seen kids in class passing notes, and how many times has he heard the teacher command them to pay attention. But never before has he received a note of his own. Never before has he surreptitiously pulled the paper the rest of the way into his workspace and waited for the teacher to look away to unfold it silently and press it into his lap to read.

It's called Advanced Math, the note says. *Is it hard?*

Angel takes a long time to reply. He considers options silently in his head and awaits the opportunity, still paying attention to the lesson and noticing that Molly does too.

No, he writes back when the time seems ripe. *If it is, I can help.* He signs the paper, *Angel.*

Molly folds the note and tucks it neatly into her binder. For the rest of the class, they pay attention only to Ms. Fitzsimmons.

But his heart is pounding.

Chapter Twenty-three

Thus begins their correspondence. Molly turns into a star, scoring goals on the soccer team and making friends in every direction. She's pretty enough to hang out with the rich kids, smart enough to talk with the smart kids, and strong enough to run with the athletes—even the boys—but she never turns on her first friend.

Every day they write their notes. They write notes about the weather, notes about homework, and notes about Veronica West's extravagant hat. Even in homeroom when they are sitting next to each other, they pass notes instead of talking. Angel learns through these notes that Molly comes from New York City, that her father's a lawyer, and that the family moved for his new job at AOL. Molly's mother is training for the Marine Corps Marathon in October.

Mom always wanted to run a marathon, Molly writes. *New York is hard to get into but Marine Corps is easier.*

Aren't all marathons hard? Angel writes back, the crucial words underlined and bold.

Easier to get into, Molly reiterates.

At first Angel keeps every single note, as if each is uniquely precious, but soon enough he throws them away when they're finished. "Is it raining outside?" . . . "It was this morning"—are not epistles for the ages, and not worth the stacking, sorting, and storage problem they were starting to become. He learns to take the notes for granted, not as irreplaceable heirlooms, but as part of a relationship he can count on.

Just as Angel used to meet kids in special locations to sell them candy, now he meets Molly to trade their latest. They meet in homeroom, math, gym, and the cafeteria line at lunch. Even that quick sprint from history to social studies isn't safe from Angel's hurried detour for a swap.

Some things are the same in middle school, but most things are at least a little bit different. Parker Carlson still wears Redskins jerseys, though a string of losing seasons have dampened even his enthusiasm. Wally Roscoe's father works for the State Department, so he and his family have moved to Brussels for three years.

Veronica West still rules the roost, making it clear which friends are cool and which ones aren't worth anybody's time or attention. Tammy Atford spends less time with Joanna Baye, who Angel learned is her next-door neighbor, and more time with Emily Hudson, who lives a bike ride away. Joanna herself seems to grow crankier and crankier until she, too, sits by herself at lunchtime—though Angel has seen both Tammy and Molly try to join her.

What's wrong with Joanna Baye? Molly writes one day. *Is she always so mean?*

Yes, Angel replies.

Really?

To me, anyway. Ask Tammy.

Angel hopes to sit next to Molly on their field trip to the Smithsonian Museum of Natural History. He imagines cozying up with her on the bus ride, then naturally working together as a team on the worksheet they've been given to fill out in the museum. But it doesn't work out that way. Kids are assigned buses by science class, not homerooms, and Angel ends up on an entirely different bus than Molly, sitting beside Alan Carrie, who spends the whole time talking to Nick Adams in the row ahead of them and shouting to Danny Franco two rows behind. Everyone is wearing their yellow Sidney Lanier Middle School T-shirts so they look like a group and they're easier to keep together.

Angel gets his yellow Sidney Lanier T-shirt from the lost-and-found. He doesn't want to buy one and doesn't have a hand-me-down, but he notices one in the lost-and-found closet. Since the closet is emptied and donated to Goodwill on the last Friday of every month, Angel waits until the morning of the last Friday and helps himself. He figures that nobody around school is missing it, and if he replaces it before the last Friday of next month, even Goodwill will be no worse off.

"You look like a banana in your T-shirt," Alan yells back to Danny, who remains slender but has sprung up in height.

"You look like a school bus," replies Danny to Alan, who eats plenty, rarely exercises, and looks like it.

Alan does take up more than his fair share of the seat. He treats Angel as nothing but an obstacle to avoid as he swings his head back and forth between his friends. "Excuse me," is all he says to Angel the entire ride, though he says it plenty of times.

Angel doesn't care how much of the seat Alan Carrie takes up, or how often he bumps him. Angel is thrilled to be on the ride, thrilled to travel someplace new, and thrilled to see the world-famous Smithsonian. The bus accelerates up the highway ramp—Interstate 66 East to Washington, says the sign—and Angel is certain he's never gone so fast. The bus is roaring and Alan is shouting as they race past cars and trucks and birds overhead. One car drives with its windows open while a dog holds its head outside, eyes squeezed shut, fur blown flat.

"Close the window!" Alan yells to Nick ahead of him.

"I like it!" Nick replies, and so does Angel.

Soon enough they reach Washington, D.C. They cross a bridge over a giant river and—*is that the Washington Monument?*—yes it is, the iconic image towering against the sky. The bus turns into a broad open street and drives uncaringly past the Lincoln memorial, with only Angel staring out the window. As the teacher announces they're nearly there, he sees the dome of the U.S. Capitol, familiar from legend and lore, hardly any farther away than his bus stop at home.

The Museum of Natural History has a dome of its own, and a triangular portico atop great marble pillars. "Leave your luggage on the bus," says Ms. Traldi as they arrive. Ms. Traldi is the science teacher and in her yellow T-shirt with long blonde hair, she really does look like a banana. "Pocketbooks are okay but anything more slows us down at security. And make sure you have your worksheets to fill out as you go. All the answers are in the museum—but you'll have to find them."

The stairway is broad but shallow, and a line of yellow T-shirts accumulates at the door as Sidney Lanier students pass one by one through the metal detectors. Angel notices that there are no tickets and no ticket booths; a kiosk sells visitor guides for two dollars, but the museum itself seems to be free, not just for students on a field trip, but for everybody. Angel and his mother had sometimes talked about traveling downtown to visit the world-famous Smithsonian but they never quite pulled it off. They never knew the price, but it being free makes it seem suddenly easier. They can visit the world-famous Smithsonian for the cost of a bus ride, and surely they can figure out which bus to use. Angel resolves to bring his mom on a Smithsonian field trip as soon as he can.

He passes through the metal detectors and up a few more steps, and suddenly Angel is in a whole new world. The atrium is vast, its arched dome as tall as the sky, light streaming in from windows on every side. In the center stands a giant African elephant, trunk raised, tusks stronger than any roof beam, ears fanned out like a gale. It's not alive, of course—the zoo field trip is scheduled for the spring—but it looks real in every way. Angel walks laps around the elephant, sees the mud caked under its feet and the gleam in its eye as it bellows to its friends and warns off predators. Birds in the grass study the elephant with awe of their own. Voices echoing in the cavernous atrium create a background throb of energy.

Up above, suspended from balcony tiers reaching toward the sky, hang giant butterflies painted black and gold. At the elephant's feet are explanatory signs about the display. Angel learns that an African bull elephant weighs twelve tons, and that African dung beetles scoop up the elephant manure and roll it into balls to store for food. A video shows dung beetles crawling around, gathering dung; a single dung beetle can move fourteen pounds of elephant manure in a single day. *Who knew?*

He leaves the elephant and walks into the nearby exhibit on oceans. Alan Carrie and Danny Franco are looking into the skeletal jaws of a giant megalodon shark, open mouth taller than they are, teeth the size of their heads. From the ceiling hangs a model of a giant whale, a behemoth in black, its mouth wide open, its flukes spread like wings on a plane; beside it hangs the skeleton from some ancient whale forbearer.

Angel opens his workbook. The first question is about the oceans.

"Right Whale," writes Angel in response, the name of the leviathan swimming overhead.

"Plankton," he writes in response to the next question. The gigantic beast survives on microscopic plants it filters from the sea with "baleen"—as the workbook asks and the sign explains. It's exactly as Ms. Traldi had promised: the answers are all around, but they need to find them. Angel never could have guessed that a creature so large could survive on food so small.

Above the oceans exhibit, a sign beckons entry to Gems and Minerals. Veronica West is already inside, gaping at the Hope Diamond with a crowd of friends, taking up so much space Angel can barely nudge through to learn the weight of the Hope Diamond for his worksheet.

Beyond the diamond and far more interesting to Angel are the bizarre and baffling formations of minerals on display. A bumpy protuberant gray stone as tall as Angel looks like it's been melted from wax. Crystalline formations look like perfect pencils, six-sided with a point at the top, some in rose, some in turquoise and one long sword in stunning aquamarine. The meteorites in the next room are exactly the opposite—ugly lumps with pockmarked faces that travelled to Earth from outer space and opened giant craters when they hit. Angel wants to touch the black corner of the meteorite but the sign says "Hands Off" and he does as he's told.

On the way down the stairs he sees the importance of not touching. The stairs themselves, though made of stone, have been worn smooth by footsteps over time. Subtle ruts have been carved under Angel's feet from people going down, and on the other side from people going up. That meteorite might have traveled from outer space, but if everybody touched it they would grind a hole as surely as they did on the staircase. He resolves to tell his mom, who probably spends more time looking at stairs than anybody else in the world.

A little girl is screaming at the entrance to the mammals exhibit, and as Angel rounds the corner he sees why. The tiger leaping from the ledge over the door is breathtaking, jaws open, claws outstretched, poised to land on the screaming child. A few steps farther in, a lion leaps onto the back of a water buffalo, raking its claws across the side and sinking fangs into its neck. The models are so vivid Angel can almost hear the scrape of hooves, the sharp intake of breath.

Parker Carlson probably loves this exhibit, but the three-year-old girl is clinging to her mother. "It's okay," the mom says. "It won't hurt you. Look! A giraffe!"

The girl keeps screaming.

Angel pauses by the girl and kneels down to her height. Her hair is blonde and she wears a white turtleneck printed with yellow ducks. Her eyes are wet with tears, but they aren't swollen or red; she hasn't been crying very deeply or very long, just a quick fright from the surprising tiger. The newcomer's intrusion changes her attention, distracts her from the screams.

"Do you have a cat?" Angel asks when she seems to be looking at him.

She studies him a moment, cocks her head in consideration. "No," she says at last, then reconsiders and adds brightly, "My friend Tammy has a cat."

"I have a friend named Tammy," Angel replies.

"Does she have a cat?"

Now it's Angel's turn to pause in consideration. "I don't know," he says, surprising even himself by calling her a friend.

The girl is all confidence by now. "You'll have to find out."

Angel nods his agreement, then points to the side. "Want to see the giant walrus?"

Alongside is, indeed, a walrus bigger than Angel's sofa at home, and the mom takes over from there. With a smile and a mouthed out "Thank you" to Angel, she tugs her daughter toward the walrus. As he walks away, Angel hears the girl exclaim to her mother about the size of its whiskers. "He needs to shave!"

Angel slows down to look at the skeleton of a lion, impressed by the difference between its slender bones and the muscular power of the model on the hunt, then stops at a film loop playing in the back. Both Tammy and Molly, working on separate teams, walk out as Angel reaches the door.

"The answer is Morgy," Tammy says with a smile.

"But it's worth watching," Molly adds.

So Angel walks in for a charming five-minute movie about Morgy, a primordial and crucially warm-blooded rodent that survived when a meteor wiped out the dinosaurs, and the answer to a question on the worksheet. Not until he's walking out does Angel notice that one member of the audience is a chimpanzee, a life-sized statue sitting peacefully in an audience chair as if it belongs there. His friend the little girl is sitting in its lap, smiling like it's a dream come true.

It's afternoon by now and many kids are going to lunch. Yellow Sidney Lanier T-shirts fill the cafeteria, where kids are laughing and lounging as if trips to the museum happen all the time; indeed they made it clear before they left that they've been here many times before and have nothing more to learn. But Angel doesn't want to lose a minute. Who knew that dung beetles could be so interesting? He skips lunch to spend time in the reptile exhibit, studying the anatomy of the turtle, its spine built into its remarkable shell.

The dinosaurs are the crown jewel. Even Angel has seen pictures of dinosaurs, from the fuzzy Barney on TV to skeletons in books, but nothing has prepared him for this breathtaking reality. Tyrannosaurus Rex towers over the entrance hall, jaws agape, teeth like knives, a carnivorous machine taller than the swing set on the playground. The "tyrant lizard"—the worksheet asks for the translation—faces down a horned triceratops across the aisle, skeletal remains crushed at its feet.

Angel thinks back to the skeleton of the lion in the mammals exhibit. How frail and scrawny it now seems in comparison to the Tyrannosaurus Rex. What muscles could have powered a thighbone like that? Like the model of the lion taking down the water buffalo, Angel imagines a T. Rex in action, scooping up the buffalo in a single bite.

Even as he walks among the dinosaurs, the other students start to gather. They've all been instructed to meet at the T. Rex at two o'clock for a final discussion and the departure home. Finally, Ms. Traldi calls them to order and starts them talking while other teachers take attendance for the ride.

"Isn't it amazing," Ms. Traldi says. "The diversity of life. One planet . . . so many different life forms! How many people saw the mammals exhibit?"

Every hand rises, Angel's among them.

"How many saw the dung beetles? Weren't they cool?"

More than half of the kids raise their hands, including Angel. A voice in the back says, "Dung beetles? Yuck!"

"It's not yucky; it's life," Ms. Traldi retorts. "How many of you saw the sea anemones?"

Half the kids raise their hands again, excluding Angel, and he resolves that he needs to come again, bring his mother, and see the sea anemones.

"Look how different it all is! Look at this T. Rex and the change over the years. The scientists call it 'tyrant lizard.' I call it obsolete. Look how we've changed!"

Angel can't stand it. He's swept up in the excitement, in awe of the T. Rex towering above them all, still mystified by the dung beetles. He doesn't usually talk at all, surely not to disagree with the teacher. But today he can't hold himself back.

He raises his hand for attention.

It's the only hand in the air. He stands out, alone. "Yes, Angel?" says Ms. Traldi, almost surprised.

Angel points straight to the T. Rex skeleton. "It's hardly changed at all," he says. "It's practically the same."

"The same as what?"

"The same as us. You. Me. People!"

A voice from the back, a boy: "The same as your mother."

A bunch of kids laugh. Another boy adds, "He doesn't have a mother."

"I mean it," Angel continues. "It looks just like us. Look! Two arms, two legs. The skull on the top. Two eye sockets."

The voice from the back, "Small brain." Angel recognizes Parker Carlson.

Angel talks past the interruption. "Big or small, the brain is in the skull, just the same. Look at the back, with the long spine in the middle made up of all the little pieces. What are they called? Vertebrae! We have them too." Angel pauses for breath. He'd never spoken so long in class and he's certainly no expert. He looks to the skeleton for ideas.

Molly offers her own. "Angel's right," she says. "Look at that leg. The big strong thighbone connects to the hip at the top. The lower leg has two bones, the tibia and the fibula. I broke my fibula playing soccer. Right there." She actually points at the skeleton of the Tyrannosaurus to show where she broke her own leg.

Tammy Atford chimes in, too. "Look at the rib cage—same as ours. Want to bet that the heart is right smack in the middle of that rib cage, nice and safe? I bet it pumps blood out through the arteries and back through the veins. Just like us."

Now Joanna Baye joins the parade. "I'm with Tammy. We all have ribs. Beef ribs, pork ribs, T. Rex ribs . . . they're all the same. I bet the T. Rex kept his heart, lungs, and spleen safe in that rib cage."

Parker Carlson: "What's a spleen?"

"I don't know, but I bet it was in there."

She's barely finished before Angel cries out, "The jaw! Look at the jaw! It's built like ours, only bigger. Only the bottom part moves."

Now Ms. Traldi enters the conversation. "Thank you, Angel," she says. "You raise a really important point. It's called a 'hinged lower mandible' and all of our jaws operate the same way. We all have ribs, we all have spines, and some of us . . . " she looks toward the boys in the back "have a heart."

Everybody laughs.

But Ms. Traldi isn't finished. "Now, what's really important. First is the diversity of life. We're incredibly different, but incredibly the same. Second, and even more important: It's time to get on the bus."

"Aw, man . . . " The sounds of discontent are overwhelming. The same voices that didn't want to waste time at the museum now don't want to leave.

Ms. Traldi leads them through the logistics of dividing into groups and heading outside for the bus. As they break, Molly taps Angel on the shoulder and passes him a torn corner of notebook paper, folded many times into such a tight little packet Molly is long gone before he works it open.

Brilliant, it says.

Chapter Twenty-four

Brilliant.

Molly Swann called him brilliant.

Angel cradles the scrap of paper the whole ride home, oblivious to Alan Carrie's bumping conversation between his friend ahead and his friend behind, or the shouting of students showing off their souvenirs. Even Tyrannosaurus Rex evaporates behind the scrap of paper, the tyrant lizard extinguished by a single word.

Angel keeps the note in his pocket for days, folded up tight, unfolding it to read when nobody is watching. Eventually, fearing for its safety, he hides it in a secret cache at home, tucked in the back of his underwear drawer. *Brilliant.* Molly Swann called him brilliant. Even if someone else saw the paper, they wouldn't know who wrote it or the importance of the word.

It keeps getting better. Mitchie Daniels asks Angel for help with his science homework and Danny Franco asks him what he thinks about *The Phantom Tollbooth.* On Friday Molly passes him a note saying their family had chicken for dinner last night: *It was a whole chicken. The body with bones. I looked at the skeleton like I never had before, and I rotated the elbow joint (I mean wing!) with you in mind. Even my mom said you were smart.*

Dinner with Molly, dinner with Molly. Angel spends his weekend daydreaming of dinner with Molly. He imagines what it was like at her house, the family gathered around the table while Molly played with the chicken joint. How he'd love to have dinner with Molly. Could he just ask her out? Where to? He can't bring her someplace fancy, and he doesn't want to bring her to his house while he boils spaghetti at their leaky sink. Molly is used to whole chickens, and he can only imagine what kind of house she has.

He knows the other kids invite each other over to play air hockey and video games, and everyone knows Parker Carlson has a tennis court. Angel doesn't lack courage to ask Molly out, he tells himself . . . but where to?

The solution leaps out in history class. Mr. Balestrieri is droning on and on about ancient Greece. Not the cool stories of Zeus and Aphrodite, but the development of city-states and how they expanded outward in search of arable land. Athens had a democracy, Sparta had an oligarchy, and the Persian Empire loomed a few mountain ranges away.

"Now for the pizza," Mr. Balestrieri declares, and everyone sits up straight. He holds in the air a coupon that Angel can see from his seat says *Brick's Pizza* across the top.

Mr. Balestrieri continues, "Everybody needs to make a PowerPoint presentation. A PowerPoint about ancient Greece. About the wars, about democracy or mythology—about anything you want. Just make it good. You pick the subject. You make it good. The best PowerPoint presentation wins this coupon, pizza for two at Brick's pizzeria."

He goes on to explain that they can use material in the textbook or do their own research, and they can work in teams if they wish. "The winner will be decided by direct democracy, Athenian style. You present. We all vote. The deadline is in two weeks." He tapes the coupon on the blackboard and draws hash marks underneath for every day until the deadline, one mark to be erased each day in the meanwhile.

"Can I use my own software?" asks Alan Carrie with more than a little brag in his voice. "My mom's a computer programmer, you know. And my dad makes documentaries."

"You can use any software you want," Mr. Balestrieri replies, "as long as it plays on our PowerPoint here in class when it finishes. Pizza for the winner."

Alan isn't finished. "My mom says there's no use learning programs like PowerPoint right now. She says the software will all be different when I grow up."

"Your mom is right. But learning how to learn a new program is something you can do right now. And presenting before a group is timeless. Do the best presentation. Win the pizza. It's simple."

Now Angel knows what to do. It doesn't matter that Alan's mom's a computer programmer, or that Angel doesn't even know what PowerPoint is. He can figure that out. He's good at figuring things out. And now he has a mission. In two weeks, he's going to win the pizza coupon. He's going to earn the applause of everyone in class, and invite Molly Swann out for pizza.

He starts after school the same day. "What's a PowerPoint presentation?" he asks the school librarian. "I need to make a PowerPoint for Mr. Balestrieri."

"Ah, the annual pizza," she says, bringing him to the computer lab. "Here you go." She shows him how to log in and make an account to save his files.

She shows him the icon labeled PowerPoint, how to double click, and what it means to make a presentation. PowerPoint is tricky at first but it's intuitive too. By the time the late bus arrives he knows how to construct a presentation and how to save it in his very own file on the school's shared drive.

He needs a security code on his account, and that's easy too. "Molly," he types, until the computer tells him he needs at least one number for security reasons. "Molly1," he types again, and the computer accepts it.

He's going to win.

The next day in Mr. Balestrieri's class, Alan Carrie points out that his favorite pizza is pineapple, and that Brick's pizzeria makes great milkshakes. "My favorite is chocolate malt," he declares. "Will the coupon include a chocolate malt?"

"The coupon will cover a chocolate malt," says Mr. Balestrieri. Then to be fair he adds, "For you or whoever else wins it."

After school that day Angel starts his research. He starts by typing words like "Greece" or "Athens" into Google, sometimes adding words like "ancient" or "myth." He's looking for ideas for the report and gets a few, but mostly it pulls up advertisements for hotels and Aegean Sea cruises that don't help him at all. He examines books on the shelf, searches some more, and soon hits upon his answer.

Molly's mother is running a marathon. Ancient Greece created the marathon. That's the key. Angel will do his PowerPoint in honor of Molly's mother. That's how he'll win his pizza.

Angel isn't accustomed to taking the late bus home, which runs a different route that drops him farther from his apartment. The trees are starting to change color for the season, maples before oaks as always, and the color reflects the setting sun so the horizon glows in orange and rose. A few tall apartment buildings like Angel's stand out, but most buildings are small brick homes with little square yards.

A woman walks past with a wiener dog on a leash, waddling along on stumpy little legs, its tail pistoning back and forth like a locomotive. Half a block behind him walk two boys a few years older than Angel, pushing their bicycles along the sidewalk instead of riding. As Angel steps out of the way he notices that the tire on the front boy's bike is flat; the second boy seems to be keeping his friend company to walk the broken bike home. The boys speak to each other in Spanish, but they thank Angel in English for making room as they pass.

Midway through the next block Angel sees an elderly woman in a faded blue dress exit her home, leaving the door open behind her, and step gingerly toward a car parked in the driveway as if every step is a challenge. The car's trunk is open, and as Angel reaches her she leans into the trunk and fumbles for a grip on one of what appears to be a trunk full of shopping bags.

Angel watches for a moment, sees how hard this seems to be, and takes the last step in her direction. "Can I help?" he offers gently.

She doesn't seem to hear, just keeps fumbling for the bag.

Angel steps closer so he's more in her way. "Can I help?" he asks again, louder.

She looks up, startled and a little bit confused.

"Can I help you unload the car?" he asks again, reaching for the nearest bag. "It looks hard."

Now understanding dawns on her face. She steps back from the trunk and steadies herself against the fender until she's sure. "That would be wonderful," she says with a smile. "That would be a blessing."

"Then I'm happy to help," he says, reaching for a bag. "You go on inside, and I'll catch up to you with the bags." He can see how long she'll need to reach the door, even empty-handed.

"Thank you," she says and starts walking.

Angel grabs two plastic shopping bags in each hand, leaving three still in the trunk, and catches up before she reaches the door. Without saying a word, he takes his place behind her and walks slowly, step by step toward her home. He's not sure if she knows that he's behind her, but she pulls over by the door.

"The kitchen is just inside," she says. "You go on ahead."

She stands on the threshold, seemingly catching her breath, in a place where even Angel can see the refrigerator. Along one wall of the living room is a threadbare couch and in the center is a round wooden table with a single wooden chair. He deposits all four bags in front of the refrigerator, then steps back out toward the car.

"I can't pay you anything," she says as he walks past.

Already past her, he doesn't reply, just continues to the car and loads the last of the bags. "Should I close the trunk?" he calls across the yard.

"Yes, please."

As he approaches her at the door, he says, "It's truly not a problem. I'm glad I could help." This hasn't set him back but a minute, and he's not in a hurry.

By the time he's dropped off the bags and returned to the door, a man is walking toward them from the house next door. He's not as old or fragile as the woman Angel's been helping, but he's long past the age where anything looks easy.

"Can you help me, too, young man?" He's wearing a tan jacket and a blue baseball cap.

"What do you need?"

"I've been sorting in my attic," he replies. "I've got boxes to keep and boxes to throw away. If you can help me unload the attic I can pay you for your time."

"I'd be happy to help," Angel replies, "but probably not now. It's getting late."

So they talk back and forth awhile, making plans. The man's name turns out to be Austin Marquette, and Angel will come over the next few days on his way home from school for short cleaning sessions. Austin will pay him five dollars every day, and maybe more in the future if all goes well.

The next day at the library Angel starts right in Googling the history of the marathon. He quickly finds some useful web pages, and he's copying notes into his notebook when Tammy pulls in next to him. "What are you working on?" she asks.

"Mr. Balestrieri's PowerPoint."

"Cool. What's it on?"

"The first marathon. How about you?"

"I'm still deciding. Probably Athena's headbirth. Maybe Helios and the golden chariot."

"Want to join me?" The computer desk next to him is empty.

"No thanks. I just need to grab a book and go. Can I show you something?"

"Sure. What?"

She reaches toward the back of the computer and calls his attention to a slot between the wires. "That's the USB port for your flash drive. It took me forever to find it the first time. Our USB at home is in front."

"Thanks," says Angel, with no clue what a USB port or a flash drive is. "I'll keep that in mind."

"Good luck with the PowerPoint," she says, lifting her backpack over her shoulder. "Brick's pizza is great."

On the way home he starts his new routine. Austin Marquette answers the door immediately when Angel knocks, and pulls what looks like a magic staircase from the hallway ceiling, "Mind your head," he says as he leads Angel up the stairs.

As soon as Angel reaches the top he sees what the old man means. The structural rafters of the roof are just a few feet above the floor, highest in the center, sloping toward the edges in a narrow triangle. Many rafters have nails, and an electric light bulb provides barely enough light to see. The attic is warm even on this mild autumn afternoon.

A row of boxes and a pair of black Hefty bags line one wall. "All of those go out to the trash," Austin explains. "Even I'm finally willing to admit that I don't need that stuff anymore."

"What's in them?"

"Newspapers I once thought were interesting. Clothes I thought I'd wear again. A couple of books. The phone book from when I bought the place thirty years ago. A lifetime worth of junk." In addition to the boxes in their orderly row lie piles of other stuff, and Austin explains his plans. "Carry the boxes down the drop-staircase and empty them into the trash can outside. That's the part I can't do myself. But bring the empty boxes back inside. I only have the four of them."

"For another load?" Angel guesses.

"Right. But not until tomorrow. Tonight I'll sort more stuff and have the boxes ready for you again tomorrow, maybe some bags. I have plenty of bags."

"Five dollars for a couple of trips down the stairs? That's too much."

Austin reaches over and actually tussles Angle's hair, like one does to a three-year-old. "We'll see," he says. "Some things won't fit in boxes and I need the help no matter what. Let me pay you the five dollars and we'll take it from there."

Meanwhile Angel is cruising on his PowerPoint. He experiments with different slide layouts and different ways to make bullet points appear and disappear. Tammy shows him how to find pictures in Google images, and how to cut and paste them into his designs. He discovers all the Word Art and Clip Art functions and spends one afternoon playing with them, but decides they're too fancy for him. Let Alan Carrie act the expert programmer; Angel will keep his PowerPoint simple and focus on his presentation, the connections between what he'll say and what he shows on screen.

By the end of the week he's ready to go. His PowerPoint is finished and Austin's attic is in excellent shape. Angel has even helped him to sort things into different piles, and to organize and label what Austin calls the "keepers." Angel is proud of both projects, and he thinks his PowerPoint can win. Between the boxes and the slides in his own presentation, he daydreams about how he'll ask Molly to pizza.

"Would you care to join me?" he imagines sometimes with a tone of formality. Or "I won!" he imagines other times with a tone of gusto. "Let's celebrate!"

"What's your phone number?" Austin interrupts as he passes Angel the final five-dollar bill. "In case I need you for something else."

"We don't have a phone at home," Angel replies. He knows well the household budget, and a phone never quite fits.

Austin seems surprised but covers it smoothly. "Well then, just stop by from time to time and say hello. I'll tell you what's up, and maybe make you a glass of lemonade."

"That sounds great," says Angel. "It's my pleasure."

Chapter Twenty-five

"Hear ye, hear ye," says Mr. Balestrieri. "Come one, come all. The show is about to begin!" He's wearing a blue suit today, with a handkerchief in his pocket and a bright red necktie.

Today is PowerPoint day, and the hallways are abuzz. Alan Carrie's been bragging about his hot new graphics accelerator and the cool video he downloaded from his mom. Veronica West has been telling people she has a "Midas touch." The hash marks under the coupon on Mr. Balestrieri's blackboard have counted down to zero.

Yesterday during class everyone handed in their PowerPoints, with their full names as the filename and the opening slide. Mr. Balestrieri spent the evening loading PowerPoints onto the laptop and setting up the projector. Everyone has been instructed on how to use the wireless mouse to advance the slides, and advised *ad nauseam* to practice their presentations at home.

"Today is the day," Mr. Balestrieri declares, grandstanding in front of his audience as he erases the last hash mark. "There's just one question left. Who goes first?"

He walks across the front of the class, eyeballing every student from the front to the back. "Who goes first?" he asks his captive audience again. "And a related question: who goes last?" Finally he pulls out a giant black top hat, holds it upside down in front of the class. "The answer is in here . . . but what is it? What's in the hat?"

The room remains silent. People want nothing but to begin.

"What'sssssssssss in the hat?" he draws out the question with the long, sibilant *S*.

Finally he reaches into the hat and with great fanfare pulls out . . . a rabbit! A fuzzy, white stuffed-animal bunny.

Half the kids laugh; the other half groans. Angel watches in silence.

"And what elsssssssse is in the hat?" Again the long pause and the sibilant *S* until finally Emily Hudson raises her hand. "Yes, Emily?" he says.

"Mr. Balestrieri, if you please," she says in a tone of exaggerated courtesy. "Perhaps you would be so kind as to tell us what's in the hat."

"How good of you to ask," he replies in kind, holding the hat toward the audience. "Names are in the hat. Everyone's name. If you are doing your PowerPoint alone, your name is on a piece of paper alone. If you are working as a team, you and your teammate are on the same piece of paper. One by one, I will reach into the hat and pull out a paper. One by one, you will go. No order. No warning." He swishes inside the hat. "Just like life, it's a surprise. I hope you've been practicing."

He strides back and forth across the front of the room. "Who will be first? Who will be last? Will it be you? Will it be her?" He stretches on and on until people want to rip the hat out of his hands and start calling names.

Finally he comes to a stop. At long last he reaches into the hat. With the class ready to strangle him he pulls out a piece of paper and he announces who goes first. "Angel Thompson," he says. "You go first. You set the standard."

Faster than anything he's done since class began, Mr. Balestrieri steps aside and turns center stage over to Angel.

It's like the oxygen has gone out of the room. Angel feels dizzy and his head goes blank. He can't believe the teacher called on him first. Some kids like to ham it up, but Angel's new to public speaking. Set the standard? *But how?*

Angel hides his uncertainty. He takes to his feet and reaches the front of the room before Mr. Balestrieri even finishes loading his PowerPoint. Angel grabs the mouse, checks to see that his name slide is on the screen in front of the class—in letters he's never seen so large—and turns to face his audience.

Everybody is looking at him. Molly and Tammy with concern near the front. Even Parker Carlson with interest in the back. Angel can't ever remember so much attention focused in his direction.

But he doesn't hesitate and doesn't wilt. He's been practicing in his head for a week, and he knows exactly what to say. "Hi, everybody," he says, his only concession to uncertainty a minor stall before the work begins. "My presentation is on the marathon."

He clicks for his first slide. His name evaporates and up pops a Google image of a runner crossing a finish line, breaking the tape, the words *Marine Corps Marathon* on a banner overhead.

"Nowadays we think of the marathon as a sport," Angel explains.

He clicks the mouse and images march across the screen. Olympic rings. Gold medals. Cheering crowds. The technology works fine, just like he practiced in the library, and he warms up as he goes.

"But actually the marathon is history."

He clicks to the next image: textbooks on a shelf.

Parker Carlson yells from the rear, "Boo!"

The next click brings a map of ancient Greece, with dots for Athens, Sparta, Thebes, and the blue Aegean Sea. "Back then Greece was arranged as city-states."

"Athens." He clicks for an image of the Parthenon.

"Sparta." He clicks for an athlete hurling a discus. They'd studied the city-states in class.

"On the other side of the Aegean Sea lurks the bad guy in this story: Persia." The next click brings an image of a warrior in a chariot, complete with shining shield and gleaming sword.

Everybody is listening to Angel. Everyone's watching with full attention, poised to hear what happens next. "Greece was expanding, you see. The population was growing and the Greeks needed land to farm." He points again to the city-states on the map. "But Persia was expanding too. Conflict was inevitable." He draws a finger northward from Athens, then another finger southward from Persia.

"Persia moved to the south with a giant army, ready to fight and planning to win. The Athenian philosophers and farmers had nothing that could match it. They mobilized soldiers as best they could, but they knew they were doomed. They needed help!"

He points to Sparta's dot on the map. "Maybe Sparta could help. Athens summoned their best runner and sent him to Sparta. They didn't have phones and email and text messages back then, so messages travelled by foot. Their star runner's name was Phidippides."

Up comes a picture of Phidippides, an ancient etching of ink on stone, a runner in full stride. "Sparta was 140 miles away. Rugged terrain over mountains and rocks. Phidippides ran it in two days, 70 miles per day. He reached Sparta and asked for help. Do you know what Sparta said?"

Angel clicks to the next slide. "*No.*" A single word typed in large font, emphasized with bold and italics, which he now reads out loud to boot.

"Do you know why?"

He clicks to the next slide: "*We're busy.*"

The classroom bursts out in laughter. The kids are really getting into this! Tammy in particular laughs audibly over the crowd. "Phidippides arrived during a religious festival. Sparta would be happy to help but not until the holiday is over.

"Phidippides explained that Persia might have won the war by then, but to no avail. Sparta said no, and stuck with it. Phidippides had to run back with his answer. No text, no phone, no email. He had to run. How far was it?"

The question is spontaneous, not in his prepared remarks. But Angel is on a roll and he feels his audience rolling with him. Mitchie Daniels calls out, "One hundred and forty miles."

"Right," Angel replies. "Another 140 miles in another two days. Ouch! But finally, he reaches Athens with the bad news, exhausted and discouraged. Do you know what the Athenians did?"

Parker Carlson: "Shot him."

"Almost. They sent him to the front to fight the Persians."

Groans all around.

"Do you know where this crucial battle was taking place?" Nobody answers. Angel clicks the next slide, another word: "*Marathon*."

"The Athenians were hugely outnumbered, but they did some stunning tactics and launched a clever surprise attack . . . and they won!"

"Yay!" Mitchie Daniels offers.

"Not yet," Angel warns. "Athens started to celebrate its victory when somebody noticed that the Persian navy was gone from the port. While the whole Athenian army was up in Marathon fighting, half the Persian troops and the entire Persian navy were sailing for Athens.

"Oh no!" Mitchie corrects himself publicly.

"It's a disaster! The city will be defenseless! Surprised and defenseless. Somebody needs to run to Athens and tell them to prepare for attack. Who can run?"

The whole class calls out: "Phidippides!"

"Right! Do you know how far it is from Marathon to Athens?"

Silence. Nobody answers.

"Come on, guess." Angel looks straight at Molly as he asks again. "Do you know how far it is from Marathon to Athens?"

She rises to the challenge. "Twenty-six miles?"

"You got it! Twenty-six miles. Poor Phidippides laced back on his running shoes—if they had shoes back then—and ran twenty-six miles to Athens.

"When he got there he did two things. First, he told them about the upcoming attack and told them to prepare their defenses. And the second thing . . . does anybody know the second thing?"

Silence.

"He died. He delivered the message, then he died."

Up goes Angel's final image: *RIP.*

"That's the story of Phidippides. He ran twenty-six miles from Marathon to Athens, and we still do it today."

The applause is loud, generous, and sincere. Mr. Balestrieri even stands to applaud from behind his desk.

Angel just stands in the front of the room, smiling into the applause, not knowing what to do next but enjoying every minute of it. He loves the acclaim and bows instinctively before he returns to his seat, and when he turns his attention back to the front the first thing he sees is the *Brick's Pizza* coupon taped to the top of the board. He can practically taste the pizza. That was all he'd ever dreamed of.

Though Angel's head is still spinning from his own performance and he isn't paying perfect attention, the next two presentations seem truly weak. The thinness of the applause compared to Angel's suggests that he really did set some kind of standard.

Tammy breaks the trend with a stunning presentation of Helios and his golden chariot that ends with a solid, enthusiastic round of applause. Molly follows her with a lovely presentation on the weaving competition between the peasant girl Arachne and the goddess Minerva, with PowerPoint lines forming a delicate weave across the screen. Molly's performance is attractive, elegant, and profound, but ends on a mournful note—as the goddess loses the duel and spitefully turns Arachne into a spider—which suppresses enthusiasm for applause at the crucial closing moment.

Veronica West does a presentation with Samantha Collins that's supposed to be about King Midas and the golden touch, but Angel can hardly tell through the arguing. Each girl takes turns presenting her own slides and spends most of her time explaining that her slide was harder to make and more important than the other girl's.

Next Mitchie Daniels does a nice presentation on coinage and the Athenian innovation of currency instead of barter, which might have been interesting if it weren't so boring.

Every time the hat has fewer names in it. Every time the few remaining people think surely they must be next, but every time it's only one of them. Angel thinks only that his chance of winning keeps getting better and better. He spends as much time daydreaming about inviting Molly as he does watching the presentations. Should he invite her right after class, or wait until tomorrow?

A few more students pass uneventfully until there are only two names left. Alan Carrie and Parker Carlson both know that it will be one of them. "No, no, after you . . . " says Parker to Alan as Mr. Balestrieri reaches for the hat. "Really, it's okay."

But to no avail. Parker is next and he bores the class with the history of the Olympics, mixing religion and sports in the city-state of Olympia in a way that makes no sense to Angel and apparently not to anyone else either. He finishes to tepid applause, the weakness made even more vivid by the excessive applause of a few football friends, until the only presenter left is Alan Carrie.

Alan ambles to the front of the room and starts plugging in speakers even as Mr. Balestrieri tries to make a joke out of pulling the last and only name from the hat.

"You said I could use these, right?" Alan asks Mr. Balestrieri as he works the speaker cables.

"Yes to the speakers. No to the firecrackers."

Speakers? Firecrackers? The class leans forward in anticipation.

Alan presses his opening buttons and the sound comes up. Wind and breeze. A little guitar, then sounds of the ocean, waves breaking on the beach. "I'm doing the story of Icarus and Daedalus," Alan begins. "Subtitled: your father is always right."

He clicks the mouse and the first image isn't a slide but a movie! Nothing in Angel's experience in the library suggests how he did that. Ocean waves roll across the screen, swelling and foaming as they break. Alan says nothing as the class watches surf take over the front of the room. Together with the soundtrack it's like a day on the beach, and the class sits spellbound, the magical effect of waves slowing down the day. Finally, Alan interrupts to explain that Daedalus was the great inventor of Athens, creator of tall buildings and tiny tricks. "But eventually, like most clever people, he got in trouble."

"The jealous king locked him up in a tower on a remote island with his son, Icarus." The next image shows a snapshot of such a tower, on an island, taken from the air.

"Daedalus couldn't run away and the island was too far to swim. But he figured out he could fly." Next comes a movie of birds in flight, soaring and swooping through the sky, another spellbinding show across the front of the room. Eagles soar; hummingbirds hover; a single feather breaks loose and flutters down, down, down all the way to a beach. Then Alan explains how Daedalus collected feathers that landed on the island and made wings for himself and his son. "'But don't fly too high,' Daedalus warned. 'The hot sun will melt the wax on the wings, and you'll crash into the ocean.'"

Angel is mesmerized by the movie. He doesn't even have a TV at home, let alone professional footage of birds in flight, played on a screen that fills the front of the room. He watches eagles soar while the soundtrack plays guitar and a gull calls in the background.

"Of course, Icarus flies too high," says Alan, as the image changes from the ocean to the sun, and not just the sun that Angel sees in the sky but close-up footage of sunspots and solar flares blasting jets of fire out to space. *NASA STEREO satellite* reads a logo in the bottom corner of the screen. The surface of the sun is a boiling cauldron of flame.

The sound changes too. No longer the peaceful ocean with the guitar strum, but an electric bass, accelerating the already exciting views of the sun. Again Alan leaves the class to sightsee, lets them enjoy the NASA footage with the thrilling bass beat. As one especially impressive solar flare arcs across the screen, Alan concludes, "Icarus's wings melted. Daedalus watched, helpless, as his son crashed to his death."

The last image is a car crash, some kind of NASCAR footage with cars racing around the track, then piling up in a flipping, flaming heap. "The end."

Even Angel leaps to his feet to applaud with everyone else. The music was thrilling, the video sensational, and even though Alan said little and explained even less, the effect was astonishing. Alan had used his technology to blend video, audio, and mythology. The class needn't wait for Mr. Balestrieri to tabulate results or recount any score. As the applause winds down and the cars continue to burn on screen, everyone knows who won. Alan Carrie will be eating Angel's pizza.

Chapter Twenty-six

THEY TOOK MY PARENTS AWAY *when I was in second grade*, reads the opening of Monet's essay for admission to college. *My parents sold our house to hire a lawyer. Five years passed before I saw my mother again.*

She's done everything to prepare for this day. She put in extra hours on her homework and on her exams. She researched colleges and stopped talking to her mother by phone to save money for application fees.

Sheila knows everything of course. "We'll just take a break," she proposed in their penultimate phone conversation. "Next week we'll say good-bye. After you get in, we'll schedule a call for congratulations." Her new prison job pays thirty-five cents per hour, plenty for stamps.

The school guidance counselor was helpful too. She didn't recommend Monet for the hardest AP or most advanced classes. Monet isn't prepared for them, and she wouldn't get credit just for trying. Better to aim one notch down and score the A's, the counselor advised.

Monet didn't have the cash for Stanley Kaplan and the other SAT test prep classes that her classmates were taking, but the library had plenty of resources for free. She built that into her schedule too, and now Monet has a respectable SAT score and a transcript full of A's. She gets a warm glow every time she looks at her transcript, every high grade a story of hard work and uncertainty.

They weren't even guilty, her essay continues. *Neither one of them. I admit that my father once sold heroin, but my mom made him stop before she would marry him. He got out of the drug trade long before he was arrested, and he never sold cocaine. He didn't even know the people dealing cocaine, nor any of the people charged as co-conspirators. But most of them are out by now, since they pegged him as ringleader.*

She'd traded drafts of Zeb's appeal by mail, and she knows his arguments by heart. Not all of them fit in her application essay, but she's picked the ones she likes.

She talks about herself, too: her weekly phone calls; her babysitting and odd jobs to pay for them (skipping Angel's candy, with his permission, because it's too complicated); her heart-stopping visit to her mother, who told her to go to college. She talks about why she wants to go to college and how she owes it to her parents to make the most of herself: *When I graduate, I'll do enough good for all three of us put together. I promise.*

The only point where Monet and Sheila don't see eye to eye is what college to aim for. Sheila wants Monet to go to a fancy white people's college—"the best one you can get into"—and beat them at their own game. Monet wants to go to a historically black college (her favorite new acronym is HBCU). She's sick of being surrounded by rich white people and wants some friends she can relate to. The best book she ever read in school—ever!—was *Beloved*, by Toni Morrison, a book that baffled the white kids. Monet was already leaning toward Howard University because it's right downtown in Washington D.C., but learning that Toni Morrison went to Howard sealed the deal.

At ninety dollars apiece to apply, they can't afford many applications. Monet applies to Howard, her favorite, and the University of Virginia because she is, after all, a state resident.

Won't it be delicious if you're in a Virginia state college and I'm in a Virginia state prison at the same time? Sheila wrote in one letter.

No, Monet replied. *It will be delicious if you win your appeal and you come home before I matriculate.* Matriculate. A fancy new word that she never would have learned if her mother hadn't sent her on this path.

Monet's last application is to Harvard, her mother's daydream and her fantasy to "stick it to the establishment." Monet isn't optimistic about Harvard, but the folks at CURE assure her that God works in strange and wonderful ways.

A week before the deadline she seals the applications and makes a special trip to the post office, Libby and Angel by her side. Libby kisses each envelope before Monet drops it in the slot.

"So long," says Angel. "Hurry back."

Chapter Twenty-seven

The death comes as a surprise. One day he was a happy member of a happy family. Tammy had bragged about the Santa hats her father had given everyone at Christmas, and how the whole family wore them to the New Year's party. "We all threw our hats in the air at midnight," she'd said on the first Monday back at school after the holidays, as if she were still enjoying the party. On Tuesday he was gone.

Apparently he was a little late driving home Monday night—too fast, perhaps?—when he bumped another car and rebounded into the support pillar for the overpass. And just like that, his life came to an end. No longer was Benjamin Eli Atford a happy member of a happy family. His death left a giant, gaping hole, a smile with a tooth knocked out.

Tammy skipped school on Wednesday but came on Thursday and told people about it. Her mom thought it might help her to go to school as if everything were normal. Angel saw her drive Tammy to school and drop her off with a hug and a kiss.

Everything wasn't normal. Tammy didn't make it through the day.

"I want to go to the funeral," Angel tells his mom when he brings home the news that a student's father has died. "It's on Saturday."

Libby doesn't say anything. "Saturday," she mutters.

"That's the funeral. I want to go." Angel repeats. "To the funeral."

Libby stays strangely silent. Not the gasps Angel heard from the teachers, nor the hugs Tammy received from her classmates. Libby registers the death of Tammy's father with puzzling ambivalence. She's troubled, Angel thinks, but differently from everyone else.

Angel's own father—Libby's husband—died in a car accident all those years ago. Just like Tammy's dad. Maybe that's the problem. Maybe his mom is having her own memories, her own sadness on top of Tammy's. "Dead father . . . " he thinks he hears her say. "I wonder if . . . "

But she's murmuring to herself and doesn't seem to want to be heard. He decides not to intrude and ask her. He gives her a hug instead.

The next day Angel learns the details of the funeral, and he stays after school to look up the bus route to Tammy's church on the same computer where he wrote his PowerPoint. He's pretty good with the computer by now, but he doesn't like what he learns. The trip will require two bus lines and nearly two hours. He copies the directions off the web page to save the printer fee, and takes the late bus home.

On the way he knocks on the door of Austin Marquette, in case Austin needs help with anything or knows someone who does.

"Thank God you're here!" Austin exclaims as the opens the door. "A gift from heaven! Yes, please! Quickly! Up the stairs!"

A water pipe has burst under the bathroom sink and flooded the room with water. Water is an inch deep on the tile floor, the bath mat in the center saturated and stuck to the bottom. Austin has shut off the water supply so it's no longer filling, but water is overflowing the threshold at the bathroom door and starting down the stairs.

Austin tosses Angel a towel. "Stop it on the stairs," he says. "I'll find more towels."

Angel drops the towel on the top stair, soaking up the water instantly, but immediately notices that more water is still trickling over the threshold. He picks up the sodden towel and lays it across the door to the bathroom like a dam.

Austin returns with two more towels. One he hands Angel and the other he drops on the top stair, where it saturates instantly. "That's all I have," he laments.

"Bedsheets," Angel replies.

"Right!" Austin rushes to a closet that's filled with toiletries, cleaning supplies and, Angel sees, linens. Austin tosses a stack of sheets toward Angel, and turns back for more.

The bedsheets dry the stairs completely, and Angel uses the sodden sheets to shore up the dam at the door, then they turn their attention to the bathroom itself. They both take off their shoes and roll up their pants, and quickly they work out a rhythm, tossing the towels on the floor to saturate, then wringing them out in the bathtub. The towels never truly dry, but enough water wrings out that they can soak up more on the next round.

Twenty minutes later the bathroom is no longer flooded, just wet. Angel finds enough dry edges in the linen they'd used on the staircase to chase the water out of the corners.

Austin walks carefully down the stairs, then hollers from below, "Ceiling seems to be okay. No damage—yet!"

He comes back up the stairs, drying his hands on a new little towel from the kitchen sink, and passes it to Angel. "Thanks goodness," he says. "What a disaster if you hadn't knocked! Like manna from heaven."

"Manna?" Angel doesn't know the word.

"You don't know manna? From the Bible?"

Angel shakes his head.

"The Israelites escaped from Egypt. They were starving in the desert, wandering for forty years. Every morning with the sunrise came manna from heaven, food for the day."

"Where did it come from?"

"That's the point. Nobody knows. It came from heaven. Like you."

"Well, I came from school," Angel says with a shrug. "But I'm glad I could help."

Austin heaps the last of the heroic linen and towels, now just dirty laundry, into a basket. "I'll fix the pipe tomorrow. It'll be like new . . . thanks to you." He presses a five-dollar bill into Angel's hand.

"That's for today's work. Next time we can do without the catastrophe."

Austin's five dollars is like manna too, a gift from nowhere that covers the long and costly bus ride to the church on Saturday. It's a cold day in January and Angel's mother bundles him up in his warmest clothes. "Sure you don't want to join me?" he asks one more time, certain this death has troubled her more than she's letting show.

"I'm sure, thanks. You go to your friend. It's good of you to go to your friend."

The trip takes two hours, but the church is beautiful, with a steeple on the top and magnificent stained glass windows. This is the first time Angel's ever been in a church, his first religious service of any kind. He sees Ms. Traldi, the science teacher, with her husband, looking somehow like her, but with a dark beard trimmed short. He sees his homeroom teacher, Dr. Eisman, sitting in a row near the front, and the school principal, Mrs. Isserow, in the back. Mrs. Isserow sees Angel and gives him a nod. Whether the other teachers see him, he's not so sure.

In a special place at the front, Angel sees Tammy, Tammy's mother, and what must be Tammy's immediate family. Tammy's mother is tragically beautiful, with a full head of dark brown hair pinned tight against her head. Before her stand Tammy and two younger brothers in order of height and, doubtless, of age. Before them lies a casket, dark wood, closed.

Joanna Baye is all but hidden in a corner, separate from everyone else in the crowded room. She has a roll of toilet paper in her lap and a wad in one hand. She's crying when Angel notices her, and she cries through the entire ceremony. She cries during the sad parts and cries during the uplifting parts, cries during the Jesus parts and cries during the family parts. She doesn't respond like everyone else, just weeps or sobs in a world of her own.

"As for man, his days are like grass," the minister intones from the dais. "He flourishes like a flower of the field; the wind blows over it and it is gone." Angel barely listens to the service, tuning in occasionally but losing it just as fast. The organ music and the stained glass are more captivating by far. "You can shed tears that he is gone, or you can rejoice that he has lived."

The service takes barely an hour, then the casket is ceremoniously loaded into a hearse and driven away for cremation. Many people stay for the reception with snacks, though Angel—with the exception of a few tasty bites—walks back to the bus.

"I was almost the only student," Angel reports to his mother when he returns home in the evening. Monet is out with some friends, not scheduled to return until bedtime.

"Did you see anybody you knew?" Libby asks. She'd boiled a pot of rice already, but held the rest to cook after he arrived. Now she starts a pot of water to steam broccoli, and breaks eggs into a bowl.

Angel peeks at the dinner prep, breaks one floret off the broccoli, and eats it raw. "I like broccoli," he says.

"I know you do. But tell me about the funeral. Who was there?"

"Some teachers. Principal Isserow. Mostly it was Tammy's family and friends. They seem to have a lot of friends."

"It's nice that you went."

"Oh, and Joanna was there. Joanna Baye. She sat crying by herself the whole time."

"Did you talk to her?"

"No. I left her alone. She hasn't been in school lately, anyway."

"Why not?" Libby is whisking the eggs with a fork.

"I'm not sure. Maybe she's sick. Kids have been teasing her."

"Why are they teasing her?"

"She has sex with her father."

Libby drops the cup of eggs in her hands. It shatters on the floor with a crash, and the impact spreads egg in goopy yellow streaks.

"No," she gasps. "No!" She's looking at Angel, not at the eggs. "What did you say?"

"She has sex with her father. That's why kids are teasing her."

Only now does Libby notice the shattered cup at her feet, the mess of eggs spreading toward the stove. Immediately she's on her knees to scoop at the mess, keeping the eggs out from under the stove.

Angel passes her a sponge for the eggs and starts picking up pieces of the shattered cup.

They spend a long time on the floor, sponging up the eggs and sweeping the microscopically small shards of ceramic. The empty broccoli pot starts to burn.

"Crap," says Libby, taking the pot off the burner. Then she turns to Angel, her face a wasteland, like she's seen a ghost, not dropped some eggs. "I can't do this. Can you clean up? I need to use the bathroom."

She drops the pot in the sink and runs for the bathroom, slamming the door behind her.

Angel takes over in the kitchen. It doesn't take that long. The mess wasn't that bad, really, just a little something on the bottom of the pot burning itself off. Angel fills the pot with water from the sink and checks the refrigerator for eggs. There are plenty more.

After a few minutes of soaking and one of scrubbing, Angel starts new water for the broccoli and scrambles new eggs. He wants to tell his mom about the funeral. He wants to tell her about the organ music and the stained glass.

But his mom doesn't emerge from the bathroom. All he can hear is water running. What's going on in there?

Chapter Twenty-eight

Dinner is cold by the time Libby returns to the table. Angel went ahead and cooked the eggs and broccoli, and started to eat, thinking she'd join him soon enough. His mom's plate rests at her place on the table, eggs on top of the rice the way she likes them, broccoli on the side.

"Thanks for cleaning up," she says when she joins him at last, trying to act as if everything is normal. She picks up her broccoli by the stem and bites off the crown. "Thanks for cooking, too."

"What's the matter, Mom? Is it Tammy's dad?" Maybe it just took a long time for his death to hit.

"No," she says after a long break. "It's not Tammy's dad. It's Joanna's."

"Joanna's?"

"Joanna's dad. He's having sex with Joanna. Is that what you said?"

"That's what the other kids say."

"How do they know?"

"I don't know."

"What does it mean, 'they're having sex'?"

"Mom . . . ," he complains, his voice dripping disapproval.

"Well, you need to find out. You need to talk to the other kids. You need to learn what they think is happening, and why they think it. Can you do that?"

"It's something about a computer."

"A computer?"

"Somebody saw something on a computer."

"Saw them having sex on a computer?"

"Mom!"

"Please, just find out. It's really important. I need you to find out what's happening. Find out what the kids think is happening. Find out how they know it. Can you do that? It's really important."

"I'll find out. I'll check at school tomorrow. I mean Monday."

"And I need to talk to her."

"Who?"

"Joanna. That's what you need to do. You need to find out what the kids are talking about. And you need to introduce us. Can you do all that? It's a lot. Can you manage? Please?"

"I'll try, Mom. Joanna's mean sometimes. She doesn't like to talk much."

Libby chews down a spoonful of egg with rice. "I'll bet."

Chapter Twenty-nine

SCHOOL ON MONDAY STARTS LIKE any other day. In homeroom, Dr. Eisman sits at his desk, busy over a notebook, grading papers or filling out forms. The windows open to another gray morning in January, barely daylight. Kids come trickling in, sometimes talking, occasionally laughing, mostly sulking like they'd rather be someplace else. It's still cold outside and many don't bother to take their coats off when they sit down.

Molly is running late this morning. Maybe she stopped to talk in the hallway or maybe her bus was late, but the room is nearly full by the time she arrives. She nods at Angel as she takes her seat, then digs through her backpack for paper and pen, and passes Angel a note.

Did you go to the funeral?

Yes. He writes back on the same piece of paper, then breaks their unspoken rule and asks his question out loud. "What's up with Joanna Baye?"

She doesn't register his change, just answers as if talking is normal, but she shakes her head as she speaks. "I don't know."

She seems to understand his question, at least.

Dr. Eisman calls the room to order.

ANGEL DOESN'T SEE JOANNA BETWEEN classes, which isn't unusual for this switch at this time. But Tammy is in math class, as usual, the first real class of the day. She looks tired but otherwise normal, like it's a Monday after an ordinary weekend. Her blonde hair is pulled back and she's wearing a heavy gray sweater, a pink shirt visible underneath.

She's standing by her desk when Angel arrives, but she walks straight to him and takes his hand in her own. "Thank you," she says.

How strange it is to be touched like this! Angel almost never touches or is touched by anybody, and certainly not in school. "What for?" he asks. Her hand is soft and warm, and squeezing him gently.

"For coming to the funeral," she clarifies. "I appreciate it." She chokes up just a little. "You were the only one who came."

"It was beautiful," replies Angel. "You have a wonderful family." He's unsure what to say. "I liked the stained glass."

Tammy just smiles. This is awkward for her too. Their hands move apart.

"Joanna was there too. Joanna Baye." Angel wants her to get credit.

"Was she? I didn't see her."

"She used a lot of tissues."

"I need to thank her. Have you seen her?"

The teacher tells everyone to take their seats even as Angel shakes his head that he hasn't. Tammy's question answers Angel's own.

JOANNA DOESN'T COME TO SCHOOL on Monday, or on Tuesday either. Angel reports to his mother at the end of each day, and on Tuesday she remarks while steaming broccoli that she "may need to take matters into her own hands." Libby speaks little during dinner, and afterwards she asks Angel to bring her Joanna's address and phone number from the school directory. On Wednesday, with nothing further to report, he does.

"Thanks," Libby replies.

Monet walks in bearing cookies she baked at a friend's house for dessert. "Why does a brontosaurus have such a long neck?" she asks with a mischievous grin.

"Why?" Libby and Angel respond in unison.

"To get to the other side!"

Everyone laughs out loud, Libby longer than Angel has heard her laugh in a long time.

Monet explains that she made that joke up in science class. "Some kids were arguing evolution with the teacher, which I'm so sick of. The teacher asked about necks, starting with giraffes, and by the time she got to brontosauruses I shouted out my answer."

"Did you get in trouble?" Libby asks.

"The teacher laughed too. I think everyone wanted a way out."

IN SCHOOL ON THURSDAY ANGEL has one period free, an elective time slot during which he sometimes has typing class, but Thursdays he has study hall. Today he's in the library researching Julius Caesar for Mr. Balestrieri's world history class, which has advanced from Greece to Rome. He still hasn't seen Joanna or learned anything about her, but three boys are gathered around a computer. They're a year older than Angel and he doesn't know their names, but they're making too much noise for the library.

"There she is!" exclaims one boy.

"Joanna?" The next boy is quieter, a library voice.

"No, her father. Alfonso Gustaf Baye. See? He looks like her too."

"A foreigner. Figures." The third boy also talks far too loud. "Foreigner . . . sex offender. They're all the same."

"Those guys are weird," says the first boy at the computer. "Come on. Let's get a soda before class."

They all leave and Angel moves straight into the vacancy, hoping maybe they left the web page open—but no such luck. He opens the Internet browser himself and starts by striking the "back" button, but the new browser has no history so the page doesn't change.

Angel opens his old friend, Google. *Alfonso Gustaf Baye,* he types, positioning his fingers on the home keys and typing properly, not hunting and pecking like before he started his typing class. Google doesn't appreciate his effort, though, and gives him a meaningless jumble of entries in return. Angel tries a few different spellings—Gustav ending with a *v*, Alfonse not Alfonso—but the results don't really change. Finally he enters "Alfonso Gustaf Baye" in quotation marks and "sex offender" in quotation marks, right next to it.

And there he is. Bold blue letters fill the screen: *Alfonso Gustaf Baye—Registry of Criminal Sex Offenders—Fairfax, VA.* Several sites have similar links. He clicks on the top link, *Watchdog USA.*

In the center of the screen appears a face, a white man, roughly the age Angel would guess for Joanna's father. Below the picture is his name, Alfonso Gustaf Baye; above the picture are bright blue words, with links in bold: *We found 039 offenders in your area. Protect your children! Details.*

Full criminal background check on Alfonso Gustaf Baye. $39.95

Credit report. $19.95.

Angel is interested but not convinced. The computer shows a name and a picture, but it still doesn't tell Angel what he's looking for. The man looks a little like Joanna, but maybe that and the name are pure coincidence. Maybe he's an uncle who lives in the area . . . so what?

A banner to the left of the sex offender registry advertises Italian vacations. A banner to the right advertises contact lenses at the top and a weight loss programs at the bottom. A little box near the sex offender's zip code links to local weather.

Angel clicks again on the name under the picture of Alfonse Gustaf Baye, and up pops the detail he's looking for.

- *Street address: 6036 Culpeper Drive, Fairfax VA 22030.* Angel recognizes Joanna's address from the school directory.
- *Family: Married. One child.* That would be Joanna.
- *Offense: Incest.*

Incest! That's the answer, right there. Alfonse Gustaf Baye is married, but relations with his wife aren't incest, and there's only one other person in the family. That must be Joanna. She's having sex with her father . . . or he's having sex with her. It's all right here. A few clicks away in the school library.

Angel is getting late for his next class, but even as he packs his bags and leaves the library he hears the chanting. "Daddy molester! Daddy molester! Joanna is a daddy molester!" A group of boys is standing near the door to outside, chanting in unison, waving their arms in the air. Angel moves down the corridor as fast as he can, but all he sees is Joanna running away.

Chapter Thirty

Every day Libby hurries home from work for the latest updates. She's been working hard recently, but the worst is behind her. Today Libby is home early and she's barely through the door before Angel is grabbing her arms and pulling her toward the couch.

"Mom!" he cries. "Mom! I've got it."

"What have you got?" She's starting to guess the answer but she still hasn't taken off her coat or her shoes. Half of her wants to push him away and beg for a minute to breathe. The door is still open to the hallway.

"Joanna. Joanna Baye. I got the answer."

Now she's fully focused. She forgets whether she's wearing a coat and whether the door is open or closed. Only one thing matters. "And?"

Angel tells her the story. He tells her what he found on the computer, and how he found it. He closes every deductive loop because Joanna is an only child, and repeats with care the important legal term. "Incest."

Even as Libby listens to him he starts to fade. No longer is she on her own couch in her own apartment with her coat on. She's back in her parents' house, sitting on her parents' bed, her father's hands creeping up her thigh, his tobacco breath hot on her neck.

"Mom, is something wrong?" Angel asks.

His voice brings her back where she belongs. "No, dear," she says.

"I thought I did something wrong."

She pushes her handbag out of her lap and gathers him in. "You were amazing." She praises his persistence and his detective work. "You did nothing wrong."

"So what are you going to do?"

"That indeed is the question." She says it like a question but she already knows. Incest. A crime out of the Bible. Her eyes travel silently to her handbag on the floor. Joanna's address is already inside.

She needs to find Joanna. She needs to become the friend she herself never had.

Libby has been working hard lately, and on Friday her boss is willing to let her slip out an hour early. "Don't make a habit of it," he warns. "But have a good weekend."

But she doesn't go home. She boards a different bus going a different direction.

The bus routes are pretty convenient: one line goes directly from the hospital to Joanna's house, another goes directly from Joanna's home to Libby's own. Barely a half-hour after clocking out, Libby is walking the short distance from the bus stop to 6036 Culpeper Drive. It's still early in the afternoon, in a leafy green suburb with large houses and empty sidewalks, save one woman walking a golden retriever on a leash.

Number 6036 Culpeper Drive is a lovely white house, with a veranda across the front and a screened-in porch on the side. A tall spruce tree dominates one half of the grassy front lawn and, on the other half, a strange but charming pelican figure holds a lamp in its beak. Azaleas that must be fabulous in springtime border the yard.

Libby hurried to arrive, but she slows down as she reaches the house and stands all but still on the sidewalk before turning onto the stone path through the yard. Here she ceases to be a pedestrian on a walk; when she turns the corner she becomes an intruder on private property.

She doesn't have a precise plan—still doesn't know exactly what she's going to say, or why this girl might talk to her at all. But she trusts that she'll figure it out. She's back up to speed by the time she reaches the veranda, certain she's doing the right thing as she climbs the steps and knocks on the white painted wooden door.

Nobody answers. She knocks again.

Still no answer.

Beside the door is a doorbell. Libby presses it and listens for the ring, keeps listening for movement or signs of life on the other side as a robin redbreast lands on the edge of the veranda and watches her quizzically. When it leaves, she presses the doorbell again and hears the ring.

There's still no answer. No signs of life.

In the center of the door is a black iron knocker shaped like a pineapple. She pounds a few times, the sound hurtling through the empty neighborhood like cannon shots.

Still no answer. She notices now that there's no car in the driveway.

And suddenly she's all out of ideas.

Her plan was imprecise, but it brought her here. In Libby's daydreams, Joanna always answers the door. In Libby's daydreams, someone, somehow, is always happy to greet her and bring her in.

Instead Libby is standing by herself in front of a strange house in a strange neighborhood, with a doorknocker that's so loud she dare not use it again.

Back down the stone path she walks, ringing the bell as if in farewell, not even waiting for the result she knows it will bring.

But she doesn't turn toward the bus stop. She walks in the opposite direction, then turns right at the first corner, past another block of similar houses, tall and elegant, with bay windows, colored shutters, and screened-in porches. Trees fill the yards and flowerbeds border the houses. One giant maple has a red baby swing tied low to one branch and a bigger blue swing tied high to another.

Libby makes two more right turns until she's back at 6036 Culpeper. Not enough time has elapsed for anything to change, but she rings the bell again to be sure.

With no answer she heads out for a longer walk, and follows her ears to a playground with kids at play. It's closing on evening by now, and as Libby arrives a mom calls to two little girls, "Come on home, time for dinner."

"Aw, Mom . . . ," they complain. "One more time?"

"One more time. This time for real."

Another mom tempts a three-year-old boy off the jungle gym with a lollipop, straps him into a bright red running stroller, and heads home at a jog.

Libby rests on the bench as the playground empties for the day, and imagines if this were her neighborhood, her home.

For millions of people, this is home. Back in the days of Happy Jack, she cleaned houses for people like this.

It's almost dark by the time Libby rings Joanna's bell one last time. She studies the house as closely as she can without trespassing too much or feeling like a burglar. No lights are on, and there's no car in the driveway. It's time to give up. She knows from the men in the hospital laundry room that if she were African American she might have been arrested by now. Joanna's not home, and Libby can't wait any longer.

Libby walks the short distance to the bus stop and is home around dinner time, a little late, but no worse than she's been all week.

On Saturday Libby does something she's never done before. She lies to both her children. Sure, she wakes up with them and they have a nice breakfast together—she can't knock on 6036 Culpeper too early on a Saturday—but then she helps the kids set up homework, games, and activities for the day, and tells them she needs to log some extra hours at the hospital. Then she hops the bus to Joanna's neighborhood and rings the bell.

There's no car in the driveway. Nobody answers the bell.

Today a newspaper sits delivered but uncollected on the stone steps leading up to the house. On her second try after a walk around the block, Libby collects the newspaper and carries it to the door. A nice gesture if someone is home, no harm in leaving it on the veranda if not.

If not. She leaves the newspaper and walks the block again, detouring toward the playground in hopes of Saturday morning traffic. Sure enough, little kids like to wake up early. Mostly dads sit on the benches, reading newspapers and talking on cell phones while the kids dig in the sandbox and climb the equipment. It's still January but warm and sunny today. Libby finds a nice spot in the sun and relaxes, watching the kids, feasting on their innocent calls and laughs.

The parents around the playground are ten years older than Libby, though their children are still playground age. Libby can barely remember Angel at this age. How fast time has flown since she pulled Angel from that trash can and made that escape! Years have passed since she saw her mother, whom she loved so dearly and never forgave for her betrayal.

But a long time has also passed since she woke up in anger. Does time really heal all wounds?

Libby walks back to the house and knocks again, pauses briefly for the silence she knows is coming, then walks another lap. Around lunchtime she gives up. They're not home today, maybe even gone for the weekend.

Libby returns home on Saturday afternoon and tells the same lie on Sunday. There's still no car in the driveway when she arrives, and another uncollected newspaper sits on the stone walkway. She brings the new newspaper to the front door and leaves it by yesterday's newspaper when nobody answers. She gives the Baye family a few hours to return home before she gives up and goes home to her own children, owing them a dinner that's far better than average, starting with the beans Libby left to soak before she left in the morning.

Now while the beans boil in one pot and rice in another, Libby and Angel chop carrots and onions, and mix dough to make corn tortillas the way Libby learned from a dishwasher who left the hospital years ago. By the time Monet gets home, they've created a fabulous multi-course meal with burritos, fried rice and cucumbers in a yoghurt sauce. Everyone finishes dinner and starts looking forward to leftovers tomorrow—which is no accident, since Libby is planning once again to stay out late.

On Monday she leaves work early and takes the bus to Joanna's neighborhood. She's walking toward the Baye residence when she sees a brown UPS truck drive away, and a young woman step out the door to collect a package.

She looks exactly as Angel described her. And Libby knows from Angel's research that she's the only child in the house. There she is. Joanna Baye.

Chapter Thirty-one

"Hey!" Libby yells, catching Joanna's attention before she turns back inside. She picks up her pace and rounds the corner down the stone walkway to the porch. "Hey," she repeats. "I'm Angel's mom. Angel Thompson. You don't know me."

Joanna has long brown hair with a wave to it, and highlights that catch the sunshine. She's very pretty in a pubescent, twelve-year-old kind of way. She's dressed for nothing more than bringing in the mail, but her jeans are attractive and they fit her well.

She's obviously surprised to be called in this way, but she isn't opposed to it. "I know Angel," she says. "He's nice. And smart."

"Thanks. He always says nice things about you too." If that's a lie, it's a little one.

They look at each other without talking. Libby started this, but she's unsure what comes next.

"Well," says Joanna. "It was nice to meet you." She turns toward the door.

"Wait!" Libby's voice is low but urgent; she takes a step in Joanna's direction. "I know about your father."

Joanna looks up in alarm, then finishes her turn to the door. "Everybody knows about my father." She takes the first step inside.

"No. I know for real."

That stops her. Joanna adjusts the package she's holding against her hip. "I'm listening. What do you know?"

Libby's voice turns low and dark. "I know about the baths he gave you as a little girl. I know how he used to rub your feet, nice and soft, and how you used to like it."

Joanna looks horrified. Repulsed but riveted at the same time.

"And I know more," says Libby without a break. "I know how he used to leave your feet and move up your legs. I know where he put his hands. I know how you stopped liking it but couldn't make him stop."

Joanna's mouth is wide open. She clutches the package in both hands like a life preserver, then she defends herself. "You saw it on YouTube?" She's trying to be sarcastic.

"I lived it. My father did it to me. We're in this together."

Joanna reaches again for the door, opens it wide enough for both of them. "You'd better come inside."

"Nobody's home?"

"Mom's at work and Dad's in jail. I said to come inside." It's more than an invitation; it's an order.

The front door opens to an entry hall with wooden floors and a thick, multicolored Persian carpet. A staircase with carved oak banisters leads to the upper floors, and a dining room with a dark wood table stands off to the side. Joanna leads Libby through the dining room to the kitchen, with floor tiles the color of daffodils and wallpaper of lilac and roses.

The kitchen is divided in half, one half for cooking with a stove, sink, and refrigerator, the other for eating, with a little round table of birch or some other blonde wood, and four matching chairs. A pot of flowering violets rests in the center of the table; spider plants and ivies hang above a bay window that looks out over a sunny backyard.

Joanna gestures Libby toward a chair and pulls one out for herself. "Can I get you anything?" Joanna asks.

"No, thank you," Libby replies.

For a moment they relax in their chairs. Both of them watch a big black crow land in the backyard, then fly off again. A pair of squirrels chase each other over top of the fence. Something has to happen next, but neither knows what it is and neither seems in a hurry.

"The plants need watering," Libby observes. "They're thirsty."

The violets are blooming but starting to fade. The ivies look a little wrinkled, and the broad leaves of a peace lily in the dining room are curling up.

"I know," Joanna says. "They're Dad's plants. I might as well let them die." She seems immediately to regret that level of cruelty toward innocent houseplants. "I'm sorry. Dad taught me how to take care of them. I do see that they're thirsty. Every day I say the same thing."

"What's that?"

"Tomorrow. I'll water them tomorrow."

Libby can't help but laugh out loud. "You say that as much as you want," she says. "You can water them when you're good and ready."

Libby plucks the fading petals off the violet at the table, and pokes her finger in the dry crust of soil at the bottom. "I'm sorry," she says, reconsidering. "Do you mind if I water them? They look so sad."

Joanna smiles. "Have at it."

Libby guesses correctly that there will be some kind of watering pot under the sink. She fills it up and makes rounds in the kitchen, starting with a few drops for the violet at the table. "I'm flooding the peace lily," she calls from the dining room. "Then you can forget it for a while." She learned all about plants as a kid; she used to compete with her brothers to grow snap peas in the yard.

Joanna joins her in the dining room, watches her flood the peace lily, and picks up a little ceramic dish made of clay coils. "I made this when I was in third grade," she says. Each coil is glazed a different color, like a rainbow, and it's still pretty after all these years.

She passes it to Libby, who turns it upside down, sees the initials JB scratched in the bottom.

"Look at this," Joanna continues, holding up a coconut carved into a smiling monkey. "We got that on the beach in Belize."

Libby examines it and passes it back. "Nice."

The two of them look around the room together until Joanna pulls a book off a shelf and holds out the front cover so Libby can see that it's her elementary school yearbook. "Check this out," she says, and starts turning pages like she's on a mission. Finally she spreads the book open wide and passes it to Libby. "That's Angel," she says.

On the page is a beautiful picture of kids in a schoolyard. In the background some kids throw a football. In the foreground, a little girl Libby recognizes as Joanna is talking to a small blonde girl. To one side stands Angel, showing off a big maple leaf for the camera. "He kept a collection in class," Joanna says.

"He told me," Libby replies. "But I never saw the yearbook."

"Angel didn't buy a yearbook?" Joanna asks, then lets the question fade away, as if maybe she's said something wrong.

Libby turns some pages in silence, then returns the book to the shelf. "Thank you."

Libby waters the rest of the plants on the ground floor, and returns the watering pot to its place under the sink. She can't help but straighten up decorations and pick up bits of lint as she goes, her habits from Happy Jack's resurfacing in a house like this.

"I'm basically homeschooling," Joanna offers out of nowhere.

"Homeschooling? What's that?"

Joanna explains that she hardly goes into school anymore. She picks up assignments and tests from the teachers, and has a tutor in the neighborhood.

"She went to our school too, but she's in college now. She's home this semester because her mother's sick. Everybody agreed that this would work okay for a while."

"Did you?"

"I don't care. As long as it's a girl. That's all that mattered. The tutor had to be a girl."

Libby sits down across from Joanna and pays attention to nothing but the girl in the room, listens while she describes her new tutor and how much easier school is now that she doesn't have to go to class everyday. "I miss my friends, though. I get lonely sometimes."

She goes back to the dining room and returns with the yearbook. The book opens easily to the same page they were looking at a moment ago: Angel with his maple leaf, and Joanna talking to the blonde girl. "That's Tammy," says Joanna.

"She looks nice."

"She's very nice. She lives nearby too. We used to be best friends."

"What happened?" Libby regrets the question as soon as she asks it. She can guess what happened; she can guess why Joanna started acting strangely and losing friends.

"I went to her father's funeral."

"I heard it was beautiful."

"I cried the whole time."

"That's what Angel said."

Joanna waits a long time before speaking again, seems to be weighing something that maybe she shouldn't say. Finally she goes ahead. "I wanted my father to die," she declares. "I hated him so much I wished he were dead. I lay awake at night, hoping for a heart attack. Or a car accident. Or a terrorist attack. I was very creative, all the ways I imagined for Dad to disappear. Then it happened! A dad died in a car accident." She shakes her head in condemnation. "But it was the wrong dad."

"You wanted him to stop," Libby replies. "That's all you wanted. It's not like you were a walking death wish. It's not like you made Tammy's father die."

Joanna grabs for a tissue from a box nearby. "Everyone at the funeral was so sad. People loved him." She blows her nose loudly and generously.

Libby notices that there are tissue boxes all around the room, so Joanna is never far from one, and she guesses that the house wasn't always like this. She looks out the window and speaks softly, not even looking at Joanna, as if she's talking to nobody in particular. "Your dad's a jerk."

Joanna seems surprised by the attack. "You can't say that," she says. "He's my dad. Lots of people thought he was a nice guy."

"That's why I said it. You can too. He's a jerk and a creep and a liar. You can love him . . . but he's still a jerk."

Joanna stands up and grabs the back of her chair, facing Libby across the table.

"You're not the problem," Libby goes on. "You did nothing wrong. Not by squirming when the stroking started, or pushing back when it got more personal. He's the one who did something wrong. He's the jerk."

Joanna walks out of the kitchen, starts pacing around the dining room, like she needs more space to hold what's inside. Libby hears her step into the living room and turn on the radio. It's playing commercials. She hits a button, but it's commercials again. She turns the radio off and sits by herself at the dining room table.

Libby leaves her awhile, then goes and sits at the other end of the table in silence. "Look!" she says at last, her eyes on the peace lily. "The leaves are perking up."

"I can't do anything right. I can't even kill plants right."

"You love him." Libby's tone is absolute.

"No, I don't." Joanna is angry. A stranger just called her a liar in her own home. "I hate him."

"That too."

"Both?"

"Yes, both. You love him. And you think he's a jerk."

Joanna looks like this possibility has never occurred to her before.

"Both are okay. Normal, I think."

"Everybody is responsible for their own behavior," Joanna declares like a formal lecture, emphasis on the nouns. "*He's* responsible for *his* behavior. That's what everybody says. *He's* responsible for what *he* did . . . not me. Personal responsibility, blah, blah, blah."

"What's wrong with that?"

"But *I* was supposed to make him stop!" Joanna's anger is coming back. "*Me!* Personal responsibility, remember? *I* was supposed to tell someone." She moves up on Libby like she's readying an attack.

Libby doesn't wait. "Did you?" she says.

"Of course I did! I told everybody. I did everything I could to make him stop . . ."

Libby finishes the thought for her. "Nobody would listen."

"I can't do anything right. I couldn't stop him right, I couldn't tell anybody right. I can't even kill plants right." A tissue box is on the windowsill, right where she needs it. She wipes the edge of her nose.

Slowly, Libby closes the distance between them. Gently, like touching a cat that might start, she touches Joanna on the shoulder. She remembers too well the pain and doesn't want to set off an alarm. "You did everything right," she says.

This time Joanna finishes the thought. "He's the jerk."

"And if I had let you, you would have killed his plants."

Joanna looks up with a smile in her eyes and clears her nose with one heroic blow into the tissue, finishing with a glance at her wristwatch. "My mom will be home soon," she says. "And I have homework to do."

"Can I come again?"

"I'd like that. I'd like that a lot."

Chapter Thirty-two

They meet the next day and the next day, take a few days off, and meet again. Libby's boss was willing to let her go on Friday, but he makes clear that two days is too much. "How much longer?" he asks, a white man surrounded by a United Nations of women.

"Not much longer, I hope."

He shakes his head in disgust. "Tomorrow I'll start papering your file. Union or no union, I can't take care of everybody. I've got floors to wax."

Libby takes the risk and gets into a routine, blasting through her morning work and cleaning through lunch. Friends offer to cover her later if something comes up, and she clocks out in the afternoon. Buses run frequently and straight, so she spends some secret time with Joanna, then leaves shortly before Joanna's mother returns and reaches her own home only a little later than usual.

"Shouldn't I meet your mother?" Libby asks. "I mean, shouldn't your mother meet me?"

"Later. Maybe. Eventually." Joanna replies. "Not yet."

The first day they prepare spinach lasagna together. It was Joanna's idea, and they actually prepare two. One Joanna puts in her oven before Libby leaves, to surprise her mom for dinner, and the other Libby takes home carefully on the bus. They can eat it later tonight or save it for tomorrow.

"You do have an oven?" Joanna checks to make sure. She seems to know that Libby and Angel don't have a lot of the things she takes for granted, but she doesn't know the lines—either what they have or what she can ask.

"We have an oven," Libby confirms. "Thanks for checking."

The next day Joanna is worried about her science exam. "Did Angel take a test today?" she asks.

"He didn't mention it. What was it about?"

"Ecosystems."

"Ecosystems? What are they?"

"Zebras eat grass. Lions eat zebras. Stuff like that."

"Was it boring?"

"Some of it was . . . but lots was really interesting. I liked the part about the human food chain. Humans grow grain on one farm and feed it to cattle on another farm . . . then we buy meat in the supermarket and put packaging in the landfill. I never really thought about all the parts."

Some parts Libby understands quite well. She tells stories about her own farm, and how the fertilizer for the soy made the creek bloom green with algae. They spend a whole hour talking about ecosystems. "How did the test go?" she asks in the end.

"It was multiple choice," Joanna replies, as if that answers the question.

The next day Libby's boss renews his warning. "If something goes wrong I'll come looking for you."

"Has anything gone wrong yet?" Libby asks.

He scowls but knows the answer.

After he's gone, Libby puts on her coat and walks out.

When she reaches Joanna's house, Joanna shows her a map. "We're thinking about moving," she says. A map of the United States is unfolded across the table, and a stack of city guidebooks rests in the corner.

"Why would you move?"

"To start again. Someplace new. Someplace where nobody knows me, where my past is secret." She waves her hand aimlessly over the map, points to the books. "City or country?" She asks. "Oceans or mountains? What sounds cool?"

Libby hardly looks at the map. "Do you want to move?"

"Not really. It feels like running away."

"Whose idea was it?"

"My mom's been talking with the Victim's Services Agency. They're trying to help. They want to give me what I want. Before Dad was sentenced, the prosecutor kept offering to give him more time in prison for me. She said that in a case like this, the child-victim pretty much calls the shots."

"What did you say?"

"I didn't want to call any shots. Putting my father in prison didn't make me happy. Putting him in prison *longer* didn't make me any happier. But the idea of him going free didn't make me happy either. Half the time I wanted him dead. Half the time I wanted him to come home and make blueberry pancakes like he used to. I stayed out of it."

"What would make you happy?"

"They asked me that too. I'll give you the same answer I gave them."

"You don't know." Libby guesses immediately.

Joanna smiles back. "One girl prosecutor told me that my father would probably get 'his comeuppance' in prison. She told me that when the other inmates learned his crime, they'd give him what he deserved. That definitely didn't make me happy. The thought of my father getting raped in prison was not therapeutic, if you know what I mean."

"It wouldn't be your fault."

"Yeah, yeah, whatever. I've been through all of that."

"You're not thrilled about moving either," Libby observes.

"The secret wouldn't last. They'd Google the new girl. I'd give up my friends and my mom would give up her job for nothing." She folds the map in half. "Then what? Move again?"

Libby knows her way around the kitchen pretty well by now. She takes two glasses from the cabinet and fills each of them with apple juice from the refrigerator. "It's good that you don't want to give up. Keep the things you like."

"Thanks," says Joanna, taking a sip of the juice. "I'm thinking about dropping out of school."

Libby almost chokes on her own sip of juice. She comes up spluttering with an exclamation. "I thought you weren't giving up."

"It's not giving up. It's starting something new."

"It's starting something that's nothing."

"I could actually learn about ecosystems instead of taking tests."

"You will not drop out of school," declares Libby, losing her temper. "You won't learn about ecosystems. You'll learn how to lie about your age and wait tables for morons."

"But you're not waiting tables."

"I clean toilets at a hospital! I mop floors after people vomit. My boss tracks how much time I spend in the bathroom." She looks around the kitchen, gestures toward the fancy appliances and grand backyard. "Standardized tests are stupid. Dropping out of school is even stupider."

Joanna watches in silence. Gone is the friendly, supportive woman who always approves, and who finds a solution for everything. Libby is an avenging angel who will not take no for an answer. It happens so fast she hardly knows what to do; she just sits there, juice in hand, idea hanging in the air like a dirigible over a firing range.

Libby moves from anger to pleading, actually gets on her knees in front of young Joanna. "Please," she says. "Please. Don't drop out of school. Promise me right now that you won't drop out of school."

"I didn't realize it was that big a deal," Joanna says, as if she can make light of her own silly thought.

Libby stays on the hard tiled floor but gets off her knees and leans back against the kitchen counter. "If I had it all to do over again, that's what I would change. I don't know what I would have done, but I wouldn't have dropped out of school." Her head is down, her eyes on the floor. "I'm pretty good at math, but I already can't help Angel with his math homework. Leaving school is the worst thing I did."

"Why did you quit?"

"I was pregnant." Libby surprises herself with the swift certainty of her answer. She's never said that out loud for someone to hear. Now she just blurts it out like it's obvious.

Libby can see Joanna making connections, a smart young woman with intuition of her own. She sees her putting the pieces together. What they have in common, why Libby came here at all.

Joanna looks Libby in the eyes, down to her tummy, then back to her eyes again. "Angel?" she asks, hardly a whisper.

Libby nods. She wasn't expecting this. She feels herself starting to panic, feels the raw pain—ancient, long buried, but still familiar—surging to the surface. She clamps down on her breathing, struggles for control.

Joanna doesn't let her off. "Your father?"

Libby nods again, then just keeps dropping her head lower and lower. She hooks her elbows over her knees and covers her head with her hands, looks down to the floor, down past the floor. She feels her mind and soul descending through the floor, through the basement, falling to the center of the earth where gravity disappears.

"Oh, my God," Joanna mutters, her eyes open wide. "Oh, my God."

Libby barely hears her, buried as she is by a thousand million tons of earth. She sits on the floor, scarcely breathing, while Joanna whispers, "Oh, my God" over and over again.

Finally Libby looks up. Lifts her head and looks her young friend in the eye.

"Does he know?" Joanna wants to know.

This time the head shakes no.

Joanna looks pale, almost sick. For a moment she heaves as if she might actually be sick, then she too drops out of her chair, lands hard on the tile floor, her back against the counter. Her breath is loud and ragged, like a runner after a race, until she too brings it under control. "I won't tell," she says. "As God is my witness, I will never tell a soul."

Libby looks up from the floor. "I know you won't," she replies. "You're a good girl. Your family is lucky to have you."

They sit together on the floor a good long time. The afternoon is moving toward evening; clouds are moving in. If Libby were cooking, she'd want to turn the lights on.

She stands up and reaches down to give Joanna a hand, helps her to her feet. "You know my worst," she says. "Now it's your turn."

"My turn? What do you mean?"

"What's the worst he did? What's your biggest fear or biggest regret?" They're standing together in the kitchen, still holding hands, facing each other like they're dancing. "Your father didn't do to you what mine did to me. He might have, eventually, but he didn't. You stopped him. I don't know how . . . but you did it. You." She wants Joanna to take credit for herself.

The sky is starting to glow with sunset, ruby red streaming through the clouds. A flock of sparrows descends upon the lawn.

"What's your nightmare when you're lying in bed at night? What comes back to you?"

Joanna steps to the window, turns her back on Libby, looks at the sunset like a tourist admiring the view. She makes some comments about the sparrows that Libby can't quite hear and doesn't bother to ask about. When the sparrows suddenly fly off as a unit, Joanna turns back to face Libby, her eyes full of certainty.

"My bed," she says. "That's the answer. My bed."

"He always used your bed," Libby replies. Her father always brought her to his own.

"My bed squeaks," says Joanna. "It has a special, squeaky squeak. I hear it every time I sit down. Sometimes when I roll over."

Libby knows what Joanna's talking about. She imagines this poor little girl teased at school, rushing home, retreating into her bed . . . and hearing the squeak. Imagines her tossing around, beating her pillow . . . and hearing the squeak.

Joanna goes on. "When I was little, I used to jump up and down on my bed, like a trampoline. My mom would yell at me."

"And it squeaked. It still squeaks." Libby knows where she's coming from.

"Some nights I give up and sleep on the floor." She wipes a tear from the corner of her eye. "I can't stand the squeak."

"Let's get you a new bed. You can pick one you like."

"My mom will buy it for me. She'll love to take me shopping. New sheets, new blankets! A bed that doesn't squeak."

"You can paint your room. It's cheap and you can do it yourself. Pick a color."

"That's easier than moving." Joanna gets it now. She's gaining momentum like a sled going down a hill. "I've outgrown my old posters. Time for new ones."

"Great idea!"

"I'll put up curtains. I'll make a whole new room."

"What should we do? Should we talk to your mother?"

"Yes," says Joanna, less like a discovery than a conclusion. "That's the answer. I don't need to move. I don't need to drop out of school. All I need is a bed. A new bed."

Libby grabs both her hands, looks her full in the face. "Do you want to talk to your mother alone, or do you want me to come with you?"

Joanna starts to reply, then she cuts herself off. Finally she declares her answer. "I can do it." She looks stronger now than she has in days, far stronger than she did when she was waving her hand over the map. "I can do it myself."

When Angel gets home, his mother is crying. She's remembering her own father, the time she spent in his bed, which also had a squeak; she remembers jumping on that squeaky bed as a little girl until she, too, got in trouble.

She was just a little girl! She was so little when she ran away. She was hardly older than Joanna when her father first penetrated her. She was younger than Monet when she pulled newborn Angel from the trash can and left school forever.

Libby never got help like she just gave little Joanna. She never figured out how to convince her mother or confront her father. She still hasn't. She doesn't even know if they're still alive.

And her secret. She'd never told anybody her secret. Angel's secret. Exposure hurts like a fresh-cut wound.

It's not that she doesn't trust Joanna to not tell. She trusts her absolutely.

But she doesn't trust herself. She doesn't know if she's making the right decisions. Doesn't her son have a right to know about his father? Is it not time to come clean? But how? How can she tell Angel the truth after all these years? How can she explain that it took so long?

Will he hate her for lying? Will he forgive her for denying him his truth?

And what about her own mother? Doesn't her mother have a right to know about her daughter—who ran out on her those endless years ago?

Libby just found a way to help Joanna and her mother heal together. Shouldn't she do that for herself? But maybe not. Maybe she's doing just fine, thank you. Maybe she should stay as she is, steady as she goes . . .

Who can advise her? Who can she ask? Who can help her the way she just helped little Joanna? She flops face down on her own bed. What would they say?

That's the moment when Angel walks in, later than expected. "I stopped at Mr. Marquette's on the way home," he announces. "I have a five-dollar bill."

Libby has enough time to straighten herself out and sit up in bed, but it's clear that Angel sees something is wrong.

He drops his backpack and races to her side. "What is it, Mom? What's the matter?"

She walks to the bathroom, unrolls some toilet paper and blows her nose. She's still wondering what to say when Angel solves it for her.

"It's Tammy's dad, isn't it?"

It takes a long time for Libby even to figure out what he's talking about.

"It's okay to cry, Mom. The school guidance counselor says it's okay to let it all out. She also says that sometimes it takes a long time to hit. But we should let it out when it comes."

The soap-opera advice from the school guidance counselor doesn't help, but the spirit in which it's offered is worth the world. Libby drops to a knee and spreads her arms wide. Angel dashes in for a giant hug, and they stay together for a long, long time.

At last Angel steps out of the hug. "We had a lot in common, you know," he says.

"You and Tammy?" She's stalling for time.

"Yes. Me and Tammy. Her dad died in a car accident. My dad died in a car accident."

Libby hardly even knows what he's talking about, but she holds herself still while she puts the pieces together, reconstructs her lifelong lie.

"It's okay, Mom," he says consolingly. "Tammy says her dad had a good life, and his time had simply come. She likes to visit his grave. It makes her feel better."

Libby gets back to her feet, and sits down gently on the edge of the bed.

"We can do that too, Mom." Now Angel's on a sled sliding downhill. "We can visit Dad. I'm sure you know where he's buried. Let's do it, Mom. Let's go visit my father. Maybe this weekend. I have five dollars I wasn't expecting."

Angel wants only to help. Libby can see on his face how hopefully he's offering a solution. She can see how disappointed he is as she dives back into her pillow. She can contemplate—or at least wonder about—her mother. But her father is a different matter altogether. One thing she knows for sure. Whether he's dead or alive, she's not visiting Angel's father this weekend.

Not yet, anyway.

Part Four

Punch and Rise

Chapter Thirty-three

Joanna gets a new bed and spends a weekend painting her room with her mother. She's started a long, painful piece of therapy, but the trends are uphill and she's feeling better. She joins Libby's family for dinner regularly—open invitation, no notice needed—until Angel is no longer embarrassed by their simple meals and rudimentary setting.

Now when Joanna lies in bed she feels like she's in a whole new place. Indeed, she tells Libby, the new bed has a few squeaks of its own, but now she likes them; the old squeaks took her someplace she didn't want to go, and different squeaks remind her she's not there anymore. The therapist wants Joanna to heal herself and stop blaming herself for her father's wrongs—but with Libby, Joanna prefers to talk about her mother. Forgiving her father seems easier in comparison; to Joanna this seems strange, but it makes perfect sense to Libby.

Monet is admitted to Howard University with a scholarship that pays half her tuition. She's rejected outright from Harvard and put on the waiting list for UVA, leaving her with a decision that couldn't be easier (HBCU: her favorite new acronym; FAFSA: the opposite).

The Lord works in strange and wondrous ways, and CURE had scheduled a trip to Fluvanna for what turns out to be the Saturday after Monet's acceptance letter arrives. Monet travels to Fluvanna to tell her mom in person, and they spend literally every minute of the visiting session holding hands under the Plexiglas.

Zeb's legal challenges are moving forward. His direct appeals were denied, but he's hopeful about collateral attacks for ineffective assistance of counsel. Attorney Simpson Mellor, who disappeared all those years ago, resurfaced when he got caught practicing law without a license in Tennessee. It's not technically relevant for Sheila and Zeb, but it sure doesn't hurt.

Libby also succeeded at some things she'd long wanted to do, including some legal work of her own. The Legal Service Society of Northern Virginia helped resolve both her and Angel's lingering problems of paperwork and identity. Now, after all these years, they finally have impeccable documentation of who they are and how they belong.

She also buys a telephone for the apartment. "In case Monet needs to reach me," she explains to Angel. "Besides, I'm a grown-up by now. I ought to have a telephone." They set it up, and it proves convenient almost immediately. A few weeks later, Angel comes home to find Libby all but hugging the new phone book that came cost-free with the service. "Look!" she says, pointing to her name in the directory. "I'm somebody now!"

Now it's Angel's first day of high school. It's early September, but the temperature is near eighty degrees already and it will hit the nineties by afternoon. Angel is wearing the bright blue T-shirt his mom bought special for his first day, and carrying a backpack filled with supplies that the school district itemized in advance.

This year Angel uses a different bus stop, but he knows exactly where it is and how long it takes to walk there from the apartment. He's practiced it many times since he received the schedule in the mail, and learned the nearby stops in case they're handy. Today he leaves plenty early so he'll have lots of time and also because his bus schedule dovetails neatly with Libby's schedule for work. Leaving together at 7:15 in the morning puts Angel at his bus stop by 7:25 and Libby on the hospital bus to start her shift at 8:00.

"So long, honey," Libby says, giving him a little peck on the cheek, a hint of moisture in her eyes. "You're a big boy now."

"Aww, Mom," Angel replies. "I'm the same size I was yesterday." He tugs on his T-shirt to prove it.

"Good luck," she says, wiping that little tear. "Have a great day. And send my love to Joanna."

Off they walk in opposite directions. At the end of the block, Angel looks once over his shoulder and sees his mom standing motionless on the sidewalk, gazing back at him like he's a sailor disappearing over the horizon. He gives her a wave and she waves back, then he turns the corner to be on his way.

A flash in the grass catches his attention. He leans down and sees it right away. A penny. A lucky penny, heads-side up.

Find a penny, pick it up, and all day long you'll have good luck. The childhood rhyme runs through his mind as he picks it up, polishes it bright, and has an idea. He calculates quickly, decides he has time, and breaks into a run, carrying his backpack in his arms like a football.

The playground comes into view at the end of the next block, already bustling with nannies, moms, and toddlers. Taking care not to attract attention, he sets the penny on the sidewalk, then hurries back to his bus stop. Now a younger child will find the penny, heads-side up, shining bright in the morning sun. Why keep all the good luck for himself?

Three middle schools converge to create Centreville High School, Angel's new home. The school bus arrives on schedule and has plenty of empty seats. Angel recognizes several kids from the neighborhood, but most faces are new, and the space where he used to sit is already taken. He finds an empty seat and looks out the window on his new route to his new school. Some kids sit quietly like him, but the bus is alive with excitement.

The parking lot is crowded by the time they arrive. Teachers greet students as they step down from the bus, and Angel can see them answering questions and giving directions. Amidst the swirl, a few familiar faces appear. He sees Mitchie Daniels struggling with a giant backpack and a tote bag that appears to be filled with books. He sees Parker Carlson and a bigger boy, probably his older brother, smack a notebook out of a smaller kid's hand.

At sidewalk level it's harder to scan the crowd, and Angel still hasn't spotted the person he wants to see most of all, Molly Swann. How was her summer? Did she travel or play tennis? Are they in the same homeroom? Angel is in 2203. Is she? He wants to know, he wants to know.

He wants to know so badly he wrote questions out in advance. The paper is folded up in his pocket. For days he's been looking forward to slipping it to her, hopefully while sitting together in homeroom like they used to. Today he'll find out.

Angel slips into a current heading toward the main building, jostled and jostling like everyone else. Ahead of him a girl with curly red hair is carrying a tennis racket in one hand and pulling a backpack on wheels with the other. Atop the backpack is balanced some kind of instrument case, maybe a French horn, and atop the instrument case perches another smaller case, probably a lunch box. The girl pulls it all slowly, minding the precarious balance on the bumpy pavement. As Angel walks past, the tower catches a wheel and starts to tip.

She feels it go and turns around in alarm; she can't possibly get there in time.

Angel catches the case on the pinnacle before it all goes over, and uses both hands and a knee to lever the whole assembly upright, keeping all the parts in order.

"Thanks," says the girl, as she helps to stabilize it all. "You saved my life."

"Do you need a hand?"

"I'm okay now," she says with a smile. She takes the lunch box off the top and holds it in her other hand with the tennis racket. "There."

"That's much better," Angel agrees. "Have a good day." They seem to be heading in different directions anyway.

On the first day of school, the whole freshman class meets in the auditorium. Angel sits near the back so he can watch the crowd while he mostly tunes out the principal's greeting. "Welcome," says the principal. "Work hard. Learn something new. Have fun; but not too much." That last line got some laughs. Most kids look excited, like it's a giant family reunion. Some kids look like they'd rather be dead and buried than back here at school.

Angel knows that his middle school is the smallest of the three, but he's impressed by how few of the faces look familiar. Far fewer than a third, it seems, and Molly Swann is nowhere to be seen. He doesn't notice her as he watches faces filing past, and he doesn't see her when he scans the audience systematically, left to right, front to back. He sees Parker Carlson again, and Veronica West, still one of the few African-American children, and conspicuously tall among the freshman. He sees Nick Adams and Alan Carrie, Emily Hudson, and Paulie Soltz. But he doesn't see Molly Swann.

After the assembly comes an ordinary day. The first class of the day is homeroom, though in high school, homeroom isn't a separate class of its own. The first class simply counts as homeroom and is scheduled ten minutes longer for attendance, announcements, and administration. Today the assembly has used up half the homeroom time, but afterward, everyone proceeds to their homerooms to start the day.

Angel's homeroom class is social studies in room 2203 with Mr. Dirksen. Angel knows where 2203 is located—he researched that in advance—but he doesn't know who else will be in it. Walking corridors lined with lockers, he sees more familiar faces but he still doesn't see Molly Swann. He sees Veronica West towering above the crowds. He sees Tammy Atford talking to a girl he doesn't know, and he sees Parker Carlson cut in line at the water fountain.

Molly isn't in 2203. The only familiar faces are two kids he barely knew at Sidney Lanier, who huddle together in a corner. To add insult to injury, Mr. Dirksen seats them in alphabetical order. "Only until I learn your names," he says. "Then you can sit wherever you want."

Angel Thompson finds himself between Oliver Swain and Kyle Winston, who know each other and busily chat straight past the new boy between them.

After the bell rings, Parker Carlson enters the room, disrupting class and highlighting the injustice. That's not a trade Angel would have made: Parker for Molly, Molly for Parker.

Parker doesn't even get in trouble for being late. He just gets pointed to his empty seat.

Mr. Dirksen greets them, tells them to be quiet, takes their attendance, and describes their social studies curriculum.

The curriculum sounds interesting enough—American history from the Constitution to World War II—but all Angel thinks about is that school is already an hour old and he hasn't even seen Molly Swann. He waits all through class, hoping for better luck in the next one, his folded note burning a hole in his pocket.

Angel and Molly haven't communicated since the last day of school last spring. *Have a great summer,* he wrote on a scrap of paper pulled from a recycling bin.

See you next year. She passed it back with a smile. It didn't occur to either of them to write, call, or try to get together over the summer.

During their middle-school years, their whole friendship centered around the writing of notes. Talking wasn't forbidden, but it was seldom used—just notes. Long and thoughtful or quick and snippy, the notes kept them constantly in each other's thoughts. A week out of school, he realized he missed her and started to write a note. Soon enough it grew into a summer's worth of forgotten thoughts, lost correspondence, and important questions, now a tidy packet of paper in his pocket.

Molly isn't in his next class, English. The teacher, Ms. Iacobucci, says they'll read *Romeo and Juliet* and *To Kill a Mockingbird*. "We'll watch the movies, too," she adds.

Molly isn't in art either, which would be a good class for passing notes. Parker Carlson is, however. He starts to throw someone's paper mâché mask into the trash can, but Ms. Boswinkle stops him and orders him to sit.

His next class is biology, the last before lunch. Molly isn't in this class, and he still hasn't seen her in the hallway. Mr. Trimble discusses dissecting frogs, which sounds exciting, but the hour takes a long time anyway.

Lunch is more of the same, only worse. The cafeteria is crowded with strangers and still no Molly Swann. Most kids stand in line to buy food, but Angel brought his own lunch in a plastic grocery bag from the supermarket.

All of a sudden, there she is. Not only in view, but standing up waving to him. Molly Swann in a bright red tank top and brand new blue jeans. Molly Swann with her long dark hair, her face tanned with summer sun. *Over here,* she says with her arms, catching his eye and pointing to an empty seat.

The table is filled with old friends. Tammy Atford opens her arms for a hug. Joanna Baye with a new haircut, very short and very cute, shakes his hand like a business partner and pulls out the empty seat between her and Molly. "Please," she says. "How's your mom?"

Molly is mid-sentence with Tammy Atford, so he goes ahead and answers Joanna. "She's great. How has your summer been?"

They chat until Joanna is distracted by a newcomer and Tammy makes a trip to the trash can. Molly turns to Angel and looks him straight in the eye, with attention for nobody but him.

Angel isn't sure what to say. "Hi," he manages. "How was your summer?" He interrupts himself. "Wait a minute." He digs through his pocket for the papers he prepared in advance. All of his questions, everything he wants to know.

But he's not alone! Even as he digs for his notes, Molly reaches into her little golden pocketbook. They both emerge at the same time with a folded-up sheet of paper, look at each other, and start to laugh. No words are spoken, but they share a vivid, joyful meeting of the minds, trade notes from the summer, and start to read.

Molly points to Angel's first two questions. "Yes," she says out loud, "Yes and yes. I went to tennis camp and I travelled too. My father had a surprise meeting in Paris. We all went to Paris for a week."

"That's great," Angel starts to say, still unsure about talking, when a large boy who looks familiar steps between them.

"*Est-ce que quelqu'un parle de Paris?*" he says.

Tammy all but leaps across the table to give him a hug. "Wally!" she cries.

Joanna, too, leaps to her feet, though she's across the table so she settles for more of a high-five than a hug.

Now Angel recognizes Wally Roscoe, Parker Carlson's friend who moved to Brussels a few years back. His blue T-shirt says *Brugge*, with a rectangle of black, gold, and red that Angel guesses must be the Belgian flag. Wally is tall with light brown hair cut short, like in the old days of his Redskins T-shirts.

Tammy takes control. To Wally she says, "My mom said you'd be back before school, but we haven't seen you yet."

To Molly she says, "This is Walter Roscoe. He lives around the corner." Collecting Joanna in the sweep of her arm, she continues: "All three of us went to preschool together. We've known each other practically our whole lives."

To Wally, she says, "I trust you remember, this is Angel."

"The Candyman," Wally replies. "Two for a quarter."

Finally she points to Molly. "This is Molly. She moved here from New York while you were away."

"*Enchanté, mademoiselle,*" he bows before her and kisses her hand, lingering a little longer than Angel would like, and even Molly seems to blush. "*Je suis enchanté.*"

But she collects herself and continues to hold his hand as he straightens up. "*Moi aussi,*" she replies.

"*Tu parles Francais?*" he exclaims.

"*Un petit peu,*" she replies. "A little bit. A tiny little bit."

"That's good because I'm sick to death of it," he says. "I'm glad to be home."

"Your French is pretty good."

"Not bad. It's getting there," he replies. "Check this out."

Next comes a monologue in a strange guttural language that sounds a little like French but mostly like something is stuck in his throat. "That's Flemish," he says at last. "The first language of Belgium."

"Is Flemish spelled like 'phlegm,' with a *P-H*?" Joanna asks with a wry grin and a bite of her sandwich.

Soon they're all talking and eating and acting like friends. Angel still holds Molly's note in his hand, though he sees her fold his into her pocketbook. When they're mostly done eating, Wally reaches across the table and taps Joanna on the shoulder with what seems like long familiarity and a playful grin.

"Tag," he says. "You're it." He stands up and hurries out of the room.

"Let's go!" Joanna cries, and a moment later they've all cleared the table and run out into the courtyard, chasing each other and tagging each other with outstretched arms.

Angel starts high school with a game he managed never to play in first grade, and it's fun.

Chapter Thirty-four

After lunch come two more boring classes, neither with Molly, though after tag he doesn't miss her so much. Finally the last class of the day is math—Algebra Two this year—and he and Molly reach the door at the same time as if it's destiny.

They sit down together, and Angel digs for the note she left him. She'd written questions about what he did over the summer, and he wrote answers during the boring classes after lunch.

It's just like the old days, only better. They sit down together and, as he pulls out his written replies, he sees that she has written replies of her own. As other kids file in and find seats, they swap notes and start to read.

"You built a porch?" Molly responds out loud to Angel's answer to her first question.

"I built a porch," he replies comfortably, as if talking is normal. "An old man in the neighborhood named Austin Marquette needed a ramp to his house and a place to park his wheelchair. He hired me to help."

"How did you know what to do?"

"Austin knew. He drew the plans and took me shopping with him to buy supplies. He told me everything and helped a lot, even though his legs aren't working so well these days. We did electricity, too. The porch has lights!"

"That's amazing. I didn't know regular people could build porches. I thought builders built porches."

Angel points to the opening line of her note. "You went to Paris?"

"I climbed the Eiffel Tower."

"Now *that's* amazing."

"Mom lost her sunglasses looking over the edge," she says with a smile.

Angel doesn't share her smile. "Did anybody get hurt?" he asks. "Underneath, I mean."

"Nobody screamed," she says. "At least we didn't hear it. We made a joke of it. Mom was pretty upset, though."

"Did she need new glasses?"

"We went out for Nutella crepes," Molly replies, without slowing to answer. "In Paris, there's nothing a Nutella crepe can't fix."

"Nutella crepe?"

So Molly tells him about Nutella, and how to make a crepe. "The Mona Lisa was crowded, though. Not worth the trip."

"Nutella is better?" Angel understands the idea.

"Much better. Now about that porch."

On and on they chat, as easy as losing your sunglasses, helped along by the notes in their hands. Angel learns about different kinds of crepes and the pyramid in front of the Louvre. He tells her how his mom took a second job at night to pay for Monet's college. "She's a junior now. Someday she wants to be a lawyer like your dad."

Angel talks a lot, but he doesn't tell her everything. He doesn't tell her that Monet wants to become the defense attorney her own parents never had. He doesn't tell her the stories that Austin told him while they worked together on the porch, or that Austin met his lifelong sweetheart in tenth grade. He courted her through high school but got sent to Korea when he turned nineteen. ("Did you know we had a war with Korea?" Austin had said. "Tucked between World War II and Vietnam, we had a whole war that most people forgot.")

They got married after Korea and had forty wonderful years together until the cancer took her away four years ago. Austin took care of her until her final weeks, right in their very own home. Austin helped her manage even as his own legs started to fail.

"I have just one piece of advice for you, young man," Austin had said. "When you meet your sweetheart, don't waste a minute of it."

Molly and Angel talk a long time, while up front the teacher is in serious discussion with Mitch Daniels. Even after the bell rings, she looks up to the class. "We'll start in a minute," Ms. Ellis says. She's young, with short blonde hair and a lavender blouse. "Keep sitting nicely. We're almost done."

"What did you do with your money from the porch?" Molly asks.

"Half for Monet and half for my mom to help around the house," he says. "She works so hard . . . "

"Nothing for you?"

"My mom took me out for ice cream. We had sundaes at Ben and Jerry's. With cherries on top."

"That's my favorite."

Angel is about to do it. He inhales as he chooses his words carefully, finally about to ask her out on that date—sundaes, no doubt—but at exactly that moment, Ms. Ellis calls the class to order.

"Okay, quiet everybody," she says. "Thank you for your patience."

The moment disappears. Molly starts folding his note and opening her pocketbook. Angel follows one heartbeat later, folding her note and fitting it back in his pocket. Ben and Jerry return unopened to the freezer.

"What's three divided by two?" Ms. Ellis asks.

Nobody answers. People are still settling into their seats and opening their notebooks.

"Come on. This is the intensified math track. What's three divided by two?"

Mitchie Daniels takes the bait. "One point five?" he says, with a hint of uncertainty, like he knows it's a trap.

"Nope," says Ms. Ellis, snapping it shut. "The answer is sixteen. Three divided by two is sixteen." She smiles as she says it, and the class knows it's a joke even if they don't know the punch line, with smiles all around and a handful of audible chuckles.

Mitchie is most betrayed. "Sixteen?" he asks aloud.

"Yes, sixteen," she says as she writes the number three on the blackboard. "Three middle schools came together to form this school." She points to the three. "Between the three schools, there were thirty-four students in intensified math. Budgets are tight and they tried to put all thirty-four into one classroom.

"But thirty-four students is too big for one class—especially intensified math. I and some other teachers fought hard to divide thirty-four into two, and we won! They broke you into two classes of sixteen students each."

"That's seventeen," says Mitchie, still sounding burned.

Ms. Ellis nods in Tammy's direction. "Her mom helped it happen. She was the hero of the PTA. Please thank her for me."

Nodding to Mitchie she finishes, "We lost two during the process."

Mitchie is glowing at catching the mistake, but Tammy looks into her notebook like she's embarrassed.

"Now for the fun part," Ms. Ellis continues. "Sixteen is plenty small, so we get to make it interesting. More teamwork and more problem solving. But first, let's get to know each other. Tell us your name and something interesting about yourself."

She pauses for an instant to see that nobody raises a hand, then she points to a dark-skinned boy in the middle of the room. "Tell us your name, please, and something we need to know."

"My name is Faisal Rahman," he replies. "I'm from Iran. We speak Persian at home."

"Terrific!" exclaims Ms. Ellis. "Nicely done."

The boy next to Faisal speaks up. "I'm Saad Kamal. I was born in America, so I'm technically American. My mom shops at the same Hallal grocery as Faisal's."

"Thanks again," says Ms. Ellis. She looks at Mitchie Daniels.

"I'm Mitch Daniels and I like to play chess," he says.

Molly says, "I'm Molly Swann and I like raspberry sorbet."

Angel can guess why she's thinking about ice cream.

The next girl says her mother and father each have two children from previous marriages, plus two children of their own. "That makes six children altogether, and our first initials together spell 'BAGELS.'"

"And what's your name?"

"Oh, I'm Sophia. I'm the *S* and I can pluralize anything." Angel had known Sophia's name for years but he didn't know about the rest of her family.

Next Ms. Ellis looks at Angel. He wasn't sure what to say and thought maybe he'd mention the porch, so he surprises even himself with his introduction. "I'm Angel Thompson," he says. "I don't have a father."

For an instant the room is silent. Somewhere in the building, a door slams.

Into the space a Chinese girl across the room declares, "I'm Maia Ruth and I have two fathers. You can have one of mine."

A gentle laugh replaces the awkward silence, though Maia Ruth isn't finished. "But sometimes I wish I had a mother."

"There are lots of ways to organize a family," Ms. Ellis says, and they keep going around the room.

Even with the late start and long introductions, they finish three minutes before the bell rings. "What's three divided by two?" Ms. Ellis asks.

"Sixteen!" Mitch Daniels declares.

"Nope," says Ms. Ellis. "This time it's zero. Three minutes early and you can go now. See you tomorrow."

Molly and Angel walk out together and don't separate until they reach the bus.

Chapter Thirty-five

Mitchie Daniels keeps a poster of Albert Einstein in his locker. Wisps of hair, a goofy smile, tongue sticking out. You can't tell from the picture that he unlocked the mysteries of space and time.

It's before school on the last day of the first week. People are loading their lockers and organizing themselves for class. Parker Carlson walks past Mitchie while his locker is open, and rips Einstein down.

A line of kids forms at the water fountain. Parker Carlson cuts to the front and helps himself to a drink.

All that was before homeroom. Once he gets to homeroom, Parker grabs a pen from a boy Angel has never met before, Tim Haack from a new school. "I need it for a minute," Parker says while burrowing through his backpack. He finds a form and leans on the desk of another boy, who tries to ignore him while he fills it out. Then he gives the form to Mr. Dirksen and tosses the pen back at Tim Haack's desk, where it skids across the top and falls to the floor.

Angel considers what he should do. But it's on the other side of the room and none of his business. He decides to ignore it.

Mr. Dirksen takes their attendance in the homeroom part of class, then moves into the semester's social studies curriculum. It's interesting enough, and now, knowing when he won't see Molly and when he will, Angel can actually pay attention.

They've studied this period of history before—all of the Founding Fathers stuff—but Mr. Dirksen introduces tidbits they haven't heard before. "The state of Pennsylvania is misspelled in the Constitution," he says. His mom will find that interesting.

Ms. Iacobucci's English class is interesting, too. She gives them one paragraph to read and think about by themselves, then they spend the whole class finding ideas in it. But art class is more than boring. They spend the entire time talking about safety and reasons not to drink the paint.

After the third warning, Parker Carlson exclaims "Yuck!" from the back of the room. All eyes turn to see Parker's lips and chin the same bright blue as the paint they've been exhaustively warned not to drink. "It tastes like motor oil."

In biology they're instructed to do a PowerPoint on weather. *Time to find the computer lab,* Angel says to himself. Lots of kids have their own laptops.

But lunchtime is worth waiting for. There's his group of friends at the table ahead of him, chatting away. As Angel approaches, Wally Roscoe joins them from the cafeteria line and sits at the far end by Joanna. Molly is one seat from the end closest to Angel, and the corner chair is actually empty.

She gestures for him to sit as if she's been waiting for him. Before he's seated she passes him a note. It's folded tightly and compressed like she's been clutching it in her hand.

Do you know Adam Zepp? it says.

Angel knows the answer right away but he takes time to think while he sits down, then he passes back the note unmarked. "No. Why?" he says out loud. He senses it's important.

Molly reaches for a pen to amend the note and looks suddenly embarrassed, then Tammy comes up between them. "My mom made banana bread last night," Tammy says. "Actually, we made it together."

Molly shoves the note into her pocketbook before Tammy notices it. "I love banana bread," Molly says.

"We used loads of bananas, and brown sugar instead of white. And lemon juice! That was a surprise in this recipe." Tammy's been unloading her backpack the entire time, and now the banana bread makes it out to the table. "Come and get it!"

Everyone knows what to do. In the time before the bell rings, they devour the banana bread, finish their lunches, and argue about whether banana bread is better with walnuts (Tammy's position) or chocolate chips (her mom's). Then they play a wild game of tag in the courtyard.

"Nice move!" Joanna exclaims as Angel dodges a high-speed lunge, but her momentum is in Tammy's direction, and a second later she tags her instead. The game is fun again, and Angel proves to be quick and slippery—but he never learns about Adam Zepp.

Yesterday the two classes between lunch and math took long enough, but today they take an eternity. The economics teacher draws analogies between the federal budget and household spending, and the health teacher is so diplomatically vague, Angel can hardly tell what she's talking about. Angel barely pretends to pay attention. His mind is on one thing alone.

Standing by the door in math class, Angel passes Molly the note he prepared in advance. *Adam Zepp. Why?*

She looks embarrassed and gestures him toward a pair of empty seats. Soon enough they're together at the desk, Molly poised with pen in hand, ready to write.

"Let's get started," Ms. Ellis announces. "It's a busy day today."

Molly folds the note up tight and jams it into her pocketbook.

Ms. Ellis tells all the students to stand, and reassigns them to different desks in an activity that treats students as variables and changes their values by literally moving them around the room. The exercise is lively and fun, and Ms. Ellis's jokes actually make people laugh—but Angel isn't paying attention as he should, and everyone gets a laugh when boys are assigned to be X's and girls are assigned to be Y's, and Angel stands when the X's are told to sit.

But it's no accident that he's standing by the door when the bell rings. He's positioned himself so Molly will need to walk past him on her way out. It's a smart plan, but Ms. Ellis runs a minute late; the buses are already lining up in the parking lot, and students are accumulating on the sidewalk.

Even as Molly steps in his direction, Tammy grabs her arm and pulls her straight outside. "Come on! We'll be late!"

Molly follows Tammy as quickly as she can, but not so fast that she can't put a piece of paper into Angel's hand. It's the same *Why?* note he'd passed her earlier, with writing on the opposite side. Sometime during class she'd found a way to answer.

He asked me out.

Chapter Thirty-six

Angel is horrified.

For years he's daydreamed about asking Molly out and, since he built the porch with Austin, he's been plotting how to do it.

A simple question would be best, he's decided. No fanfare and no romance; he'll just ask her out like you'd ask the time of day or the likelihood of rain. No big deal. Just ask. He's been waiting for the right time, of course; but between lunch, tag, and talking, he figured it wouldn't take very long.

He didn't realize it was a race. He never realized he was on deadline.

Now here he is, just days into school, more comfortable with Molly than he's been in years—and suddenly the door is closed. He's on the outside; Adam Zepp is alone in the lead.

Angel packs his bag for the evening and he's about to board the bus when he realizes he's making a terrible mistake. Molly asked him a question: she wants to know about Adam Zepp. He owes her an answer. It's not too late to find out.

Back he turns away from the bus, back into school and in toward the library. He has hardly any homework so early in the year, and he can take the late bus home. He needs to learn how to use the school computers and create a new student account anyway.

A minute later, he's talking to the librarian. Five minutes more and he's creating his log-in. Ten minutes after that, he's sitting at the computer looking at pictures of Adam Zepp on the screen. Adam Zepp is tall and handsome, with brown hair and an athlete's body.

Adam Zepp gets plenty of attention around the school. From the school newspaper to the school Facebook page, there's no shortage of information.

He didn't come from their middle school.

He's a junior, not a freshman. There's no reason he and Angel would know each other.

Zepp's only a junior, but he plays striker on the varsity soccer team.

He plays soccer year-round, but he sidelights on the track team. Last year he set a record in the hundred-meter dash.

He was only a sophomore at the time.

He says he'll break his own record next spring and set a new one. "It was too easy," he said of a mark that lasted fifteen years. "I need to set a higher bar for the future."

But Adam Zepp is more than just a jock. Last year he was a semi-finalist in the science fair. His project was on imparting spin onto a soccer ball.

He won an award for raising the most money for kids with leukemia.

People call him "A to Zepp."

Click after click, link after link, the headlines accumulate. Angel's ignorance turns into jealousy turns into awe.

Angel can't compete with this. Adam Zepp is out of his league.

But finally, by the time he's finished his research and packed his bag for home, he realizes he doesn't have to.

Adam Zepp isn't Molly's type. Angel has known Molly for years. He's watched her every move and pondered every syllable of every note (and requested clarification when needed).

Adam Zepp may have fallen for her at first sight (Angel understands that), but that doesn't mean it will work. Yes, he's a hotshot; yes, he's a star on varsity before he's even a senior. Molly may say "Wow!" at first, but she'll come around.

Molly's too modest, and Adam produces too many headlines. He's too fabulous and she's too pure. It's not a fit. Angel sees that now. He just needs to be patient.

"That smells great!" Angel says to his mother as he enters the apartment. It doesn't smell merely yummy, as it often does when Libby beats him home and starts to cook—tonight it's fabulous. "What's going on?"

"It's just spaghetti," Libby replies. "I'm making sauce from tomatoes."

Angel told Molly that his mother had taken a second job to help pay Monet's college fees. He didn't mention that it was at a restaurant, *Ristorante Firenze*. She's still just cleaning—overnight, in this case, after the hospital during the day—but her boss is more flexible at least. Moses Pizzigati is the restaurant owner and she works directly for him. Libby estimates him as roughly sixty years old, unmarried and child-free, and she says he runs his business like clockwork. Moses knows the difference between truly clean and just clean enough, and he expects Libby to make it truly clean.

Libby earned his confidence during a trial period over the summer, and now he trusts her to work unsupervised all night. He doesn't care what time she starts or finishes, which part she cleans first or last, or if she takes a minute to rest or use the bathroom—as long as it's done in time, and done well.

That she does.

Moses also pays her fairly and, working in a restaurant, she has access to leftovers, day-olds, and produce that's starting to turn. Since taking this job two years ago, Libby's family isn't only earning more money, they're also eating better and spending less on food.

Yesterday a whole box of tomatoes was starting to go bad. Moses yelled at the chef for not noticing it and using them earlier; he yelled at the prep cook who manages stock for not rotating the new tomatoes to the back and the old ones to the front; then he visibly, conspicuously carried the box to the dumpster.

The tomatoes weren't that bad, though, Libby thought. Everything Moses said was true, but probably not as true as Moses made it sound.

After everyone left, Libby took the tomatoes home.

She already had onions and garlic in the pantry, along with an impressive collection of herbs and spices. She saves fresh herbs from the restaurant when they aren't fresh anymore, dries them out at home and places them in jars in neat little rows, like she lined up seed jars as a little girl back home on the farm.

Today Libby finished early and clocked out from the hospital as a bus was pulling in. Her speed plus Angel's decision to stay late has the house smelling as good as the kitchen of the Firenze by the time Angel arrives.

"Wow," he says again. "It smells great."

He tells her about his day as he unpacks and helps serve dinner, focusing on his social studies class and skipping Molly in every way. "They misspelled Pennsylvania in the Constitution," he explains while sipping a spoonful of sauce as if it were soup. "At the signatures at the end. Every delegate from every state signed their name under their state. The delegates from Pennsylvania signed under the word *Pensylania* with only one *N*."

"That's funny," she agrees. "Who were they?"

"We didn't talk about that."

"There's a brand of disinfectant we use at the hospital," she continues. "The warning label says it's 'hazardous to humings and animals.' Are you a huming? Do you know any humings? I hope there aren't any humings at the hospital, because we use it all the time."

They laugh about warning labels over dinner, and finally when the dishes are put away (plenty of sauce left over for tomorrow), Libby confesses that she's tired. "I'll sleep awhile before I head to the Firenze," she says, looking at the clock on the stove. "I can get maybe five hours before I have to go. You know Fridays are hard—in early, home late—but I'm not working tomorrow. I can sleep all day."

Angel twirls his spaghetti while they plan for the weekend. He refills both their water glasses as she describes the building air conditioning and why she's happy the weather is starting to cool.

He has nothing else to do this evening and he doesn't want to spend his time thinking about Adam Zepp and Molly Swann. Finally he asks a question that seems suddenly obvious. "Can I join you?"

"Join me where? Laundry on Sunday?" She'd mentioned that, too.

"Join you at the Firenze tonight. I can help. We can keep each other company. Maybe you'll finish faster."

"That's sweet, but you're tired."

"I'll nap now too."

By now they're finished eating and the dishes are mostly done. The kitchen's not as clean as the Firenze in the morning, but it's clean enough for now.

Libby clearly doesn't like the idea but can't see any reason not to let him come along. She sometimes brought him with her to work when he was younger—if for no reason other than that she didn't have anything else to do with him, so he would sit quietly and read a book—but that hasn't happened in years. During Libby's time at the Firenze, Angel has been barely farther inside than the lobby, and certainly never to the kitchen, where Libby spends most of her time. "I can help," he says again.

"Okay," Libby replies at last. "I'll jostle you when I wake up. You can change your mind and stay in bed if you want."

Angel closes one last cabinet and heads for his bedroom. "Nighty night," he says. "See you soon."

Chapter Thirty-seven

Angel surprises himself by how quickly he falls asleep, and he's ready to go when his mom knocks on his door. She's still dragging while he washes and dresses, and he suggests that they walk the two miles to the Firenze even though it's a straight shot by bus.

"Including the wait it takes the same amount of time," he says, knowing that she knows it better than he does. "But with two people we'd pay twice the fare."

"Then we can walk," she replies, matching his stride. "But you have to scrub the stove."

And off they go. It's not truly late yet, still before midnight, so a few people are still out, walking their dogs or hurrying home. Several times they see the last lights go out in a home, leaving it dark as it goes down for the night.

As they reach the Firenze, Angel turns to the front door, but Libby gestures him around the side. Together they skirt the edge of the parking lot and a dumpster in the back to where an open door is flooding light into the night.

The heat strikes them before they even reach the door, gusting into the night like a blast from a furnace—and bathed in the flavors of olives, onions, and spaghetti bolognaise. Angel isn't hungry but the smell makes him want to eat.

Beyond the door is what Libby describes as the prep cook's alcove, a narrow corridor between the main kitchen and the door to the outside. To Angel's left stands a tall rack with condiments, herbs and spices. To his right, the counter top is one long cutting board, a large knife in the center, surrounded with spots of color where it had chopped green peppers, red pimentos, and yellow squash. Above the cutting board are shelves of utensils crammed tight—beater, blender, grinder, and more than Angel can name.

Moses, the owner, should be gone by the time we arrive, Libby has explained, and the head chef too. Nobody should be left but the dishwasher, Santiago, a young man from Bolivia who's working hard on his English and even harder to become a U.S. citizen. Libby said that Santiago starts at the Firenze before lunch, works until dinner is clean, and sends part of every paycheck home to his parents.

"*Que sorpresa!*" cries Santiago as they round the corner to the main kitchen. "Young man, what a surprise!"

Santiago is working at a sink on the opposite side of the kitchen, wearing a sleeveless tank top in the heat and hot water. He's not large, but his slender, sinuous strength is clear as he cranks shut the spigot at the base of the tall, arcing faucet.

"*Hola,* Santiago," says Libby. "This is my son."

Santiago steps back for a better look and breaks into a giant smile. "*Felicitationes,*" he says. "Congratulations." He dries his hands on a nearby towel while Libby explains why they've come for the night, then reaches out to shake Angel's hand in a proper greeting.

Angel has never seen such a hand, bleached pale from the water but crusted with callouses, encased like barnacles. It feels to Angel like he's grasping a lobster's claw or a horse's hoof, smooth as glass in some places, coarse as sandpaper in others.

"Dishwasher hands," Santiago explains, reading Angel's thoughts.

"Can't you wear gloves or something?"

"It's too hot," Santiago replies. "And they make me drop things . . . " He nods in Libby's direction, "Then she has to clean them up—and Moses has to buy new ones. *Guantes son malos,*" he concludes. "Gloves are bad."

"Shall we?" his mother interrupts, gesturing with a bucket she picked up while they were talking. "It's late and we have much to do." With a knowing smile at Santiago she translates herself. "*Mucho que hacer.*"

Santiago smiles back. "Get to work."

They'd walked past the stove on their way to greet Santiago, and now they turn back to the dominant feature in this hot little space. Heavy and cast iron, the stove looks like an artifact from a different century. Eight blackened burners in two rows line the top, and the edges are spattered with sauces and gravies, burned and crusted from a night of drips and heat. Above the burners is a giant aluminum hood that captures smoke as it rises. Above but behind is a metal frame dangling with fry pans of every size. Plenty of times at home Libby has described how the chef at Firenze reaches overhead for a clean fry pan as he starts every dish, and exchanges it for another one when he finishes.

The other side of the kitchen, Santiago's side, is divided in two. Half is Santiago's for the sink. The other half is a salad station, where the salad chef grabs handfuls of lettuce, tomatoes, or cucumber slices and portions them into dishes.

Angel is still looking around, but Libby has attention only for the stove, serious when she told Angel he'd be scrubbing. Now she sets him up with scrubbers and detergent, and shows him how Santiago will let him fill the bucket and change the water in the sink. "Gloves for you, though," she says, giving him a pair and pointing him to the spatters on the side. "If the stove isn't clean tonight it will be smoky tomorrow."

While Angel works the stove, Libby works the rest of the kitchen, starting with the salad station. Each little drip of dressing has left its mark for the night, and every tomato slice that fell eventually got stepped on. Watching her work as he focuses on the stove top, Angel sees how this division makes sense. Angel's job is hard but easy. Just scrub. Libby's job requires knowing her way around the kitchen, and putting things back where they go. She and Santiago perform a practiced dance, carrying knives, bowls and cutting boards back and forth between Santiago's sink and the prep cook's alcove, and staying out of each other's way.

But when Libby removes the garbage bag from the garbage can to take it outside, Santiago whistles for her to stop.

She understands immediately and steps aside, resting and watching, as he roots through the garbage.

What's he doing? asks Angel with his eyes.

Wait and see, his mother replies with a gesture and a nod.

Soon enough Santiago emerges with a dinner roll with one bite removed and a half lemon that's been squeezed. "*Perfecto*," he says with an easy smile, setting them beside his sink and getting back to work.

It's not until Libby finishes in the salad station and leaves to work in the prep cook's alcove that Angel sees what it's all about. Santiago steps away from the sink, swings the garbage can out toward the stove, and tosses that dinner roll high into the air.

Staring straight at Angel as if he's forgotten the roll, Santiago stands still as it falls down, past his face, toward the floor that Libby just cleaned so carefully.

But the roll never reaches the floor. At the last instant, Santiago gives a little flick with his foot.

The roll bounces off his foot and back into the air.

This time as it drops, Santiago bounces it on his knee.

Then his other knee.

Then back down to his foot, all the way up to his head, and dropping off his back before flying up again from the tip of Santiago's toe in a spin move that makes Angel gasp out loud and burst into applause.

He's seen kids on the soccer team juggle soccer balls like this, keeping the ball aloft with knees and feet, but he's never seen a performance like Santiago with his once-bitten dinner roll in the tiny space between the sink and the stove in the Firenze in the middle of the night.

Santiago tries the lemon half too, but he seems to like the dinner roll better—and after a few minutes he puts them both down and turns back to the sink. "*Mucho que hacer,*" he says with a sigh.

"Much to do," Angel replies, and turns his attention back to the stove.

After that it gets tiring. The kitchen is hot and the early fragrance of garlic and onions has been replaced by the smell of detergent and cleanser. But Angel cleans without stopping, even when the stove top is finished and his mom asks him if he wants to take a rest.

"Are you taking a rest?"

"I'm scheduled to be here," she replies. "You're scheduled to sleep."

"I'll rest when you do," Angel insists. So she shows him how the stove top is clean ("Great work!") but the wall behind the stove and the oven alongside are still spattered with grease and sauce, so there's more to do.

Santiago takes a few little juggling breaks, but eventually the dishes are all clean and the last of the fry pans is drip-drying on the rack over Angel's head. Santiago heads out for the night, leaving Libby and Angel alone in the restaurant. Ahead of schedule with both of them working, she gives him a tour of the rest of the restaurant, especially the basement with its food storage and giant walk-in refrigerator, then she brings him back upstairs to the oven.

Angel already cleaned the outside, but Libby opens the door. "It doesn't need cleaning every night," she says. "But tonight it could use some."

"Didn't you used to bake bread?" Angel asks in reply. "Monet says you baked bread when I was a baby."

"For a while we lived in a house with an oven big enough to bake bread."

"Monet says fresh bread is the best thing ever. She used to talk about the smell alone. She says it's delicious before you even eat it."

Libby leans against the edge where the salad chef loads salad bowls. "She's right."

By now Angel has the oven door open. He's exploring the inside and thinking about how much scrubbing it needs and how long it will take. "This oven is big enough for bread," he says at last.

"Plenty big."

"Let's do it, Mom. Let's bake bread. We can use this oven."

Libby doesn't say a word while she thinks. She looks at her baby boy with his head in the oven, looks around the kitchen and the pots and pans, clean and unused. "I think you're right," she says at last. "We can use their oven and their pans to mix it up—but we'll use our own ingredients and clean our own dishes."

"Tomorrow night," Angel declares. "I'll shop during the day to buy ingredients. Tonight I'll clean the oven so it's ready tomorrow."

"Not tomorrow," Libby replies. "Tomorrow you need to sleep. Do clean the oven now, though. Some night we can bake a loaf of bread."

Chapter Thirty-eight

Angel works through the night, never taking a break no matter how much Libby suggests one, and they return home around sunrise. Again they pass dog walkers, though people are now waking up for the morning instead of bedding down for the night. Newspapers have been delivered all along the street, and at some homes with long staircases, Angel gratuitously tosses the newspaper from the sidewalk to the top of the stairs.

"It might be more convenient," he explains nonchalantly.

But that's the end of his energy. He doesn't say another word before they reach their apartment and he goes straight to sleep, ignoring the sticky feeling on his arms and the oven grit in his hair. Within minutes he's fast asleep.

Angel wakes up around three in the afternoon, feeling great, takes a shower and starts his homework. Libby has already been awake a few hours, doing some chores around the house.

"You didn't go shopping, did you?" Angel asks. He knows it's on the list for the weekend.

"Not yet. I figured you might want to join me. Do you?"

"You bet." Angel knows that there's still shopping to do even when treats come home from the restaurant. Right now they're low on toothpaste and shampoo, and he'll need a sandwich loaf for lunch next week. "When do you want to go?"

The plan for shopping becomes a plan for the day, and Angel insists on returning to the Firenze overnight. Libby cautions him about school on Monday but eventually gives in, and a few hours later they're walking the familiar aisles of their local Safeway.

Angel lets his mom tend to soap and toothpaste while he heads straight for the flour. It's sold in five-pound sacks, and the coincidences keep lining up in Angel's favor. Flour is on a "buy-one-get-one-free" Safeway sale, and there are recipes on the bag. The gingerbread cookies and blueberry muffins are interesting but irrelevant, but one side has a recipe for "Grandma's old fashioned sandwich loaf." Perfect! The recipe becomes a shopping list.

Sugar and salt are easy, and good to have at home. Yeast is trickier since Angel's never bought it before, but Libby is happy to help. They settle on Fleischmann's Active Dry yeast, and buy a three-pack of bright red and yellow envelopes filled with yeast for $1.99.

"What about a loaf pan?" he asks. The recipe says to bake the dough in an eight-inch loaf pan.

Libby isn't sure, but she thinks they probably have an eight-inch loaf pan at the restaurant. "If not, we'll figure something out," she says.

They walk to Firenze past homes shutting down for the night, not as late as last night but still past most people's bedtimes. In one hand Angel carries a grocery bag with the heavy sack of flour; in the other hand he carries the bag with sugar, salt, yeast and other incidentals. The back door of the Firenze is open again, and they can smell good cooking as they round the corner behind the dumpster.

Moses Pizzigati looks up in surprise as they enter. He's dressed in a classic suit and tie for his customers, but wearing an apron and chopping green scallions in the prep cook's alcove.

"All set," Moses yells to Arturo, the cook who's bending over the stove in the main kitchen.

To Libby he adds, "We had a late rush for risotto and ran out of garnish. Oh, and hello." He turns back to the main kitchen without waiting for response, removing his apron as he walks. "Behind you," he says to Arturo as he squeezes behind.

"That was Moses," Libby says to Angel, taking the groceries from his hand and setting them on the edge of the prep cook's alcove. "This is Arturo, the head chef."

Four burners are going on the stove, each with a pan over the flame. Arturo grabs one pan and gives it a flip so what looks like spinach leaps into the air, flips upside down, and falls back into the pan with a sizzle. Even as it sizzles Arturo opens the oven Angel cleaned last night and pulls out a tray of lasagna.

He slides two slices of lasagna onto two separate plates, returns the tray to the oven and divides the spinach in the pan he just flipped evenly onto the plates. He tosses the empty pan into a bin near Santiago's sink, where it lands among other pans with a clatter, then he ladles sauce from a large pot on the back of the stove onto the lasagna slices. Finally, he sprinkles slivers of almond on top of the spinach and lays a slice of lemon on the edge. No sooner has he set the plates by the door than a waitress comes in and swoops them away.

Before she's out the door, Arturo is filling two bowls with risotto from burners near the back of the stove. He makes a quick dash to the fresh-cut scallions Moses left on the cutting board in the prep cook's alcove, and spreads the green rings around the edge of the bowls.

When the waitress returns, Arturo slides the plates across the service tray. "Regular risotto," he says of the first. "Fennel risotto, extra garlic," he says of the second.

"I love you," says the waitress as she grabs the plates and turns her back.

This entire time, Libby has stayed out of their way and Angel has pretended he doesn't exist. But now Arturo addresses them both together. "Summer is over and school is back. It's the first Saturday . . . time for lasagna!" He points to the oven. "Moses estimated three trays would be enough, but I had Dante prep five before he left. I put them in one after another, and now there's only one serving left." He glances at the clock on the wall. "I think we'll make it."

Never has it been so clear to Angel why his mother comes home with odd portions like a single serving of lasagna at the end of the night. That's just how it worked out.

The waitress returns before Libby says a word. "Dessert for table five," she says, sliding a slip of paper into a clip over the stove. "Table eleven just left and table two sends compliments on the veal. A party of four just arrived. Moses locked the door behind them."

Then she's gone. Libby guides Angel down the stairs toward the walk-in refrigerator. As they descend, Santiago steps away from his sink with a handful of clean pans to hang overhead by the stove. "Behind you," Santiago announces to the chef focused only on the flames in front of him.

Downstairs by the refrigerator Libby explains to Angel the inner workings of the Firenze. Dante the prep cook works in the alcove by the door, slicing and dicing since before lunch and laying out material for Arturo to cook as orders arrive. Dante starts earliest among the cooks and goes home first, as dinner winds down. Libby rarely sees him.

Sylvia is the salad chef who works beside Santiago on the opposite side of the kitchen from the stove. She preps her own station during the afternoon, chopping lettuce and slicing cucumbers and tomatoes, and makes some of her own salad dressings. Meals are a matter of assembling components at high velocity with no mistakes.

Angel was here only last night, and he's amazed by how dirty the space has gotten in just one day. Boxes of lettuce that were stacked yesterday have been transformed into flattened rows of cardboard scattered with lettuce leaves turning brown. An empty jug of sour cream that missed the recycling bin now sits upside down, dribbling whitish fluid, surrounded by footprints and skid marks.

Libby and Angel organize the mess as they talk. Unlike last night, when Angel scrubbed the stove top by himself, tonight they work closely together as Libby explains precisely what to do and how to do it. Order quickly emerges from the chaos. The sour cream jug goes into the recycling bin (obviously!) and the empty lettuce crates are stacked to carry outside after the kitchen slows down for the night.

"Let's try the storage locker," says Libby.

Angel follows her to a room off the side where the shelves are filled with equipment, and Libby quickly spots what she's looking for. "Eight-inch loaf pans," she declares. "Seek and ye shall find."

"Five of them," says Angel, as his mother passes him the stack. "Can we make all five?"

"Let's start with one. See how it goes."

Maybe an hour later, Moses and Arturo come down the stairs together.

"Some night," Moses says.

"More nights like that and you'll need a second chef," says Arturo, his white chef coat spattered with color.

"More nights like that and I can retire," Moses replies.

Arturo grabs a set of clothing from a shelf and heads for the storage locker. Moses grabs a hat from a rack and turns to Libby and Angel. He has either guessed or been told who Angel is, and reaches out to shake his hand.

"Pleased to meet you," Moses says. "Your mom is terrific. She makes everyone's life a little easier."

Angel swells with pride. "Mine too," he says.

Soon enough Arturo is back, dressed in regular clothes, looking like someone coming home from dinner, not like someone who just cooked a hundred of them. Farewells are exchanged all around, and the two men head up the stairs together. "Good call on the lasagna," Angel hears Moses say to Arturo as they turn away at the top of the stairs. "I never thought we'd use that much."

Angel launches immediately into action. He gathers his bags from home, races up the stairs, and unpacks in the prep cook's alcove. He brought his own measuring cups, and he quickly identifies a big bowl and strong spoon for mixing. He sets everything in order while Libby cleans around him, starting with the cutting board counter top, creating a functioning workspace for everything else.

Angel reads aloud from the recipe on the side of the flour sack. "Mix the yeast with warm water, salt, oil and sugar."

"No," says his mother. "First mix the water and yeast alone."

"Not the rest?"

"Not yet. First the yeast. Make the water nice and warm. Too cold and the yeast stays asleep. Too hot and you'll kill it. First mix it in water, then feed it the sugar."

"Kill it? Feed it? You make it sound like it's alive."

"Yeast is alive. It's a tiny little organism sleeping in the package."

"Can you eat it if you're a vegetarian?"

"Wait 'til you see what happens once you wake it up."

Angel opens the package and peeks inside. The yeast is tiny grains, like sand, but each speck exactly the same size and shape, a tiny light brown cylinder. "It's alive?"

"Mix it in water," says Libby, who is pouring detergent into a bucket by the stove.

So Angel measures out a cup of warm water and adds a teaspoon of yeast. Nothing happens at first. The yeast just dissolves into little clumps, though a minute of gentle stirring turns it into a thick, tan, soupy fluid like a soup. Even through the strong smells of dinner, Angel notices the fresh, loamy aroma of the yeast rising from his cup.

"Sugar?" he asks his mom

She looks up from where she's scrubbing the stove. "Sugar," she agrees.

Angel stirs in two tablespoons of sugar, sees no change, and turns his attention to the dry ingredients. He measures three cups of flour into his big mixing bowl, and adds a teaspoon of salt.

"Mix the salt around in the flour," counsels Libby from the stove. "Make sure you spread it around. Otherwise you'll get lumps of salt."

"Yuck." Angel can guess what she's talking about.

Soon enough he turns his attention back to his yeasty soup. "It's bubbling!" he exclaims. Tiny bubbles are rising from the bottom of the cup and fizzing toward the top.

"It's waking up."

Angel spends five more minutes cleaning his workspace while he watches the fizz on the yeast cup build up into a head of froth that soon rises all the way to the top of the cup.

"You can pour it in and mix it anytime," Libby advises.

The loamy smell is stronger than ever as Angel pours the frothing liquid into the white mound of flour in the mixing bowl, then adds the oil too. "Now mix," he instructs himself aloud.

It's hard work, though. The tiny cup of water disappears into the floury mound, and stirring seems only to move things around rather than truly mix them together. The more he angles for the edges or speeds up the motion, the more the handle of the spoon slips from his grip. "Can I use my hands?" he asks.

"What do you mean?"

Angel doesn't answer. He just pulls the spoon out of the bowl, reaches in with his hand, and muscles the batter around the inside with his fingers. "That's better!" he exclaims as he scrapes, mixes and squeezes batter in his closing fist. Soon enough the heap of flour turns into a tan glob of dough.

"Good work," Libby says. "Nice technique. Now we knead."

She dusts the cutting board with flour and they spend ten minutes pressing and kneading the dough together. She shows him how to press the dough down hard into the cutting board, then lift it, fold it over itself, and press it down again. "Look how it changes," she explains, as it transforms from a sticky batter to a dense, elastic solid.

"What next?" he asks, when she pronounces it finished.

"Nothing," she replies. "Now we wait. Let the yeast do its work."

Back they head to the main kitchen, leaving the mound of dough lying on the cutting board. Santiago lets them use his sink to wash their hands up to the elbows, then they get to work.

Angel starts again with the stove top, though he takes a break to help himself to that last slice of lasagna that's still in the oven and still pretty warm. The mound of dough on the cutting board is bigger every time Angel looks at it. "That yeast does good work," he says.

"Just you wait," his mom replies.

And she's right. An hour later the mound of dough has more than doubled in size. "Now we punch it down," she says.

"Punch it out?"

"Punch it down. One's mean. The other's yummy. Wash your hands again."

So Angel washes the detergent off his hands and, under his mother's instructions, presses the dough in a slow motion punch, fist clenched, so it deflates gently, exhaling a whoosh of warm, yeasty air as it goes. Once it's back to its original size, he folds it and presses it a few more times, like the original kneading but softer. "Now what?" he says at last.

"Now nothing. Now we wait."

"Again?"

"Again."

And they wait. There's plenty to do around the kitchen, though two of them working gives them plenty of time to play tic-tac-toe with detergent on the oven wall and hangman with soap on the bathroom mirror. When Angel notices that Santiago is down to his last load of dishes, he offers to wash them for him so Santiago can go home early.

Santiago looks to Libby for confirmation. "Is it true?"

"Trust him," Libby replies

Santiago's smile is as wide as the horizon as he hugs them both and hurries out for the night.

The last step is called "proofing" the bread, and it's like punching down but even more gently. This time, instead of leaving the mound on the cutting board, they shape it into a cylinder that fits neatly into the eight-inch loaf pan. And this time, instead of leaving it uncovered on the counter top, Libby covers the pan with a wet washcloth. "So the crust doesn't get too crusty," she explains.

Next they leave the kitchen to clean the front floor of the Firenze, where the customers sit to dine. They empty the trash cans, mop off tabletops, and straighten the blinds. Libby makes sure all the napkins and tablecloths are collected in the hamper for the laundry service, and asks Angel to bring the vacuum cleaner up from the storage locker.

But she doesn't start vacuuming when he arrives. "Time to preheat the oven," she says.

It takes them a moment to work out the controls and make sure the racks are positioned where they want them. "Set it for 350 degrees," she says.

"That's 175 degrees Celsius," Angel adds for no reason, since the control is in Fahrenheit.

"Really?"

"Near enough. I rounded a little."

By now it's after three in the morning. The kitchen is cool and the air is clear, no longer smelling like Italian cooking or even detergents, with most of the heavy cleaning behind them. Angel peeks under the washcloth and sees that the dough is rising again, swelling now so it almost fills the eight-inch loaf pan.

They vacuum the front of the restaurant, Libby driving the machine, Angel moving the tables and chairs out of her way as she goes and replacing them again behind her. When they're finished Angel carries the vacuum back down to the storage locker while Libby checks the oven temperature.

"All set," she announces. "You do the honors."

Taking care not to bump it lest it deflate again, Angel places the loaf pan in the center of the oven. Libby sets the timer for fifty minutes.

"It will probably need a whole hour, but we should check it early in case it's done," she explains.

This time Angel accepts his mother's invitation to take a nap. He curls up in a corner, with one tablecloth folded into a pillow and another over top as a blanket. "Nighty night," his mother says with a smile as she tucks him in.

He didn't think he'd fall asleep, but an hour later his mother is jostling him awake. The restaurant smells delicious. Now at last Angel knows what Monet was talking about for all those years. He rests on the floor a moment longer, enjoying the smell of fresh-baked bread, while his mother wishes him good morning.

"You do the honors," she says again as she returns the table clothes to the linen hamper.

Angel climbs to his feet and checks the oven. Apparently his mother has turned it off but done nothing else. He takes the bread, with its golden brown dome cresting high over the loaf pan, out of the oven and sets it on the clean, dry cutting board in the prep cook's alcove. It smells better and better every moment.

Libby advises that they let it cool a minute, then she pops it out of the loaf pan.

Now it sits in golden brown glory in the center of the cutting board, looking like the idealized fresh loaf from artwork and movies. "Can we eat it?" Angel inquires.

"Give it a few minutes to cool and harden," Libby says. "Then I think it's breakfast time."

Chapter Thirty-nine

They set themselves a table with fresh linen, clean dishes, and glasses of ice water. The freshly sliced bread is so sweet and tasty they don't want butter, cheese, jam, or extras of any kind. They just sit across the table, smiling at each other over their night's work.

"Worth every minute of it," says Angel.

"Worth every minute," Libby agrees, then pauses as if she means even more. "It was worth everything." She takes a bite as a tiny shadow flits across her eyes.

"I miss Monet too," Angel says, guessing about the source of the shadow.

"I used to bake bread with Monet."

"I know."

Again comes that long pause and hint of a shadow. Finally Libby continues, "I used to bake bread with my mother."

Angel says nothing. He knows that too—because Monet told him—but he doesn't say so. His mother never talks about her mother, and he doesn't want to get in her way.

"We had a big, beautiful kitchen on a farm," Libby continues at last. "A big window looked out over the field, with sheep in the closest paddock. My horse, Shadow Dancer, stayed in the barn behind.

"My mother and I used to bake two loaves at a time because it wasn't worth the trouble to make only one. She had her own special motion to blend and knead. Even when we used the same batter, her half always rose higher and faster than mine did. I never knew how she did it. She had some special twist and flip with the dough." A sad smile lights up her eyes. "I tried but I could never knead as well as her. The whole house smelled from the baking. In the summer with the windows open you could smell it from outside. Fresh bread. No matter where you were, you knew it was time to come to the kitchen."

Angel ventures to speak at last. "I'm sorry about your mother."

The shadow returns. "You don't know the half of it."

"Tell me," he says, picking up crumbs from the tablecloth.

But Libby is already moving on. She stands up and collects the dishes, rushing as if to put something behind her. Soon enough the table is bare and she's doing dishes at Santiago's sink.

Angel just watches. The Firenze is clean and their bags are packed. There's nothing left to do.

Libby finishes the final dish and puts everything in place as if an ordinary work night—everything clean, no bread baked. "Good night, Firenze," she says. "Thank you for a lovely evening."

Angel follows her to the door. "Tonight we can make all five loaves," he adds.

Libby smiles as she locks the door behind them. "Tonight you'll sleep. It's Sunday. It's a school night."

But Angel is right. They head home for a full night's sleep, and by early afternoon they're awake and taking care of their day. Angel does homework. Libby does laundry. At what might have been bedtime Libby is packing up to head out for the evening, and Angel simply packs a bag alongside her.

"Where do you think you're going?"

"Making one loaf is hardly worth the cleanup," Angel replies.

"It was totally worth it," she counters. "You said so yourself."

"I said it was worth it. But not *totally* worth it. Not yet," he pleads. He gives her a hug like he hasn't in years, taller now than his mother. "Please?"

He knows he has her. There's nothing left but negotiations that he'll rest during the baking and rising, and catch his bus to school the next morning. He makes every promise she requires.

So Angel spends another whole night at the Firenze. By now he's learned a lot about what to do and where things go. As soon as the kitchen empties for the night, he takes over the prep cook's alcove, but this time he multiplies the recipe by five. Five cups of warm water, not one; fifteen cups of flour. He's glad he got that second sack of flour, and he finishes his entire three-pack of yeast.

Again he uses his hand to mix the batter. Again he and his mother knead side by side on the cutting board. He watches her press and flip, but experiments with techniques of his own, curious if it can make a difference.

He cleans up their workstation and helps his mother vacuum the restaurant floor. He agrees to nap during the first rise . . . but apparently he falls asleep deeper than he thought because the next thing he knows his mother is waking him to "do the honors."

"Time to punch them down?" he asks.

"Time to take them out of the oven," she replies.

"They're finished?" He's alarmed but he doesn't have the heart to complain. His mother looks tired and he knows it was extra work for her—five loaves to knead and proof, and less help with the cleaning.

He turns off the oven and takes the loaves out, one by one, five golden-brown treasures in eight-inch pans, a beautiful crest on top where the yeast did its work. Angel pops them all out and slices the first in half, even though it's still hot. "Was it worth the trouble?" he asks his mother.

She inhales conspicuously over the slice in her hand. "Every minute of it."

They sit down for a peaceful meal in the center of the Firenze, though both are quiet today. Angel is relaxing; Libby looks tired.

After breakfast Angel cleans up their dishes and all five loaf pans, and returns to the prep cook's alcove where the remaining loaves sit in a row. He grabs a bag and starts counting them out.

"One loaf for breakfast," he says, pointing to the restaurant floor where they just ate. "One loaf for lunch." He takes the next loaf and cuts it in half. One half he gives to his mother, and the other he sets aside for himself.

"What about the other three?" Libby inquires.

Angel is already putting them in a bag. "I'll bring them to school and see what I can get for them."

Chapter Forty

Thus, the Candyman becomes the Bread Basket, as his classmates take to calling him. He sells fresh bread, still warm when he arrives at school, for five dollars a loaf to students and teachers alike.

Molly and Joanna split a loaf every day at lunch. Two more loaves easily sell around the cafeteria; he has a crew of regular buyers, though the individuals vary day by day. Ms. Iacobucci buys one in the teacher's lounge every morning so hers is warmest. A math teacher named Michael Codrington, who's also new to Centreville High School, buys a loaf most mornings too.

Angel quickly diversifies his selection. A combination of research and invention creates a tasty herb-onion bread, a spicy pepper-cheese bread, and a sweet bread made with oatmeal and honey. He tries roughly to reflect his customers' preferences, though they still choose from what he brings rather than him bringing what they choose.

His daily total is eight loaves, four pans on each of the oven's two racks, though he's learned to take the herb-onion bread out a few minutes sooner than the rest. Angel and his mom eat one loaf for breakfast and another for lunch, leaving six loaves to sell at school. He even finds a different bus stop closer to the Firenze, which shortens his commute by fifteen minutes every morning.

Two weeks later Molly passes him a note. *We broke up,* is all it says.

What happened? Angel writes back.

Obsessed though he'd been by Adam Zepp asking Molly out that short while ago, Angel has nearly forgotten by now. The momentary nightmare has been kneaded, scrubbed, and punched down to oblivion.

Nobody is around so she answers out loud. "Everyone acted like we were a match made in heaven. He's only a junior . . . but already starting on varsity. I'm only a freshman . . . but already playing JV. Obviously we were made for each other."

"But . . . ?"

"But he wanted too much! Too much, too fast, I mean. It's one thing to sit together in a dark movie theater . . . but I'm only a freshman! It was too much. I'm done with him."

"But you're still playing soccer?"

"Of course, I'm still playing soccer. Sometimes I think of him when I kick the ball really hard." She stops talking and searches for a piece of paper. A moment later she passes him a note.

Where did you get this bread? it says. It's lunchtime and she just bought a loaf.

Nobody had yet asked him that question. It doesn't seem hard to guess, but still he isn't sure what to say. Fortunately, at that moment, a car peels out of the school parking lot with a screech of sound and trail of black smoke where the rubber was burning.

"That's Parker Carlson," Molly says. "His older brother got a new car."

"Going to McDonald's for lunch?"

"Probably. Now about that bread." She's not letting him get away. "Where do you get it every day?"

But Angel is saved again, this time by Tammy Atford. "Tag, you're it," she says tapping Molly on the shoulder.

Angel can see that his crew is heading outside. He follows without answering.

Tag is fun, as usual. Angel makes a few particularly nice moves and escapes one trap where Molly Swann and Wally Roscoe come at him together. Angel finds himself beside Molly again at the end as they walk in for class.

"You're pretty fast," Molly says. "Want to join the track team?" Track is her winter sport after soccer winds down in the fall.

"No, thanks," Angel replies. "I'm busy after school."

"Busy with what?" Molly knows he isn't on any of the organized sports teams, drama clubs, or extracurricular activities that most kids do after school.

"Busy sleeping," he replies.

"Can't you sleep at night?"

"I'm busy at night."

She looks at him quizzically. His tone isn't sarcastic but surely he must be teasing her. She goes ahead and falls for it. "Busy with what?"

Now it's Angel's turn to stop talking. It's inconvenient by now—they're walking in for class—but he digs for paper and pen. Last before the bell rings he passes her a note with only two words: *Baking bread.*

Chapter Forty-one

In homeroom the next morning Parker Carlson arrives early and so does Angel. Just the two of them are alone in the room. Even Mr. Dirksen isn't there yet.

Parker tugs Angel's shoulder, points him toward a corner.

Angel considers his options and decides to go with him.

Parker guides Angel all the way into the corner and stands in front of him so Parker's larger body blocks Angel's view from the door. Angel is trapped. Parker reaches into his pocket and fumbles to dig out something that's obviously important and confidential.

Is he dealing drugs? Angel wonders. Parker used to buy Starbursts back in elementary school. If he wants a loaf of bread he can buy one.

Parker pulls from his pocket and holds tight against his chest a roll of money. Hundred-dollar bills, it seems to Angel. He can't see how many, but the wad is thick and round.

"That's right," says Parker. "Hundred dollar bills. Ten of them. How much is that?

"A thousand dollars," says Angel.

"Right again. A thousand dollars. It's my birthday. My father gave me a thousand dollars for my birthday."

"In cash."

"You'll never have this much money in your life."

Angel has never even seen a thousand dollars in one place at one time. He's doing well with his bread sales but he deals in fives and tens, sometimes twenties. At the end of the week he's grossed $150, but he still has to buy supplies.

A thousand dollars is a month of food and rent at home. It's more than Monet pays for her books and school supplies when she comes home to complain about the cost of books and school supplies. A thousand dollars would easily cover the costs Zeb and Sheila need to print transcripts to advance their appeal.

Angel can't help but look at the roll of bills as Parker rattles on about how much money he got and the new stereo he plans to buy.

When Parker's bragged enough—and by now other students are starting to arrive—he steps back from the corner and releases him.

Angel expects Parker to tuck the money back in his pocket, but he struts the classroom, showing it off until Mr. Dirksen calls the class to order.

The next few classes are boring as usual, though Angel sees Parker walking the campus displaying something in his hands, often to kids who look like they'd rather be doing something else.

Angel doesn't connect with Molly at lunch. Their table is crowded and the cafeteria is unusually noisy. They end up in seats at opposite ends, and don't even pass a note. Angel is rarely happy not to see Molly, but today it's a relief. She might pursue her question, and he still hasn't figured out how to talk about baking bread in the kitchen his mother cleans overnight.

But it's not Molly he needs to worry about. It's Parker Carlson. At the end of the day, as Angel is heading down to the bus ramp, he sees Parker showing off his wad of bills to a pretty girl Angel doesn't know. Parker jams the bills into his backpack and sets it down beside them, then starts fingering something on the girl's shoulder, moving what seems to Angel uncomfortably close.

As Angel walks past, Parker's older brother leans on the horn of his new Audi convertible in the parking lot at the top of the hill.

"Damn," says Parker, turning and running up the hill.

The girl starts walking Angel's direction toward the bus when Angel realizes that Parker's backpack is still on the ground where he left it.

"Wait!" he calls in Parker's direction. "Your backpack!"

"Later, loser!" Parker yells as he hops over the door into the waiting Audi.

Angel drops his own pack on the ground, picks up Parker's, and starts running toward the parking lot—but he isn't even close. The Audi takes off, burning rubber.

A boy in the front seat gives Angel the finger.

Angel is breathing hard by now. The quick sprint was uphill with Parker's heavy backpack. He turns and runs back down the hill, gathers his own backpack, which is sitting undisturbed where he left it, and barely makes it to his bus on time carrying both of them.

At home at this time, Angel usually makes himself a snack and either goes straight to sleep or does homework until he's tired, then goes to sleep until they head for the restaurant a little before midnight.

Today the first thing he does is open Parker's backpack. On top is a single piece of paper; jammed down beside it is the roll of hundred-dollar bills. Angel pulls it out and looks it over, counts all ten of them—but he barely daydreams. It's not his. He doesn't even think about taking it.

But he does read that piece of paper across the top before he closes the bag.

It's a homework assignment from Mr. Copeland, whom Angel knows teaches remedial math. The details at the top of the sheet say it's due tomorrow, period two, the first period after homeroom.

Parker Carlson can't possibly get this done on time.

The assignment is about negative numbers, a subject Angel studied in fifth grade. The first question is 4 + -3. Parker already wrote the answer, 1.

He got it right.

The second question is -2 + -4.

Here Parker struggled a little, with scribblings and corrections in the margins, but he has circled what is, in fact, the correct answer, -6.

Angel takes out his pencil and fills out the rest of the page in a passable imitation of Parker's handwriting, including some scribbles so it looks like work. Then he puts everything back in its place and starts homework of his own.

The Firenze is a little tricky that night. They arrive shortly after midnight and see Moses as they enter through the door behind the dumpster. Libby immediately turns on Angel and chases him back outside.

"What's the matter?" Moses asks Libby as she enters the restaurant alone. Angel listens from behind the dumpster.

"Nothing," Libby replies. "I thought I saw a rat. It was a squirrel."

Angel has never heard his mother lie before. He's impressed by how quick and smooth and plausible she sounds, but he hangs around outside for a while, walking around the dumpster, appreciating why a restaurant owner might be worried about rats.

Nearly half an hour later, his mother ushers him inside. "I'm worried about Moses," she confesses.

"Are we in trouble?"

"He doesn't know. He saw you one night, which was fine. But he might not want you here every night."

"And he doesn't know we're using his oven."

"He doesn't know anything. I haven't told him anything. Everything seems okay . . . but I'm worried about it."

Angel knows exactly what she's talking about. Honesty is the best policy, of course, but Moses doesn't really need to know. And he might make them stop.

Angel isn't ambitious about baking that night. They're a little late getting started and it's been a complicated day. He makes four loaves of regular white bread and four loaves with oatmeal and honey, the easiest of his other choices. He doesn't have energy to slice onions for herb-onion bread or grate cheese for the pepper-cheese option.

He helps his mother vacuum the front floor during the first rise. He's always happy to share the work, of course, but this is the only job that goes genuinely faster with two of them, with one person driving the machine and the other moving the furniture.

He punches the loaves down, and he rests but doesn't sleep during the second rise. He's awake when his mother leans down to kiss him gently on the forehead.

The next morning in homeroom Parker Carlson again arrives early, looking far more grim and not nearly as smug as he did the day before.

Angel gives Parker his backpack. "Everything is in there," he says.

"Everything?"

"Everything."

They part without another word. Some other kids are in earshot, but even if they were listening they wouldn't know what they were talking about.

The bigger surprise is at lunchtime. As Angel is heading out to play tag with his gang, Parker Carlson pulls him aside.

Not just aside, but all the way aside. To a tiny corner out of everyone's view.

"Thank you, man," he says. "That was huge. That math homework especially. Mr. Copeland said he would call my parents if I was late again. You saved my life."

"It wasn't so hard," Angel replies.

"I felt so rich yesterday," Parker continues. "I was going to buy a thousand-dollar stereo. Now I don't have enough money."

"What about your birthday present?" Angel asks in alarm. "It was all in there."

"Not anymore," Parker declares. He puts something in Angel's hand.

He looks down. It's a hundred-dollar bill.

"Finder's fee," says Parker Carlson. "Thank you again. You saved my life."

They talk a moment more, visiting as if it's normal, until Parker asks him, "How come you're so good at math?"

"The same reason you're good at throwing a football. It's easy for me . . . and I practice."

"Yeah . . . practice. That's what everyone says. But negatives are tricky."

"No they're not. Negatives are like money. If I owe you ten dollars, that's negative ten. If I borrow ten dollars more, that's adding another negative ten. Negative twenty."

Parker is quiet awhile before he answers. "You make it seem so easy." Then he asks another question that's clearly hard for him. "If I pay you, will you tutor me?"

"No," says Angel. This just doesn't seem right. "I'll tutor you if you ask."

Chapter Forty-two

It's the strangest first date ever.

It's nothing close to what Angel imagined when he daydreamed about asking Molly out. Not in his early daydreams over Mr. Balestrieri's pizza coupons or his recent daydreams involving ice cream sundaes. When Austin Marquette advised Angel not to waste a minute, surely he wasn't thinking about this.

They had to get permission, of course.

It was strange when Molly asked her parents to spend a night out with a boy they'd never met. Not just an evening, but a whole night out, overnight, followed by school the next morning.

First, Angel provided a note from his mom. Then they arranged a brief meeting in the parking lot after school so they could talk eye to eye, mother to mother, about the safety of her daughter out overnight with an unknown boy.

Ms. Iacobucci provided crucial testimony that Angel reliably (and mysteriously) brings fresh warm bread every morning. Molly said that tipped the balance.

They choose a Sunday night. Molly will still need to stay awake in school all day on Monday, but at least she can sleep the day before. Friday and Saturday nights have the advantage of letting Molly sleep the next day—but Angel doesn't work on Friday and Saturday nights because there's no school the next day and nothing to do with all his bread. So they settle on Sunday.

Now here it is. Sunday night. Molly's parents deliver her to Angel's apartment with a change of clothes and her school bags for the next day, then they all walk together to the Firenze just like any other night.

Molly wondered where Angel gets his fresh bread. Now she'll find out.

Sunday nights are usually slow at the Firenze, so Moses and Arturo are long gone by the time they arrive. Santiago knows all of their secrets, of course, and he's immediately gracious from his position behind the sink.

"Libby is a national treasure," he says to Molly, "and her son is truly an angel. Welcome to the neighborhood."

Angel has been talking with Santiago in English while they work at night, and he notices that Santiago's English—pretty good to begin with—is even better after these couple of weeks, especially the accent.

Molly replies with a little curtsey that this Bolivian dishwasher has surely never received in any language. "Thank you for having me," she says.

Santiago bows in reply, then returns to the sink.

Immediately they start to work on the prep cook's alcove, first clearing it off and cleaning the cutting board. Molly had requested cranberry-raisin bread "like my grandma makes for Thanksgiving." Per Angel's request, Molly brought cranberries, raisins, and the recipe.

Most everything overlaps recipes of his own: flour, sugar, and so forth. Her recipe calls for more butter than most of his, but that's easy to figure out. They decide to bake four loaves of regular white bread tonight, and four loaves of Molly's cranberry bread.

"Four?" she exclaims. "I only need one."

"But look," he replies, pointing to her entire bag of cranberries and package of raisins. "You'll be surprised."

They start the yeast in water, then feed it the sugar while they soften the butter and measure out the dry ingredients. Half of the dough they separate for regular white bread and half they give extra butter and—on Angel's impulse—a little extra honey. Then it's time to knead.

Angel stands beside Molly to show her how to press the dough, fold it over itself and press it again, sounding exactly like his mother explaining it to him just a few weeks ago.

Angel doesn't mention that he's been experimenting with different flips and twists in the interim, and that he numbered each pan individually so he can track the results. Clearly, he has learned, the kneading technique affects the speed and height of the rise. Angel wishes he could test himself against Libby's mother.

He shows Molly how the dough grows more elastic as they knead, and how it tears when stretched, leaving little cables stretched across the divide. After a while they add the raisins and cranberries to the half with the extra butter.

Once they're finished they leave the eight little mounds to rise and help Libby clean the tables and vacuum the front floor.

When they come back, the little mounds have doubled in size. Molly knew what to expect, but still she's thrilled to see it happen.

"Are you tired?" Angel asks after they punch it down.

"I'm having a blast."

"Do you want to call your parents? Tell them everything's okay?"

"It's two in the morning," she replies.

"Oh, right."

Santiago leaves soon enough, and Angel and Molly work on the stove until it's time to punch down and proof the loaves for the final time. Finally they preheat the oven.

This last stretch always seems longest, and Molly does seem to be getting tired. Angel shows her the place he often naps on the floor, but she insists on staying useful so they help his mother with the salad station, which is nearly done anyway. This is the time when Angel usually does any homework he hasn't finished—but since it's Sunday and they're well prepared, neither student has any left before school the next day.

By the time the bread goes into the oven for its final bake, the three of them are playing twenty questions to pass the time. Libby goes first. "Vegetable," she begins.

"Do we eat it?" Molly replies.

Halfway into the hour for baking, the scent of fresh bread starts to fill the air. This is Angel's favorite part of the night. Outside, the sun is rising and birds are starting to sing. Inside the aroma grows and swells until you can taste it.

Around 5:30 it's time for breakfast. Of course the cranberry-raisin is everyone's choice and, of course, it's superb.

"Better than Grandma's," Molly declares.

"But you won't tell her," Libby cautions.

"Of course not."

The remaining loaves they divide for lunches and sales, but Angel separates one loaf of cranberry-raisin bread for Molly to take home to her parents. He puts it in a bag with a note. *Proof,* it says.

Chapter Forty-three

Monday night they arrive at the Firenze late enough that Moses should be long gone, but he's in the kitchen and seems to be waiting for Libby to arrive.

"You know we aren't a breakfast restaurant," he says, instead of a regular greeting. "We do lunch and dinner."

Libby and Angel have walked in together. Clearly he sees both of them.

"I know," Libby replies.

Angel can see she's stalling for time. They can only guess why Moses is talking about breakfast.

"I've missed you lately," Moses continues. "Everything is done in the morning, but you're coming in later."

"Angel's been joining me," she says. She can't hide it, so she makes it obvious. "Together we finish a little faster. Everything's okay, isn't it?"

Moses shakes his head in a gesture of concern. "We start work around ten in the morning and start serving lunch at eleven. Most restaurants that serve lunch at eleven have to open earlier. But our staff is amazing, especially Dante. We can open later and still be ready for lunch on time. Obviously lunch doesn't really get busy until noon—and we can prep dinner during the dead time from three to five."

Libby knows all of this. She still doesn't know why he's saying it.

"I often come in when we open at ten, and sometimes Arturo does too." He sounds like he's reaching his final point. "Sometimes when we arrive it smells like fresh bread. Just a hint, nothing strong. But our lives are in cooking and we notice these things. Do you know why? Do you know where the odor of fresh bread is coming from?"

Libby says nothing.

"It's a nice smell. Very pleasant, obviously. Nobody minds. But we don't know where it comes from. It's as if someone has been baking overnight."

He raises his hands to the sky. "Nobody knows. You're here at night . . . and you're the only one I haven't asked yet. Do you know? Do you know why it smells like bread in the morning?"

Libby answers without making it look like a confession. She gestures Angel in the sweep of her arm. "Together we can arrive late, and finish faster," she says. "And my son likes to make bread while we work."

"I'm getting good at kneading," Angel adds without invitation.

"We use all our own ingredients and—as you know—we clean up afterwards as if it never happened."

Moses shrugs his shoulders in a gesture of relief.

"Is it okay?" Libby asks. "Do you need me to pay rent for the gas or the stove?"

Moses reaches forward and gathers both Libby and Angel in a generous hug. "No, no, no!" he says. "No need for rent or anything else. It's exactly the opposite. I'm delighted you're putting it to use. Why waste a perfectly good oven overnight?"

Moses is satisfied but Libby isn't. The next day, Tuesday, she sends some inquiries during business hours and learns Moses's home address, which turns out to be a condominium nearby.

The day after that, Wednesday morning, she detours on her way home from the Firenze and leaves a loaf of fresh bread by his door.

Moses thanks her at midnight, gushing about how the bread was still warm and how good it smelled when he sliced it open in his little kitchen. After that, without invitation, Libby and Angel start a rhythm. Every Wednesday and Friday morning, they take Moses a loaf of bread. It's warm when they deliver it around six in the morning, and Moses knows to bring it inside when he wakes up around seven.

One night at midnight Moses is waiting for them. He says his neighbor wakes up and gets jealous of the smell in the morning. "She wants to know about the bread wizard," he explains. "She wants to know how she can get a loaf."

Angel doesn't give Libby a chance to answer. He speaks up for himself. "Eight dollars per loaf," he says. "Delivered to her door."

The next day at school Angel makes his first email address, *mannafromheaven.01@gmail.com*. If Moses's neighbor sends him an email before he leaves school on Tuesday or Thursday, she'll get a loaf at six the next morning.

Part Five

Making Manna

Chapter Forty-four

"Hear ye, hear ye. The honorable Virginia Court of Appeals is now in session." Striding into the well of the court, the bailiff transforms from an irrelevant brown uniform into the physical embodiment of the state. Chevrons on his shoulders, badge on his breast, white handlebar mustache across his aging face, he looks like a character from an old TV show. "All rise for the honorable Michael Young." A swoop of his arms commands everyone to stand.

The judge in black robes enters from a door behind the bench. Blond-haired and a generation younger than the bailiff, he grins whimsically. "Thank you, Charles. Are you having fun?"

"I love my job, your honor," the bailiff replies.

The judge turns to his audience. "Take a seat, everyone."

Everyone consists of nobody but Angel, Libby, Monet, and some man in the back who seems only to be using a seat while he reads his newspaper.

"No newspapers in my courtroom," says the judge.

The man folds his newspaper and walks out.

Angel is a senior in high school, and for him this is like a family reunion. Libby he sees every day, of course. He comes home from school for dinner, and they spend every night at the Firenze. Today Angel is playing hooky from school and his mom is skipping work. Neither gets sick in real life, but today they're pretending. Today is for family.

Monet he sees less often. She's in her second year at the University of the District of Columbia School of Law—and not just because it's an HBCU or because it's inexpensive for D.C. residents, which she is after four years at Howard. Monet chose UDC because of its extraordinary curriculum built around clinical programs and actual practice. The notion of getting academic credit for providing legal services to poor D.C. residents is like getting paid to eat dinner. And next year Monet will be a lawyer. A dream come true.

Angel has never seen Sheila or Zeb in person, but they've been an invisible presence for as long as he can remember. From saving money for their Friday phone calls to Monet's life-changing trip to Fluvanna that put her on her path to UDC, Sheila and Zeb have been the ghosts in the machine.

They'll be here for their hearing too, of course. Monet's enthusiasm has been more than infectious. They've been counting the days for months.

"Daddy got a hearing!" she came home yelling one day. "Daddy got a hearing!"

"What does that mean?" Angel had to ask.

Libby already knew, but Monet explained the details. She described how Zeb had been appealing his conviction for years. Zeb drafted letters and pleadings for himself and Sheila, and sent copies to Sheila to file on her own behalf. Monet and Zeb had been exchanging drafts and sharing comments since high school, and after all these years, she'd showed his material to her favorite professor at UDC.

"Your dad's a good jailhouse lawyer," Professor Broderman had said, then read further and changed her mind. "Strike that. He's a plain good lawyer." The hearing had been granted on his claim of ineffective assistance of counsel.

The courtroom is surprisingly bare. The three of them sit in rows of empty seats. The bailiff has returned to his innocuous space along the wall, and the judge sits at a grand desk in the center. The flags of Virginia and the United States stand on one side; two people who appear to be administrative assistants sit at a separate desk on the other, and one man who seems to be the state's attorney sits at a desk flipping through papers. The furniture is wood and the walls are white. Now that they're seated and everyone has taken their place, nothing moves.

Monet said she researched the judge after he assigned the hearing. He's new—recently appointed to the bench—and Young in more than just name. She couldn't find much about him. He's a former prosecutor, though. She doesn't like that.

Judge Young turns to the bailiff. "I'm ready to go. Where are the bodies?"

The bailiff all but salutes in return. "The male is in transit from the holding block. The female is in the anteroom."

"Bring in the female."

It happens so fast Angel doesn't even see it. He's watching the judge and the assistant who seems to be taking notes when the door opens and the female—Sheila—appears.

Monet rushes for the bannister that separates the audience from the floor of the court, and Sheila breaks free from the escort who brought her in from the anteroom. The two meet at the bannister and hug each other across it, arms wrapped around each other's bodies, pressed tight. Both burst into tears, and Angel can hear the cries from his seat, their voices wrapped into one.

They break themselves apart even as the judge slaps his desk.

"Control yourselves," he commands. "Order in the court." To the bailiff he adds, "You'll need to search her again."

Another door opens and in walks Zeb. Angel has never seen him before, not even a picture, like Monet sometimes brings home of her mother. Not until he sees him does Angel realize that he has no mental image of Zeb, no idea what to expect.

Zeb looks like a prince.

Not the orange prison jumpsuit—Sheila is wearing the same—nor the yellow legal pad in his hand. But something in his posture, something about the way he stands before the court, watches his wife, and assesses the judge, makes Angel feel like he's in the presence of royalty. Tall and strong, with close-cropped hair and a perfect shave, Zeb Blackstone is a leader among men.

Monet returns to her seat, her face wet with tears.

Sheila moves toward the bailiff who brought her in, and offers her arms for handcuffing.

The bailiff declines the handcuffs and directs her toward the judge.

The judge waits until everyone has found their proper places, standing like Zeb has already established.

"The court is now in session," Judge Young affirms.

The clerk to his side presses some buttons.

"In the case of Blackstone versus the Commonwealth of Virginia, the petitioners are now present. Petitioner, do you have counsel?"

"No, Your Honor." Zeb seems to answer for both of them, and the judge accepts it.

"For the state?"

Now the prosecutor stands for the first time. In age he's closer to the bailiff than the judge, and the overhanging belly that went unnoticed in the chair is conspicuous when he stands. Sounding bored and barely paying attention, he intones, "Alan Pembroke for the Commonwealth."

"He could lose a few," offers Libby quietly from her place in the audience.

"Let me explain where this case stands," announces the judge, looking in turn at his clerk, the audience, and then the petitioners. "This case was originally heard, guilty pleas accepted, and sentence declared by the Right Honorable Judge Horace Winters. Judge Winters, however, retired shortly after accepting the plea and before acting on any subsequent petitions.

"The case was reassigned to Judge Frances Weinman, who was transferred to the family court before taking any action on the matter. It does appear that the case remained on Judge Weinman's docket even as Judge Weinman's docket was scheduled to consist entirely of family court matters. It's unclear what happened after Judge Weinman left the family calendar.

"Petitioner Blackstone"—he looks quickly at Zeb—"wrote letters and filed multiple motions on the matter, some of which were attached to the jacket and some of which make references that suggest that some writings may have gone missing. In any case, it's fair to say that a good deal of time has elapsed and this jacket may not have received the attention it deserves.

"The petitioner's latest letter hit its target, however. He welcomed me to the bench and called the likely lapse to my attention." Judge Young surveys the audience one more time before turning full attention to Zeb, still standing silently before him.

"Now, petitioner, it is, as they say, your day in court. Use it wisely."

Zeb stands up even taller, looking more than ever like a prince at an affair of state. "Thank you, your honor," he begins. "I appreciate the court's time and attention."

For the first time he turns his attention to Sheila and the people in the audience. "First, if I may, I'd like to introduce my family. My wife, Sheila, you know, of course. Petitioner Sheila Blackstone."

The judge nods acknowledgement. Sheila, too, is properly before the court.

"Behind us is our daughter, Monet."

Monet stands and nods toward the judge. "I'm in law school at UDC."

Judge Young seems to indulge the impropriety. He nods in recognition.

Zeb turns next toward Libby and Angel. "This is our old friend Libby Thompson and her son. I can honestly say that none of us would have made it—and Monet would not currently be in school—if it weren't for Libby Thompson."

"Pleased to meet you," says the judge, then turns to Zeb with a clear motion of expectation. "Now to business."

How is it that Zeb somehow seems to keep standing taller? Every time he straightens it's as if he grows another yard and everyone has to look at him anew.

"I'm here today with two legally unrelated but substantively identical claims," he says. "First is ineffective assistance of counsel and, in the background, insufficiency of evidence."

"Go on," says the judge. The hearing was granted on only the first claim but the judge doesn't seem to be counting.

"As you may know, our attorney, Simpson Mellor, didn't last very long. Shortly after he handled our case he was disbarred in Virginia for mishandling client funds. The next time he showed up, he was caught practicing law without a license in Louisiana, then again in Alabama. I found him arrested for fraud in Texas. He was sentenced to twelve months of unsupervised probation and I haven't found him since."

The judge turns to the prosecutor. "I assume your files confirm the allegations in the petitioner's pleadings?"

The prosecutor nods indecipherably but the judge accepts it as agreement.

"And I assume you subpoenaed former defense counsel for this case?" Turning to Monet in the audience he explains, "It is routine in cases for ineffective assistance to produce the attorney to explain his actions and also—" with a glance at Sheila and Zeb "—to castigate the defendants."

"Subpoenas were issued, your honor," says the prosecutor.

"No response?"

"No response, your honor."

"Do you have anything to add regarding the conduct of counsel?"

"No, your honor."

"Petitioner Blackstone, do you have more to add?"

"Your honor, I'd like to make a confession."

Judge Young looks at him quizzically.

"I used to deal drugs. I confess it in all honesty. I dealt small quantities of heroin for years. But Sheila wouldn't marry me if I was dealing. Eventually she forced a choice. It took longer than she wanted, I think—" he pauses to watch her smile "—but I got a better job and went completely clean. That's when they arrested me. Long after I'd stopped. For crimes I never had anything to do with. Not one single bit, and with codefendants I'd never met. And Sheila . . . " for an instant his composure breaks ". . . Sheila never broke a law in her life."

Judge Young looks troubled. He turns to Sheila. "But you pled."

"I didn't mean to!" Her voice sounds less like a lawyer's than a cry for help. Even the prosecutor looks up.

The judge sounds a mixture of kind and confused. "Tell me what happened."

"I never would have pled to anything that long." Her voice sounds like an eternity behind bars. "Our lawyer guessed a sentence of four years, tops. Minus some time off for good behavior and time already served, I thought I'd have another two years, maybe one if I was lucky. I'd spend practically that much time in jail awaiting trial. And everybody warned me that if a black woman takes a drug case to a Virginia jury, the sky's the limit."

Sheila looks over her shoulder towards Monet. "She was in second grade . . . "

The judge turns to Zeb. "By your own admission—and the records before the court—you had more experience in the justice system. Why did you plead?"

"Same as her. I did the math. Black women have it tough . . . but black men aren't exactly treated like puppy dogs. And there's one thing more. Here I'm different from Sheila."

"Go on."

"You're fully aware, your honor, that codefendants are legally presumed to have different interests. Those other codefendants fingered us as the leaders."

"Codefendants always do."

"But married codefendants are different. As we both know, though I did not know at the time, special procedures are needed for the same counsel to represent both parties in a marriage. Our interests might be legally adverse—but they might be legally shared. Married codefendants are supposed to sign a waiver . . . "

"True enough," says the judge. To the prosecutor he adds, "Does your file show any evidence that petitioners were warned of potential conflicts of interest? Were permissions granted or waivers signed?"

The prosecutor shuffles through a file that's obviously not very thick. "No, your honor." Defensively, and with a little more paper pushing, he adds, "But *their* waivers wouldn't necessarily be in *my* file."

Judge Young turns back toward Zeb. "Go on."

"Codefendants aren't the only people who can make things up. I can make things up, too. If I knew what was coming, I would have confessed myself as ringleader in a heartbeat. Myself alone. I would have traded anything to get Sheila off easy. Cut my legs off. Lock me away forever. I don't care. Just send Sheila home to our baby girl. I would have confessed to anything to save my family."

Judge Young gazes out to the audience, then back to the folder in front of him.

"Now on the insufficiency of evidence, if I may, your honor."

"Be brief."

"I never saw any evidence of any kind. Our lawyer never showed us any and, as far as I know, the prosecutor never produced any. I don't know what drugs were involved or who sold them. Were there recordings? Fingerprints? Police reports? Was there anything that tied either of us to the drugs? I never saw anything and I don't think the case file contains any evidence at all . . . because there isn't any."

The judge turns to the prosecutor. "What do you have?"

The prosecutor turns a page. "They were convicted of possession with intent to deliver nine kilograms of cocaine."

"I see the judgment of conviction. My question is about evidence. Where is the evidence supporting the conviction? Petitioner Blackstone raises questions that ought to be answered right here in the jacket. They're not. Tell me about the facts."

The Commonwealth's attorney stands again at his desk and leans forward across the file, turning pages. His belly again comes into evidence, along with the fact that the file is thin and can't take long to investigate. "It's not clear on cursory examination, your honor."

"Is there a sentencing report to support the 'ringleader' enhancement?"

"Not at this time, your honor."

"Let's do this," Judge Young declares, closing the file before him as if a decision has been made. "Go back to your office. Reexamine your files and exhume the colleagues you need. Produce some kind of evidence that supports this sentence in some way. It's a low threshold but I need something to suggest some semblance of proof . . . or that there ever was any. Even just a police report. Show me some evidence that Simpson Mellor didn't con these people, and that the prosecutor didn't help." In closing he sounds less like a judge than a prosecutor dismayed by the standards of a colleague.

"It's been a long time, your honor."

"I understand that."

"The petitioner has the burden on appeal. We met our burden of proof when they pled."

"I understand that," says the judge. "But the passage of time affects more than just your files." He's looking straight at Monet. "You don't need a whole trial. Just show me something that suggests how you met your burden of proof back then."

"It will take some time, your honor."

"Thirty days. Go find your supervisor, get her permission. Check your files. You have thirty days to show that some rudimentary fairness was afforded."

"Your honor, it takes twenty days just to open the archives. I can't possibly get this done in thirty days. Sixty, if you please."

The judge rises from the bench. "Forty-five days. They're in prison."

He passes the file to his clerk and turns to the bailiff. "This hearing is concluded. Charles, return the bodies to the holding pen. If the family wishes, you may afford visitation in the counsel block until lunchtime."

Chapter Forty-five

It's fall of his senior year and most kids are looking at college. Joanna is shooting for Haverford College outside of Philadelphia. "I like the Quaker tradition of peace, community, and nonviolent dispute resolution," she says. Molly likes Wesleyan up in Connecticut. "It's artsy without being silly. And it's close to New York."

Tammy is the most conflicted. "Sometimes I want a small school like Wesleyan or Haverford. Sometimes I want a giant school or a giant city, with the whole world around me. Obviously I should go to NYU." Fifteen minutes later she changes her mind. "How about Reed College in Portland, Oregon? It's smaller than our high school! With pine trees and mountains! Or maybe Carlton College, in the twin cities . . . ?"

Angel has no interest in college. He bought a third rack that fits in Moses's oven, so now he's up to twelve loaves a day. Roughly half of these he sells at school for five dollars each, and roughly half he sells in Moses's condominium for eight dollars, doubling his margin.

He bought an answering machine at home to go with the phone. Condo customers need to place their orders before 10 P.M., first come, first served, though he turns the ringer off so he can sleep through the afternoon.

While other kids long for college, Angel longs for a larger oven. He daydreams business plans, starting with Moses's condo but expanding throughout the neighborhood. Fresh bread in the morning, delivered to your door. Who can resist?

The area contains multiple high-density residential areas where large numbers of customers can be reached with ease.

He took the elective course on web development and he's ready to create a web page that takes orders and processes payment.

The margins on bread are low, so he'll sell side dishes to pump up the cash. A few dollars for jam, jellies, or cheese—maybe even drinks. He figures he can buy giant tubs of jam and sell tiny jars at high margins. If all goes according to plan, he'll pick up the empty jars at the next delivery and credit the return.

It all feels so real—easily within reach—but other times it feels like a fantasy daydream. He estimates he needs $300,000 to get started, but really he should have twice that to be safe. Where can he find money like that?

Neither Angel nor Libby can possibly qualify for a loan, no matter how sound their business plan. Moses is looking to retire and in no position to help. "I'll sell my house and liquidate the Firenze," he says, "then take the slow boat to Italy."

Angel even puts Parker Carlson to work during their occasional math lessons.

- "If the oven has three racks and each rack can hold twelve loaf pans, how many loaf pans can the oven hold? What if there are two ovens?"
- "If each oven costs $5,000, how much do six ovens cost?"

But it's not all baby math. Sometimes Parker is genuinely helpful. "What about the car?" he asks one day.

"What car?"

"You're planning to deliver, right? You need a car. Maybe more if you need to get to too many places during the morning rush."

He's right about that. Delivery costs money.

"Do you need me to drive? I can go fast without getting caught."

Angel already has a regular base of customers. Ms. Iacobucci and Mr. Codrington at school, plus his friends, like Molly and Joanna. At Moses's condo he sells to Geneva Clarke and Peter Campbell, neither of whom he has ever met in person. He also sells to Rooj Chopra, a delightful young woman from India with surprising blue eyes and a blazing smile. Angel knocks gently on her door when he makes his delivery and she always says good morning.

One morning he meets Bernard Farley by the lobby door. In his forties and wearing a business suit and a Yankees cap, Bernard doesn't know Moses and has no idea what Angel is doing there—but the smell of fresh bread stops him in his tracks. Even as Angel explains the connection between his paper bags and the bakery smell, the man's telephone emits a little chirp.

He pulls it out of his pocket. "It's my secretary's birthday," he remarks. "Always be nice to your secretary."

"Bring her a loaf of bread," Angel suggests with a smile. "Maybe more, but at least a loaf of bread."

"You're right," Bernard Farley replies. "And I haven't had breakfast, either. How much per loaf?"

They talk business for a minute—herb bread for Bernard and wheat for his secretary, they decide—until Bernard realizes he has no cash on hand and needs to hurry for his morning meeting. "Can you take a Visa card?"

"Too hard to set up, and the transaction fees would kill me," Angel replies. He pushes the loaves into Bernard's hands. "Take your bread. Pay me tomorrow."

Bernard hesitates but as his phone chirps again, he accepts the loaves. "That's credit the old-fashioned way," he says. "See you tomorrow."

Chapter Forty-six

Four in the afternoon and the telephone is ringing.

Angel has just cooked and eaten his afternoon meal. Libby seems to be late today and Angel is tired, so he left her meal on the stove and moved to turn off the phone for the evening—when it starts to ring.

"Hello," he says. Probably this is a bread order. It would be easier to take the message off the machine, but it's smart to visit with customers.

The reply is slow in coming. Angel is about to hang up when he hears a woman's voice, thin and uncertain. "Is Libby home?"

"She's not here. Can I take a message?"

Silence on the other side.

Angel repeats himself. "I said she's not here. Who is this? Can I take a message?"

The voice is stronger now. "This is Eva Louise Thompson. Her mother."

This time it's Angel who's slow to answer. "I'm sorry, ma'am. Libby's mother is dead. She died some years ago."

"No I didn't." The answer comes sharp and fast. After a pause, she continues. "Is this her son?"

"Yes, ma'am."

Again the pause. "Are you seventeen years old?"

"Yes."

Another delay. "Is your birthday in August?"

"Yes, ma'am." Maybe he shouldn't be giving information to a stranger over the telephone, but she seems to know already and doesn't sound threatening.

"Are you in school?"

"Yes."

She's all confidence now. "Of course, you're in school! How she loved school."

"Excuse me, ma'am, but how do you know all of this?"

"Seventeen years ago she sent me an envelope with your picture in it. You were a baby. But you looked so beautiful and happy. And so did my little girl."

"Your little girl?" Angel is slow putting the pieces together.

"Libby. My little girl. Someday you'll understand."

Libby's mother. "That makes you my grandmother."

"Bless you."

"You're alive."

The woman is talking quickly now. "I asked everywhere for your mother. I kept thinking she'd come home. I was sure she'd come home. Finally I got that letter. It was postmarked Fairfax. I telephoned Fairfax directory information right away, but she wasn't listed. I tried again every few days, then every few weeks, then the next year on her birthday. But there's no Libby Thompson listed. There are several L. Thompsons and other sorts. I called them all."

"What happened?"

Strange sounds are coming over the phone. Gasping, almost like crying. "I didn't know what else to do! I didn't have any other ideas."

"What happened?"

The crying is clearer now. "None of them were your mother." Angel hears a deep sound, almost a sob.

"That was seventeen years ago!"

"Every year on her birthday I call Fairfax directory information." She takes several breaths to pull herself together. "People think I'm crazy. But I don't know what else to do. And I don't want to give up hope. I want my little girl to come back to me. Someday, I want my little girl to come home."

Angel is fighting his own tears now. It doesn't make sense . . . but somehow it helps make sense out of other things that don't make sense otherwise. "I'll tell her to call you," he says. "What's your number?"

"Tell her that her brothers are okay. Both of them. And they have two little boys each. My *other* grandchildren."

"She has brothers?"

"They moved off the farm. Did your mother ever mention the farm?"

"Yes."

"Did she talk about her horse, Shadow Dancer?"

"A little."

"He missed her so much after she was gone. Nobody ever rode him like Libby used to. He died a few years after she left."

"What about my father? Tell me about my father!"

Again comes that long delay but with no sound at all, like the crying hit a wall and stopped.

Angel repeats his question. "What about my father?"

"Libby's father passed away some years ago. A few years after the accident. The burns were really bad."

"The car accident?"

"What car accident?"

"Never mind." In some ways they know what each other is talking about, but in other ways they're having separate conversations.

It's a long wait while nobody speaks. At last she starts anew. "I've called this number before. Nobody ever answered."

"We just got the answering machine." Until recently, if nobody were home, the phone would just ring and ring.

"Please tell her I called." The woman is fully composed by now.

"What's your number?"

"She knows it. It hasn't changed. But I'll tell you to be sure."

Angel keeps pen and paper by the telephone for bread orders. He writes down her name and number.

"Tell her I called."

"Of course."

"Good-bye."

Angel hangs up.

A minute later, with Angel still staring at the paper in his hand, still trying to make sense out of the phone call, Libby enters the apartment.

She looks tired tonight and Angel can see she made some kind of detour. She puts a shopping bag down as she takes off her shoes.

"Your mother called," says Angel, before she even stands up straight.

Libby looks at him quizzically. "I don't have a mother," she says.

Angel steps in front of her in confrontation. "She says your brothers are doing fine. They have two kids each."

Libby stands speechless.

"She says Shadow Dancer died. So did your father."

Now Libby is more than speechless. She looks like she's been punched in the stomach.

"She left her number for you to call back."

At last Libby speaks. "Give it to me."

Angel passes her the slip of paper. She jams it in her pocket.

"You'll call her back?"

"I told you. I don't have a mother."

Chapter Forty-seven

It's Thanksgiving, and Monet returns home for the weekend.

"Dad's petition was granted," she declares as she walks through the door. "Yesterday. The judge vacated both their convictions."

For an instant Libby and Angel stay shocked in silence, then both of them leap to their feet and cheer. "Hallelujah!" Libby cries, an expression Angel has never heard her use before. Libby races to give Monet a hug and soon all three are hugging together.

"Are they coming home?" Libby asks the obvious question.

"We don't know. We're still trying to figure that out."

"What's to figure?" Angel wants to know.

"The judge vacated the convictions and remanded the case for a new trial," explains Monet, sounding more like a professor than a student of law. "Now it's the prosecution's move."

"Uh-oh."

"Exactly. The prosecutor." Monet, with a sour look, says "prosecutor" like it's a dirty word, then tries to make light of it. "I have good news and bad news."

"Good news first," Libby replies.

"The good news is that the new prosecutor recognizes that the evidence was never very strong, and has deteriorated over time. He offered them a plea bargain for a lesser amount, with a sentence of time served. They could come home immediately."

"The bad news?"

"They need to plead guilty to get it."

The room is silent as everyone works through the implications.

Monet isn't finished. "Now I want to be a prosecutor," she declares. "I used to want to be the defense attorney my parents never had. Now I want to a prosecutor who doesn't pull this kind of shit. Why make them plead?"

For a moment she sounds like the little girl who misses her parents, but quickly she turns back into the law student and future lawyer. "The case has been remanded for a new trial, and the state bears the burden of proof. In the absence of compelling evidence, the prosecutor could simply decline to proceed. The ABA says the prosecutor's duty is 'to seek justice, not a conviction.' The case would disappear instantly. He doesn't even have to say he's sorry."

"What are they going to do?" Libby asks quietly.

"That's what we're trying to figure out. Mom wants to plead guilty and be done with it. Dad doesn't want to plead twice to a crime he didn't commit. He's certain the state can't win at trial."

They're still all standing by the door. Only now does Monet fully enter the room, take her coat off, and hang it neatly on the rack.

"What do you want them to do?" Libby asks at last.

"A criminal record is tough," Monet replies. "If they come home clean, they can get on with their lives. If they plead guilty, they come home with a record. They'll never find work. Nobody will ever hire them. Certainly dad won't ever get a job in a law firm."

Chapter Forty-eight

They decide to plead.

Zeb swallows his pride, does the math on incarceration pending trial, and decides his time left on Earth is too short to spend in a cage.

It never occurs to them to decide separately. Sheila and Zeb will stay together as a family, though Monet is the crucial liaison since they can't talk directly to each other from their respective prisons. They rack up impossibly high phone bills over the Thanksgiving weekend, but finally they reach a decision.

They'll return to Fairfax next week—or approximately, pending the judge's scheduling calendar—to enter their pleas.

"No audience," says her mother. "Please don't come."

After the plea they'll be transferred to the county jail to process their exit, probably the next day, since the county doesn't like state inmates congesting its facilities.

"If all goes smoothly," Zeb cautions.

"If all goes smoothly," Monet echoes, many times burned and now a law student to boot. "Do you want a coming-home party?"

"No," says Sheila.

"No," says Zeb.

"I love you," says Monet.

Just because Sheila and Zeb don't want a party doesn't mean that Libby can't do something for Monet. She looks up recipes from cookbooks in the storage locker of the Firenze and changes their shopping list for a day. The next night Angel bakes fewer loaves of bread and leaves room in the oven for a cake.

A chocolate cake with chocolate frosting, they decide together, and for Angel it's an adventure in a new kind of baking. No rising yeast and punching down, the cake uses baking powder for leavening and as much sugar as a whole week's worth of bread. While Angel mixes, Libby makes frosting from a stick of butter and a whole bag of chocolate chips. When they're finished, it's a sight to behold, with colored candy sprinkles on top.

"Magnificent," says Angel, who's never seen anything like it.

"She'll come home for dinner tonight," Libby confirms.

Monet does come home for dinner, but nobody cooks. All they eat is cake. Bite after bite, piece after piece, frosting rinsed down with soda. They eat and laugh until everyone is stuffed to the top, and still there's cake left over for tomorrow.

"Thank you," says Monet, when the dishes are clean and their faces are washed. "That was wonderful."

Angel adds, "What's for dessert?"

Chapter Forty-nine

Bernard Farley stops Angel as he enters the door of his condominium. "I'm glad I caught you," he says. "I'm hungry."

Bernard never orders in advance, but they often pass each other in the foyer in the mornings. Bernard likes to take his chances on what, if anything, Angel can spare that day.

Angel is carrying his bread duffel, a satchel of thick, soft cloth that keeps heat inside and protects against bumps. As usual at this time of day, Angel has ten loaves inside—twelve loaves, minus one they ate for breakfast and one Libby took for lunch. In theory, another loaf inside is for Angel's lunch, but he's been known to sell it and not eat until after school. The satchel folds up nice and small to carry home when it's empty.

Six loaves have been reserved in advance today, leaving plenty to sell as he goes. "I have herb-onion," Angel says. "Your favorite."

Bernard doesn't look thrilled about his favorite this morning. He thumbs the visor of his Yankees cap nervously, and laments that his new secretary isn't as good as the previous one. "It's hard to find a good secretary these days," he complains.

Angel doesn't know much about hiring secretaries but he has good choices this morning. "I have cranberry-raisin today," he says. "It's sweet. The opposite of herb-onion. But the cranberry gives it tang."

"I have cash today," says Bernard taking out his wallet. "How many loaves do I owe you for?"

"This is the third."

Bernard puts two twenty-dollar bills in Angel's hand. "That's an advance on the next two."

"It's a pleasure doing business with you," replies Angel, passing Bernard the cranberry-raisin loaf and continuing inside to make his deliveries.

"Wait, a moment. If you please."

"Sir?" Bernard is wearing a suit. Something about it brings out Angel's formality.

"What do you do with all the money?" Bernard asks. "Do you buy clothing and concert tickets? Like my ex and her daughters?"

"'*Her* daughters?'" Angel notes his choice of words. "Not yours?" He still hasn't worked things out about his mother, the missing piece of paper, or the phone call that Angel believes really was her mother. His grandmother. He has family on his mind.

"We've been divorced for years," Bernard explains. "I'm just the ATM for child support. So what do you do with the money?"

"Half goes back into the bread," Angel replies. "For ingredients and other marginal costs. Half goes home—to help my mom pay for food and rent, and my sister's tuition. Half goes into savings—so I can grow the business and someday buy ovens of my own."

"That's three halves."

"I'm rounding."

"What would it mean to 'grow the business'?" Now it's Bernard's turn to notice Angel's choice of words.

Angel explains all his plans, delivering to condominiums and other high-density residential locations. He thinks he can do a morning shift around this time and a dinner shift in the evening. He even explains his daydream of selling side dishes like jam. "McDonald's asks, 'Do you want fries with that?'" Angel jokes. "I'll ask if you want jam."

"Coffee? If you offer coffee you'll be golden."

"Drinks are different," Angel declares. "Sometimes I think about drinks, but it's complicated. I almost certainly can't offer a cup of coffee like people want. Probably I could bring them a jar of orange juice, but . . . " his voice trickles out, leaving the doubt to speak for itself.

" . . . but it strays from your core line of business." Bernard finishes the thought for him.

"Exactly."

"You're smart to stay with the core. How much do you need?"

The question comes from nowhere but Angel handles it like a loaf hot from the oven—tricky but familiar. "Easily $300,000," he replies. "For space, primarily. Furnished kitchen space with ovens. A little more for pans, ingredients, and delivery costs. Maybe $300,000, but probably more than half a million to be safe. I don't know how fast the customers will come."

"You can't get there by saving a dollar a loaf."

"I know," says Angel. He's worked it out too many times. "But I could pay back a loan over time."

Bernard straightens his tie and stands up like a businessman ready to do business. "I'm thinking the same thing," he says. "You have a good plan and low overhead. You know how you rounded three halves when you talked about your saving? I know investors who don't see much difference between $300,000 and $600,000. It's a rounding error to them. I'll hook you up."

Angel sets down his satchel and frees his hands. "What do you need me to do?"

"I'll need something written. Some kind of prospectus or business plan."

"Written prospectus or business plan," Angel replies. "Check."

"I'll bring you some examples. So you'll know what they look like and what they'll be looking for."

"That would be helpful." Angel nods in agreement.

"And you'll deal me in. When it's all done, I'll get some cut of the agreement, at least, maybe a percentage over time. We can work that out later."

"Unbelievable." This feels to Angel like good fortune out of the fairy tales.

"Believe it. I'll be your sugar daddy. I'll connect you to money and step out of your way. If it's useful—and to protect my investment—I'll help with some of the tricky stuff. Negotiate with the landlord, apply for a business license, things like that." He closes with gentle sarcasm. "It might help that I'm old enough to sign a lease."

Feeding his daydreams, Angel had once investigated the process for opening a business in Fairfax County. It was trickier than he'd ever imagined. Food service, in particular, requires all kinds of inspections and approvals. Working with a partner with a stake in helping him succeed is more than a dream come true. He'd never even dreamed things could work out so well.

"All I need to do is write up the business plan . . . "

"Don't count your chickens too soon. I don't have the money yet."

"Let it rise," Angel says.

"What?"

"Add the yeast, and let it rise," Angel reiterates. "Like baking bread."

"Exactly," Bernard agrees. "Some things take time."

"Sugar and time." Angel is on a roll. "And it matters how you knead."

Chapter Fifty

"I'm in heaven."

They're Zeb's first words when he walks through the door.

He walks around their little apartment, and says them again. "I'm in heaven."

"It's so quiet," Sheila adds. She says nothing more, and everyone understands what she wants. Nobody says a word.

Outside, birds are singing. Otherwise, it's silent.

Monet went with a friend with a car to pick them up at the Fairfax county jail. They expected to be out around ten in the morning but it was four in the afternoon when they finally walked through the doors.

Monet's friend, Angela, was upset with the delay. She felt abused by the misinformation and had other things to do.

Monet helped her put the few hours in perspective. They waited it out together.

To Angel, Zeb still looks like a prince. Something about his height and bearing makes him royal, and his narrow musculature makes him strong. After years of hearing about him, followed by his larger-than-life performance in the court, for Angel it's like meeting a president in person.

Zeb steps around their tiny apartment, examining every detail, moving as if in slow motion. He looks at the counter in the kitchen, steps past the couch along the wall, and soon reaches the window in the back, his arms pressed close against his sides.

"It's okay to touch things," Angel says, for no good reason.

Zeb smiles in understanding. He picks up an empty glass that someone left by the window, examines it awhile, then sets it down exactly where he picked it up. It's just a dirty dish carelessly left behind, but he handles it like treasure.

"Glass," he intones softly.

That catches Sheila's attention. She walks over and picks up the glass like she's never seen such a thing, turning it around and around in her hands, examining it closely. She peers at the setting sun through the transparency and smiles like a baby.

A tiny tear escapes as she cradles the glass to her bosom. Angel watches her suppress the tear and sit back down on the couch, holding the glass in her hands, gazing at it like a talisman.

Angel thought there might be more tears at the homecoming. He'd seen them on the telephone and remembered two wet faces in the courtroom, but the homecoming is silent. Every step is gentle, like it's the floor that's glass, not the ordinary drinking glass in Sheila's hand.

Zeb walks to the kitchen cupboard and opens it, then steps back to admire what's inside.

Glasses.

Angel watches Sheila catch her breath as she, too, sees what's inside. Half a dozen drinking glasses lined neatly in a row.

Now Zeb seems to realize that what they're doing must look strange. "Glass is dangerous contraband," he says, pointing inside the cupboard. "It's been sixteen years since I've held a drinking glass in my hands."

He pauses as if it's too much to ask, even as he already knows the answer and knows he's being ridiculous. He removes a glass from the cupboard and walks to the sink. "May I?"

Everyone laughs.

Zeb fills the glass with water, sips it down to the bottom and fills it again.

He walks to where Sheila sits with the empty glass cradled against her chest. He gets down on one knee like he's ready to marry her, and offers to exchange her empty glass for his full one. "Please," he says.

Sheila silently accepts the gesture and trades the glass, tastes the water now in her hand.

Zeb walks back to the sink with the dirty glass, fills it and walks again to the window.

Monet sits on the couch beside her mother, pressed up against her side, touching from thigh to shoulder.

For a long time no more words are spoken. Angel moves into the tiny bedroom that was once his but will now be taken over by Sheila and Zeb, while he sleeps on the couch in the living room. He straightens the last few corners and makes sure the new double bed is neatly made.

"Are you sure you don't mind?" Monet asked, those several long weeks ago.

"Of course not," Angel replied. "For as long as necessary."

In the living room, Zeb is gazing out the window. Angel sees him laugh out loud, and realizes he's watching something. He steps to the living room to look over his shoulder. Together they watch awhile.

Out the window is a tree. Nothing extraordinary, just a suburban maple, leafless in December. Squirrels are dashing up and down the branches, leaping and chasing each other through the air. Zeb catches his breath as one leaps over a void to an electrical cable, then runs away until it's gone.

"In D Quad on the Northeast tier there used to be a tree," Zeb says. "Everyone wanted to be on Northeast D. For a few months I had a bunk on level three. You can't control it. You go where you're assigned, but for a while I had a world-class spot on Northeast D. Up on level three where the leaves are.

"It's not that close. Maybe a hundred feet away. But close enough. There were squirrels. That's why everyone wanted to be on Northeast D. We could watch the squirrels."

"That's lovely," Libby says. "Finding beauty in a place like that. Did they let you keep animals or pets in prison? They could nurture your nurturing instincts."

Zeb turns away from the window and looks her dead in the eye. "They cut the tree down," he says. "When the warden found out, he cut the tree down."

Libby looks down at her feet. She doesn't understand prisons, and she knows it.

Monet leaps to the rescue. "It's nearly dinner time," she says. "Who's hungry for dinner?" She walks to the refrigerator and starts calling out choices. They stocked well in anticipation.

"Hamburger," she says, "or chicken wings. Spaghetti. Omelets with cheese and eggs." She turns to her audience. "If we don't have it, we'll go get it. You name it. What do you dream of for dinner?"

"A hamburger," says Zeb. "A hamburger sounds perfect. If you can make a hamburger, I really am in heaven."

Monet looks to her mother. "Mom?"

Sheila is sitting in the couch, holding herself, the glass down by her feet, hands across her chest like she's holding something inside . . . or keeping something out.

"Mom?"

Sheila starts rocking back and forth in place, still clutching herself.

"Mom? What's wrong? Do you want something for dinner?"

Sheila opens her mouth but no sound comes. She opens her mouth and tries again. At last comes a pitiful whisper. "I don't know."

"Would you like a salad? It's probably been a long time since fresh lettuce."

"I don't know."

"You don't know?" A pointless echo.

"I don't know!" The words pour out in an angry torrent. "We don't make choices in prison. We don't decide *anything*! They tell us when to wake up and when to go to sleep. What to do and how to do it. They don't ask what we want for dinner! They don't even ask if we're hungry. We come to chow when we're told and eat what we're served. We don't make *choices* in prison. We do as we're told.

"They give out toilet paper by the square!" She's on her feet now. "They treat us like babies. They *turn us into* babies!" She whirls around the room, looks everyone in the eye.

Then she loses speed. "Now I'm out. I'm free. I can do what I want . . . and I don't know what to do. I don't even know what I want for dinner." She collapses back in the couch. "It's too much."

She smiles and shakes her head as if she's making fun of herself. "Freedom is such hard work." Her face is wet with tears.

Monet sits beside her on the couch. "It's okay, Mommy. You're with us now." She wraps an arm around her mother's shoulder and touches her cheek with her other hand. "You take your time, Mommy. We'll take care of you. You take as long as you want."

They sit together on the couch for a long, long time.

Zeb watches the squirrels until the sun fades away.

Libby and Angel cook hamburgers for dinner.

Chapter Fifty-one

They celebrate Christmas together, and New Year's too.

All Sheila and Zeb want is to be together. It seems to Angel that they spend every minute holding hands.

Soon the household finds its new routines. Monet goes back to campus at UDC, and Angel returns to school during the day while cooking and cleaning with Libby overnight. Sheila and Zeb keep the house—not that there's so much to do—and learn how to be free. They explore the neighborhood during the day and Sheila—Sheila!—decides what to cook for dinner. They share a family meal together every afternoon at four o'clock, often with Monet.

They have a family conference to discuss the budget. They can't afford a bigger space, they decide, but they need to do it.

"Bernard will come through with the funding," Angel says. "My business will grow."

"I'll find work of some kind," says Zeb.

"I still have my Visa card," Libby offers.

In February they move into a new place a few blocks away. It's still tiny and the windows aren't as good, but Libby has a bedroom, Sheila and Zeb share a bedroom, and Angel has a room of his own. Monet sleeps on the couch in the living room when she's home from school for a night.

Zeb has some friends from the inside who help with the move. They'd do it for free, but Angel insists on paying some cash. "We need to share our good fortune," he says.

"They'll appreciate that," Zeb agrees. "Most people don't have it this good."

Angel's bread money no longer goes into savings to start his business. Every nickel goes to survival but, as Bernard observed, he wouldn't accumulate half a million dollars of venture capital one loaf at a time, anyway.

Bernard is excited about one prospect in particular. "He's practical but adventuresome," he explains. "His practical side will appreciate fresh bread for breakfast. His adventurer will enjoy working with a teenager."

Bernard explains that his friend is coming in May. He has big meetings in D.C. but will come to Fairfax just to see Bernard. "We're old friends and we've had some hits together."

A meeting in May gives Angel time to polish his prospectus, and he and Bernard even find time to look together for space. "Kitchen space that's ready to use doesn't come up that often," he advises. "We should survey our options and be ready to move."

Angel stops charging Bernard for bread in the morning. It seems the least he can do.

The new apartment opens new horizons in every direction. The kitchen has a full-sized oven, and soon Sheila learns how to bake bread and sell fresh bread around the apartment in the evenings—testing Angel's model for business development at the same time that she helps pay her way and makes some friends.

In March Sheila learns that the apartment has a community garden on the edge of the property beside the parking lot. A few years ago, tenants got the landlord's permission to turn what used to be an unused strip of grass into space for vegetables, flowers, and herbs. Sheila signs up for a four-by-eight plot of her own and, after years of daydreaming, she lets loose her natural talent for plants. She starts by tilling the soil—which she calls "playing around in the dirt"—and learns from the neighbors that it's not too soon to start planting spinach, radishes, and peas.

Sheila also learns how to make tasty sprouts in a jar in the kitchen from beans she buys at the supermarket, causing Libby to remark that she used to do the same thing when she was a little girl on the farm.

"With your mom?" Angel inquires, giving her a dirty look.

Libby doesn't reply.

He still doesn't know what she did with that piece of paper.

He learned the hard way that the phone company wouldn't divulge the number that called in. "Not without a court order," the agent told him. "You can buy caller ID if you want, but we protect customer privacy."

While Sheila digs in the garden, Zeb learns that local men who need work hang out by the Home Depot, where homeowners go for cheap hourly labor. With his good looks and perfect English, Zeb learns that he can catch several hours of work or sometimes several days in a row digging ditches or clearing brush. It pays for his bus ticket to the Home Depot and helps with the month's rent, though it's not a real job and not what he dreams of.

Real jobs are proving hard to find, though. Most job applications ask if he has a felony conviction, which excludes him before he even reaches the starting line. He can't apply for bottom-end jobs because of his felony conviction and he can't apply for financial aid in hope of getting an education and maybe even finding work in a law firm. So he settles for the Home Depot and longs for more.

"You'll be my general counsel," Angel declares. "Once my bakery delivery is up and running I'll need all kinds of help with business and paperwork.

"Great."

On Sunday evening, April 1, Sheila makes a special dinner. Some tasty leftovers and barely usable zucchini came home from the Firenze the night before, and Sheila turns it into ratatouille. After dinner Sheila and Zeb head out for a walk—with deep appreciation of the freedom to turn left or right as they wish—while Libby and Angel begin to turn in for the night.

The telephone rings, and Angel picks it up right away. After only a few words he calls across to Libby, "It's for you. It's your mother."

Chapter Fifty-two

"Yes," Angel says into the telephone. "She's here. You can talk to her in a moment. But before I give up the phone, tell me again, what's your number?"

He makes it sound so casual, an ordinary question for an infrequent caller, and of course his pen and paper are right by the phone. He doesn't say that he's out of patience with his mother, but his eyes burn into her as he passes her the phone.

Looking helpless and uncertain, she takes it.

Then she disappears. She flees into her bedroom and closes the door, and a long time passes before Angel even hears her talking. He doesn't exactly stand by her door listening in, but he doesn't run water on those last few dishes or disappear into his own room for the night. He finds little things to do quietly around the living room, picking up a newspaper and sweeping some stray dirt out of a corner, ears trained on Libby's bedroom.

Libby stays on the telephone for nearly an hour. Angel is conscious of the time, scratching out a few ideas on his business prospectus but knowing that his heart's not in it. Right now, he's supposed to be asleep. So is Libby.

Instead he listens to her voice rise and fall in the other room, sometimes barely audible, sometimes almost a shout, until clearly she says good-bye. The apartment goes silent.

Still he waits. It takes all his willpower, all his seventeen years of patience not to knock on the door. But still he waits, expecting that soon enough she will emerge to hang up the phone, or at least to use the bathroom.

"We're going to visit her," Angel says.

Libby hasn't fully stepped into the room before he announces his decision.

"Give me a minute," she replies.

"Seventeen years wasn't enough?"

But she takes her minute. Walking to hang up the phone, then use the bathroom and wash her hands.

"Okay," she says when she comes back out. "We can visit."

"Really?" After all this, he didn't expect it to be so easy.

"You're right. It's time." She says it like she's decided what to cook for dinner.

He doesn't hug her, doesn't shout for joy. He just puts away the notebook he had in his hand when she joined him.

"It's far away," she continues. "It's not easy to get to."

"It's in Virginia. That's the only thing you ever told me about your family. They're from Virginia. All of us were born in Virginia."

"There's no bus." She sounds helpless like never before.

"I'll drive," he affirms.

After that, it's just logistics. Libby doesn't have a driver's license and doesn't need one, but it makes sense for Angel. Most kids in school have licenses by now, or at least a learner's permit. He knows how easy it is to get a learner's permit: study an hour in the library, take a test at the DMV. That's it. Even the fee is cheap.

The full driver's license is harder. Classes cost hundreds of dollars and take weeks in an official car, including a driving exam—but he doesn't need a full license at this time. The permit will allow him to drive with an adult, and Libby is good enough for that.

They're discussing rentals when Sheila and Zeb return. Renting might be hard with only a learner's permit.

"My friend Curt would lend you his car for a weekend," Zeb announces, barely knowing what they're talking about. "When do you think you need it?"

Chapter Fifty-three

The next morning, Monday, Bernard is waiting for Angel at his apartment building. "My target is coming on Friday," he declares. "My prospect."

"Your friend the investor?"

"Exactly. His business is bringing him to D.C. earlier than he thought. I've arranged to meet him at four o'clock on Friday. You'll be out of school by then, no?"

"As if it would matter?" Angel replies. "Where?"

"The Common Grounds coffee shop." Angel knows the Common Grounds, though he's never been inside.

"My business plan isn't finished, you know." Angel is proud of his plan but thought he'd have more time for the final formatting, typing corrections, and a last look at his budget.

"It's done enough. He's an old friend. He'll get the idea. Half the reason to write the business plan is to solidify your own ideas, and you're rock solid there. You're ready. I'll take care of the rest."

"Friday. Four o'clock."

"Dress your best."

Molly greets Angel as he arrives at school, and he seizes the opportunity to ask about learner's permits. "Just look up 'Virginia driver's manual' on any computer," she advises. "Read it and memorize. It won't take you a whole hour."

Tammy is nearby. "We're talking about Angel," she adds. "It will take fifteen minutes."

Parker Carlson guesses exactly what they're talking about. "If you flunk the test you can take it again. But you have to wait fifteen days in between."

Angel recognizes the voice of experience. He'll get it right the first time.

While Angel is thinking about learner's permits and business plans, the rest of the school is thinking about the senior prom, the big dance in May. The hallways buzz with ideas and intrigue. Two girls by the door in homeroom are comparing catalogs of dresses. Three girls in the back are trading opinions on jewelry and shoes. At lunchtime, Veronica West walks around the cafeteria in a hat that looks to Angel like a helicopter, asking everyone (except Angel) what they think of it. Boys talk about renting tuxedos and whether to wear black or something creative like burgundy or blue. Parker Carlson announces that he's going in gold.

The biggest question is who's going with whom. The couples are obvious enough. Parker Carlson is going with Melissa Brinn, whom he's been dating for months. Joanna Baye isn't dating Wally Roscoe, but the old friends decide quickly to go as a pair. Faisal Rahman will go with Amrita Patel, and the scandal it raises in Faisal's family produces a rolling seminar about Islam, Hinduism, and the history of religious conflict in West Asia.

Angel knows it's happening but he isn't even dreaming about it. Sure, he'd like to go. It even sounds like fun. But the price of the tickets alone—skip the tuxedo rental—makes it impossible. He tunes out those conversations and doesn't even consider it. Too much needs attention before prom tickets.

Angel takes an hour after school to study the Driver's Manual on a library computer, then stops to visit Austin on the way home. He doesn't do Austin's chores anymore, but he likes to check in and say hello sometimes; if he has a loaf left over, he leaves a gift. At first Austin protested that an old man like him couldn't use a whole loaf of fresh bread, but then he started bragging how he makes croutons when it gets stale.

Today Angel has much to report. He tells Austin about his learner's permit and the trip he's planning with his mother, though he skips most of the personal details.

And he updates about his business plans with Bernard Farley, whom Austin does not trust at all.

"What's he paying you to write the prospectus?" Austin asks.

"He's not paying me. He's helping me think it through. He'll make money later off his investment."

"Sounds to me like you're writing his business plan for him. He'll take it to his investor and *whoosh!* He's the millionaire. If you're lucky, he'll give you a job."

Chapter Fifty-four

Angel's agenda after school is fixed for the week. On Tuesday after school he takes a bus to the DMV and takes his permit exam. It's on a computer and feels almost exactly like the practice tests he took at the library. He passes easily and walks out with a receipt. His permit will arrive in the mail within days.

"Once it arrives you can drive with another licensed driver in the car," he's reminded as he finishes the paperwork.

"Not just an adult?"

"No. A licensed driver."

Angel already knew that, and his mother does too. But she's an adult and she says she grew up driving tractors on the farm and pick-up trucks to the dump. She says they'll be fine.

Tuesday night his mother suggests that he can skip baking at the Firenze if he wants.

"No, thanks," he replies. "Cash flow."

On Wednesday after school he takes a bus to the Fair Oaks mall. Sheila and Zeb join him to shop for a suit.

Angel rarely goes shopping, and Sheila and Zeb haven't been to a place like this since before they were locked away. They walk the mall with eyes of astonishment and awe at all of the affluence, all the excess and all the *choices* people can make.

But they focus on their mission, too. Sheila and Zeb can come back as tourists anytime they want. Today they choose a classic gray suit for Angel, with a blue shirt and red tie.

"How do I tie it?" Angel asks.

Zeb gives him lessons right there in the store. Over the top with the wide end, then up from behind and through the hole in the middle. Angel masters it on his second try, but does a third and fourth anyway.

Zeb convinces him to spend an extra thirty dollars for "while you wait" tailoring. "Sometimes you have to spend money to make money," Zeb says.

Sheila tugs on a little looseness around his shoulder and points to the extra length on his sleeves. "Make it perfect," she declares.

So Angel stands while the tailor tugs the fabric snug around his shoulders and measures his sleeves. Then the threesome walk wide-eyed around the mall for an hour. The food court is most exciting of all. "So many choices!" Zeb exclaims.

"None of them healthy," Sheila adds. But they go ahead and accept a free sample of chicken from Hunan Wok, even with no intention of buying a meal.

Back at the Men's Shop a whole new person looks back at Angel from the mirror. Gone is the scrawny teenager in the old slacks and worn T-shirt. Those are in a bag on the floor. Now he's a young man ready for action.

On Thursday after school he's back in the school library to Google map the directions to Libby's family farm near Chatham, Virginia. He takes his time looking at the map, zooming in and out, trying to understand the area—off Highway 29, not far from the mountains to the west. The satellite view shows lots of green, but zoomed in he can see the actual cleared fields of the farm.

His mother grew up there. That's her home. The answer to his mystery is on the screen in front of him. He smiles at the irony that his first view of his mother's home is from outer space. It doesn't feel homey yet, he realizes, but it will. Soon.

Feeling like a grown-up, he presses "print" and pulls the text directions and a map off the printer.

In the old days he would have copied the directions and sketched the map longhand into a notebook, to save the printer fee. But he's a businessman now. Like the suit and tie, the printer fee is worth spending money on.

Bernard is supposed to bring a hard copy of his prospectus to the meeting, but Angel wants to be sure. He prints that, too, with Zeb's counsel on "spending money to make money" echoing in his ears. Ninety cents on the printer is really okay.

Friday is the big meeting. Should he go to school in the suit? Angel decides not to risk it.

Last before he leaves the house on Thursday night he packs his suit into an extra gym bag, Libby folding it carefully along the creases. He'll change after school on Friday and put his school clothes into the empty gym bag.

His prospectus goes in the same bag.

He's ready.

Chapter Fifty-five

School lets out at 3:02. Angel takes a school bus that goes the direction of Common Grounds, then walks. On the way he stops at a supermarket to change his clothes in the bathroom. He doesn't want to enter Common Grounds and find Bernard and his investor already there, waiting for him and finding a schoolboy.

When he enters Common Grounds at 3:45 he looks like the other young professionals drinking coffee and typing at laptops.

Bernard is nowhere to be seen. Fine. Angel expected to be early, and he is. He picks a table by the window, with empty seats.

At 3:55 Bernard has not yet arrived.

At 4:00 sharp he has not yet arrived.

At 4:10 Angel starts to worry.

Around 4:15 he gets a dirty look from one of the servers, a young woman in a brown Common Grounds uniform with her hair tied up in a bandanna. Angel is occupying one of the best tables and hasn't even bought anything.

At 4:20 he starts studying the menu.

At 4:30 he buys himself the cheapest thing he can find, a chocolate chunk cookie for $1.95 plus tax.

He has homework to do but he'll feel like a child if the investor comes in while Angel has textbooks spread across the table. He keeps his printed prospectus and a blank notebook in plain view, but does nothing else. He tries to be patient. He tries not to worry. Surely, the investor's meeting went late. Surely Bernard is stuck in traffic and feels terrible to keep Angel waiting. He makes excuses on their behalf, practices his gracious acceptance of their apologies.

He keeps practicing his pitch, as Bernard advised.

"Tell me about yourself." He has an answer.

"What's your business plan?" He has an answer.

"But you're so young! Shouldn't you get experience in someone else's business . . . then start your own?" Angel has an answer.

At 4:45 he's been waiting a whole hour. Where's Bernard? Has something gone wrong? He doesn't have an answer.

He sits there and sits there. The cookie is excellent, and he stretches out his nibbling as other groups of customers walk in, look at him sitting by himself at a table for four, and squeeze in someplace else.

By five o'clock he's truly out of patience. Has Bernard done him wrong? What if he leaves and Bernard arrives five minutes later? He'll give it another five minutes.

Then another five minutes. He spends the whole time pondering the very same question: *When should I give up? When should I leave?*

At 5:30 he gives up. They're an hour and a half late, if they're coming at all.

But Angel doesn't go home. He takes the bus to Bernard's condominium. He's been here many times with bread for Bernard or bread for others. The security officer recognizes him when he arrives.

"Gone, gone, gone," he says. "Your friend, Bernard Farley? He's gone, gone, gone."

"What do you mean? We had a meeting."

"Process server came on Wednesday. Civil suit for sexual harassment. Not his first. Farley gave notice yesterday and moved out of state. He says he'll get in touch about forwarding his mail and cleaning out his stuff."

"Cleaning out his stuff?"'

"The landlord is already showing his unit." He points to a bulletin board with a vacancy announcement. "Hopes to have Farley out and a new tenant by the 15th."

"Thanks," says Angel.

"You look nice," says the officer.

Angel has no Plan B. The work he put in with Bernard didn't convince him that he could do it himself, didn't inspire him to take the leap on his own. It showed him it's nothing but a daydream. Nobody will lend half a million dollars to a kid with no track record, and he can't accumulate half a million dollars one loaf at a time.

He needs Bernard. There's no other way. Bernard isn't the only one "gone, gone, gone." So is Angel's dream. There's no other way to make this happen. He heads home feeling discouraged like never before.

And his suit is tailored. It isn't returnable.

At home the apartment is still. Sheila and Zeb are out, and Libby is fast asleep.

On Angel's pillow is an envelope. His learner's permit arrived in the mail. On the envelope his mother wrote a note: *Tomorrow.*

Chapter Fifty-six

At six in the morning Angel hears Libby return from the Firenze. She enters his bedroom and shakes his shoulder. "Zeb is outside with a car," she says. "I'm going to take a shower. Go take a driving lesson."

Zeb is on the street with a white Ford Focus and a full tank of gas.

"Where's Sheila?" Angel asks. He's so used to seeing them together.

"In bed, silly. It's barely daylight. Now come here." He shows Angel how to sit in the car and adjust the mirrors. As someone who's rarely even a passenger, it's all new to Angel.

Zeb shows him how to start the engine, turn on the lights, and put it in gear. He fastens himself into the passenger seat and counsels Angel through some low-velocity driving to an empty parking lot, hours before the stores even open.

Soon enough Angel has the hang of it, and he's weaving around the empty lot with velocity and confidence. "There's just one more problem," Zeb says.

"What's that?"

"Other cars."

Zeb gives him a long warning about other cars, unpredictable drivers, and taking it slow. "I didn't tell Curt you don't know how to drive," he concludes as Angel pulls back up to their apartment. "Don't mess us up."

Libby steps out the front door with some extra clothes and bags of food.

Angel rolls down his window. "Let's go."

At first it's all about driving. Angel takes it slow and Libby tells him to look out for this or he's too close to that, mixed in with directions about which way to turn until they reach the highway.

The merge is easy, but fifty miles per hour feels fast to Angel, and Libby says that's fine. "Let them pass us."

After that, both are silent for a long time. Angel is nervous behind the wheel and Libby looks tired. Finally, after novelty gives way to boredom, Angel breaks the silence.

"Why didn't you tell me?" he asks.

Libby says nothing. She's awake and listening but she says nothing.

"I'm going to guess to save you some embarrassment," he continues in a lighthearted tone. "You got knocked up by a local boy. Your parents disapproved. You ran away." Angel isn't a child anymore. He can make adult guesses.

Libby says nothing.

"Am I right? It's not a bad story. You wouldn't be alone." He tries to make a joke. "Was he cute?"

Libby says, "Look out for the little blue car."

She's right. Angel hadn't noticed the little blue car swerving and weaving just ahead. As they pass, the driver is talking into a cell phone and adjusting the radio. "Let's put him behind us," Angel says.

A mile later he tries again, pushing further in the same direction. "Maybe there was more than one boyfriend," he offers. "More than one possibility, and you don't know who. That's okay, too." He's trying to offer an easy way out. "You still wouldn't be the first."

Now Libby reacts like she can't stand it anymore. "He wasn't my boyfriend, and he wasn't cute." Her voice is a hammer. The final blow strikes his head. "It wasn't consensual, either."

Angel almost jerks the car off the road, looking so hard in her direction. He recovers control quickly enough, but still he's horrified. He wishes he could swallow every word. He thought he was being so clever. Now he sees how much of the world never occurred to him. He's shocked by his own ignorance and intrusion. Had his mother been raped? Raped by a gang? What if she'd been raped and impregnated?

Might she not want to talk about that? Why is that not okay? Who is he to drag it out like this?

Maybe she needs therapy. Maybe she needs to talk.

Or maybe she just needs to put it behind her and leave it there. Is it fair for him to take that away?

He thought he had the right to know. He thought he had truth and justice on his side, the right to push. Suddenly he's not so sure.

As the miles roll on, he replays in his own mind everything he knows about his father, every time he asked a question, and what his mother said in return. It's so little, such a small number of words. But that shortage helps him remember more precisely, since every word was gold. Nothing she ever said on the subject was inconsistent with what might be the terrible truth.

From nowhere his mother says, "Exit 43. Turn south on 29."

Angel doesn't even reply. He could be so wrong it's almost like he's lost the right to speak. Besides, he remembers the map from the library. Three hours south on Route 29 brings them home.

"Wake me up before we arrive." She squints as a flash of sun hits her eyes. "I'm tired."

The next three hours are like an awakening. First, he's new to the open road. Even sixty miles per hour doesn't seem so fast anymore. When he swerves around bends or accelerates up hills, he understands why people like to drive.

At the same time, he watches his mother sleeping in the seat next to him. She looks relaxed and comfortable in a way he rarely sees. His mother is usually nothing but business; even her free time gets scheduled in. He sees her in a whole new light, and himself as well. What if she's not a closed-mouth keeper of secrets, but a surviving hero? What if he's not a victim of schemes, but an aggressive intruder? His reaches a simple conclusion: Better to keep your mouth shut.

Eventually he gets hungry and manages to unpack the bag at his mother's feet. Garlic bread from the Firenze. It would have been better hot and fresh, no doubt. But along with an apple from another bag, it makes a nice breakfast.

Just shy of Chatham they stop for a railroad crossing. Angel was close to awakening his mother, but she stirs for the crossing, which makes it easy.

They visit for a moment but it's hard in the hullabaloo. With the end of the freight train out of sight in the distance, they get out of the car and amble along the tracks, the massive machinery thundering alongside

"When I was a little girl, we'd put bottle caps on the track and pick them up after the train ran them over. They'd be flatter than a pancake."

"Sounds like fun," Angel says.

"Lots of things were fun back then." Libby's tone is also flatter than a pancake.

Soon enough they're back in the car and driving along Route 29. It's like a main street here, not a highway. It slows down for cross streets and traffic lights. On the far side of town they catch up to a woman walking on the side of the road. She's tugging her child's hand, and Angel can see "Hurry up!" written all over her. As they pass they see the child, a girl, maybe five or six years old, dragging her feet as her mother pulls her arm. Up ahead is nothing but distance, probably miles before the next town.

"Pull over," commands Libby as they pass.

"What?"

"Pull over. Turn around. We need to give them a lift."

"Do you know her?"

"Pull over."

Angel pulls over to let another car pass, and even as he calculates how to turn around, his mother opens her door and hops out.

A moment later the woman and child are climbing into the back seat. "Thanks so much," the woman says. "We're heading for my sister's house—"

"Cousin Abby!" interjects the child.

"—and we missed the bus. It's two hours before the next one, and we want to be there by brunch. It's only a mile or so."

A few minutes later, in hardly more time than the explanation and some introductory chitchat, the woman is interrupting. "Here we go. This will be fine. Thanks so much for the ride!" She's pointing to cluster of homes on a long driveway, and the little girl is already zipping up her coat. A moment later they've both bustled out with final thanks and farewells.

"You bet," says Libby. "It was literally the least I could do."

Angel starts to talk but his mother waves him off, and Angel has learned to not to press when she does. "The least I could do," she repeats. "I couldn't do any less."

Angel keeps listening. He can see her thinking hard.

"I got a ride once," she says. "People around here give rides all the time. It's no big deal. But this one ride in particular. I was going the other direction. I was traveling north." She peters out. Angel can't tell if she's just tired, if the memory has faded, or if she's hiding something.

"Where were you going?" he tries to help. He's slowing down now, having caught up to a truck traveling slowly. He doesn't mind the delay.

At last his mother continues. "I didn't know where I was going. Away, I guess. Away from home. I was probably traveling north because our driveway hits the road on the northbound side of the street."

Angel sees some pieces fitting into place, even the ones he'd guessed at. "You were running away?"

She nods.

"Was I with you?"

She nods.

"How old was I?"

She doesn't answer for a long time. Eventually he tries again. "Why were you running away?"

She still doesn't answer.

Finally he prods her onward. "Things were bad at home."

She nods.

Acutely conscious of his ability to make mistakes, he tries to put himself in her shoes. He starts with his mother running away, and wonders what from. She loved her horse, loved the farm-fresh food, and loved baking bread with her mother. Her father is the biggest mystery, the father who disappeared. Maybe it was something about her father . . .

Suddenly, many pieces come together at once. He remembers how Libby reacted when she learned that his friend Joanna Baye—not even his friend at that time, someone he hardly knew—was being abused by her father. Libby moved heaven and earth to help someone she didn't know. Somehow Libby knew Joanna needed help, and that police and prosecutors were beside the point. Something in her own experience taught her what Joanna needed.

Angel still doesn't know what to say, but television news and Joanna Baye give him the vocabulary. "You were abused," he says.

She looks at him in alarm.

"Sexually," he adds.

She nods again, and he risks one step farther. "By your father."

Libby goes dark.

Angel doesn't know what happened or how, but suddenly his mother changes. A minute ago she was part of a conversation. Worried, for sure, maybe upset, but utterly present and engaged. Now it's as if she's disappeared. She isn't looking at Angel, or anyone else. Her lights have gone out.

A wide shoulder opens on the road ahead. Angel pulls over and shuts off the engine. He doesn't trust his driving, and this needs full attention.

With the car stopped and the windows opened, Libby finally looks up. "Yes," she says. "My father. Joseph Warren Thompson."

For a long time he looks at her. He sees the next step coming into view. The last step, and he wants to leave it unsaid but he can't. "That's where I fit in."

Even as he says it he wants to vomit. The sick feeling starts in his stomach and rises.

Libby nods again, but this time not just in agreement. Now it's as if she wants to say something but doesn't have the words. She moves her mouth like she's gasping for air, until finally she gives up and leans back against the seat.

"You never told me," Angel says. He wants to sound wounded, expects to sound wronged, but even to his own ears it sounds like a childish complaint, a tiny injustice at the bottom of a much bigger pile.

His mother rises in ire. "Of course I didn't tell you! I didn't know what to say. If I don't tell you, then you don't know. If I tell you . . . " her voice trickles off. "It's not clear that you're better off."

A big truck pulls in alongside them, and a line of cars that had been stuck behind the truck all accelerate past. When the last car is gone, the truck pulls out, engine roaring, black exhaust belching into the sky.

He starts to talk again, partly to her, partly to himself out loud. "What if you . . . " but he trickles off.

"You never tried to . . . " but again it goes nowhere.

Another car whizzes past, bright red and moving fast. Angel shakes his head with knowledge that in moments it will be stuck behind a slow-moving truck.

"I didn't know what to do," Libby says. "I didn't know what to say."

Angel turns on his engine and puts the car in gear, pulls out behind the red car, knowing full well that soon he too will be stuck behind the truck. As he reaches cruising speed he says to his mom, "I don't know either."

Chapter Fifty-seven

Angel doesn't have any preconception of what the farm will look like. He hasn't imagined anything in advance, not a storybook farm with hayrides and apples, nor a destitute backwater of tobacco and filth. He doesn't know what to expect when his mother slows him down in the final mile, making sure he won't miss the turnoff that Libby might not recognize and his Google print-out doesn't show with precision.

Finally, after five minutes of creeping along, getting passed by every car approaching from behind, his mother says the magic word: "There."

She gestures toward a mailbox attached to a tree where a long, nondescript driveway reaches the road. Angel turns left into the driveway on the northbound side of the street and keeps on driving, nice and slow.

It's full spring by now and the leaves are emerging from their slumber, pale green against a clear blue sky. Yellow daffodils line the driveway, and other early flowers flash bright colors against awakening grass.

"I planted the daffodils," Libby observes. "At the end of summer it's tiger lilies."

In another moment the house comes into view, a modest bungalow with yellow clapboard siding. A newish Toyota is parked in front, along with a big old pick-up truck. Some distance behind the house is a barn, and other smaller structures are scattered around, with big fields fading into the distance.

Eva Louise Thompson emerges from the door. She's shorter than Libby, and Angel too, as well as heavier. She's wearing a faded blue dress on top of blue jeans, and a pretty cardigan sweater with flowers. Her hair is tied up in a bun. As she steps out of the house she's tucking something into her pocket.

Libby and Angel get out of the car, and the silence is awkward. No tears are shed. There are no exclamations of joy or jubilant hugging. Three strangers stand in a driveway, not knowing what to say. Libby straightens out her jacket and brushes hair from her eyes. A small gray bird lands beside the car.

Eva Louise breaks the silence. "You must be tired. Can I get you something to drink? Please come in and use the bathroom."

They follow her through the door to the kitchen. The kitchen is all wood, even the floor, with large windows and blue gingham curtains. Each window has a broad sill filled with fresh-cut flowers, small plants, and ivies that reach all the way to the floor. An old cat scurries into the next room as they enter.

On the table, a nice breakfast looks ready to go. A bowl of fruit has been sliced, and ceramic dishes arranged in order. Eva Louise lifts a towel to reveal a tray of muffins. "Tea or coffee, perhaps? Eggs?"

"From our chickens?" Libby asks, the slightest ache in her voice.

"Of course, from our chickens." To Angel, Eva Louise says, "Wait until you meet our chickens!" Placing a hand on Libby's shoulder, she adds, "Your mom used to love taking care of the chickens."

Libby flinches away from the hand, walks to the other side of the room.

Eva Louise goes on. "Your mom used to love the flowers, too." She points toward the windows. "I picked tulips for you. And some of your daffodils."

Libby doesn't seem to be listening, but Eva goes on.

"Remember the house used to be white? It needed paint a few years ago and I was tired of white. It's always been white. White's boring and I live alone now. I needed something to brighten me up. What do you think? Do you like the yellow?"

Libby peers around the corner where the cat disappeared.

"We have a new chicken coop, too. Your brothers came down one weekend and we spent the whole time building the new chicken coop. Wait until you see it. It's fabulous."

Angel sees it all happening. He sees poor Eva Louise struggling to start a conversation, trying to break the ice. He sees his mother not even listening. He knows where her mind is, too. He knows what barrier remains unspoken between them.

"We had chicken for dinner that night. The poor dears! They watched us all day, and we ate the biggest one that night. What do you think, Libby darling? If we build them a new house, can we eat one for dinner?"

Libby shakes her head like Angel has seen her do so many times, if he's complaining about something or making excuses for doing something wrong. He recognizes her earnest disappointment, her distress that someone is missing something obvious. "I don't care about the chickens," she says at last, her voice quiet, then gaining in strength. "I didn't come here for the chickens."

Eva Louise defends herself. "But you loved the chickens!"

"And I like the yellow, too," Libby replies. Then suddenly it's like she can't take it anymore. "It's me, Mom. Libby. You can't act like nothing happened. You can't act like I'm visiting for breakfast."

"I thought, maybe . . . "

"You thought what, Mom? You thought maybe I'd forget what happened? You thought maybe I'd forget you never helped?"

Libby strides across the room to her mother. "How did you let it happen?" Her voice is rising in anger, years of torment finding release. "*Chickens?*" she sneers. "You could have done something. You could have helped. *Why didn't you stop him?*"

Angel has never seen his mother like this. Her face is red, her eyes ablaze. This isn't the sweet reunion Angel was expecting. Her anger is terrifying.

Eva Louise retreats until her back is against the wall, her hands pressed flat against the surface. Angel sees no doubt in her mind, no confusion. She knows exactly what Libby is talking about. Eyes down, talking to her feet, Eva mutters softly, "I didn't know."

"You didn't know?" Libby's words are poison, dripping with venom. "How could you not have known?"

Eva lifts her hands helplessly. "I can't know everything that happens in the house. Or on the farm. I can't see everything behind every door." She gains energy as she defends against the attack. "How could I know? *How come you didn't tell me?*"

The accusation seems to push Libby over an edge. She jabs her finger toward her mother like she's poking holes. "How come *I* didn't tell *you*? As if I didn't tell you. I told you! You weren't listening."

Now Libby races back to the other side of the kitchen, as if she can't get far enough away, then turns and shouts, "I didn't tell you? What about the time I showed you the bleeding?" She points almost obscenely at her crotch. "You bought me a new saddle."

"It was a nice saddle," Eva protests. "We didn't have money for it, and I bought it anyway. For you!"

"I liked my old saddle." Libby's hand is still on her thigh. "Why do you think I showered at three in the morning?"

Eva says nothing.

"When he heard me in the shower, he'd wait for me in my room until I came in to get dressed. The middle of the night was the only time it was safe." She's hugging herself across her chest by now, as if hiding her breasts from onlookers. "If I brought clothes to the bathroom, he'd barge in anyway. Don't you remember I asked for a lock?"

Eva seems to know exactly what she's talking about.

"I installed that little deadbolt on the inside. You made me take it off."

For an instant Libby's composure breaks. She's no longer a demon of anger but a little girl pleading for help. "I needed you. *I asked for you.* You refused." Tears almost begin but the rage chases them away. "Don't you dare tell me I didn't do enough. *How could you not have known?*"

Now it's Eva Louise who's on the brink of tears. "It was so far beyond," she says. "I just couldn't believe it. I didn't believe my own eyes. I just couldn't imagine." She's crying all the way now, pulls a towel from beside the sink and wipes her eyes. Suddenly she points at Angel. "Then came the proof." She pulls the towel away, uncovers her eyes. "There's no denying the proof."

Angel wishes he could disappear. He feels like a bystander to a terrible accident, unable to help but unable to look away. He's an intruder in someone else's personal drama.

But no, he's not a bystander. He's not an intruder. He's the proof.

"The burns were bad," Eva Louise is saying, as if Libby would know what she's talking about. "Burns hurt a lot, you know, and they're slow to heal."

"But you took care of him, I'm sure."

Eva's voice drops in loathing. "I let him take care of himself," she replies. Angel can taste her bitterness—her own betrayal by the man she'd built her life with, the man who did things that she literally could not believe. "He called his own doctor. He drove himself to the appointments. I didn't care how much it hurt. If he couldn't reach it, it didn't get the salve."

Eva accepted the small justice that came to her but it didn't heal the wounds, didn't make things right. She opens her hands and drops them to her sides. Her eyes are on her daughter. "I'm sorry," she declares. "I didn't do enough. Can you ever forgive me? I was wrong."

In a movie, Angel knows that this is the part when the parties joyfully hug and all is forgiven. But it doesn't turn out that way. With Eva Louise repeating herself, all but begging forgiveness, Libby turns and leaves the room.

When she doesn't come back after a minute, Eva Louise walks out the other door.

Now Angel is by himself in the kitchen.

Chapter Fifty-eight

He's hungry by now. He helps himself to a muffin and pours a glass of cider from the refrigerator. He sees the eggs in a row and thinks about frying a few but decides he shouldn't cut off a speedy exit.

He thinks his mother will come back. He sees a happy ending maybe about to happen; he just doesn't know how it gets there.

He steps outside to look more at the yard, hoping to see some other signs of life, but other than two chickens scratching behind a bush he's all alone. The two women are somewhere in the house.

In a nearby tree, a bird sings a sudden snatch of melody. Somewhere behind the house another bird matches the call, and the first bird flies off in that direction. Angel stays awhile, listening to the songs of nature, a low hum of insects and birds he rarely hears in busy Fairfax. The scratching of the chickens sounds like a racket in comparison.

"Don't you want to go to your coop?" he asks the chickens. "I hear you have a great new coop."

The chickens don't answer. Eventually Angel gets cold, and heads back to the kitchen.

The moment he enters, he notices a smell that maybe had been there all along, though certainly it wasn't this strong. The smell can't come from nowhere, and surely has a source right here.

He puts a hand on the oven. It's warm.

He opens the door. A fresh loaf is on the shelf.

He closes the door quickly before the heat escapes, and as he turns around, Eva Louise reenters the room. "I prepped it this morning," she says. "I put it in when you arrived. I figured you'd want fresh bread soon enough."

It all makes sense to Angel. The scent increases as the dough warms.

"What kind is it?" Angel asks.

"Your mother's favorite. White bread with too much butter."

Angel can feel the history in the room. He knows his mother used to bake bread in this very kitchen, with this very woman beside him.

"Show me how to knead," he says.

Eva Louise looks at him quizzically.

"Mom says you have some special trick to kneading. She says your loaf always rose higher than hers."

Eva Louise knows exactly what he's talking about. "Your mother never quite got the knack of it. Good thing she has you."

When his mother comes back, the first loaf is out of the oven and Eva and Angel are wrist-deep in dough for the next.

Angel shows Eva his favorite easy recipe with oatmeal and honey.

Eva tells Angel about cornmeal and rye, options he's never really explored.

They swap techniques while they knead.

Libby arrives unnoticed from behind them. She simply puts her hand on her mother's shoulder and says, "Yes."

One word says it all. Whatever the questions were—and Angel doesn't remember them all—every one of them now has the same answer. "Yes." The hugs begin. The hugs and the tears.

It's not all fixed yet, even Angel can see that, but it's started. The years and the distance are starting to shrink.

Over bacon and eggs, Eva Louise talks about the future of the farm. One brother runs a little lawn care business in the suburbs of Richmond. "He uses the skills he learned on the farm, but he's not coming back here," Eva explains.

The other brother is assistant manager at a Safeway in Charlottesville. ("Safeway!" say Angel and Libby together. "Our store.") He, too, is settled down and won't be coming back.

"I guess you don't need a used-up old farm, do you?"

Libby shakes her head sadly.

"The vultures are after it," Eva continues. "Every week another shark comes by talking about tourist resorts and summer homes. That piece by the lake seems especially attractive. Last week some guy offered me half a million in cash to sell off that little parcel."

Angel's ears perk up at the mention, the specific irony of not just what he needs, but the exact amount.

Libby sees him and wags her head, no.

"Why not?" he says aloud.

Without waiting for Libby to respond, Angel turns to his grandmother and says what's on his mind. He explains about his plans for a bakery, and the investor who never came. He worries about upsetting the new truce in the room, but the future seems suddenly much closer than the past.

Libby holds her peace while Angel talks; Eva Louise smiles the entire time.

"Yes, why not?" Eva Louise echoes when Angel has run his course. "I want to die on this farm and I plan to die on this farm. But I can lose that piece by the lake in a heartbeat. You kids don't swim in the lake anymore, and I won't even know it's gone."

"Please," says Angel to his mother.

"It's blood money," she replies. "I won't take it."

"I did you wrong," says Eva Louise. "Let me help you now."

"No," says Libby.

"It's not for you. It's for him."

Back and forth they go until finally Angel can't stand it anymore. "I'm sorry!" he asserts from the sidelines. "You guys are arguing about my *existence!*" The women stop abruptly and stare at him. "Clearly people did you wrong. Your dad for sure, and maybe your mom. But if they'd done you right, I wouldn't exactly be here to witness it."

He stands and walks over to Eva Louise's side of the table. He crouches down beside her. "Do you really think you could do this? Would Libby's brothers be upset, your other children? Is this really possible?"

"You let me worry about my otherlings. If you say yes, I'll make the sale. You'll have half a million dollars as soon as I can manage it. More, if I can get the sharks to fight amongst themselves."

Angel holds out his hand to Eva Louise. "Yes, please," he declares. "I accept your offer. I would very much appreciate that money. Someday I might even be able to pay you back. You or your 'otherlings.'"

Next he turns to his mother. "As for the rest of it . . . you two take your time."

He gets up to check the bread he'd been working on. It's been rising while they talked, resting on the warmth of the oven. The half that he kneaded and the half that Eva Louise kneaded are both the same size.

Chapter Fifty-nine

At school on Monday, Molly spots Angel in the computer lab, staring at a map of Southwest Virginia, apparently doing nothing at all.

"That's not your web page," she observes. Everyone knows he's been working on it.

Angel closes the screen as if he's been busted. Veronica West parades past, dressed up like a flamingo on stilts.

For Angel it's enough to change the subject. "Are you going to the prom?" he asks Molly.

"I hope so." She sits down at the computer next to him.

"You're not sure?"

"I'm waiting to be asked."

Angel is astounded. He doesn't know the deadlines, but he knows the dance is soon and it seems like most people are settled already. "Nobody's asked you?"

"Sure, people have asked me. I haven't said yes yet."

"Why not?"

"I already told you. I'm waiting to be asked. What about you, Angel? Are you going to the prom?"

Angel looks embarrassed, like he did in the old days, when they were still passing notes. "I don't know," he says. "I haven't been thinking about it. And it's expensive! Tickets and a tux. It's not so easy." Whatever the future holds, cash today is tight.

"I already have tickets," Molly says. "Two of them, in fact. For me and my date. And look here." She pushes the computer keyboard out of the way and moves her pocketbook into its place, hunting for something that's lost or deeply buried. "Here it is. A fifty-dollar gift certificate for a tuxedo rental."

She holds it out in front of her, all but waves it in his face. "Now tell me. What would I ever do with a gift certificate for a tuxedo rental?"

Angel is looking at his feet. "I don't know. Give it to somebody. When you go to the prom, you could just give it to your date."

He can feel Molly looking at him like he's a moron.

"As I said," she declares. "I'm waiting to be asked."

Finally Angel gets it. After all these years, all his pent-up longing, Angel finally understands what's waving in front of his eyes. "Molly Swann," he inquires politely. "Will you come to the prom with me?"

"Funny you should ask."

Chapter Sixty

For Libby, nothing is different and everything is different.

She reports to work on Monday when she returns from the farm and spends the day scrubbing toilets and mopping floors. At midnight she heads for the Firenze to scour the stove. The sponges move and the floors are clean, but she spends the entire time thinking about her mother.

Eva Louise said she was sorry.

She said she was wrong. She could have known. She should have known. She made a mistake.

Everybody makes mistakes. Libby can understand mistakes. She understands that people don't see things they don't want to see. She understands that her father's behavior was unexpected, to say the least.

Her mother wasn't an accessory to evil.

She was just wrong.

Libby can live with that. She can move past the damage and search for the love she's buried. Eva Louise said she was sorry.

No, Libby's life didn't unfold the way she'd imagined when she was ten years old. Yes, it turned out okay in the end. And no, she wouldn't trade anything in the world for her Angel.

In early June, Eva Louise's check comes through, as she promised. Eva set the sharks fighting amongst themselves and delivers a check for $560,000, even after taxes and transaction fees.

The blood money passes right through Libby's fingers. The light that shines in Angel's eyes clears any doubt whether it's the right thing to do.

Angel calls Eva Louise immediately to thank her and report safe arrival of the check, but Libby talks to her for an hour afterward. Indeed, Libby's been spending so much time on the phone with her mother, Angel jokes they'll need a second line.

Libby gives Moses plenty of notice but stops working overnight at the Firenze. She keeps her day job though, for now anyway, partly for health insurance and partly for an insecurity she's not yet ready to shake.

Chapter Sixty-one

GRADUATION DAY.

Friday, June 21, summer solstice at nine in the morning.

Angel is wearing a black gown and a classic flat mortarboard graduation cap.

His whole family is with him. "We'll invite Eva Louise, right?" he'd asked his mother two weeks before.

Libby didn't seem to have thought of it, but she replied, "Of course."

Graduation is at George Mason University's Patriot Center because Angel's high school doesn't have a space big enough for all of the students and all of their families. Right now they're all in Eva Louise's Toyota, on their way to the ceremony. Eva's driving, with Zeb beside her in front, and Libby, Angel, Sheila and Monet all crammed across the back.

Monet's in the middle, with her knees pressed almost to her chin and Sheila's shoulder jammed into her neck.

"Are you okay?" her mother asks.

"I'm right where I want to be," she replies.

Monet is in the summer of her second year of law school at UDC. She struggled long and hard over what to do this summer, a major step towards a career.

At first she wanted to get a job at a law firm, make some money, and help out after all those years of support.

"Don't you dare," said Libby. "We put in those years so you can do what you want."

Next she considered the U.S. Attorney's Office—aiming to become the right kind of prosecutor—but in the end she couldn't do it. "I'd spend my early years locking up nickel-bag drug cases and being evaluated on my conviction rates," she explained. "Later, when I'm senior enough to maybe make a difference . . . I'll forget where I came from and be part of the problem."

She ended up at the public defender's office. Her biggest surprise was learning that half the job is getting brain-addled drug addicts to show up for court. "If they miss their court dates, the penalties keep piling up. Extra love and care make a big difference," she declared as she announced her decision.

Most conversation in the car is about which way to turn and where to park, with a little "move your elbow" mixed in. But soon enough they arrive, park, and start toward the giant white Patriot Center, which rises in front of them like a mushroom sprouting in a field of parking lots. The day is beautiful and clear, with billowing clouds in a bright blue sky. Sheila, Zeb, and Monet walk holding hands, three in a row, until the growing crowd forces them apart.

Behind them walk Libby, Angel, and Eva Louise, not holding hands, but three together.

Soon enough they enter the stadium, and soon enough they need to part, with signs directing families in one direction and graduating students in another. "Congratulations, young man," says Zeb, taking Angel's hand in his own. "You made it." They shake hands firmly, then step into a hug.

Sheila's hug lasts even longer. "Thank you for everything," she says.

Monet opts for a fist bump, but she can't keep a straight face afterwards and reaches out for a hug of her own. They stand together for a long time, brother and sister, raised together, smiling in each other's eyes.

Eva Louise's hug is merely cordial. They're still getting used to it. "I'm glad we found you," she says as they break.

Libby comes last, and she's crying, a used tissue clutched in her hand. But these aren't the soft, gentle tears of parting. So much more seems to be going on behind her eyes.

"Congratulations, Mom," says Angel, taking her hands in his own.

"Me?"

"Yes, you." He gestures to the celebration all around them. "You brought me through. You did everything right. Congratulations. I mean it."

She brightens just a little, finds a smile.

Angel gathers her in for her hug, strong arms around small shoulders. "Thanks, Mom. Thanks for everything."

Off they go in separate directions. Angel follows the signs for students and soon reaches signs for each letter of the alphabet, arranging the graduates in alphabetical order for the processional. Angel proceeds in the direction of T.

Someone smacks his head gently from behind. He turns to find Parker Carlson, on his way to C no doubt. "Hey, genius," he says with a smile.

"Thanks for all those math lessons. "I'm heading for Providence College in the fall. Football practice starts in August. I probably wouldn't have made it without you."

"It was my pleasure," Angel replies. "Go, team."

He's hoping to see Molly Swann, of course. He expects it won't be hard once he reaches the S-T zone, but the crowds are thick and he hasn't seen her by the time he arrives. It's still early, though. He leans against a wall on the edge and watches the crowd swirl around him. He nods to Oliver Swain as Oliver takes his place in line, probably the space just before Molly.

Angel's bakery will be fine, he knows that now.

He never doubted that Eva would come through. He slowed his overnight cooking almost as soon as he came back from the farm. The last few loaves he delivered were less about sales than an opportunity to say farewell and discuss his plans. While his classmates were slacking on exams and packing for holidays, Angel was working full time on his bakery, now officially christened *Manna from Heaven.*

With Zeb's help, he found a perfect kitchen, far better than anything he saw when he was scouting with Bernard—though Angel could recognize it immediately thanks to that scouting. Zeb negotiated a terrific lease, too, but Eva's sale still hadn't closed, and they lacked the cash when the landlord needed a financial commitment. For a minute, things looked dicey.

Austin Marquette rode to the rescue. He dipped into his savings that very day and drafted a money order for the landlord. Two weeks later when Eva's check cleared, Angel brought him a check for the same amount. Austin insisted that the loan be interest free, but Angel included a separate, hand-written piece of paper with the check. *Free bread,* he wrote. *All you can eat.* On the back it reads, *Make your own croutons. No expiration date.*

Moses Pizzigati created a little christening ceremony the day Angel moved into the kitchen, with a yellow ribbon tied across the front door. "Manna from Heaven," Moses declared. "Let it rain." Along with the christening, Moses offered a torrent of advice about starting a restaurant, and boxes of cooking gear. "We don't use this stuff much around the Firenze," he said, "but it will be perfect for a bakery."

Angel is turning the advice over in his head for the thousandth time, still looking for Molly Swann, when Veronica West plants herself in front of him. She's always tall but today she must be wearing heels, the way she towers over him, demanding his attention. "Most of us are going to college," she announces, pointing toward the crowd behind her. "You're not." Her tone is harsh, almost accusatory.

She's right, of course, but Angel doesn't understand what she's getting at.

"College is obvious," Veronica continues. "It's simple, it's obvious, and it's the right thing to do." She gestures toward the line of caps and gowns, but her serious eyes are directed at him alone. "You're not going to college. You're starting a business. That's the bravest thing in the world."

Angel starts to speak but she isn't finished.

"All of us are being obvious. You alone are being brave. Good luck, Candyman."

She turns on her heel before Angel can reply, and strides the short distance to the sign marked W.

By now Angel must head for his own space, but as he takes his position he feels a tap on his shoulder. "Tag," says Molly, hurrying past. "You're it."

Soon enough the principal raps the microphone and welcomes everyone to graduation. "A day to celebrate," he declares. "A day to remember." After a few words that Angel can barely hear, the band starts to play the processional, the famed "Pomp and Circumstance" that even Angel recognizes.

The front of the line must be moving, Angel knows, but back here in the T's nothing is happening. They are all standing in the hallway, fidgeting, waiting their turn. A burst of applause probably indicates the first students have entered the auditorium.

Listening to the steady beat of "Pomp and Circumstance," Angel finds his hands and shoulders starting to move. He realizes with a smile that he's kneading bread in his mind, translating the steady beat of the march into the motion he knows so well. Press and turn, press and turn, press and turn.

At last they begin to move. Stationary fidgeting becomes a forward shuffle, which eventually becomes measurable progress down the hall. Finally Angel steps under an arch and into the open air.

The stadium is enormous. Thousands of people fill thousands of seats in the biggest crowd Angel has ever seen. He advances with his procession, down the aisle, past parents and siblings and aunts and uncles all looking at their own families alongside him. He feels the energy, the human thrum of love and expectation. He has no idea where his mother and family are sitting, but he knows they're here.

Eventually the procession reaches Angel's row, and the students one by one take their seats.

The band plays on while the rest of the alphabet files in. "Pomp and Circumstance." Beat after beat. In Angel's mind, *knead, knead, knead.*

After the last student is seated the principal starts to speak. He's followed by a local minister, who's followed by some students.

Angel is hardly listening. They all say the same kind of thing. Remarks of hard work and great expectations, good times behind and good times ahead.

The exception is the president of the school board. Itemizing highlights of the year, she lists the performance of the girls lacrosse team, finalists in the National Science Fair, and "our own fresh bread in the morning."

Angel looks up like someone blew a whistle, even as the president continues. "If I understand correctly, soon we'll all have access to the same Manna from Heaven."

Near Angel, where the students know him by name, heads turn in his direction. Someone behind him pats him on the back.

Angel smiles at first, then puts his head down, embarrassed, and keeps on smiling where nobody can see him.

When the speeches finish the names begin. The vice-principal reads every name, calling every student across the stage to receive a diploma. Angel waits patiently as his classmates are called ahead of him—people he knows well, a little, or not at all.

Angel thinks about how long it's been, how much he's seen.

Joanna Baye walks across the stage like she belongs here. Parker Carlson raises his arms in the air like he scored a touchdown. Little Mitchie Daniels strides across the stage, better than six feet tall now and a star on the cross country team.

An hour later comes Faisal Rahman, who speaks Persian at home, followed closely by Wally Roscoe, whose French is nearly perfect by now. Soon enough Molly Swann crosses the stage, the most beautiful of them all, shakes the principal's hand, and accepts some special congratulations from the president of the PTA as she descends the stage.

When Angel walks across the stage he looks out to the audience, feels again the electric hum in the air. Thousands of bright eyes and happy faces are sharing his experience. Angel shakes the hands of the principal and other school leaders, and accepts a diploma of his own. As he walks past the teachers, on the way down from the stage, Ms. Iacobucci reaches out to touch his hand. He looks back at her with thanks in his eyes, then continues toward his seat.

Not long after Angel the last student is called. The applause is riotous and the caps fly into the air. Angel tosses his as well, then changes his mind and grabs one that landed nearby in case someone wants the souvenir.

By now everything is chaos. No signs tell people which way to go, and everyone is going everywhere at the same time. Even as Angel heads outside to look for his family, Zeb taps him on the shoulder.

They exchange a whole new round of congratulations, and they all take turns looking at Angel's diploma, passing it from hand to hand. Monet makes a joke of reading it pretentiously out loud. "This certifies that Angel

Thompson has satisfactorily fulfilled the requirements for graduation, as promulgated by the State Board of Education."

Everyone laughs, but Libby reaches out for the diploma again and studies it in earnest. She turns the certificate over in her hand, reading the simple text, looking at her son. Her pride is clear and her joy shows in her eyes. But Angel can tell something is wrong.

He pulls her to the side. "What is it, Mom? What's the matter?"

He hasn't pulled away as clear as he'd hoped, though, because Sheila interrupts. "Her little boy is growing up," she says. "She's allowed to be sad."

"No," replies Angel, looking earnestly at his mother. "It's more than that."

Libby hugs the diploma close to her chest and makes her confession. "I don't have one of these," she declares. "I loved school. I loved my brothers' graduations. I was looking forward to my own graduation someday."

Libby turns so she's looking at her mother. "I wanted to go to college. I was going to be the first person in our family to go to college." She looks sadly down at her feet and passes Angel's diploma back to him. "I'm sorry. I didn't mean to cause any trouble."

Angel's not having any of it. He brightens up as he reaches out to hold her hand. "I'm not going to college," he asserts like it's a triumph. "I'm going straight to work."

Eva Louise sees quickly where he's going. "Your brothers didn't go to college, you know. They didn't even try."

"You'd still be first," Angel concludes.

"Get your GED. Go to college." Eva Louise charts the course.

"Simple as that," say Sheila and Monet in unison, as if they'd planned it out in advance.

Libby looks at them all, gazing around her big new family.

"You know," she says. "I think I will."

THE END

About the Author

Eric Lotke has cooked in five-star restaurants and flushed every toilet in the Washington, D.C., jail. He has filed headline lawsuits and published headline research on crime, prisons, and sex offenses. He is author of *2044: The Problem Isn't Big Brother, It's Big Brother, Inc.*

CPSIA information can be obtained
at www.ICGtesting.com
Printed in the USA
BVOW08s2155151117
500160BV00002B/90/P